Experimentally she touched him, her hands for a moment less weightless. He was fighting now. To quiet that voice of cold water running he kissed her and kept her mouth. He let her slip from him only momentarily, then fastened on her again.

Slowly her breasts heaved, her breath quickened. Fringe of lashes screening her sliver of gaze, wary still. Plumage tones in the flesh that slightly gave to him and answered. She was with him edient, following, though the eyes would not go under. He did

She was small, not be sure she was

"Do it," she whisp o it."

Also by Marge Piercy:

BREAKING CAMP

HARD LOVING

DANCE THE EAGLE TO SLEEP*

SMALL CHANGES*

WOMAN ON THE EDGE OF TIME*

LIVING IN THE OPEN

THE TWELVE-SPOKED WHEEL

THE HIGH COST OF LIVING*

VIDA*

BRAIDED LIVES*

CIRCLES ON THE WATER

PARTI-COLORED BLOCKS FOR A QUILT: POETS ON POETRY

STONE, PAPER, KNIFE

FLY AWAY HOME*

MY MOTHER'S BODY

GONE TO SOLDIERS

*Published by Fawcett Books

GOING
DOWN
FAST

Marge Piercy

FAWCETT CREST • NEW YORK

A Fawcett Crest Book
Published by Ballantine Books
Copyright © 1969 by Marge Piercy

ACKNOWLEDGEMENTS

"The Elephant Is Slow to Mate," by D. H. Lawrence. From *The Complete Poems of D. H. Lawrence*, Volume I, edited by Vivian de Sola Pinto and F. Warren Roberts. Copyright 1929 by Frieda Lawrence Ravagli. All rights reserved. Reprinted by permission of The Viking Press, Inc.

From "Earthy Anecdote," by Wallace Stevens. Copyright 1923, renewed 1951 by Wallace Stevens. Reprinted from *The Collected Poems of Wallace Stevens* by permission of Alfred A. Knopf, Inc.

"Done Laid Around," by Paul Clayton, Larry Ehrlich, Dave Lazar and Tom Six. Copyright, ©, 1958, 1966 by Sanga Music Inc. All rights reserved. Used by permission.

"Barnyards of Delgaty," by Pat Clancy, Tom Clancy, Liam Clancy and Tommy Makem. Copyright, ©, 1962 by Tiparm Music Publishers Inc. All rights reserved. Used by permission.

ISBN 0-449-24480-6

This edition published by arrangement with Trident Press, a division of Simon & Schuster, Inc.

Manufactured in the United States of America

First Fawcett Crest Edition: January 1982
First Ballantine Books Edition: February 1984
Second Printing: February 1988

Cover art © Roberta Ludlow, 1987

TO SOL AND ADRIENNE YURICK

Friendship Stretches

Leon

August

The four-story building on the corner with bulging spinach green bays was coming down. The crane, taller by a couple of stories, was eating it. With clumsy delicacy the crane grazed, detaching a mouthful of two-by-fours and pipes and walls. A cloud of dust swirling on the wind that smelled of stockyards almost hid the iron ostrich neck. Even on the far side of the street where Leon stood the noise deafened him. Fine dust settled on his sweaty forehead.

The workmen on top had taken off their shirts. A husky Negro straight across from him sat astride a brick wall four floors above the sidewalk and swung a sledgehammer just ahead of the grasp of his thighs. Leon felt the impact in his arm, his thick arm under the faintly damp weight of his one still good summer jacket. Great work. Smash the city. Look at them sauntering over the gaps. Last week in demolition for an expressway two had been killed when a wall collapsed, and they got paid worse than he did.

The crane bit into a shiny yellow room, turned and with a tidy jerk spat the chewed wall in a dumptruck. Swinging back, the crane in passing knocked off a section of facade. Thunderous rubble fell. His legs shook. Chaos inside a fence of tulip colored doors. The crane poked around to the front, seized the fire escape, let go fumbling, then fixed on it again. Groaning, the metal held. The teeth twisted it like an arm till the tension sang and all at once it tore loose and boom,

1

was thrust in the truck. Kids all around him stared, house-wives with shopping carts. His attaché case against his leg. He'd miss the interview. All those dim bedrooms opened like cans. On the ground floor, through the smashed front window he could make out the graffiti-scrawled rooms of the bar where one of his early films had been given a showing. *Rat-Men of the Jackson Park Lagoon.* Bastards hadn't known what to make of it.

Turning he saw that Anna was watching from her room, kitty corner across the intersection, standing a little back from the windows so the workmen would not notice her. Why wasn't she downtown teaching? Summer semester must be over. Was Rowley there? He waited for Rowley to appear behind, touching her. No, she was alone, she looked alone. Naked face watched the walls crumble. She held herself across her full breasts. Her mouth looked as if it might be slightly open. He imagined her eyes melting. Would she identify with the crane or the walls? The walls, of course, or something behind them.

What if he was a little late to the interview? Looking over his shoulder he went back to his car to get his camera. Never knew when you could use demolition footage. The falling bricks rumbled through his body. Down the sidestreets Chicago was a murky late afternoon August green, moist as a swamp.

Anna

Rowley said something and Anna woke confused. She took a moment to understand that she was in his apartment and that his voice was the FM. Then she jumped up to turn the radio louder, annoyed with herself for dozing off during his own special show. His voice came out deep, persuasive and rough in spots like a good rum, talking about some blues singer. Then he played Ma Rainey:

If your house catches on fire and there ain't no water round,
If your house catches on fire and there ain't no water round,
Throw your trunk out the window and let that shack burn down . . .

She went into his small kitchen to splash her face at the sink. Sleep still clogged her limbs. Her head felt big. Her dark hair swung forward into the stream of water. She had been up all night on a Greyhound from Cleveland, part of the time preparing lectures for the new class in the family she had been promised, part of the time in the stupefied depression trundling across Ohio and Indiana induced. Seemed as if she couldn't stare at that flat repetitive landscape for long without asking herself, what have I done with my life? where am I going? am I going? Rowley had not wanted her to make the trip using up some of their rare free time together, but once a year she thought she should see her family.

3

She found herself staring into the shelf of cookbooks over his stove, loose recipes stuck in unsorted, useless. The night coming through the open windows smelled of trees and cars. Strange, his voice in the livingroom talking not for her but for anybody with a radio, and yet as if it were the man, worked on her, coaxed and teased. Twice as disconcerting since it was a tape unwinding tonight. He might have left the studio already, might be drinking with pals, playing a session, listening to some group.

Making a face she took an armful of cookbooks down and began to sort the stray pages. Now he had with him an Irish girl who sang pleasantly but dwindled away in shyness and he was flirting gently, drawing her forward into the mike. Rowley was talented but not ambitious and that gave him an ease, a natural shaggy courtesy with others: he admired, he enjoyed, he wanted to share. This recipe for veal in sour-cream had been used at least once, for one corner was splashed and the paprika measurement corrected. On the back what record had she entered?

ASHER	ANNA	ROWLEY	JOAN
47	32	58	17
39	41	54	8

She turned and without thinking closed the nearest window. The first time Asher had invited Rowley over. Was it, come over Saturday and have dinner, my wife's a good cook? No, that wasn't Asher's voice. Only the intonation of *my wife,* gray word signifying possession and function. My wife, my broker, my dentist. They must have played some game. Indeed. Joan was a fairhaired British secretary Rowley had picked up at the Art Institute, taken to bed, forgotten as she had that game. She had not liked Rowley that first night. She was proud of that. Loud and arrogant she had told Asher and he had protested her quick judgment, judging her. Because Asher classed people by their opinions and competencies, he imagined himself free of prejudice, but he . . . *Stop.* The long argument called marriage was broken off. She thought of Asher as permanently wounded, but he was digesting his steak and airmail edition of the New York *Times* together not a quarter mile away. She sighed, combing her hand through the weight of her long thick hair, and folded the loaded recipe into her purse. She could not throw away scraps of the past even if they cut her fingers.

Rowley's voice came through like a heavy hand falling on her shoulder. Singing, oh god. He had been backing up the girl with tactful inventive guitar—he played powerfully and well and she liked him singing blues. But his voice suffered like a beaten hound, in dialect yet. Bellowing away, the overbearing bulk pranced out through all those radios:

> *When I go to the kirk on Sunday*
> *Many's the bonny lass I see*
> *Sitting by her mother's side*
> *And winking over the pews at me.*

Ha ha ha banged the guitar.

> *Now I can drink and not be drunken,*
> *I can fight and not be slain,*
> *I can lie with another man's lassie*
> *And still be welcome to my own!*

Like those signs shops used to hand out, fish-shaped for the fish-market, shoe for the cobbler: a great neon phallus, here lives Rowley the Rod, Satisfaction Guaranteed.

He was playing backup again beautifully when she heard him whistling outside. Hearing him too the cat Yente woke hanging over the top shelf of the bookcase. Someone ran down the front steps. Yente leaped from the shelf with a loud graceful plop and making for the door with his splayfooted gallop, set up a welcoming yowl.

As Rowley pushed the door open, Yente rose hugging his knee until he lifted him. "Hey Annie! Where are you!" He came toward her with the cat walking on his shoulders, leaning to lick the ends of his buffalo hunter moustache. On his big frame, six feet and broad as a wall, objects were slung: red and black hunter's jacket looped over his shoulder, rec-

ords in a shopping bag, the *Sun-Times*, mail that had come
at the studio, and the worn overnight case he used as a briefcase bulging through all its cracks.

Behind him in midsentence came his landlord Harlan Williams, who lived above him on the first floor. Though Harlan
was about Rowley's height and age he looked younger, because of his quick nervous gestures, because of the hard neat-
ness of his body, and because his dark redtoned mahogany
skin was smooth and unlined except for one fine wrinkle that
ran up from the top of his nose like a decoration. He was
brandishing a newspaper and the line showed. "This is the
end, man, I can't believe it. They're going to seize our land
and throw us off!"

"The University can't seize anything. Keep your cool."

"For married student housing. They can't call this a slum,
but these are black blocks and that's enough. We can move
back and sleep in the ghetto streets." He let out his barbed
laugh.

Tossing his stuff on the kitchen table Rowley took the
neighborhood paper from Harlan and sat down to scan it.
Harlan leaned against the sink drumming his fingers. She
was glad she had straightened. Rowley and Harlan were
bound in a sparring friendship from years before she'd met
him. Harlan, a minor official in welfare, seemed to like her,
but wafts of his wife Shirley's disapproval chilled the basement from time to time.

Handing her the paper Rowley pushed to his feet. "Their
real estate lobby put through legislation downstate that lets
them move to *prevent* slums. But I can't believe they expect
to ride over so many people without protest. This announce-
ment is to open the bargaining."

"The University doesn't bargain, not with us. They're
South Side slumlords, at the same time they've set up dummy
organizations to keep their backyard white. You think I didn't
try to buy a house over there? Every time I found one it would
mysteriously go off the market."

She looked up from the map. "Surprise number two. I
notice on the big renewal plan that my own building's been
added. I'm getting evicted too. It's not a fancy building, but

it's solid cheap housing of a sort that's getting rarer and rarer—''

They both looked at her blankly and Rowley mumbled something about, So move in, and then they turned back man to man and resumed. As if there was room. As if Shirley would put up with that. She had been about to make a point about new construction, anyhow. Most of the women Rowley had dealt with, and they'd been many, had been casual lays and he was not above treating her that way in front of old friends, though if she challenged him about it he claimed she was imagining.

Rowley was pacing. ''A university is a sensitive body. Can be embarrassed. Pressured.''

''A university, man, is a biggish corporation. If it acts like General Motors or U.S. Steel, why be surprised? Who are the trustees, anyhow?''

''Look, I'll ask around the station and see if I can find out what this means. I can't see how a private corporation can get eminent domain over people's homes.''

Harlan unpropped himself from the sink. ''Depends on who the people are, looks like.''

''You want to leave me the paper?''

''No.'' Harlan smiled at his own truculence but took it anyhow as he left.

Involuntarily she took a breath and braced herself. Whenever they were alone she felt her internal balance shift, she drew together more compactly. He smiled from his wideset tilted eyes and stooped to kiss her. She tasted beer and the remnants of spice on his tongue, leaning into him and holding tight. Good to be back. Um, tired. She felt like curling up in his arms and being loved.

''Annie—'' He tilted her head back. ''Want to go to a party?''

''A party?''

''Nothing much. Just Caroline Frayne is back from Europe.''

She shrugged. ''I didn't expect her to turn up again around here. I though she'd gravitate to more glamour.''

He tangled his hand in her hair. "Leon called, said we should drop over. I said we would."

She pulled free. Without asking her, again. "How is he?" She went into the bedroom to put herself together.

"How is Leon ever? The same jagoff. He's on a rampage about his exwife. I don't know what he thinks she's doing but he's sure it's his business." He lolled on the bed stroking the cat. "Feed Yente?"

"Sure." She combed her hair. "You're friends with Leon only because you roomed with him. If you met him cold at a party you'd think, there's a loudmouthed operator."

He shrugged evasively, tumbling Yente. "You're too hard on him."

"I hardly know him," she said equably. As she reached for her purse, he pinched her behind, and she cried out. "I don't like that!"

"Then you shouldn't have such a sweet ass or wear tight skirts."

She tugged at her striped overblouse. "Is my skirt too tight?"

"No, Christsake, come on." He steered her out. Rowley's apartment was on the ground floor, a couple of feet below the dirt line. They left by ducking around the broad staircase that went straight up to the Williams' front door.

As she climbed in her side of the VW, she noticed his guitar in back. "Are you going to perform tonight?"

He shrugged. "You didn't say how you liked my show?"

"It was very interesting."

"Interesting—what does that mean? Did you *like* it?"

"Your selections are always first rate."

"What are you getting at, Annie?"

"Nothing!" If only she had told him right out she had missed half his program, but he had Harlan with him when he came in. He had called her in Cleveland to ask her if she would be back Friday in time, and it was unlike him to fuss so much, and puzzling. They had left the predominantly black blocks where Rowley lived and drove through the campus, quiet between terms.

"All right, damn it, what are you not getting at?"

"I don't know why you will sing that sort of thing!"

"I see. You're having a bourgeois puritan hangup about a fine old song, *The Barnyards of Delgatty*."

"You'll say a lot of people like it." Something knocked in her stop, stop, but she could not. "Well, some of your friends would encourage you to eat glass if you took that into your head. If you started stripping at parties, they'd say it was wonderfully earthy."

He stepped on the gas and burst into the thing again loud as he could, which was loud. Looking sideways at him with his black hair rumpled, his moustache waving, his big head flung back, she smiled and could not believe they were quarreling. He was taking out his annoyance at her leaving town. Through the brick leafy streets of faculty houses as he stomped on through the song she cast about for some way to signal her apologies.

But he said loudly, "So lady sociologists find me vulgar. I wouldn't offend you for the world, baby, but I'm just naturally offensive. It's all those yes-men stoking my ego." He parked and hopped out to cross Leon's, between a second-hand bookstore and a closed-down coffeehouse. Leon had lived for years in one of a row of faded red concession stands put up for the Columbian Exposition of 1893 and used ever since for shops or artists' studios or apartments.

He strode ahead and she trotted after. His rambling, loose-jointed walk. She wanted him. If only she could take a deep breath and start over. "Why is Leon giving the party? Is Caroline his girl now?"

"Back when he was married I think he screwed around with her. Used her in a film."

"Which pray god he doesn't show tonight."

But Rowley would not smile, rapping on the door. Leon let them in, framed in the lit door with his bulky hirsute body and massive head like a chimpanzee. He grinned at Rowley who gave back the same calculating grin as they sidled round each other.

"How are you making it?" Leon said in his high harsh voice. As if contemptuous of height he slumped, leaning to look up at Rowley out of narrowed eyes.

"Not busted yet. How's the single life?"

They spoke and looked at each other with the same mixture of distaste and curiosity and warmth. Leon shrugged. "Doesn't make much difference, my marriage was never what you'd call a fulltime thing. It wasn't something all-over demanding like going steady or being engaged—hey, Caroline?" He turned toward the couch—a piece of Danish modern that looked as if an unclean elephant had nested there. Caroline sat beside another, younger girl, thin and black. When Caroline caught their gaze, she held up her hand with the diamond.

"In Firenze," she called, "but he's American. He'll be here next month. Rowley, aren't you going to say hello? Don't you ignore me a minute longer!"

A dozen people milled around the large front room that had changed little since the time Leon was married to Joye. Inside the peeling walls, the flaking paint dabbed with squashed roaches and old film star posters, stood the furniture one or the other prosperous family had given them for marrying each other. Festooned from the ceiling were Joye's stubborn attempts at decoration: a net of pebbles, a wobbly mobile of bicycle parts, some gourds and Indian corn strung up wizened and miscolored as shrunken heads. Leon's editing table stood against one wall with a rack of clips by the small splicer. The screen was furled in its case, thank god, beside a flood without a bulb. Books were piled on the floor and boxes stood under tables or on chairs, half packed or half unpacked. Old butts lay in drifts against the walls with old paper splices.

She would call no one here a friend, nor were they currently Rowley's. There was one black filmmaker and his boyfriend, who left shortly, some stray girls, but the knot of men around Leon had known each other at the University. Their talk bristled with names at least one of them would have forgotten. Remember, said the natty one as they stood outside the kitchen, and they laughed ritually and the fat one slapped his thigh. Rowley would not join them: he used but did not sentimentalize his past. He had many pasts and she was always discovering a new one like a corridor opening out of a casual sentence: "One time in Duluth when I was working on the ore boats . . ." "When Kirk and I hit Baja California in his jeep . . ." "So my old man sent me down to the picket line at the East Gate . . ."

"*Owen*," Leon was saying. "Course you haven't seen him around. He's locked up."

"How come?" the natty one asked. "What did he do?"

"Heard voices, man. His folks committed him." Leon drew his finger across his throat. "This time he'll never get out."

The fat one shook his head, his jowls drooping in mournful folds. "What a rotten deal. Poor old Owen."

"Shut up, Fisher!" Leon's voice rose like the whine of a saw. "I came to you asking you to find him a job in your father's snot-works, and all you had to say was, gee I'm busy. You sent him up there too, and don't forget it."

Fisher flailed his arms shouting as Anna finally slipped past into the kitchen to get a beer for herself and another for Rowley, still chatting with Caroline. He took it and thanked her without breaking the rhythm of his story, standing with one foot on the rung of a chair. Climbing in the High Sierra. One good reason she did not enjoy parties as much as she used to.

He certainly was not handsome with his crooked nose and scar and his droopy walrus moustache and strange upslanting eyes, his ruddy face, his hair long and shaggy. He had a good body but thick in the waist. A fine man to cook for, with eagerness to try and strong belly and good teeth. In the bathtub he played like a porpoise and sang. He dropped to sleep like a ton of child. His other accomplishments were, alas, obvious. She had little against him except that he did not know he was mortal.

Caroline was lit up for him, signals hoisted. The girl beside her, looking the room over with a wondering disgust, contrasted strongly. She was perhaps nineteen with coppery black skin very smooth against the mattress ticking of her shift. Her hair was cropped close to her head in tight natural curls, set on a long neck. Black swan. Coltish long arms and legs. Her face, unmoving, had the slightly flattened precision of a mask. She brought out Caroline's coloring—the brown-blond haziness, the camelshair pastels. Next to her Caroline looked sexy, full of sap, but also a little obvious with her brows and lashes heavily made up, large complaisant mouth, a bigboned hippy selfconscious body that men would call childlike without meaning that. Regular soft features that Leon kept showing in that pretentious film wrapped in slimy seaweed or with beetles crawling over.

Turning away from Caroline and Rowley the girl got up, slight and graceful. Anna intercepted her. "Like me you don't know these people? I'm Anna Levinowitz."

The girl looked up with a chilly appraising stare. "Vera Jameson. I've known Caroline for years. We're both from Green River, Michigan."

"Are you going to school here?"

"No." Sparks. "Teaching it. And you too, right?"

Anna nodded. "At the University extension."

"From the manner, you had to."

Put down, Anna smiled stiffly. "So you've known Caroline a long time. What brings her back to Chicago?"

"She's staying with me, though she'll be moving into her own place Monday." A cool high spring clear voice. "If you're interested in her plans, why don't you ask her?"

"As you see, she's talking to someone."

"Oh, to him." Vera's manner was not hostile, merely remote, she decided. "But I thought you came with him?"

Anna nodded. "As usual." Like talking with a precocious twelve-year-old. That was why she had thought Vera so young. Lovely in a fragile way, like those teacups mothers collect on bricabrac shelves. Small ears bared by her cropped hair. Lithe body designed for the sort of shift she was wearing, pleasant, summery, cool.

"Then why don't you go over?"

But her sharp teeth and candor bit. "I think people talk best by twos." Why didn't she? Afraid to be thought to interfere. Too proud. Too stubborn.

Vera considered that gravely. Then with a broad but fleeting smile, "That's true, that's very true. Because the two of

you work out a shorthand way of saying things. You don't
have to spell everything out.''

Surely Vera was thinking of a man.

''Listen, Fisher, I'm tired of you talking a good game!''
Leon shouted and they both turned. The fat man, Fisher, had
his coat on and was plowing toward the door with Leon
urging him on and the natty friend hanging on both their
arms. ''You're living like a fat fungus off the past. You think
because you smoked pot seven years ago with some musi-
cians, that makes you a radical. I'm tired of you coming
around beating your gums. Come back when you're ready to
change your life. Now go home and stew in your smell!''

''Who made you an expert on how to run my life? I'm
married to my wife. I still got my kid. I support them. I hold
a good job—''

''Get out, Fisher, or I'll break your jaw!''

Caroline had come near with a loosemouthed, excited
look, while Vera backed away with a grimace. ''Why are
they screaming?''

''Unclear.'' Anna watched Rowley steer them outside,
then shut the door against those who pressed after. With a
graceful moue of incomprehension, Vera turned and moved
off. She behaved as if she did not know what a party was,
did not sense the mandate to behave as if she was enjoying
herself. Since the filmmaker had left she was the only Negro,
but that did not seem to explain anything as she examined
the prints on the wall, stood on tiptoe to give the mobile a
poke, looked over the people with the same detached curiosity, and when spoken to replied literally to questions. Probably she had come as a favor to Caroline. And if she were in
love, of course the room was empty.

Anna turned, meaning to talk to Caroline, but found her
path blocked by a soft plump young man with the face of an
ill-tempered rabbit who must have been staring at her. ''I'm
Leon's brother,'' he said with a damp menace.

''Hello, Leon's brother, did they run out of names before
they got to you?'' She did not have any desire to flirt with
him, but he looked so sorry. Like calling on a longwinded
student for the sake of his ego.

He was Sidney. "I'm only invited because he wants to borrow my Porsche. Probably he wants to pretend it's his in front of some girl, so she'll take off her clothes for his movies. He calls it art." Sidney snickered into his glass.

Nuts at parties, the ones with a bomb or a grievance in their pocket or their pants, always sought her out. Leon came shambling back in alone to squat on his haunches before Caroline.

"You didn't get into a fight!" Caroline said.

"With Fisher? He wouldn't have the guts to hit his kid."

"What did you do with Rowley?"

"He's out there playing peacemaker. So what's this about being engaged?" He rocked back on his heels.

Caroline held out her ring as if she expected it to speak.

"He goes around and he tries to make me loan him my Porsche," Sidney was saying peevishly, "and he gets money from our mother and presents, all behind the old man's back, and he calls them both by their first names. If I ever called Mother by her first name she'd slap my face, but he does it all the time."

"What does that mean?" Leon was rasping. "You love him?"

Caroline shook out her lush shoulderlength hair. "Well of course."

"That's never of course," Leon snarled. "Why aren't you with him?"

Rowley came in alone and was stopped by an acquaintance. She heard his laugh boom.

"He wheedles in, he says tell me this, old Sid-boy, tell me about that, and then he's trying to run my life," Sidney hissed, leaning close. "All he cares about is sex and freeloading."

"Honey," Caroline argued, "can't you see that's no way to begin? He's in Santa Barbara on business." She patted Leon's cheek. "In the meantime I found a great job. I'm working in the Rising Sun coffeehouse. We wear mesh stockings and slinky short tops—"

"If you're in love with him, why aren't you with him?"

"I think it would be a miserable way to begin a marriage

with me sitting in a motelroom all day twiddling my thumbs." She leaped up. "I'm dying for a beer."

A moment later she reappeared to dodge across the room calling, "Rowley! You have your car, *n'est-ce pas?*" She took his arm. "Crisis! We're running low on beer. Let's go foraging."

Leon went after her. "Low on beer? Hold on, I'll go."

"No, honey, that'd be silly. You bought the first load."

Vera crossed over. "Drop me off then. I'm sleepy."

Anna stepped forward but Sidney was not nearly done and he blocked her without breaking the thread of his righteous lament. After they had driven off she stood in fitful apprehension with Sidney's voice slopping over her. "Everyone in the family's sick of him because of the way he acts. Then he has the nerve to come up to my apartment and put his feet up and ask for Scotch and tell me I should quit working for my uncle and go on a diet and lift weights and take LSD and be as crazy as he is."

What was Caroline dying to say that she had to catch Rowley alone? Or did she merely want to escape Leon? Great interest in what need not concern him. She could feel her attentive smile hardening across her face. Finally the beer really did run out and people began to leave all around them. At one point she noticed Leon sitting on the couch, bowed as if tired, and knew he was listening to Sidney. Twice he looked up at his brother and his face was contorted with pity.

Finally he broke in. Pounded numb with boredom she collapsed in a chair. Then she saw that only the three of them remained.

Sidney offered with sullen humility, "Come on, I'll give you a ride in my Porsche."

Heat rose along her body. "No thanks, my friend's coming back."

As Leon shut the door after Sidney, making sad sucking noises, he said. "So sure?"

"Why not?" She wanted to sound calm but sounded only silly. She paced once around the coffee table, then afraid of showing her tension, sat again. Vera had invited them in. Caroline had a real problem to talk over with him: why him?

All beer stores closed. Flat tire. An accident. Accident? That damn billygoat!

Leon clasped his hands behind his thick neck, stretching. "They've had time to brew that beer. Face it, we've been deserted."

"Why assume the worst?" She drew up her long legs into the chair.

"If it happens to be true?" His eyes studied her legs, then withdrew as if shyly. "Coffee?"

She nodded. Pushing his glasses back on his nose, he shambled into the kitchen to make instant coffee and bring back two hastily rinsed cups. Returned to his seat he looked at her steadily: looming head with a brow ridge over the eyes. The eyes behind heavy glasses were a milky opalescent gray-blue, far apart and commanding. Hard pale eyes that fixed on her with hesitant friendliness and unwavering inquisition. His jaw protruded squarely, his mouth was large and lax. His reddish hair was cut short, showing a small bald spot on the crown, hair that grew longer on his arms and the backs of his hands than on his heavy skull. His broad shoulders sloped out to big elbows, outsized knuckles. The eyes brooded on her with tender patience, waiting for her to admit her position.

She held the cup between her palms, sipping. He had turned out all lights but those around the island of couch and chair, separated by a teak coffeetable pitted with cigarette grooves, ringed with coffeecup stains, bleached by alcohol, loaded with forgotten glasses, old film magazines, rumpled cigarette packs, a weary tie, an infant's blue knitted sweater, very dirty.

"My poor ball-less brother. He thinks life would be easier if he'd been the oldest and got everyplace first. I keep telling him, go to a new place then, kick them all in the teeth, me too. . . . You got brothers and sisters?"

"A younger sister, Estelle." The hour, the island of light, his brother's confession, his manner all conspired to create an artificial intimacy. She had a fear she labeled irrational that he was about to make a pass.

"And does she hate you too?"

"She doesn't know me well enough."

"Hating can be a form of honest response." It seemed to her he was looking at her with the same pity he had shown for Sidney.

She burst out, "You think they're in bed." Her voice husky. He opened his mouth but she forstalled him, picking the phone off the floor to dial Rowley's number. Ring, pause. The phone stood on his bedside table. Ring, pause. Ring, pause.

"Hello?" Rowley's voice went through her.

Her hand came up to her breasts, protecting. If only he had not answered. He always thought it might be his father taken a turn for the worse, the studio, someone in trouble.

"You bastard." She slammed the receiver. Bending she put the phone back and rose turned away so that she need not meet Leon's gaze too quickly. Slowly she moved, feeling her body tear. What she had done to Asher had come back to punish her. "I've got to go home. I'll call a cab."

"I'll give you a ride." He got up.

"Don't bother, please. A cab is easy." She wanted to run out of his sight.

"I'll drive you." He was holding open the door. As they walked out, the phone rang. Leon looked at her, raising his brows.

"Answer if you want to. Only I'm not here."

"Let it ring."

At his old Buick Leon paused to look at the street, turned by the moon into empty facade. She stared too, wanting conversation to ward off pity or condolence. "Lived here long?"

"Six, seven years. They're going to tear it all down."

Faded gaiety of prim carnival houses with spooled storefronts silvered by moonlight. Down they would come to a pile of warped boards.

"My building's condemned too. Urban removal. They're going to dig a great hole with their steamshovels and throw us in."

"And my old man Sheldon will be in the driver's seat piling dirt on my head."

She was puzzled but too weary to care. "Turn right. I'll show you . . ."

"I know."

As he pulled up he reached across and gripped her door handle. "Look here, you wouldn't rather go have a drink someplace?"

"Thanks but I'm dead tired."

"Guess you and Rowley will make it up tomorrow." He let go of the handle.

She got out at once. "You guess wrong but it doesn't matter. Thanks again." Inside she could not climb the stairs, dim, steep, straight up. She stood by the mailboxes. The steps were a sacrificial pyramid. She would climb, mount her stone bed and her loosened heart would be torn free and fed to a god of justice because she had done in Asher, because. With heavy thighs she pulled herself up.

She let her purse drop and trudged into the other room. As she threw herself on the bed the mirror snapped her, black hair hanging forward, face strangely calm. She lay prone. She could not move. Hours ago she had found out and she knew it and knew it and knew it, him with Caroline.

Pounding on the door. She groaned. More pounding.

"Annie! Open the door!"

She stumbled up. Stopped and automatically smoothed her hair. He did not have a key. Her hand froze to the knob. Let him go away.

He beat on the door. "Annie! Let me in."

A door opened up the corridor. She turned the knob. "Yes?"

He pushed in giving the door a cuff shut. His face was furrowed with anger, his eyes hot. "What the hell are you trying to do?"

She eased away, staring at a point above his shoulder. He seemed huge and bright, he hurt her eyes. "Nothing to say."

"Short but sweet, like on the phone."

"It would have been more convenient if you'd been fit to drive me home before laying Caroline. Or was I supposed to amuse myself with Leon?"

"Get off it, Annie. I didn't plan this. I was coming back. It's trivial."

"Everything's trivial! Don't you put any value on yourself, if you don't put one on me?"

"If you didn't want to wait, all you had to do was call a cab. You're not silly enough to be jealous?"

"Are you a public accommodation? A filling station?"

"You say I'm rude. Well, I can't think of anything ruder than slapping down some chick who's offering what she's got."

"Are you as nice to horny old ladies and dogs?"

He grabbed her by the upper arm. "Now look here, Annie—"

"Let go of me!"

Meeting her gaze he let go. "Why do you have to react this way?"

"Why do I yell when you kick me?" She clenched her hair in both hands.

He smacked his fist into his palm, turned away, swung back. "Anna, I've done nothing to you, nothing, except take a little long getting back."

"I knew from the start what would happen, but I'm such a fool!"

"No, you never trusted me. You've always been hanging back." He stood there hands working, and then he shoved them deep in his pockets. "As if it was my fault I met you married to that poor meticulous bastard who couldn't hold you. You hung back from the time we met, dragging your heels, always ready to accuse me. You were born mistrustful!"

"Not born! How can I pretend to trust you?"

"You've said enough, Annie."

"You don't care, just so you can prove yourself! How can I live with a man who doesn't believe in consequences?"

"How can you?" He shrugged, a bitter mask freezing over his face, buttoned his jacket and walked out.

She stood staring. On the door she had tacked a photograph of the Cretan great goddess, in shape like a chesspiece: not the well-known barebreasted figure from the empire but

a later back-country goddess of a defeated power with stoic
face and pillar body, arms stiffly raised past the head in bless-
ing or surrender. She stared now at the worn face. She sat
abruptly on a kitchen chair, her thighs loosely parted, her
legs watery. She stared and stared at the door. He had closed
it so quietly. The earthen woman stood aghast, signaled stop,
the end. Anna groaned and then asked out loud, ''What have
I done?''

Monday—Wednesday, September 15—17

Monday Anna woke at seven alert with misery as she had
the day before, the day before that. Light poured in the five
windows on the rounded outer wall, more light since the
building on the other corner had come down. Sun danced on
the thread-bare red rug. Idly she disentangled her hand from
the sheet and touched the rug. Roughness like a morning
beard. Her skin froze.

He must have been waiting for a chance to break off. She
searched through the days before her trip. He did not need
her. Why had she insulted him? What else could she have
done? She was preserved by disbelief, by pockets of fierce
optimism. He would call yet, he had to: it would be so bad
if he didn't. She had only to stretch out her hand and dial.
She would pretend she assumed Friday meant nothing. Say
Rowley, guess what. No, could not.

She rolled out of bed. Why couldn't it be Friday again,
for one minute? But inevitable. She put on her robe before
facing the mirror. Bluish smudges under the eyes. A grave
look, yes, two days in the grave. How much of her life was
she going to waste hauling from man to man?

Her bedroom had been a dentist's office: she imagined its

old floorboards saturated with pain. The receptionist's office was her kitchen which she crossed to the hall bathroom. She shared it with a fairy in his late forties, Matt Fenn, who spoke often of his Show Biz days, and he had taken tickets at Riverview for the Ferris wheel. He was nosy but left the bath clean. She watched the tub fill and let herself into it. Suddenly, looking at her big body flushed and wavering underwater, she began to cry.

As she was toweling herself, she stopped. A phone. Hers? Wrapped dripping in the towel she ran. Him, please, him. "Hello?"

"Yeah, it's Leon."

"Oh." Water rolled down her legs. "How are you?"

"Just called . . . to find out how you are . . . and things." Limping.

"Yes, I'm just dressing to go to registration."

"You don't feel like having lunch then?" His voice raveled into silence so that she could not be sure he had finished.

She made excuses, preoccupied with a chill in her scalp. He is interested in me. Don't be absurd. Yes he is. Discourage him quick.

Registration was hectic and boring and she was glad of it. She sat in the gym riffling the catalogue, dividing and stamping forms and yawning, yawning. Beside her worked an older man and one her age who talked only to each other. The associate professor did not approve of females and the younger man was a PhD bucking for tenure. She was happy to be ignored, for she feared if anyone smiled warmly or asked how she were, she would burst into selfpitying bloom.

An old student came to register, a paperclip bowed and thin boy with blotched shy face under tumbled hair. She loved him and had spent hours tutoring him in the drafty room she and the other tweeny teachers shared, and she wanted to whisper, Freddy, I am so sad. She had never told him anything that had happened since she was ten. Long mutterings among stacks of graded test papers, books loaned and returned, papers passionate as love letters on Caste vs. Class as Concepts in Social Stratification, Draft Dodgers or

Culture Heroes: a Survey of Student Attitudes toward CO's.
She always had students she granted hours before or after
classes. Now she would feel less neutered in that exchange.

Although she did not have her PhD she was being re-
warded with a small class in the family this fall. If a subject
bored her, she maundered, but if she were interested she
could find rapport with the class like a handle hidden under
the desk and bear down. Not that she did not hate the textbooks. She had dropped out of graduate school because sociology seemed such a lot of scholastic, pseudoscientific
obfuscation. The kids went into sociology because they had
a sense of something wrong, a sense of their society pushing
on and warping people and they wanted to understand it and
change it. But their professors were working for the Department of Defense or market research firms or IT&T or General Dynamics. When she had been a student at Inland with
the University still trying through homeowners associations
to keep its neighborhood white and with bopping gangs fighting in the streets, there had been no course in the department
which confronted racism. There had been, however, professors working on pilot counterinsurgency projects for pene-
trating black militant groups and putting down the expected
riots.

She was a popular teacher and the other teachers patron-
ized her for that. She was confused herself. She did not want
her students to die slowly or at once. They streamed through,
always too many to deal with, and if she selected a few to
teach, that was in spite of her job, not through it. If she had
anything to teach them, it was the opposite of the course,
and never as authority-surrogate.

She managed to pass the day without speaking of herself,
without turning her face to anyone. How many days would
go that way? She felt chilled traveling home on the El looking
into ashy backyards of the Black Belt. Her building was integrated: one prune-faced spinster who had come back to
school for an MA in education. Her landlady celebrated her
liberality by ending repairs and telling blacks who applied
that she had Done Her Bit. Even so she felt martyred to her

principles, brought on by a flunking medical student who drank a container of insecticide in his room.

But the roaches seemed not to mind integration. They flourished and filled the walls. Chicago roaches were large shiny waterbeetles that could wear the eastern cockroaches for shoes. She found them even in the refrigerator. No one grew used to them, but anyone could learn to live with them. Like other things, including loneliness.

She walked from the trolley stop, the pink air of sunset still warm behind the silhouettes of the turn-of-the-century three- and four-story apartments with stores on the ground floor that lined the street. Her street was like a bright grimy fringe on the green carpet of middle-class housing that stretched toward campus. Weeds were beginning to grow on the corner lot, and already a shortcut was trodden across. She stopped at the candystore for a paper. Mrs. Feldman leaned her fat arms on the counter, reading a column of classified ads with a spoon for pointer.

She sat on a stool and ordered coffee to put off going the last block home.

"Hey, Mrs. Feldman, looking for a job? Going out in the world and leave Mr. Feldman to cook his own hamburgers?"

The woman laughed politely, but the lines around her mouth did not ease. "They won't say when they're tearing us down. . . ." She waved her hand at the stamped tin ceiling. Like her parents' store. "What can you do? Mr. Feldman says we should give it all up, but I say we have to find another place—what else can we do?"

Feldman's coffee was no longer good. It tasted of rust.

Wednesday afternoon the phone rang. She sat rigid over the work-plan she was typing. A bolt went through her, holding her painfully but securely to the chairback. Him. Of course not. Don't think it. Him. She tore free and picked up the receiver.

"Miss Levinowitz?"

No. Not. Why should he? A few minutes passed then before she understood what the polite voice wanted. Secretary of her department chairman.

"What, you're taking my classes away? What are you talking about? I'm down for four."

"As I said, Miss Levinowitz, Mr. Bodford is very sorry, but the fall registration was misestimated, and we're forced to cut back our classes."

"But one class. I can't live on one class. You know it's too late to find anything else. It's unfair."

"If you'd like to talk to Mr. Bodford!" said his secretary prissy with annoyance.

"You're damned straight I would."

"Well, Miss Levinowitz," said Mr. Bodford, pronouncing her name as if it hurt his jaw. "We regret this very much and I want you to know how much we appreciate and nothing personal and no contractual obligation and our PhD's and impossible to estimate and with any fairness and one of the risks of the game and perhaps next semester and perhaps we could arrange a second class if we juggle our schedules and try to understand and . . ."

"One course I can't live on, two courses I can't live on. This is a fine time to tell me. I eat as much as a PhD. You can keep your course. I quit!"

She hung up and sat quivering with surprise. Her head prickled with remarks she should have made. Yet she was half shocked that she had had the courage of her indignation. She couldn't live on what they were offering, but it was a start. She hoped the other little shits would draw comfort from her gesture.

At least she was finally out of debt. She ripped the prospectus from her typewriter and flung it in the garbage, sent her notes and exam ideas sailing after. No job and no man: she ought to leave this town. Damn them, she was a good teacher. She felt a pang for her students, those hers already, all her parttime children, her carefully distanced lovers. She rescued her notes from the garbage and brushed off the grounds. Some other time maybe. She had a forgiving disposition. Up to a point, up to a point.

She took out her checkbook and worked at it, soothed by figures. The dirty sun filtered through the steelmill fumes and permanent sootstorm the South Side called air to expire on her face without warmth. She brushed the thick springy hair from her eyes. One hundred ninety-eight dollars and twenty-three cents. She was good at being frugal. She began to work out a budget.

If she got sick or had an accident, it would be gone. Even a string of bad cavities. No one had to care what became of her. Oh, her parents, in a formal sense. Like gentle gray hamsters they lived in the old flat in Cleveland and ran what had been a drygoods store and was bleakly surviving as a cheap clothing store that still sold a few patterns and yarn and thread, with new fluorescent lighting under the high stamped tin ceiling. During highschool she had worked behind the counter. She could still smell the mothball odor of certain drawers, see the packets of needles on which women dressed in the mode of 1920 sat sewing.

Her parents knew nothing of her. "My oldest dotter, she teaches college out West, in Chicago. Yes, in college she teaches." A photo of her stood on the buffet taken at highschool graduation (big, sleepyfaced, shy, oddly inert in the robes), fortunately almost obscured by the many many pictures of her sister's two boys. Three years younger, Estelle was already the ageless housewife with a strong resemblance to their mother emerging. Estelle now treated her as if she were younger, but seemed so naive she thought of Estelle as stuck forever at eighteen. Estelle and Ben had a house twenty minutes by car from her parents, and there was a great deal of visiting.

From a distance she loved them, loved to shop with extravagance for birthdays and bring them pretty things they would never buy themselves. Visiting them, she was exhausted after half an evening. A numbing gas that turned her bones to lead seeped from the television. She could never believe how little they knew or cared about her life and the world it was lived in. When her father, who was slumped comfortably with his round shoulders in the roundbacked chair eating decorously a dish of chocolate icecream, remarked that America oughtn't to let those Chinese reds threaten us, but we ought to go in with a couple of big bombs and show them who they were talking to, she felt in their

innocence a streak of evil and sat bemired biting her tongue.
While she was married to Asher they had taken an interest,
but since their loud reactions to the divorce, little. Except for
one conversation with Estelle.

She had been helping Estelle put away clothes warm from
the dryer, when her sister paused with a folded sheet held to
her plump breasts. "So now you're on your own, where do
you live? In a dormitory? Or one of those co-ops like you
used to?"

She had been startled. "No, in an apartment. I have a
small apartment."

"To yourself? My, isn't that strange." Estelle thought
about it, still holding the sheet. "It must be kind of nice
coming home and stretching out with all that room to yourself. But aren't you scared at night?"

Did Estelle really think she slept alone? With embarrassment more for Estelle than herself she looked into her sister's
large deepset brown eyes that mimicked her own. She hardly
felt proud of it, but everyone who knew her at all knew that
if she were taken down to Antarctica and marooned, when
they came to dig her out she would have evolved a passionate
entanglement with a seal, she would be enmeshed in a violent and harrowing triangle of penguins.

Something must have shown. Estelle, who had married
from home right after highschool graduation, stepped closer
to peer at her. "Do you date now? Do you go out with boys?"

Boys. "Yes." And she had thought she would tell Estelle
about Rowley, by way of trying it out. What she had antici-
pated: Yes, I know he isn't Jewish, but . . .

"That must be . . . fun." Estelle was looking at her carefully, trying to read something. "Do you tell them you were
married? Do you call yourself Miss or Mrs.? Don't they
wonder where your family is?" Estelle's blind strong curiosity gave off whiffs of dissatisfaction. "Of course you don't
have a place to ask them in to sit . . . How do you make
them bring you back on time?"

Remembering, Anna sighed. They had never been as close
as Rowley and his baby sister were. He was helping Sam
through school—his parents couldn't with his father sick and

his mother a woman who had never worked outside the home. Sam was a bright kid but strongwilled, and one of these days she and Rowley were going to have a battle . . .

With a start she came back to the room seeing the stained lecture notes and columns of halfmade budget. If only she could forget for a whole day, for half a day, for an hour that he existed.

At seven as she was broiling a lambchop, he called. When she heard his voice she thought he was going to ask her to supper. She would not say a word about the chop. But he asked, "You want to come over and pick up your things? If you want to."

"Yes, of course. Tonight. If you're . . . if it's convenient."

"Anytime. When you want."

"I'll be over about eight."

"I'll pick you up."

"Don't bother."

He did not argue.

By then she could not eat the chop. Changed her clothes. Decided she looked too dressed, too arranged, and changed again. Walking through the darkened streets, a scrappy chill wind on her back coming in spurts off the lake half a mile east, she played over and over again their brief exchange. An excuse to see her? He needed none. No, he wanted her gear out, he wanted the clean definition of a break. She almost hated him as she approached his house, past the cavernous old apartment houses the University was always secretly buying and then making a scandal by evicting all the old tenants, into the streets of frame and shingle houses. Hating was sordid. She disapproved of women who spoke with venom of men they had loved for no reason than that they had stopped. She disapproved! She always was disapproving of something. One would think her a moral animal. I try, I try, she muttered.

The house pulsed light: probably everyone home, the relatives upstairs, the Williams in between, the downstairs Rowley. She did not want to go in, not at all. The tension that had caused their breakup came from this house, for if

Harlan were to lose it and Rowley had to move around the
same time she was put out, they could not have gone on as
they had. Whether they decided to live together or not would
be a decision, a judgment: and they must both have perceived
that subconsciously. As she hesitated, she thought that he
might look out and see her dawdling there. Down the walk
she marched to rap briskly. She must give him back the key.
To save the price of having a new one made for Caroline?

"Hello, Rowley." For a moment she was tempted to use
his first name, George. He hated it, saw that few knew it.
Rather than face him she passed into the livingroom, bruised
to see it looking as it had. Did she expect the walls to run
blood? Yente howled welcome, climbing her leg, pawing and
complaining and butting his head until she took him up. On
her shoulder he set up loud rough purring, kneading her and
in his excitement letting his claws unsheathe.

Rowley's mouth tweaked upward in restless unease. He
crossed the room rubbing his scalp, setting the coarse dark
hair on end. "I don't suppose this is the half of it, but it's
what I turned up. Don't take my word for it. Better look
around." He had piled pans and kitchen gadgets on a chair
along with clothes, a box of tampons, her toothbrush and
hairbrush, Navaho rug, wineglasses, a wide strawhat, books.
It came to her that if she had not gone on pills two months
before, her diaphragm would be on the pile too, and she was
thankful.

"The Klee drawing in the bedroom. That's mine." She
longed for a squabble about possessions to relieve them both.

"Sure it is." He strode off. "You know me, I buy things
to listen to, but not to look at."

She resolved that her dignity consisted in not following
him to that doorway. She stood clutching Yente.

"Look, have a seat. How about a drink?" He brought the
drawing back and stood against the heaped chair.

She accepted, grimly. She had begun to dread the moment
she would walk out. How she hated endings.

His hand as he gave her the glass was steady, but his eyes
broke from hers, returned with a strange vivid black stare

that felt familiar, as if a long time before she had seen him look that way. "How are your classes?"

The room was tilting toward him. She could tell him. Yes. That would rally him to her because it would let him off from being wrong. As if she were sliding across she set her flesh against him. She would not use her trouble as bait. She would not trust again. "Please don't let's talk for the sake of making talk."

He hopped from his seat to pace around the chair laden with her things. "Fuck it, Anna, you think something's more real if it hurts?"

She told him more items and he fetched them. She was tortured by the feeling that all she had to do was laugh or touch him, and the savage coldness would rip aside.

He came to stand in front of her. "Take Yente."

"Don't be silly."

"I'm not home much. He's used to you."

She kept looking at the cat so she would not have to look up. "I don't think I'm allowed to have pets."

"Your landlady afraid they'll bother the roaches?"

"Besides, I can't support him." She pulled the cat off her shoulder and handed him over. Resentful, Yente twisted free and trotted into the kitchen, tail high.

The phone rang. He dodged into the bedroom. "Rowley speaking." He scooped it up and walked to the door cradling the receiver against his shoulder, his eyes still on her. "Oh, it's you." His gaze turned to the wall. "No, I am not . . ." He turned as if casually and walked back into the bedroom. "I'll call you back. . . . Yeah, yeah, later. . . . Now shut it off. I told you she would be . . ."

She caught herself holding her breath. Caroline? Or another, what matter. The contemptuous intimate tone hurt more than pet names. He was sure of this girl already. *She* knew that Anna was here and was jealous. Need not be.

"I said I'll call you. Goodbye." He hung up.

She rose. "I'm just going. You needn't have cut that short."

"Of no importance." His eyes were hard. "You have everything you want?"

"Everything that belongs to me. I wouldn't be wanting anything else."

They stood face to face and she in the heat of her anger sustained his gaze.

"A safe attitude. I suppose if I'd held it, I'd have saved us both a lot of trouble."

His face was dark and bitter, making her forget the insult of her tongue. "Oh, Rowley, I'm not gong to start blaming you for that now—"

"Start?"

"I wasn't happy with Asher. We'd have broken up eventually." Ashamed of letting her truculence slip, she turned and loaded her arms with objects from the chair.

As he was putting a box into the backseat, he said over his shoulder with his teeth showing, "You're a fair woman."

"To everyone but myself. There I'm fowl—a sitting duck, no?"

He straightened up and glared.

"Let's not talk," she said. "Help me get this stuff to my rooms and don't say any more. Not any more."

He shrugged broadly but he kept the silence. Without more than directions exchanged—"Hold the door would you?" "I'll take the clothes"—they finished loading the car, drove to her place, and carried her things upstairs. Letting him make the last trip alone she began to put kitchen supplies away. She did not turn when he brought the books in, put them on the table and stood looking at her. Feeling his gaze on her back she thought loudly, oh please, please don't let him say anything, please don't let him speak. Keep his mouth shut and send him away. Please.

The door closed and his footsteps cascaded down the stairs. Weakly she leaned against the refrigerator and looked with blank stupidity and fatigue at the baggage piled on her table, residue of a finished small life.

Tuesday, September 23— Tuesday, October 7

Anna stayed out of the bars Rowley frequented, and since they were the only ones she felt comfortable in alone, she did not drink. She changed restaurants, stores and laundromats, avoiding Rowley and incidentally their friends. That suited her. She would keep away till she was less pitiable, but she was cut off from the usual job channels at the University, the station, the journals and institutes, and thrown back on the newspaper.

In the Lotus Gardens where for less than a dollar she could escape her walls and her own company, she sat eating chow mein. It was a slot between stores with a cramped row of booths and a take-out counter presided over by the Grand Canyon at sunset. The proprietor's fourteen-year-old daughter, who waited on tables with a transistor radio clapped to her ear and her neat butt twitching, looked on customers with disdain for anyone who would eat in such a crummy place.

She was rereading Veblen for comfort. She had an old crush on his clumsy integrity. He had been a tweeny too in this city and fired eventually. She looked up from her book and plate to see Leon waiting by the take-out counter. She started to wave, thought better. She did not want to talk to him and slid down. But a moment later he stood beside the booth, slope shouldered and scowling.

"So how are you?" he said heavily as he slid in the opposite bench. Rumpled and careworn he rubbed his hands loosely.

She smiled for answer still hoping to evade him, but he went on, "How's Rowley? You make things up?"

He must know, he was a friend of Caroline's. "We're not seeing each other."

"Oh?" His bushy eyebrows met. "From that night?"

"I think we'd about reached the end of our rope."

"You don't have to try to act cheerful. You look like hell."

She snorted. "Oh, that was only the first blow. I'm out of a job too." Briefly she told him what had happened.

Taking off his glasses he rubbed his eyes hard with his palms. His voice had a builtin sneer, undermining whatever he said. The words seemed to come out at a slant. "What kind of job you want?"

"Just one to keep me, modestly. Not bore me out of my mind or cause me to do harm to myself or others. I can type, run a switchboard, I've done editing. I've timed rats and taken care of shell-shocked lab monkeys. I've had some statistics . . ."

"Okay, I think I can get you something at ISS." The Institute for Social Surveying.

"You could?" She did not believe him but the offer was well meant. "That would be fine. You work there?"

"Yeah, and it's not fine. A place with the jitters. But there are always openings, the door swings out, the door swings in. I'll ask around. Eat, don't mind me, your food's getting cold."

She obeyed. It was already cold. After a minute he asked, "He seeing Caroline?"

She kept her eyes to her plate. "Can't say that I asked him."

"I knew that engagement was a farce. Just wanted the ring. Look, girls, stone of my own. She won't marry him."

"If she wants marriage, she'd better stick to her boyfriend."

Leon shrugged, still harried. He frowned at her as if trying to figure something out. But he did not speak, and then his named was called.

Two days afterward he phoned. "Looks like a good deal. I got a bit interviewing on what people think we should do with old folks—like should we gas them or just let them starve—but the opening for you is inside. Norma Clay needs a helper—mainly secretarial, some technical stuff. Come on sociological. Her last is having a baby. Call her tomorrow— a fat old dyke if you don't mind that—but uh don't tell her I sent you if you want the job.''

A week and a half later Anna began work for Norma Clay, a squarish bedeviled sociologist about forty who wore tweed suits with dainty frilled blouses, as if she had once been told to assert her femininity. Miss Clay had a high girlish voice that belonged to a much younger, slenderer woman, but everything else was soldierly. She walked weightily with a slight frown of decision and threat. The major business of the institution, Anna discovered, was jockeying for position within it. Miss Clay was not a natural conspirator. The con- stant effort to maintain her place, to wangle her share of foundation and industrial monies and to counter plots to oust her had soured what must have been a gentle, rather phleg- matic disposition, so that she had become awkward but dan- gerous, like a cornered cow.

Anna shared an antechamber with a middle aged woman who looked her up and down and sucked in her mouth. Mrs. Cavenaugh had been with ISS from the beginning. Sociolo- gists came and went, but the secretarial staff abided in full security elaborating Byzantine rituals. Mrs. Cavenaugh ate lunch at her typewriter, arrived before nine, left well after five and spoke of the director with an elderly flutter. In her view her most important task was to keep the technical per- sonnel from getting their hands on the office machines and supplies.

As she left Tuesday, Leon was perched on the reception- ist's desk. He rose and came after her. "So, you got the job?"

She thanked him effusively, awkwardly. She felt she had been rude, remembering things she had said to Rowley, worse things she had thought. He had gone out of his way to help her, either willing to excuse her rudeness or unaware of how she had felt.

"I told you it's no great job, so forget it." His voice was cold and distancing. In a prickly silence they walked a block, crushing the brittle cottonwood leaves underfoot. He said, "Have supper with me at Parks, I hate to eat alone."

To make amends she agreed. Though Rowley seldom ate there, she felt a great relief when she looked quickly over the sandwich shop. How long before she need not do that at every entrance?

He stared at his hands on the table as if they were something the waitress had neglected to clear. "Yeah, I hate to eat alone. Leftover from marriage. Got to have someone across the table to yell at."

"You get out of the habit of being alone. I was married once myself."

"Good experience for a woman. Makes her useful." He grinned. His teeth were his best feature, strong and white. "What happened?"

"I met Rowley."

"Oh." His eyes, milky blue and arctic, studied her. "Like that."

"He was a lever for prying myself loose."

"How come you got stuck to begin with? Why so young?"

She played with her food. If she said she married Asher for his reform politics, because she had soured on the department? "Because at twenty-one I felt older than I do now. Because a couple of other people hadn't married me. Because I thought Asher—my husband—loved me, needed me. Because I was feeling a little shabby. I wanted to get out of the wind."

"I got married because . . . it seemed the thing to do. Joye kept yakking about it. I was worn out with her thinking she was knocked up every month." He grimaced, his face tight. "You know she's got my kid."

"Your kid?" Vaguely she remembered Rowley arriving late, drunk and amorous from celebrating the birth. "I guess I did know you have a boy."

"She's got Jimmy, not me. Because of a trick I pulled when we were fighting our way through the courts she doesn't have to let me see him for a year." He tucked his chin into his ski sweater. "She's got the bit in her teeth these days and she's tearing around whining about how I treated her. I hear she tells some gory tales." He stuck out his square jaw. "All of them true."

"We had a quiet divorce. Asher's a gentleman. Once he'd given up trying to change my mind he wanted no more fuss than necessary to comply with the law. But I was the guilty party. And I felt like it."

"But *you* would have anyhow." His strange eyes lit with amusement.

"Too true." She smiled. "That's the nicest thing anybody's ever said on the dreary subject. But it in no way detracts from the sense of guilt I keep polished."

"Defense."

"Guilt as defense? Against what?"

"Believing in anything the way you must have in your marriage. Getting cheated again." He sighted along his finger at her. "When you talk about your marriage you get an expression on, like you're remembering a bad joke somebody played on you."

She frowned. "Only myself. Yes, I'm scared of being taken in."

He rubbed his cheek roughly, giving her that shy feral grin that was as close as he came to smiling: As if the shame of his awkward hairy body was too great to allow spontaneous gestures, only gashes through which his reactions could escape. He was not entirely ugly. He had remarkable eyes and good teeth, and a squat powerful build. But she remembered Joye, conventionally pretty and fluffy like a nice highschool girl. Blond-brown hair, turned up nose, okay legs. Joye had been crazy about him. At parties she had clung to him until he turned lowering and shook her off, when she would retreat to a corner and watch him with lonesome eyes. She could hear Joye talking, giving his name two full syllables: Leeyon doesn't like carrots, Lee-yon says opera is for Maggots, Lee-yon says I'm a masochist, do you think so? Joye would drink too much and end up passed out on the bed with the pile of coats or crying on a man's shoulder. He had punched someone's nose for comforting her, so Rowley had told her as proof Leon cared for his wife. Marriage was a three-legged race uphill. Foolish to blame Leon for Joye's unhappiness when all it meant was that they should never have agreed to bungle along under one roof trying to make each other's discomfort complete.

"Think there's a good chance of you making it up with old Rowley?"

"Not a chance." She bit the words off.

"Why not? Unless he's shacked up with Caroline."

"I have no idea—except there's sure to be someone warming that bed. We're both too proud. We won't put up with each other's demands, and neither of us will back down."

"Ummmm. He's had an eye on Caroline for a long time."

"I don't think so!"

"How would you know? I've seen him looking her over. It won't last—he won't care for her. But he was willing to toss you overboard to get hold of her."

Her cheeks felt swollen. "It's just that he can't resist prancing around and proving himself."

"Was it spontaneous when he took you away from your husband? Listen, I know Rowley. Didn't I share a pad with him for two years? Not that he means to be ruthless, but he's introspective as a bulldog and all he does is follow his nose— or his prick. When he wants something he wants it so bad he manages to make you think for a while, maybe a long while, that it means something. Then he can't be bothered. I used to get his girls crying on my shoulder."

She had great difficulty meeting his gaze. He was unjust, jealous. Or did she want to protect her pride?

"I don't mean he's a bastard. Only he gets into situations and then loses patience and wants out." When she did not answer he added harshly, "I suppose you think I'm a shit talking about him that way. Doesn't show much gratitude."

"Gratitude?"

"Sure. For his big rescue."

"What?"

"You know. His heroic bit."

"What are you talking about?" she cried in irritation.

"Strong silent type. He saved my life. Big deal. I took an overdose of sleeping pills. The bungler's way. If you really mean it, you don't take pills and wait for somebody to stumble over you. You borrow a gun and blow your head off, you cut your throat. You jump out a tenth-floor window. You don't fuck around with pills.''

"He never mentioned it." She was not sure how to react. "You must have been very depressed."

"No more than usual." He picked his nose.

"That was before you got married?"

"That's what I did to myself instead. Like the pills it didn't live up to expectations." He reached for the check. "I half hoped she'd lead me out to green suburbs, but I was too strong for her."

"You were involved with Caroline, weren't you?"

"Me?" He paid the cashier, turned and walked out. Under the blinking green neon sign he stood hunched as if against a wind. "While I was married. Shouldn't have mixed with her then, bad idea." He shook his head mumbling, "A hard scene, all the way round."

So he felt guilty about Caroline, hence the paternal concern. Another blondbrown girl with nice legs. He must collect them. She said, "I never use my head for anything useful. When I'm interested in a man my brain shuts off. Perhaps that's what you were saying about Rowley."

"You're still soft on him."

"Not true! But I don't dislike him."

"Good." He caught hold of a no parking sign and swung around the pole, stopped to face her. "If you mean I dumped her, you're dead wrong."

"I know nothing about it."

"People always think they do," he said stubbornly but walked on with her. "I'm afraid that's how she sees it."

She thought in surprise of their supper. She was not usually loosemouthed, but his harsh selfabusive honesty drew her open. More common ground than she would have guessed. They were both people who had become aware of the barbs in their own acts.

"Here's where I live."

"Like last time."

He showed no sign of saying goodnight. Reluctantly she asked him up for coffee.

"Your place is too small." He slumped in a chair, still wearing his coat. "It depresses me."

"Lately it depresses me too."

He sat with his big head bowed, his hair the color of tomato soup under the overhead light. As he drank off his coffee and set down the cup he gave her a bleak grin. "You uh . . . want company tonight?"

"No!" She spoke without thinking, then got scared she had insulted him. He had asked with the grace of someone emptying a bucket of slops.

"Good," he said heartily. "Better. Wouldn't pry either of us out of the muck."

"Why ask then?"

"Never hurts. After all." With a broader grin. He looked at his hand, made a fist and hit it on the table. "You're not going to get mixed up with someone right away. You're still in shock, like someone with a limb cut off. We just settled the issue between us. But we can be useful. You're low on bread, right? So I buy a couple of steaks and you fix them. Or we eat in Parks. Like I said, I hate eating alone. We pass the time, *going places, doing things*." His voice rose satirically but he watched. "See a flick, eat icecream, toss a ball around."

Faintly possible that this was his oblique approach to bed but she was not committing herself to anything agreeing to see him now and then. He had found her a job, he had been interesting to talk to. She was as poorly equipped to endure loneliness as she ever had been: a few weeks in her rooms and she'd be across the street at Woody's bar seeking proof of her attractiveness, her existence, seeking relief from the pressure of walls and memory and anxiety. "By the way, was that your standard approach?"

"I have no approach. I let women do what they want to."

She laughed. "I don't know if that's indifference or the cleverest trap of all."

"The door's open. That's all. All the doors are open."

Saturday, October 25

A clear racy day with the wind smelling of leaves. Even the grubby sparrows in the gutter showed not uniformly sooty but brown-capped and blackthroated. Content to be alone Anna walked toward the lake, a blanket over her arm and a book Leon had pressed on her—an interpretation of Blake he claimed was his theory of film—tucked in her cow of a purse. As she passed under the echoey railroad viaduct she wondered in which lakeside tower Leon was lunching with his mother, in these blocks almost entirely white and largely vertical. The managers, the lawyers, the middle echelon administration men lived over here in grandiose well kept apartment hotels or new glass walled skyscrapers. Cliffs of money on the lake.

The point was a crowded rookery of sunning students and neighborhood people sprawled under the small trees. She clambered down from rock to rock, folded her coat and leaned back. In a clean curve the lake arced away to the Loop's compact facade. Below her a man fished, clutching beer in a paper sack. Once an hour the fuzz patrolled. From daylight on men fished, old men joined on the weekend by young black guys. The old men fished with two or more poles, with pulleys, balls of stout line and bells to warn of a nibble. They muttered encouragement and chaff as if each was afraid the other would quit before he did.

She turned toward deep water, let her eyes close and the sun melt the muscles in her face. The noises grew discrete, each cry, bike chain, transistor or motor boat. Then they receded and she felt calmer than she had in a month and a half. If only she could live more gently. Her trouble was in

overresponding to events, to people, to touch and words and
the ordinary flotsam of living. Somehow her volume control
had got turned too loud. A giant baby resided in her grabbing
at things, then letting go with a clatter—responding hypnot-
ically to stroking, clutching the penis like a breast for com
fort. Time and again she saw clearly and acted irrationally
crying, Now what have I done?

Yes, these rocks. A mild April night with a damp wind
lapping over the water. The evening had begun badly. Asher
had agreed to take her to a Yeats play in which her friend
Marcia was dancing. However, the Independents for Botts
threw a party, and they must go there instead in order for
Asher to talk to someone who'd be making an appearance.
Then he did not like her dress and kept after her till she
changed it. She had always suspected that the women Asher
approved of were hipless girls with elegant bony shoulders.
He had been under the impression the party was to be more
political than alcoholic, and he was wrong. After he failed
to persuade the man to vote for a park proposal, he wanted
to go home. She said no. She did not like the group, she did
not want to be at this party, but it was Saturday night and
she was not going back to their apartment, not yet she wasn't.

Asher left, and she glared around the room waiting for one
of those stuffed green olives to ask her what had happened.
She got herself another drink and stood backed into a corner,
a grimace of desperate malaise spreading over her face. The
next morning she could count on Asher's voice regular and
relentless as dripping water:

"Now let's try to understand why you did that. You'll
agree, I think, that it was a strange thing to do? A little
immature? What did you plan to say when someone asked
you where I was?"

She swallowed her drink and went to get her coat, as Rowley came in with a group. He lagged behind to speak to her.
"Where's Asher? Out there fighting for a cleaner Chicago?"

She felt silly enough to tell him. Smiling he took her arm.
"I'd give you a ride, but I came with Cal. Come on and I'll
walk you home."

By the time they had gone the few blocks to the townhouse

she and Asher were exorbitantly buying, they had come alive to each other and besides the night was mild with spring after the long craggy winter so that one or the other had suggested walking further. Eventually they had strolled out on the point and sat talking on a rock. She felt feverish: she thought she could feel the blood fizz through her veins, the hair growing in her scalp. She had told herself her joy was a freak of the thaw, but she felt a desolate loss when suddenly she saw the the east was turning gray and sat bolt upright remembering she was married.

"God, it's morning," she had interrupted. "I have to go, *now*. I have no idea what I'm going to tell Asher."

In answer his face went somber, heavy. She thought she had angered him. He pulled her into his arms and kissed her. When she drew free the rim of the sky was lighter, and she knew with a fierce pleasurable terror that she wanted him. She was shocked and gratified. Standing she gave him her hand, and he took her home. She did not expect to see him again unless she ran into him with Asher.

Asher was asleep, and she made her bed on the couch. In the morning when she told him she had gone out for coffee with Rowley, they had one of their bad arguments. She had felt no guilt that morning, only a sense of delight she was hard put not to try to share with Asher. She could not keep from telling him she had been with Rowley not only because truth was her habit but because saying his name was a sharp pleasure. Somehow she expected Asher to understand: a walk with Rowley in the spring was not to be disparaged. As if she had been on vacation, she perceived in herself new readiness to try to fulfill Asher's ideas of wifehood. She longed for a chance to demonstrate her strengthened patience, promptness and fortitude. She got it.

Three days later Asher had gathered data on Rowley. He reported it with obvious distaste for the resemblance of this transfer of information to gossip. She listened in squashed fury. She had to question the night and ask if he had been simply on the make. His words and gestures began to haunt her. All of the time like a steady lowpitched hum she found herself thinking of him. She felt raw and sore, she wanted to

call him to account, she wanted to justify him. The next time
she saw him, by accident in the Loop, she had formed de-
fenses.

Not, to be sure, sufficient. Her marriage just might have
been salvageable had she not seen him at all, but she could
not let go feeling alive. Each time she saw him she resolved
to give nothing, to take nothing. Each time he met her believing she would break off. That tension had perhaps never
died.

She opened her eyes and watched a gull maneuver and
dive over water blue and soft as morning glories. A pity they
could not be friends because there was no one like him. She
was glad to have come through the pain of breaking and out
the other side without resorting to hatred. She was heartily
glad.

The afternoon was turning chilly when Leon found her.

She walked with him to the car. "How did it go with your
mother?"

"Okay, okay." He scratched his head in annoyance, his
voice surly. "Fern gave me a lecture, but she gave me some
money too."

"Does she do that often?"

"Not often enough. Think I'm ashamed? They have more
than they know what to do with." He snorted. "Not that *he*
ever hands any over. Fern does it on the sly."

She glanced over her shoulder and saw that the backseat
was filled with packages. Frozen sirloin and porterhouse
steaks and lambchops they loaded directly into the freezer.
The bag Leon toted in with care held a pot of stuffed cabbage. "Put that on, heat it up for supper. Fern's stuffed cabbage is the greatest."

She would make her stuffed cabbage for him. She would
not be outdone by anybody's mother. Out of another bag
came two sportshirts with pins still in them, a Scottish sweater
with a mothhole, a bottle of good men's aftershave used perhaps twice, recent issues of *Commentary* and a pair of ice-
skates. Another bag held Chinook salmon, kosher soups,
sardines, asparagus, fancy mixed Chinese vegetables, water
biscuits and red caviar.

The kitchen table was hidden by a grove of empty pop bottles, forcing them to eat in the livingroom. "Film's expensive," he mumbled as he ate. "Those damn foundations swimming in money, you'd think they'd give a little but they wait till you've made it halfway, and then who needs them? Scared of being caught wrong. Fern can't see my stuff for shit but she tries, anyhow."

"You're closer to her than to your father, right?"

"At least she's a human being, or she used to be. Sheldon sounds like a vulture, he acts like a vulture, he thinks like a vulture. He even smells like one. Fern married him for security, and I bet she's sorry. They stayed married for the children's sake, my poor ball-less brother Sidney and me." He had turned up cranky but now he was relaxed. She did not set out to adapt to his moods or shape them, but she could not help taking on a certain amount of protective emotional coloration from a man. He was old to be wrapped up in his family, but perhaps seeing his mother stirred up a swarm of annoyances from the past. He was still talking about his father, a passionate bitterness thickening his voice. "Sheldon's in love with the dirty work he's doing for the University—facilitating renewal. Like pulling strings and putting the pressure on where it hurts. He thinks the University is pure and that makes him pure. He's always been self-righteous, but now he's impossible, he's leading a damn holy crusade against the lowdown and the unworthy."

"Tell your father he's forcing you—and incidentally me—out of our snug homes."

Leon laughed: the teeth of a saw catching one by one on his larynx. "That's the idea, gang. Sheldon believes in the good, the true, and the beautiful. He wants to be where the good people are—only heaven is here and the points are bread and status. He's prepared to sacrifice for his ideals. Like old Abraham he's all set to knife his son. Anyhow, he has another." He got up abruptly. "Let's get our asses out of here. Let's wash all this rot down with some beer."

She should not have let him talk so long about his family. On her side of the rusty Buick she curled up. Leon was likable once you came to know him: prickly and stubborn but loyal. He always had some project afoot to get a friend something he thought they needed, a job, a woman, away from home, back into school, into analysis. Coming near him she stepped into a palpable field of interest. The converse was an equally strong pull for sympathy, a tugging at the breast she suspected him unaware of. She did not mind that pull for nothing came more cheaply than empathy with a man. He had only to capture her attention.

"When Joye and I got married he offered us a thousand bucks if we'd swear to keep a kosher kitchen. Ace, I told him to shove it. You don't give presents with clauses. He's such a barefaced hypo. You know, when I was getting bar-mitzvahed, I got hooked on Hebrew and serious about the stuff and I was even thinking about being a rabbi, dig that. He made me feel like a worm. You don't take that shit seriously, he let me know, it's bad manners, it's only poor *schlumps* like your mother's family who really let it get in the way."

Woody's bar was jammed. Once in the door they were brought to a halt. In the lead he forced a slow way, squeezing between the tables and the crowd along the bar. As he inched forward gouts of words came over his shoulder in the uproar. "Always got to be right . . . bigoted old bastard . . . got me thrown out of school . . . tell you some time." Then he turned. "There's your friend," he hissed.

She followed the direction of his gaze and ran against Rowley's table. A hot wave of confusion flooded her. All in green Caroline leaned toward him, the fingers of one hand just grazing his. Outstretched graceful hand of possession. She snagged almost at once on his eyes. She caught her breath, shocked at the anger in his frowning stare, shocked that he had not, did not greet her. Blood knocked in her temples and throat.

"It's crowded, it's too crowded. Let's go!"

Leon turned, looked her full in the face, and then took her arm and led her out.

Leon brought out a bottle of scotch that they attacked in the island of light on the couch set in his dark lofty apartment.

"What did you expect? You annoy him. It's damned inconvenient of you to turn up in his world."

"But I don't hate him! Why should he hate me?"

"You will. You have to. He rejected you."

"But we loved each other."

"Rowley never loved anyone but Rowley."

"You don't know!"

"Nobody has ever loved you." He chuckled dryly. "If someone had loved you, you'd never have left him."

"How could he not speak to me? How could he do that to me in front of another woman?"

"Why not? You'll cut him dead next time."

"Now I want to. I want to march past him with fourteen other men."

"You couldn't make him jealous. Seeing you with another man probably relieves his conscience."

"My, you're cheering me up."

"You want lies or reality?"

Scotch and shock were breeding a sponginess in her brain, but through it she studied him. He was trying to tear from her what she considered her history and he considered illusion. He was strange and dangerous and this peculiar struggle was not healthy: but it was absorbing. She was not confident she was fit for anything better than to sit with Leon late at night over the wreckage of her own and other lives.

"You keep saying he didn't love me. All right, he doesn't give a shit now—granted, after tonight, granted! But he did care. You don't know how well we got on. Just simple things like eating together . . ."

"Sure, he's easygoing, long as he has his way. So why didn't you get married?"

He buffeted her with questions from retreat to retreat. "Why should you care?"

"I believe in caring." He lay back plunking his feet on the abused and stained teak table. "When we die we're meat, and in the meantime nothing's worth bothering about but people. Not words, actions. Anybody can say *love, love, love*, but will he cross the street to do you something? First he has to find out what you need. Who you are. Right?"

Yes. The slow warmth of recognition. He talked on and her murmurs of agreement rounded his sentences.

"What matters is handling others not like things but setting up a connection. A live circuit. You have to keep trying to get through. When you give up, you're dead: walled in."

He told her a story. "Once upon a time there was a woman came to a man and said, Baby, love me. He said, Ech, you? A plain dumpy broad like yourself? Go on. She said, Baby, love me and I'll be anybody you want me to be, please. Man said, How about Cleopatra. So the woman turned into Cleopatra, and the next morning, man said, That wasn't half bad. So they got married. After a while, man got tired of all the snakes in the bathroom and he had her turn into Marilyn for a while, and then he had Harlow and Garbo and Lucretia Borgia. Everything went fine till one morning he woke up first and there she was too pooped to play her role. Who the hell are *you*, said the man, and where's my gorgeous wife? I am your wife whom you love, said the woman, but he kicked her out of bed. Women are ever deceitful, he said, and went to bed with his officeboy. The woman went to a fortuneteller to ask, Why did he stop loving me?"

She was lying on the couch. She rose on one elbow to look at him through narrowed eyes. "You're clearly not talking about Rowley now."

"Or how about this one? A man got himself a pretty bright-colored bird because he liked the way it sang. He took it home and put it in a cage, but it wouldn't sing where it couldn't fly around. Every day the bird got smaller and smaller, it wouldn't eat and drink, and finally it got so small it flew out like a mosquito through the wire mesh. That goes to show you, the man said, I should've invested in a better cage."

"Or a better behaved bird." She was sitting up. "So you knew Asher?"

He laughed like a kid. "I saw you with him. That's all."

She shook her head wonderingly. "I don't remember meeting you."

"I'm an old girlwatcher. You know. But I was just figuring the odds. I'll tell you one thing. That whole year with Rowley was just a game. The problems you have to solve were the ones bound up with your marriage.''

She lay back on the couch. She had kicked off her shoes and slowly she flexed her toes. ''Sometimes I feel as if I killed some small, pretty, fluffy but vicious animal—like a rabbit with fangs—and I go around with it hung in my hair wondering why I smell something bad and what hurts.''

''Kid, we're topnotch rabbit buriers around here,'' Leon rasped, ''but you'd be surprised how many people can't walk upright if they don't have something heavy in their hair.''

Hard to believe in a world beyond this island of light caulked by darkness. The brown couch was low and scarred with cigarette burns through which foamrubber showed. His baby's sweater lay on the table, growing dirtier. Looking at the film of grime and ash, she decided she would have to clean.

Wednesday—Sunday,
October 29—November 2

Wednesday: Anna learned that Rand Grooper of ISS had got a grant from the housing administration to do an objective study of democratic participation in the processes of urban renewal planning in the area. He had farmed out a piece to Miss Clay in return for her name on the proposal. Miss Clay enjoyed a reputation in Washington since she had run a monumental study on re-enlistment among WACs. Anna had handled the volumes of the report, full of mathematical tables demonstrating among the sample of five thousand WACs that the desire to have offspring negatively correlated with re-enlistment intentions; favorable attitudes toward authority systems, on the other hand, demonstrated positive correlation. The project had caused a stir in military and governmental circles, and her services were in demand.

The ISS board of directors interlocked with the University. Grooper was an ambitious young man. One arm of the University was preparing the renewal plan. Anna was reminded of her foray into market research, when she had worked briefly for a consumers' testing organization that specialized in producing tests for companies who wished to demonstrate the superiority of their products.

Thursday: Her friend Marcia called her. "Meet me for lunch, no excuses. I won't have you hiding in a sulk."

They had lunch in Woody's bar where the hamburgers were the best around, the noon atmosphere dim and relaxed, the dark beer on draft cheap. At first she kept glancing at the table where she had seen Rowley last.

Black stretch pants showed Marcia's musculature of a dancer, under the layers of red and purple poncho and thick auburn hair. Her scrubbed face would have been gentle, a little tired around the mouth, but over it Marcia painted a luminescent landscape. Today jade green and cobalt ringed her sad brown eyes and several sets of furry lashes fluttered bravely under brows drawn concave. Nevertheless, Anna thought, we both look like nice healthy Jewish girls, a bit battered but with centuries of chickenfat embedded under the skulls, welldeveloped laps and heavy emotional runoff in damp weather. She was arming herself, certain from Marcia's forward leaning posture that she was in for it. "Who told you?" she asked.

"Jennie Rosen. Her husband asked Rowley to come to dinner with you. I couldn't believe it! What did he do?"

She smiled at the question's form, then with a twist of her lips, paused, paused, and briefly told.

"That jackass! An ego as big as his head. But don't tell me you couldn't make up. Sore pride—that's your problem. Understandable, but not much for gals our age."

"Come on, don't rub my nose in it. I have another forty years to sit on this *tuchus*."

"You shouldn't throw away a good thing. All day I meet

people. Maybe ten percent of the things that shave are *men*, and they're married with six kids so I can look anyhow. Rowley has his troubles—who hasn't?''

"Maybe it's significant that he isn't married." Echoing Leon but why not? "A man who's never been willing to commit himself—"

"Anna! What man do you know who committed himself? Some woman got him."

"Some woman's got Rowley, so this is academic and a mite painful."

"Oh god. Who? Do I know her?"

"Caroline Frayne."

Marcia caught her breath. "You mean he gave her that ring?"

She sighed. "No, that's from the guy she's supposed to be engaged to. She can't still be wearing it." With a frown she pictured Caroline in green pants, green shirt, hand just touching Rowley's: no ring. She could not be sure. "You mean when she first got back from Europe."

"Anna, I saw her in that chichi little coffeeshop with the folksingers last night—she waited on us. Jennie's taking my class at the Y—a riot, you should see her prancing around."

She itched with shame. Her they had talked about. "Did Caroline hear you?"

"I don't think so." Marcia looked upward trying to remember. "We weren't yelling. And part of the time she was singing. The chap who runs the place lets her start the program." Marcia wrinkled her nose. "A grapefruit has more talent."

"Still!"

"She is pretty. That innocent slutty look. To think I left her a tip."

"Are you sure she's talentless? I never heard her. Remember I told you I got edgy whenever he was backing up an attractive singer, because I had to be on the fringe of his music, not really sharing it. I can't carry a tune across the room."

"Oh pooh. What *have* you been doing with yourself? Jennie swears she called your place nine times, and I'd just about given up hopes of finding you in.''

''If I don't keep busy I feel like a sack of last winter's potatoes.''

''Who have you been busy with?'' Marcia waited, her eyes bright.

The sum total of places one went was too small. ''Oh, mainly Leon Lederman.''

''Leon Lederman . . .'' Marcia absently scratched her nose. ''Do I know him?''

''Probably not.''

''What does he look like?''

Vaguely, defensively she described him, but to her sorrow it worked.

''*Him*. Isn't he married?''

''Divorced.''

''Ummmm. That loudmouth.''

''Come on, Marcia, you said you don't know him.''

''I remember him now. I had to throw him out of a party for starting a fight.''

''But I'll bet it was a good cause. Let me pay for the beer.''

Friday, Halloween: Miss Clay's office had new decorations: a vast aerial photograph of the neighborhood, and a map with crosshatching indicating blight and decay. Anna stood in front of the photo, mesmerized. In the foreground the gray battlements of the University swelled, dominating the landscape. The photo slanted one way toward the white teeth of the lakeside towers, and shaded the other way into the amorphous sootiness of the Black Belt, crowded even denser by the curvature of the wide-angle lens. White and black, high and low, the photo was almost schematic. Her own building was a bump a nudge could topple.

The review board for the renewal study had been appointed, consisting of a mayor's appointee to the downtown planning office whose further advancement was connected with the local project's success; the chairman of the division of social sciences who hoped to find time in between testifying for the redevelopers at hearings on their movement into Rowley's neighborhood and his services to a Presidential blue ribbon panel on crime control; and a clubwoman distinguished for her organizational work among other upper-middle-class liberals, who had thrown the weight of her group behind renewal.

It was hoped that such a wellinformed board of review would greatly facilitate the work of the project in investigating renewal.

Friday was the climax of the week for Anna's officemate Mrs. Cavenaugh. On her because of age and righteousness devolved the delicate task of cutting the Friday afternoon cake. It was understood, Anna found the first time she took a piece to shocked stares, that pieces diminished with seniority and status.

The coders, interviewers and minor technicians were not permitted coffee till the others had finished. Building rumor claimed that the wee folk used to be given coffeebreak with their betters. Certain graduate students serving out their peonage at the Institute, however, had been observed making a meal of the cake.

When she arrived at Leon's, he had been buying candybars, good ones, he said, the kind he had wanted to be given. He was good with the tinseled children, had a deadpan way of kidding they played up to. "Do you really live here?" the kids asked. "Is this a store?"

"Sure it's a store. This is a store where we give words away. Do you want a long one or a short one? How about rococo? or snorch? or troglodyte? Grunt's a good word."

When the last kids disappeared from the streets, he sat down and methodically ate all the remaining candy. They went to a triple horror bill in the Loop. Chewing buttered popcorn in the balcony she had the disturbing sensation of having grown constantly younger since leaving Asher. Leon had days when he wanted to plunge back into his own or an imagined adolescence. He would begin to bolt quantities of Pepsi-Cola and pseudo-foods: potato chips, donuts, peanuts and confections named Korn Kings and Tayco Twists and Nutniks.

On the way home as she looked at his lowbrowed face set in a scowl over the wheel she realized he was depressed and had been so all week.

Saturday: Leon had an appointment with his lawyer at ten thirty. He insisted that she come, then left her in the outer office to leaf through magazines. His voice boomed through the closed door. He emerged pale from anger.

He drove up to the near North Side and then slowly along a street of large wellkept apartment houses, searching an address. Parked.

"What are we here for?"

"Justice."

She looked at him narrowly. "Who lives here, chief?"

"Who do you think?"

"Why didn't you take me home first? Why drag me along at all? Okay, march in."

"Can't. Got to wait for Joye to come out."

"You could have left me in the Loop, idiot. I'm in the way."

"Don't be funny. Joye's seeing some dentist, I just found out." He drummed on the wheel. "Haven't I told you I'm a madman?"

Joye did not appear, with or without his child.

Sunday: After a late brunch of waffles Leon said, "Let's go see Vera."

She said hopefully, "She's a strange girl . . . isn't she?" But he would not comment.

Snow was falling lightly. The wind skimmed the flakes along the ground and heaped them against curbs and stoops and hedges, except where they caught like ashes in the grass. Church-goers in new-looking winter coats were pouring out of pumpkin-colored St. Thomas. On Vera's street the Nation of Islam—women stately in white habits and men in dark suits—were chatting in clumps outside the yellow brick mosque.

The worn name on Vera's building advised that it had been Granada Courts. They buzzed JAMESON and after a long pause she buzzed back. The doorlock was broken anyhow. The lobby was vast with rough plaster walls and Moorish archways. In the weedy court stood the remains of an ashtray shaped fountain surmounted by half a cupidon. They climbed one of a maze of stairways. Vera was standing just outside her door, peering blankly down. Barefoot, she wore slacks and a deep blue sweater above which her faced burned with a dark jarring intensity.

Anna had a foretaste of discomfort. She was intensely sure that Leon hardly knew Vera and contrary to what she had thought, was barging in unexpected and maybe unwelcome. By this time Leon had followed Vera. Testily she went after. He must be interested in Vera to come charging over here—but why drag her along?

Vera lived in a large light room with a corner kitchenette and a skyfilled view of apartmenthouse roofs and the bare twiggy summits of trees. Anna felt even more an intruder when she saw the boy sprawled in selfconscious but stubborn languor on the bed. Cheese, French bread, dairy orange juice and butter lay on a table before the windows, while a percolator steamed on the hotplate.

Vera offered the food and coffee, sitting primly on the bed's edge. Leon sat in an armchair, she in a highbacked wicker rockingchair. She had a sense of being watched, and then she noticed the masks on the wall. "Those are your work?"

"Of course," the boy answered for her. "Who else would make such crazy things?" He poked Vera hard. "Introduce me, stupid."

She told them that he was Paul: just that monosyllable. A jealous lover, this black wedgewood girl. Anna smiled. The boy was rangy, with a slight but good build, skin a few shades lighter than Vera, and a highbrowed sensitive unfinished face. Large awake eyes. He was still arranged in what must be meant to represent a relaxed sprawl, but finally he bounded up to help himself to bread and cheese. In his movements a natural grace fought it out with stiff selfconsciousness.

"Aren't they gorgeous fetishes?" He waved at the bizarre masks put together of scraps of corduroy, satin, velvet,

denim, bottle caps and corks, a bit of a pencil, a salvaged
cigar butt, some wire. "She's been making them since she
was seven." He was talking to them, yet half turned away.
He lifted one from its hook and swung on them, spangled
leer and long green satin nose with frayed rope ends for
moustache and brows of steelwool. For just a moment she
thought . . . she was obsessed, she saw him everywhere.
Letting his hands dangle and flap, Paul went hopping sideways, whirled and tossed the mask at Vera. "Naturally they
were cruder then."

"They were never crude or natural." Vera smiled—she
would have said with amused tenderness except that reactions
touched Vera's face and were gone too quickly to judge more
than the afterimage. "I brought a bunch into school on Friday and let the kids put them on. Of course they all got
destroyed, but the kids had a party. Even Carla, one of my
girls who won't even speak but sits with her head on her desk,
was running around and laughing. Finally I even got them
doing a play."

"Well, that's how the masks got started, so why not?"
Paul said.

"You've known each other for a long time," Anna said.

They stared blankly. Leon looked over his shoulder.
"Sure, kid, they're brother and sister."

Then she saw that they were. "Oh. You're going to school
here, Paul?" Quick before they realized what she had
thought.

"He's a real student," Vera said. "School bored me. Kindergarten wasn't bad, but after that, it got less inventive."

Paul pouted. "Then why did you do so well?"

"Because I didn't care."

"A real student! I'll never get my degree if I can't pass
that science class. It's ridiculous. I'd get my degree in June,
but I'm flunking the same course I dropped once before.
Imagine, I was going into archaeology."

"So you're flunking nat sci," Leon muttered.

"I don't mind your giving up archaeology . . ." Vera's
voice was clear and sad. "But you won't give thought to what
we're going to do."

Paul reached overhead for another mask made from the top of a bathroom scale. "I'll be a clown."

His sister ducked her small chin, considering. Then with a pleasurably malicious smile, rolling her eyes white, "No. You aren't funny enough."

"Bitch. Mean bitch." Drawing his bare foot up he shoved her off the bed. She sat hard on the floor with a surprised giggle.

Perhaps Paul enjoyed the masks because they freed him. She felt for his rangy awkwardness, his embarrassed glib efforts to entertain them. Vera was closed, did not care what they thought. She must be the older but they seemed twins. Old daydream: boy twin, agreeable other. First sexual phantom. Much better than dumb tagalong sister Estelle. Her periodic efforts in more recent times to get through to Estelle (through what? into what?) brought puzzled resentment. She envied Vera a brother, a man to love her no matter what, with full visibility and loyalty.

"How's Caroline?" Leon asked between mouthfuls of cheese. "What's she doing with herself?"

Her breath caught. He was testing her nerves.

Paul wrinkled his nose and declaimed in a loud bored drawl, "Princess Grace. Does she ever do anything?"

Leon persisted, "She break her engagement?"

Vera wriggled her toes. "Break it?"

Paul asked her, "Did she ever pay you for that whopping big phonebill?"

"Naturally." Vera's lips shut tight. Turning her back she plumped up the pillow, piled the used plates, put the leftover juice on the outside windowledge. After she had watched the weak snow littering down, she turned around with a yawn.

Anna rose. "At any rate, I have to be going."

As he got up Leon said to Paul, "If you really are flunking that course, get in touch."

"Oh, Paul hates to be tutored. He's too stubborn," Vera said.

"I wasn't offering to tutor. Still, I can guarantee you'll pass." Leon let out a slash of grin and ducked out, tramping downstairs. The door across the landing opened an inch, an

eye surveyed them. As she descended through the gloom sh
heard Vera's windchime laugh and the door bang shut.

That evening he spoke of them. "Sick scene, eh?"

"All those masks and dolls? It would get on my nerves."

Leon shoved them away with a thick palm. "Not the de
cor. The way the kid is eaten up by his sister. She answer
for him. She decides what he'll do. You hear that bit abou
'we'—if you aren't going to be an archaeologist, what wil
we do? She acts like she's married to him."

"Well . . ." They had charmed her, the sense of play and
private pastures and the longlegged games of young giraffes.
"I'm not sure how much one controls the other. They both
obey a certain style. He answers for her too."

"Style? She's an ordinary domineering bitch with a kid
brother under her thumb. Another sick family all hung up on
each other. What choice does he have? Probably doesn't see
what's happening. Doesn't see the obscene trap he's grown
into."

"Then you aren't interested in her."

He snorted. "That frigid tank? A real castrator. Those
managerial chicks, spade or white, they freeze my blood."

"I thought maybe that's why we went."

"Uh uh." He slumped on the couch, with his massive
head bent forward on his chest. With his sleeves rolled halfway up the hairs in the light made his arms look dipped in
water. Slowly the lids over his milky eyes settled. When he
did not speak she thought he had dozed off and took up a
book to read.

"Very few things I want. Most of them I can't have. Not
ever." His brows were yanked together, his pale eyes fixed
on nowhere. "What you don't see is I care a lot about her."

She looked at him blankly. "Vera?"

"No! Caroline!" He rasped. "I have to find out what's
happening. I have to know. It sticks in my throat. It gnaws
on me. She's dying step by step and nobody cares. Nobody
sees her but me—and she can't see me."

Her stomach dropped like a fallen cake. He was in love
with Caroline. Seemed like everybody was.

"I had her, and I screwed up. The way I screw up everything." He slammed his fist on the table. "Everything. I can't deal with people, can't deal with things. That I get anything done, that I feed myself and get through a day and maybe make a short film once in a while is a miracle."

"How did you happen to break with her then?"

"Joye was pregnant. Finally she really was." He wiped the sweat from his forehead. "It's taken me a long time to undo the damage I did then. I got excited, I got desperate. I wanted them both to keep their heads and they both panicked. Joye wouldn't even talk rationally."

What the hell did he expect her to do?

"But by not asking anything of Caroline, just being here, always being here so she knows she can come for help when she needs it . . . I've got to play it cool. Then she got this idea to go traipsing around Europe, running away from herself, from me. Comes back with that rock. What do you do with a person who says she's in love with somebody else? Even if you know it's a lie."

"But do you think she loved you?"

"She's not capable of love. But I'm the chance she has."

"Why?"

Again he struck his fist on the table. "It's a thing I saw—something I knew from the first time with her. Only I couldn't believe it then. Not being with her is hell. Who can tell what it's like at night when I'm alone. I hit the walls. I have to scrape myself off the ceiling. I think I'm losing my mind. She turns everything on me, and I can't con myself with anything less."

When he talked about Caroline she had the feeling he was reciting an incantation, a formula. She believed and disbelieved.

"So I had a month, one month, between her sashaying back in here with that sparkler and the time her beloved gets here. And Rowley has to fuck up. He just has to."

By midnight Anna was exhausted, while Leon's voice had lost its sullen thunder. He was finally cheerful and had her make cocoa. Her chest felt hollow, her head ached. Why should she mind if he loved Caroline? They decided she was

to spend the night on the couch. Obviously he liked that. A
he said, he hated to be alone.

As she was making up the couch he said offhand, ''Don'
know why you live in that rathole. They won't even tell you
when it'll come down around your ears.''

''It's cheap.'' The curse had left. She liked her rooms
again.

''You ought to move in here—plenty of room for two.
three. . . . Save yourself money and be comfortable, ha
ha.''

''And fight like caged cats, ha ha.'' She sat on the couch
and kicked off her shoes. ''You're genuinely domestic, but
I'm not.'' He was out of his mind to imagine she would live
with him in bloodless brotherhood!

''No? Who asked you to clean this barn?''

''That's not what I mean.''

''Evidently.'' Leon grinned.

For the first time she felt a polarization of the air, a sexual
question between them. I wonder, she thought, I wonder how
real that obsession with Caroline is.

Leon

November

He kept noticing the building as he came from Woody's bar or her apartment, not because they were tearing it down but because they had stopped. A foot of snow fell on the weekend. The next day the air softened, the sun poured down melting snow that froze that night in a jagged crust. His car was soldered to its parking place. All week in the brittle cold, the wolf wind sinking its teeth in his neck, he kept passing the building.

The doors had been ripped off and stood as a fence. The windows were broken, the roof kicked in. Part of the facade had been knocked away. The apartment—built on rough gray stone the color of Chicago—stood against the night sky half buried in its own rubble and ominously dark. Buildings are hardly ever that dark. Moon froze on its streaked walls in ghostly almostpinks and almostyellows. In the wind a forgotten chandelier tilted and swung.

From looking at that building every time he came past, he noticed a light in the redbrick tenement next door that he had thought empty. A glimmer showed at one second-floor window. A wavering light like a flame.

In Woody's he found out that an old woman clung there barnacle-like, alone. He saw her a greatgrandmother, outliving children, forgotten by her descendants. In the day-time she crouched at a window with its cracks stuffed with rags, looking out at the busy street. People said she had

59

lived there thirty years. People said she was crazy. She beamed at the Saturday street of shopping carts and dragged babies and drunks and linked couples. The electricity, the gas, the heat had been cut off. The city had delivered written warning the water would go next. They had given her every chance, they said. Now when he walked by he watched for her lamp.

He came past one morning in blurred dawn and saw that they had begun wrecking the gray apartment again. The crane reared above the shattered torso, ready to strike. In the halflight he saw the rats come out in lines, in slow deliberate rows, then the stragglers alone and hurrying after: he saw the migration of the rats from basement crannies and wall bowers of the broken building. They did not go into the old woman's tenement next door. They poured in orderly measured haste toward the houses in the street behind, the townhouses with their shoveled walks and snowcapped hedges. He stood with his worn tweed overcoat pulled up around his ears and watched. In ten minutes they were gone. A case of relocation in superior housing.

Rowley

Saturday, October 25

He woke feeling great. The night before he'd been drinking, but he had burned it up. The bedroom faced the next house across two feet of hard earth, but lying in its gloom he felt sure the day was good. Harlan's boy was whamming a ball thump off the steps. In the next room Yente was chasing something.

Last night he'd barely made it from the studio in time to take over from the second singer at a hoot. He had done his show live because of turning up another Black Jack record. He swung out of bed, sat scratching his toes. The song seeped through:

> *For each time I make it it's seven times I lose,*
> *Yeah for each time winning it's seven times I lose,*
> *That's how come I got the California Boulevard Blues.*

House of detention. Jack Custis' rawhide voice working it over, voice from the late thirties with the flab and lilt scoured from it, a black singer who sounded as if the grit of a dirty world had honed him mean and powerful.

He stumbled on the first record by accident in a second-hand store, in a pile that looked like nothing but Guy Lombardo. Opened his September twelfth show with it. One side was a battered verson of "Jail-House Blues," the other "Why Don't You Get Out Of Here and Get Me Some Money, Too."

Sung by a man that was audacity. Turned the song on its noggin. He quit scratching. Imagine Annie not digging it. She had lit into him for something he'd sung and nothing about his find. He shrugged and got up as a crash came from the livingroom.

He sauntered over to pluck Yente from the door where the cat was cliffhanging. From his leaping point, the top of the bookcase, books had cascaded. Near the ceiling a fat horsefly buzzed. Rowley reached up, held off a minute, grabbed. Bringing his hand slowly down with the fly knocking against the palm, he released the fly in Yente's face, laughing as the cat spilled forward.

Then the second disc with two original blues. In the meantime a listener wrote that Black Jack had been in Chicago during World War II and performed around bars on the South Side. So he told his listeners and urged that any tapes or records be dug up. If Jack himself were alive he should get in touch and the same with anyone who knew him. Just after he went off a woman phoned. She said her son had called her in the middle of the first song, he had FM and he was a student at Roosevelt. That was surely Jack Custis, but he hadn't sung she thought in a long long time. Yes, he'd been in Chicago, got a janitor's job, but right after VJ day they fired him and she lost track. However, his sister Lucille had married a man named Thomson in the post office. Lucille had three sons, but she helped Jack after he got turned out of his job. She told him the church Lucille had belonged to and where she'd lived.

The day was bright and clear with a long clean wind off the lake. He carried his typewriter out and answered his mail sitting on Harlan's steps—the straight flight leading to almost secondfloor level was a local style dating from the era when Chicago was filling itself out of the mud and nobody knew what height the sidewalks would be. Yente thrashed around in the cottonwood leaves on the lawn. Touch football in the street. In a backyard little kids were playing some counting game, shrill, rhythmic.

He stopped upstairs on his way out, tried to get Harlan to come with him. Harlan at the dinette table with documents on federal urban renewal laws a foot deep around him. "No I'm not going to go playing hide-and-seek with some rickety old race hustler all around the South Side. I got twenty phonecalls to make. And I thought you were going to help me put up posters?"

He had lunch at his favorite rib place full of the spicy smoke and ate an order with hot sauce standing. Then he drove west. Everybody was out riding around and it took forever to get by South Park and 47th, with cars making turns from the wrong lane and Bobbie Blue Bland drawing a crowd at the Regal. He did not think he would find Jack Custis today or next week, but he was sure he would find him.

He'd never taken himself seriously as a performer. He played for the pleasure and the cash. The women sometimes. He had good presence and rapport with an audience, but he liked best playing backup for somebody first rate. He wanted to play behind Jack Custis.

If only Harlan had come, that would heighten the game as well as increase the chances for success. They would be kidding and hustling each other. They didn't get that much time together any more.

He found the big yellow apartment house the woman had described though it was on the corner of 43rd and not 41st. No Thomson. No Thompson, Tomson or Tompson. He rang the super, which did nothing. Finally stumbled on him at the back basement entrance.

The super was not a heavy man yet he looked flabby. Gray had worked into the brown of his skin and his hair was grizzled, but he had all his teeth and he locked his jaws together. No. He didn't know nothing. No, no Mrs. Thompson, Thomson or otherwise lived there or ever had. He had been super more years than he could remember. No, nobody else would know. His eyes narrowed, his jaw set and he said No, No, No. Rowley tried to explain. Hatred flashed off the super like the blinding beam of a lighthouse.

He drove back slowly. He still had a lead: the Baptist church Lucille had belonged to, but next time he would try to go through helpful channels. He stopped to comb new releases at a shop that carried a lot of rhythm and blues and stopped again to pick up posters Harlan had ordered.

"You can't just go around putting those posters on people's property!" Shirley said. Her smooth brow puckered. Shirley was a thin bigboned woman with honey skin and a high rounded coiffure worn just to her nape. She was a fierce housekeeper and an earnest mother and without trusting Rowley admired him—he could never figure why since she disliked music with more thrust or grit than Mantovani. Harlan's previous girls had been ones to make men's heads turn in a bar rather than to warm a teacher's heart at the PTA. But he had to admit the kids were great. Harlan spent a lot of time playing with them, going over homework or teaching them to make things (often with a how-to book in hand, since his own childhood had been anything but what he was providing).

When neither of them answered Shirley folded her arms and said not loud but passionately, "Harlan, you can't go around plastering those things all over people's property. You'll get in trouble, and you're bound to upset people."

"If this neighborhood doesn't wake up they're none of them going to have any property to worry about," Harlan said. "Come on, Rowley."

The job made them silly. They got very quick. They hit trees and buildings as they went at finally about two minutes a poster.

" 'The Assyrian came down like a wolf on the fold!' " Harlan declaimed, looking back at the street. "You think anybody's going to pay attention? Think anybody's going to come Tuesday night?"

"Why not?" He said back:

When you hear this wolf howling, howling at every woman I see,
When you hear this wolf howling, howling at every woman I see,
Yeah, I'm only howling, well, well for what belong to me . . .

I learned that off a Champion Jack Dupree record."

"Why you might've been a good blues man if you had a little of the blood. And a voice."

"Guess who I got a date playing backup for?"

"What you get paid for that?"

"Standard union rate. I'd do it for nothing. He's good."

Harlan stepped back to admire, saw that the poster was crooked, shrugged. "They wouldn't let you do it for nothing."

"I'm crying. . . . Remember Jack Winder?"

"Small guy, played lousy jazz guitar."

"I ran into Jack the other day in the Loop. Will that hold?"

"Half of them be ripped down before tonight. What's become of the old fire-eater?"

"Working for his uncle. Office job. Married. Couple kids."

Harlan grinned. "Baby, don't say that like a fatal disease. Some of us like that, some of us think that's living."

"Remember when the FBI pressured his girl into giving them lists of everybody came and went in his pad?—and he was a mixer, he gave big parties. When she confessed, lot of people got a bad chill. Everybody was scared in those days."

Harlan made a sour face. "We were all against the reds but we'd never for sure seen one—like the tales uncles tell you about timber wolves when you know there are things on two legs in the city much scarier. When I was fifteen I felt obliged to cut anybody who looked at me too long, and I guess I was meaner than any ordinary gray wolf."

Rowley thrust out his finger. "Just observing. The older you get, the tougher you were. By the time you're fifty with your first granddaughter and a beer belly down to your knees, you'll be claiming you were a numbers runner at age ten."

"Beer belly, ha. Speak for yourself, baby." Harlan poked Rowley in the midriff. "I was a mean kid, but I loved my mother." Nailing up the last poster he made a sign of the cross.

> *"Oh why don't you work*
> *Like other men do?*
> *How in hell can I work*
> *When there's no work to do?*

> *Hallelujah! I'm a bum*
> *Hallelujah! Bum again!*
> *Hallelujah! Give us a handout*
> *To revive us again!''*

Rowley was waiting for a can of chili to heat while he wrote his reviews for the local folksheet. He had an open box of hard catfood and everytime he finished a sentence he reached in and tossed a little rabbit turd for Yente to chase and crack between his teeth. If he took too long on a sentence Yente would come and nudge his foot.

He got the cat last winter. He was cutting through an alley taking a shortcut to Annie's when he saw something move in a garbage can outside the barred back door of a store. He was startled to come on a rat in daylight. Then some sudden curiosity made him question that faint noise. Cautiously he lifted the lid. Among the spoiled celery and moldy copper green oranges three kittens were bedded, tiny and wet and dabbled with the harsh green ooze of rotting spinach. He thought they were dead. Gingerly he touched them and immediately one began mewing, butting his hand for milk, while another stirred. The third was cold. In high anger he began kicking on the door, found it open and charged into the stockroom of a grocery.

"Get those dirty things out of here," the manager said when contact was made. "I don't know nothing about them. What are you doing snooping in garbagecans? I'll call the cops."

He ended up carrying the two live kittens to Anna's. He was disgusted to find himself involved in warming milk and shopping for pablum. One kitten died that evening, but the one who had butted his hand thrived. Then Anna's landlady announced she did not allow pets.

"What do I want with a cat?" he asked her. "Isn't there some agency you call and they come and get them?"

"And gas them. You shouldn't pick things out of garbage cans if you mean to throw them back!" Her fine, dark, dogmatic air. He took Yente home.

He sang at Yente,

> *"Oh Dunderbeck, oh Dunderbeck*
> *how could you be so mean*
> *to ever have invented*
> *the sausage meat machine?*
> *Now all the rats and pussycats*
> *will never more be seen.*
> *They'll all be ground to sausage meat*
> *in Dunderbeck's machine."*

Herb from the station was throwing a party and later he might drop by. He was learning a blues off the newfound Black Jack record, and he looked forward to sitting down after supper to work it through.

> *"She gave the crank*
> *a hell of a yank,*
> *and Dunderbeck was meat!"*

Someone knocked.

"Evening, honey." Caroline was carrying a bag. He had carefully said nothing about tonight. That ended the chili because she unpacked steak, beer, and frozen frenchfries.

"Another Care package. Do I look starved?"

She tittered happily. Coming up behind she put her warm arms around his neck. "Don't you like me to make supper for you? You just won't admit it."

She made him feel brutish, forever shaking free and growling at the hundred and two gifts she tried to dump on his head. If he sat still she would tie bows all over him. "Look, I did my own shopping. You don't have to haul in supplies like this was Hudson Bay."

"Don't you like steak? I know you—you just open an old can. Go right ahead and work as if I wasn't here, and I'll call you when everything's ready."

She began ostentatiously tiptoeing about setting down pans with many "Oh dears" and "Shhhs" to herself.

"Look, don't go shushing around. Live!" So she began singing "I gave my love a cherry." The last two reviews he wrote were high in acid. She had a soft contralto and her parents had bought her singing lessons. But learning a song she learned the singer's style till she was a whole sampler of other singers' feelings. All a bit slicked up.

He smelled the smoke before he heard the crackling because he had been trying not hear anything. He swung around just as she yanked the broiler open. At once the burning steak set fire to the potholder in her hand. She shrieked.

"Drop it!" he shouted.

She let it fall and he stamped the flames out. He shut off the broiler, pulled out the steak, cut off the charred fat, put the boiler back two notches lower and relit the oven. "Like this," he said mildly. He was ready to sit down and laugh except that she looked crushed. He tousled her blond hair, wavy and lush reaching just to her shoulders. He had told her once she had 1940's hair. Soft to touch, it tangled about his hand and followed after: Caroline all right.

Peering into the cupboard she asked, "Where're those salad tongs?"

"Don't know." he relented then. "Think I saw them in the front closet."

"The front closet!" She went to look and came back with the tongs. "How'd they get there? I used them in the kitchen just last week."

"No idea." He shrugged. "Maybe the cat dragged them in."

She seemed satisfied although she continued to talk to the tongs as she made the salad, wondering how they'd learned to walk. She had indeed turned them up out of a drawer on Wednesday. They were Anna's and after Caroline went off to that coffee box where she "worked," he'd decided to take them over and give them back. Why not? It had been a few weeks and all that shouting around ought to look pretty silly. Meanwhile his little bit of strange had turned into his daily wonderbread.

He had gone over after ten. He didn't know her new teaching schedule but her latest possible class would get her home by then. Her apartment had been dark, however, and his knocking roused no one. Funny. He'd checked the time in Woody's bar across the street where he stopped for a beer, and it was ten thirty. He'd fallen into an argument about

Cuba. When he left he glanced up at her windows, still dark. He had wondered, briefly. He wondered now, sealing the envelope on his reviews.

All their friends must be fussing about her, telling her what a shit he'd been. One thing he was sure of: she wasn't with a man. Not yet. Smiling he recalled their duel in the early days. She could turn from a woman to a blockhouse in nothing flat. No, she was out with the gang from the department. Then he saw that Caroline was returning his smile, her eyes shimmery. Caught off stride he went over and put his arms around her. In a way he had been relieved that Annie was out that night, in a way.

They set out to see a new Italian flick, but since the line reached the corner, they went to Woody's instead. Though the bar was crowded too deep, he saw nobody he felt like drinking with. They night was freakishly warm, one of the last good nights when you could walk at leisure without your nose breaking off. A loose nostalgic wanting filled him but he could not fix on an object. The first girls in his first car with fuzzy sweaters and sharp elbows, sticking their gum to the dash before necking? Then he would have gone for Caroline. She was wearing a sad, cheated look, but at the meeting of their eyes she perked up and took his hand beside the pitcher. Green made her face fresh and pinky. Sometimes she looked pretty enough to startle him, a radiance that belonged to paper, not to flesh.

He was not often nostalgic, yet he felt it like a warm tide of dark beer pulling his mind under. For what? the oreboats? ought to get more exercise, get Harlan to take up handball . . . on the bum? student politics in the peace union? early days at the station when the electric company was threatening to shut off their power? He missed something he'd had. He had done what he wanted then as now. His mood puzzled him and he was frowning when he looked toward the door and saw old Leon plowing through the mob, talking all the time over his shoulder.

He felt a wave of relief. That was what he wanted, someone he'd known through years and changes. Leon's gaze met his then, and a fierce blank hostility lit his pale eyes. Leon looked from him to Caroline with his face tight as leather. Turning he hissed something. A girl behind stepped sideways to peer around him. Then Rowley understood: Anna. "Or did you expect me to amuse myself with Leon?"

He read at once Leon's stare, the two of them turning up in Woody's on Saturday night so wrapped up in each other they almost walked over him. He understood, yet he did not believe it. Like a nincompoop he sat staring while they turned around hurriedly and went straight out.

"That was Anna What's-her-name with Leon, wasn't it? They acted too embarrassed, really," Caroline said.

Leon, for Christsake. He'd never fathomed Leon's success with women. He'd seen Joye with a black eye and another time Leon had knocked her down. He'd always had girls on the side, easy lays like Caroline maybe, but still a married man had to go out of his way for things a single man tripped over. Leon had fathered a kid the court wouldn't let him near. This was the guy Anna couldn't wait to start mixing it up with. Always losing jobs or quitting in disgust, he never worked at anything, never found anything he thought worthy. Even the films he made were kind of daydreams.

"Come on, let's split." He stalked out and she came hurrying behind. Driving home he asked, "What's so attractive about Leon? Not what you'd call a goodlooking guy."

"I don't know, I'm sure," Caroline said. "Are you jealous about her, still?"

He was irritated enough to say, "I'm not supposed to know you were Leon's girl?"

"I was terribly young. You know."

They'd just got in bed when the phone rang. He reached across her to answer it. "Rowley."

"*Sam*." She laughed. "Trying to get you all day. Going from one payphone to another clinking my quarters. Hey, give me my big brother, I'd say, and the phone would answer, nobody like that here."

"I was out trying to find an old blues singer nobody's seen since 'forty-five."

"But you're going to find him and make him rich and famous."

"Maybe I can get him a recording date anyhow." Good to hear her voice, low and chesty and bubbling. "How's school going, Sam? How come no letters?"

"My anthropology is great, but lit class is a bore. Rowley, I need money."

"What for? Didn't you get your allowance?"

"I need thirty dollars."

"You need clothes or what?"

"I'm coming to Chicago in two weeks for the weekend. I'll explain all then."

"Okay, come ahead and explain and I'll round up the money then."

"Slob, I need the money to get there."

"By chartered plane?"

"Someone's coming with me."

"Who can't pay their own busfare?"

"Let me talk to Anna. Is she there?"

"Don't change the subject."

"I'm not! I have to talk to Anna. I need her advice."

"What is this? No, you can't talk to her, she isn't here."

"Then give me her number and I'll call you back. Can I call collect?"

"I will not. Look, Annie and I aren't going together."

She caught her breath loudly. "What happened?"

That's what came of introducing a girl to his sister. "Nothing for you to fuss about."

"You needn't be so glib. What was it, you wouldn't marry her? Don't you ever dare use me as an excuse."

"Button your lip, Sam. You're young to be giving advice. I appreciate that you liked Annie, but life is more complicated than that and things don't always work out the way you might imagine."

Sam snorted. "If you could hear yourself! If you want to know, I've met a wonderful person, and I love him, brother."

"How serious is this? It's early on in the term and you have enough to run you ragged—"

"You sound like the dean of women—her standard lecture to freshmen. Next thing you'll say is be sure you make him respect you, young ladies, by always being just that."

His stomach sank. "Maybe you better come next weekend."

"No! I have a big paper due."

"Just tell me why you expect me to pay his busfare. What kind of jerk is this?"

"Stop prejudging. I'm shocked at you, coming on parental. It's you and the folks want to look him over—he's not going to enjoy that one bit. Besides, he's broke. I told him we could trust you."

"Finagling doesn't become you, Sam."

"Then stop making me finagle."

"How old is this kid?"

"Twenty-one. So quit calling him a kid."

"Anybody whose busfare I have to pay is a kid."

"Forget it. I'll get the money somewhere else."

"Damn you, Sam, you goad me like an ox."

She laughed again, high spirited. "My blue ox. So we'll be hearing from you?"

"What's this guy's name?"

"Gino Warwick, brother. So, see you!"

Caroline was hunched up on her side of the bed, pouting. "If you want to talk to that girl so bad, why don't you go see her and take me home? Calling her Sam, pretending it was a man."

"That was my sister and Sam is short for Sandra." He swung out of bed. "Get dressed and I'll take you home."

"Sister?" Her voice trailed up. "I didn't know you had a sister."

He reached for his trousers. "One. Tonight that's too many."

"You're mad because I thought it was a girl?"

"Not mad at all." He put his hand on her bare shapely shoulder. "There's nothing in this scene for you. I noticed your ring came off last week."

"I thought . . . you know . . ."

"I won't string you along. You're not getting much out of this and no wonder, because I'm not putting much in. Let's call it off before you get angry at me for real."

"You sit there and won't discuss anything. You don't really listen. I might as well not be here half the time."

"Right. You're entitled to more than that. But not from me."

"I don't understand you," she began bitterly.

"Not worth your time to try."

He was afraid she would cry. Her brown eyes grew moist and wavery, but then she shook her head and got up. "You change so radically from one day to the next, I don't understand."

For the next twenty minutes until he had dropped her in the lobby of her apartmenthouse, among the turquoise chairs and doorman in rig and plastic bonsai trees in pots—he tried to concentrate on her and leave her feeling good. He worked to keep his mind off Sam and the phonecall. He felt a little guilty toward Caroline, as if he had been lacking common courtesy. Yet when he left her in the garish lobby, he felt only relief. He would still have time to work on that song before he went to bed.

Tuesday—Wednesday,
October 28—29

The shadows crept across him as he walked north out of the Loop across the Chicago River that flowed backward with the city sewage, up Michigan Avenue broad and washed in the recent rain, past Tribune Tower (he spat ritualistically) which his old hero Louis Sullivan said had a spider perched on top: Gothic skyscraper with itchy bricabrac as if the gray stone had dripped crazy in the rain. Tuba of newspapers willful windy hollow and fat with hatred.

Walking past the pretty shops of North Michigan, the French restaurants and shoe salons and branches of New

York stores, he was walking a razorback ridge of money which dropped steeper than a toboggan slide down into slums. Good rock group, kids from there he'd tried to push but the lead guitar got busted. He was walking to Oldtown planning to eat in a little German place, then to take the subway back in plenty of time for the meeting at Harlan's.

As he walked north between the lake and goldcoast apartments, the tall buildings created twilight but the sky was a mustard yellow barred with low surly clouds. A brisk damp wind came off the lake. The waves folded into humps of whitecaps. Far out the world had no waist. Lake blended into sky. Against the teeth of the wind he pulled up the collar of his hunting jacket.

Ahead a woman whose gorgeous freeswinging high ass he had been admiring stopped to let her woolly Afghan shit enormously on the sidewalk. "Caesar, you pig," she drawled complacently. Her voice made him hasten his step. No, couldn't be. Three years? She stared through him as he caught up, then suddenly saw him. "Rowley! What do you mean sneaking up on us? How are you!"

Nina: as gorgeous, more gorgeous. She was five feet ten with a helmet of yellow hair and high hardlooking breasts. He used to run into her all the time when her husband worked for UNA, the neighborhood organization, and always he was conscious of her in a room and knew that she opened up when he spoke to her. She was quiet, and he thought her shy. Once at a fund raising party she had danced with him. That was all. Only he would watch her following Tom Lovis out, towheaded baby on her arm, and almost, almost envy Tom.

"Have you finally moved around here?" she asked.

"Still in the same place. I'm on my way to eat."

"Here? You mean with someone."

"No, I'm walking to Oldtown."

"Hiking you mean. You are crazy." She took his arm. "Have a drink with us if you're really not meeting a friend. It's been ages." The building she steered him into had a Japanese rockgarden in the lobby for contemplation. As they rose in the elevator she leaned against one wall contemplating him. "You've gained weight, darling, like a married man. Careful!"

Anna's contribution, and Nina had not used to call him by false endearments. "How's Tom?"

"Still with Penman and Bates. They think a lot of him."

"The PR boys doing the University whitewash?"

"Don't be pseudo-wise. The University has its own PR staff. Tom is simply serving as parttime consultant to the planning arm. Anyhow, they don't listen. At least finally his connections there are doing him some good."

The livingroom was white, red and black, and Tom was nowhere to be seen. As the dog gamboled in shaking itself, he wanted to laugh. A nice big turd on the Danish longhair area rug, please. She mixed martinis and made them double.

"Don't keep dripping disapproval all over the poor room. We have a decorator in, and why not? You never forget you came from Gary, do you? Union boy from a company town." She made her eyes large. "I don't mean to scold. Don't stand there disassociating, you make me nervous. Come sit." She patted the white leather expanse of sofa.

Obediently, reluctantly he sat. Through an open door he could see the unmade kingsize bed. He didn't particularly want a martini, he didn't particularly want her: not this way, now. She took his arm conversationally in a grip of steel. "Why not move up here? Chicago is drab otherwise. Why hide down there in a dirty dangerous neighborhood that's getting worse all the time."

"The sight of the lake gives me rheumatism . . . You used to like it well enough."

"Where you can't leave a package in your car without someone breaking in. Where a woman isn't safe on the streets."

Looking at Nina he thought she was strong enough to hold her own.

"It's such a bore—I don't know why you stay there." Her hand slid up to his biceps.

"The best thing you can say is that in pockets anyhow it swings." His muscle tensed under her hand.

"We have a Negro doctor and his wife in the building."

The clock was long, low, black and chromium with a vaguely trapezoidal dial. He had to count blobs around the circumference to figure the time. "What's the University doing, Nina? They don't think they can kick people out for their convenience?"

"Don't be sentimental. Have any idea how many families are displaced by every expressway? The University needs an urban environment that can attract middle-class students—and hold middle-class faculty." Her hand moved up to his shoulder.

He had forty minutes maximum. The graceful thing would be to gather her up and haul ass into the bedroom, but he was afraid he could not lift her except in a fireman's carry. "When is Tom arriving? Soon?"

"Don't worry." Her golden throat tilted back. "Not till after eight. And Rhoda's at her grandmother's."

So he kissed her muscular tanned throat, and her arms sprang around him. Six minutes later he was fucking her on the vast slab of bed with candy striped sheets. The bedroom clock was easier to read. Her body tensed under him, tan except for the imprint of a bikini. As she arched backward with her nails digging in his back, every muscle stood out discretely. This was a wrestling exhibition. Her belly was hard and bouncy as the mattress. Harlan would never forgive him if he missed the meeting. He could remember lusting after Nina's ass. Then Nina had lived for civic good works and mild causes. She wore homemade dresses and carried her baby in a sling and sat behind a card table red-cheeked with wind and cold raising money for CARE or collecting books for somewhere. That Nina had been a silly woman of easy indignations and patched-up opinions. This one had won a statuette in a woman's golfing tournament, which swung Fore at him from her dressing table.

He was propped on set arms pounding at her teak body. Her eyes kept opening to keep watch, then shutting as she concentrated on the building of her tension. He was trying his strength on the carnival strength machine. If he hammered at her cunt long enough the bell would ring and he could climb off. Maybe he would win a cigar.

Finally her mouth came open, her lips thinned and her eyes popped to glare through him. With her teeth clamping into his shoulder she came. He finished quickly and got out. Efficiently she rolled out of bed and dressed, then as he was dressing, made up the bed and smoothed a sheepskin coverlet over. Then she looked carefully at the clock as she brushed her hair flat and retouched her makeup. "Like one for the road?"

"Tell you what—make me a sandwich."

"What?" She glared over her shoulder, asking if he were making fun of her.

"A sandwich," he said patiently. "I don't have time to eat now. Anything out of the icebox."

"*Icebox*? So sorry I made you late . . ."

"My pleasure. Leftover meat? cheese? pickles?" He ended making himself two sandwiches from a can of Swedish meatballs.

"I used to think you were a fantastic person," she said as she put the cocktail glasses in the top of the dishwasher. "But it seems to me you've been standing still. How long have you been with that arty little station? You say PR as if it were a joke, but Tom is making something of himself. You'll see."

He had some olives, potato chips, and then he rode down in the elevator eating an apple he took at the last minute from a bowl.

Walking briskly west along the dark wet streets toward the subway, he thought that at this rate he would be trim again in no time. He could do with three more sandwiches like those he had eaten—but not too much like them. Ground beef meatballs extended with oatmeal and potato parings in snotty gravy: not unlike the canned petfood Yente turned up his nose at.

He hoped Yente had bummed supper. Shirley had a soft heart for animals. Right after he'd polished off a pile of gizzards at home, Yente the bum would go upstairs tail high, meowing, and rub against her ankles acting starved. Bolt their table scraps and beat it home before Harlan's kids started hauling him around by his pudgy middle. He caught the time on the corner of State and turned south to a quick standup hamburger, just a couple blocks. Tonight he'd bet the tomcat had gone better than the man.

Fuzzy Afghan dropping that enormous turd on the sidewalk. She had prepared to outstare him. Exorcising something with him. Walking under the canopy of a restaurant he shrugged. Woman not safe on the South Side streets? Man not safe on the sidewalk up here. He had been had. Yes indeed, subpoenaed, made to perform, and kicked out without a thankyou or a decent bit to eat. Grimly and neatly used.

Now look here, he summoned Anna, what was I supposed to do, say No thank you and scoot out the door like a frightened deer? Come off it. Anna leaned against something vague, arms folded, and looked back at him through halfclosed eyes with an insolent and sensual smile. A public service. She nodded and faded.

After his hamburger he turned north to the subway past Bughouse Square. The rain had washed some of the trees bare. Nobody was exercising right of free speech guaranteed under deed of park to city. A few bums huddled on the wet benches, but nobody exhorted them. IWW used to house itself around here, and hereabouts speech hadn't always come free. Haymarket to Bughouse. August Spies to the hangman before they closed his mouth with the hood. *There will be a time when our silence will be more powerful than the voices you strangle today.* Any bets, August? Who here has heard of you? This city gave its name to anarchists who argued that unions should avoid opportunism, guard against betrayal by leaders, rest on direct action of the rank-and-file, and stress equality. A week ago he had picked up a history of unions, among them his old man's, which started with a disclaimer of any interest in ideology, as irrelevant. . . . *all government, in the last resort, is violence; all law, in the last resort, is force* . . . People he knew would find that relevant yet, but history was buried in libraries, and the official history was lethal as mustard gas. This neighborhood was unslumming and would be expensive. The IWW had gone north. Born in Chicago, smashed in Chicago when one hundred leaders were jailed.

We hate their rotten system more than any mortals do,
Our aim is not to patch it up, but build it all anew . . .

On the train he wrote commentary for a couple of string quartet programs and a note to himself. Think about this: the modern state is a machine for making war. Ninety percent of our budget. But grafted on a notion of state was force arranging economy and ministering to needs and wishes of its citizens. Making good environment. So can have states combining at least slightly humane domestic policies with classic colonial interference and aggression and chauvinism overseas. Toynbee's external proletariat of the Roman empire exists today. One outcome of civil rights struggle could be incorporating all in middle-class. United fat America squatting on a billion peasant necks. We are five percent of the world's people and consume fifty percent of its goods. Who can stop us, ever? Selfrighteous cannibals.

As he came down the block Harlan's porchlight was on and he could hear voices. Yet he was shocked to walk in— two steps was all he could manage—and find maybe fifty people packed in the little square livingroom and dinette. Harlan had borrowed chairs from his neighbors but not nearly enough. The room was full of a tense worried anger. Four or five were white. The rest knew if not exactly who was fighting them then exactly why. He found a place along one wall.

Sam Short, a highschool teacher in his late forties, was chairing the meeting heavily, wary of the excitement in the room. The louder the voices rose and the higher the whine of pressure behind the words, the harder he leaned on Robert's Rules. A broad-faced man got up to say, "The University can move us all out anyhow. You can't fight city hall—"

"Why not, if they fight us?" a woman yelled, clanking her thin arm loaded with bracelets.

"The chair recognizes only Mr. Watson."

"Well, I don't recognize Old Watson, giving up before we start."

Watson went on, "Why not play ball and we all get the best prices we can? Why wait till they come in and condemn us and we have to take what we can get? We can't stand up to the University and the city and the mayor and the Federal Government. If they're going to expand, they're going to expand, and we might as well get good prices while we have a choice.''

He had murmured support, but most speakers stood for resistance. The gist of their speeches was injury. They had had enough trouble finding this house, this flat. What would they do? Move back into the slums with their kids? Here their kids had yards to play in and if the schools were crowded, well, at least they learned something.

"I'm just a renter but I got to say, first we have to move for the expressway, and then another project, and then we live in a place and the landlord stops repairs. We so sick of moving I just want to bawl when I think about it."

Blanche, the skinny hardbitten woman with all the bracelets, insisted on being heard. She could outyell Short. "We was sold a bill of goods with all this renewal stuff. We was told they were going to improve this community and fix up the streets and the schools and give us garbage pickups and stop signs, and it turns out what they mean by improve is getting rid of us. The same real estate men who made a fortune letting us in are going to make a fortune throwing us out. Here I am and here I stay and I'm not ready to budge myself for nobody!''

"How can the city call my house rundown?" A small man with a small voice, mumbling. "Me and my brother-in-law painted it and fixed it up and my wife planted flowers."

He was reminded of something. Then he frowned, remembering. Late gradeschool. His old man had been active for a time in a neighborhood improvement association—which except for a hassle with the city about streetlighting existed to keep their dirty depressed blocks white and Christian. The same air of earnest hope overriding fear and poverty and mangled ambitions. The air of being beleaguered in their manhood. Worse, he remembered sitting impressed beside his old man—who'd been of course an official—and thinking this is like the union. Voting, electing, discussing: this is what they mean in school by a town meeting. Democracy in action: shoulder to shoulder, fence to fence against the Jews and colored. Jews had not been real to him, but the colored they were keeping out were the same kids he went to gradeschool with.

About halfway through Harlan took the floor. "You can feel sorry for yourselves all night." Strain and fatigue were etched in his face. "You can sigh and complain and curse the University right to the day they tear your houses down. The University doesn't hear you. Nobody's listening tonight. We're just a bunch of black nobodies bellyaching and they won't hear us unless we make so much noise they can't shut us out." Shrill at first, his voice deepened as he gained confidence. "First, we need an organization. Second, we need members, every one of you to go out and convince your neighbors we mean them. Third, we need money, fourth, publicity, fifth, a lawyer. Sixth, we got to apply what pressure we can swing on our alderman, on the mayor's office, on whoever we can push on so they feel it. We can't afford to give up. We can't afford to wait and see and send polite little feelers and wait for the hearings. We know what we'll see—the bulldozers coming. Nobody cares except us here in this room and our kids who'll have to grow up where we can squeeze in. We all know what conditions are like back in the ghetto. We can't take our kids back there. Nobody ever will care unless we make them listen by making so much fuss and noise and trouble that they can't shut us out. They think this is going to be an easy move. It's our job to make it hard for them."

Harlan stepped backward, wiping at his forehead. He looked at Shirley, sitting with arms clasped as if cold, looked quickly around the room, and gave up the floor to his neighbor J.J. to read the resolution they had drawn up establishing the Defense Committee.

When the resolution came to a vote some hands shot up at once: Harlan's, J.J.'s, Blanche, and the little man with the soft voice. Others looked around and then slowly raised their hands. Finally about two thirds of the people in the room were voting yes. Sam Short and Watson were among the negatives. Rowley noticed that Shirley did not vote.

Afterward Shirley made coffee for the six who stayed. Harlan was still high, his face quick and fiery. His hands shook. "I felt helpless and put down all week. But when they started coming in tonight . . . something happened. Just because we made some calls and tacked up some rotten posters. Now we have a weapon. They think we can't organize fast enough, but they're in for a shock."

Rowley reached across and took one of Harlan's cigarettes—not because he needed it but to make contact, for he was struck that they were in a fight now, a real fight, win or lose.

They planned a block party to raise funds. He would entertain and dig up black artists. He told about his pursuit of Jack Curtis, and J.J. knew the minister he was looking for. He walked down as Yente rose howling welcome from under the front steps, with Harlan leaning out still yelling instructions for moneyraising and publicity.

Wednesday night the wind was blowing like a mean bastard when he parked. The plate glass of the cafeteria was steamed up so he didn't catch sight of Caroline waving until he was in line waiting for a slice of rib roast. She was sitting with the thin black girl who'd been at Leon's, and she gave him a nervous smile. The cafeteria was crowded and what the hell, he'd been firm enough. He sat with them.

"You remember Vera." Caroline was beaming. Vera gave him a brief icy glance, lowered her chin firmly. Why did she mind him joining them? He had met middle-class black girls who asserted their virtue by being rude to him, but somehow he did not think that was her pitch. Embarrassed, Caroline dug under the table. "Friday's Halloween, so I asked Vera to make me a mask. Something I could work into my act at the Rising Sun." She put a bag on the table.

"Why did she ask *you* for a mask?"

Her face was one. She made the smallest of motions with her delicate shoulders and went on eating.

"Vera makes them. Don't you remember—But of course you've never seen it, I mean, it's over my bed."

Vera pouted. "I did that when I was seventeen and it looks it. Give that back sometime, and I'll give you a better one."

"How about this? Can I keep it?" Caroline held up the bag.

"Why not?" A voice clear with the shivery sound of a tuning fork.

"What would you think of somebody who painted pictures and then gave them away?" Caroline asked, her eyes large and melting. "Because to me Vera's things are works of art."

"Why did you give her the mask you did so long ago if you don't like it?" Stubbornness set his jaw. He was hung up on making her speak.

"Because I was seventeen when I gave it to her: I thought it was pretty. I didn't know any better," she chirped acidly. "I was very small town, very primitive " She was wearing a boyish white shirt, and her long neck bore her face high above the open collar. Her wideset eyes slashed him and turned away.

"Now you're twenty-one, big city, very cool."

"Twenty-three soon, thank you." With her wide nostrils dilated she turned toward the steamy window. Reaching into Caroline's lap he took the bag and pulled the mask out. From the corner of her eye Vera caught his action and swung around, making an immediately checked gesture at taking it from him. The mask was made from a piece of beige silk, and the lank hair from unwound gold tassel. Even in the distortion created by spreading it flat on the table, the face painted on the silk was a fallen, an aged Caroline, a caricatured bled dry Caroline. Couldn't she see that? "But what will you use it for?" he asked her.

"Because I'm going to sing 'The House of the Rising Sun.' Isn't it beautifully relevant?"

He wanted to beg her not to. That mask with Caroline's trained doggy contralto. None of his business. "I want to see more."

"Come to Vera's with us then. She has dozens. Why don't you come?" They were sitting over coffee.

He looked at Vera. "I'd like to."

For an instant her face held irritation, contempt and humor. He almost doubted his observation for the mask slipped back.

As they got up he saw too late that Caroline was toting her guitar. The rain had stopped but wind swept water from the pavement in long running waves. At the car Vera climbed hastily into the backseat piled with junk and Caroline's Martin. Under cover of the front seat Caroline gave his thigh a squeeze.

He set his teeth. He was tempted to drop them and go on home. He was helping Harlan prepare arguments and his briefcase was heavy with reports on urban renewal projects he had to slog through. He had some of it figured. The redeveloper got the land for building expensive apartments (sound financial basis) through the government at about a third or less of what that same developer would have had to pay on the open market. Not to mention that a lot of the people would never have sold to him if they had any choice. He wanted to work on the program on the Defense Committee's fight he meant to talk Cal, his boss, into letting him do. In the rearview mirror he looked at Vera. With her dark raincoat drawn up she seemed monochromatic, cut clothes and all from the same curve of wood. Passing lights seized her face with a remoteness that piqued him. Sitting with her coat drawn to her, sitting as little as possible on the dirty cluttered backseat, she had leaped into herself and let the lid fall. Wrinkling his nose so his moustache tickled the nostrils, he smiled at his curiosity.

He parked near Muhammed's Mosque Number Two with its perennial message *Justice for the Black Man in Islam*. The wind had shifted, sharpened. The night was clearing and getting colder, the sky was littered with rags of torn cloud. In the vestibule Vera stopped to check her mailbox.

Caroline swung her guitar impatiently. "Expect the mailman to come back after supper?"

"Paul would put a note in, if he came by."

He asked, "Boyfriend?"

Caroline tsked-tsked. "Silly. Her kid brother."

The vast lobby had been hot stuff in the era of Valentino movies. Wee bulbs in heavy iron brackets lit it feebly from the squat pillars and rough plaster walls. Here and there against a pillar a leather chair exposed gored intestines. The back wall of French doors leaked puddles on the marble floor through broken panes.

Up a side stairway following Caroline's hippy pink pants. Then the room. He let it come in. Wall of faces. Wall of judgments. Society which must jar and rub on her, cuff and molest her, insult her daily in banal and trumpeting ways, she looked back at through its blind faces. She worked with anything. A few masks were painted on cloth or canvas, but most were constructed of household trivia.

"Do you start with an idea? Or do you find components and build from them?" Deliberately he sat on her narrow bed, under the faces.

Vera curled up in a tall art nouveau wicker rockingchair extending way over her neat head. "Not a black or white case," she said with a thin unfriendly smile. "I keep an eye out for pieces I like the shape or feel of. Every time I'm in a department store, I check the remnants table. There always seem to be things around I don't need. As my mother used to say about casseroles, they get rid of leftovers."

Caroline sat artfully. "I knew you'd be impressed. But she won't do a thing with them. I've tried and tried to get her to exhibit." She made a Z of her legs in pink pants.

"So they can talk about African influences. I make them to amuse me—and Paul. If other people want masks, they can make them."

He fished for her eyes. "Still I'd like to know how you work."

"Would you?" Her voice limpid, mocking. She sauntered over to a screen to push it clacking against the wall. A table covered with odds and ends, a portable sewingmachine, a dress laid out and pinned, a pile of egg cartons. Standing with one hand on her hip. "Well, watch. The entertainment begins."

Caroline sat forward, throwing him a look of entreaty to make sure he was paying attention. In some funny way she took credit for Vera. Vera took one of the egg cartons, emptied buttons from it, then broke it across. "Tonight it's fast and sloppy." With rubber cement she fastened a cornucopia of green satin, reached in a drawer for what looked like a jump rope. Snip, snip. Then she tied something. He caught the glitter of tinsel. Then she worked with the scissors, slashing and trimming.

Caroline leaned toward him, said in a flat voice, "I got a letter from Bruce today."

He looked at her hand. Ring was back. She was just being friendly.

"He's arriving Saturday by plane."

Did she want him to drive her to the airport? Vera passed them taking something from the sink, tore and glued. Swung around. "Crude, simple—as you see."

Caroline drew her breath sharply, then slid down in the armchair gasping with laughter. "Oh, oh, she has you to a T!" The mask was all leer and droop, part hound, part lecher and smug with satisfaction. Huge green nose, brows of steelwool, moustache of a frayed jump rope unraveled and slack, with wicked little tinsel pigeyes and great fat satisfied tinsel smirk. His vanity sputtered and yet he was tickled. He wished he were alone with her, damn it.

Still giggling Caroline swung the mask like a severed head. "Rowley, sometimes you do look just that way! Give it to me."

"No," he said. "I want to hang on that wall for a while."

"Headless men can't talk," Vera said. "But no, you can't have it. Paul hasn't seen it yet."

"But then?" Caroline poked it carefully in the green snoot.

"Maybe you won't want it. It was too easy." She watched through her lashes to see if he showed anger. "Don't knock it apart."

"I'm sturdy stuff. I take a lot of punishment."

"I guess so." For a moment as she took the mask from Caroline she smiled but this time without that edge of contempt. Then she put the mask on the worktable and drew the screen to. A silence built and stood between them. Caroline had her guitar before he could forestall.

"I've learned a new song." She gave him her performing smile. "I was thinking you'd particularly like it . . ." She launched into "Which Side Are You On?" Sweat broke out on his back. He wanted to throttle her. He could not stand

the damn songs, not to listen to them anymore. They gave
him a feeling of awful embarrassment, as if some gross bag
with eight chins had begun to flirt. He imagined cramming
Caroline's Martin right down her wide mouth. Wham. Just
the pegs sticking out. He could write songs for a fat union:

> We know just what we are for:
> the more, the more, the more, the more:
> burn the gooks, deport the spics,
> for a wider, whiter, annual fix,
> screw the reds at home, abroad:
> Three cheers for NAM, HUAC and GOD.
>
> Insularity forever,
> Insularity forever,
> Insularity forever,
> for Privilege makes us strong!

His old man rotting in Gary. Still if he heard middle-class
types jawing about unions he got blazing mad. Some heritage.

The moment she paused he bounced to his feet. "Got to
be going."

"I'll go with you. I mean, can you give me a ride?"

He turned at the first bend to look back, but Vera had
already shut the door. He heard the click of the chain sliding
to, the clack of the lock engaging. Down the dim worn car-
peted stairs after Caroline who descended slowly, so slowly
he finally thought of asking, "Want me to carry the guitar?"

At the bottom she turned but instead of handing him the
Martin, made a choking noise and flung her arms around his
neck. The guitar landed case and all with a boom that made
him wince. Jesus, she didn't deserve that instrument. "Oh,
oooh," she burst out. Tears ran down her face against his
throat. Cringing he put his arms around her. "There, Caroline, hey, what's all this. Hey come on, baby, don't carry
on."

Holding tight she rubbed her face into his throat, ground
herself against him in passionate complaint. "I don't want
to marry Bruce, I don't want to!"

"So give his ring back and flick him."

"Who'll marry me then?"

"Why should anybody?" He leaned awkwardly against a wall, a bracket with a broken bulb next to his head.

She sobbed harder. Her hands worked under his jacket. He lost his balance, ended up sitting on the last step with her sprawled across him. "You don't want to marry me! You'll make me marry *him*."

"Marry anybody you want." He made an effort to get up but she had the leverage. He lay on the steps with her treads digging into him and her soft but substantial body squirming all over. His tool was knocking against his belt buckle and the breath whistled through his teeth.

"You don't even like me! You don't care about me!" Her hands worked his shirt loose and crept under. The tears dripped like warm milk across his neck.

He felt like yelling, Hell no! Something sloppy, opportunistic, sly and shiteating in her that he hated. But her breasts squirming against him raised the vivid image of her body, a body that naked in bed had never excited him as much: the jutting hips, smallish breasts, soft thighs and bony knees that now lit him up like a welder's torch, at the same time the steps were breaking his back. His hand closed on her ass and he began trying to roll her over.

"You do want me. You do!" Her crying stopped. She put a hand on him, hot through his levis. A door opened somewhere up the stairs. He got up at once with her clinging. Stairs ended here. Space underneath closed in. Stepping down into the lobby for one minute he started for a burst red leather chair, but then he noticed the French doors and pushed on through the nearest with her, knocking it shut behind them.

They stumbled into tall wet weeds and grasses gone to seed, broken bottles and beer cans shining in the dark: unpromising. He backed her against the squat fountain in the middle, propped her on the rim. She was fumbling with him again, but he brushed her hand aside, got himself out, unzipped her slacks and pulled them just far enough out of the way along with her panties.

The angle was steep. He went thumping against the concrete rim, but she was excited and helping, and he shoved in. Then he realized they were in a patch of light. He looked up. No one at a window yet. The court echoed with television laughter, a manic avalanche of marbles. Anyone looked out, they would set race relations back a decade. He yanked her over into the dark.

Even as they jockeyed back and forth locked in uneasy balance and his excitement sharpened and sharpened, he still was half afraid he would blow the whole thing by collapsing into laughter. Over her shoulder he faced the bottom half of a castrated cupid. Lost it one damn wet night. They'd left the guitar in the hall.

"I've come," she hissed suddenly. "You go ahead. Please." He did not believe her, but then he was not sure she ever did come, in any sense he could understand. She was crazy, out of her mind which wasn't roomy to begin with. Her ring dug into the small of his back. He could feel her sudden nervousness, twitching on the wobbly rim. Once again he felt close to laughter. He went off the bottom feeling himself buck, but even then he thought, this is the end, not on a silver platter or a feather bed, I am not tangling with this one any more.

Saturday, November 8

He was hanging around the entrance to the 53rd Street Illinois Central station when Sam came sprinting down with her friend behind toting a dufflebag. They were both in levis and denim shirts like Bobbsey Twins, but she looked great with her dark hair slapping between her shoulders and her rosy face beginning to smile. She gave him a sharp wild hug and yelled in his ear, "Hey, this is Gino Warwick! Look."

He looked. Gino was of middling height and skinny, even scrawny, with his hair worn long and a silly fuzzy goatee. His face set sullen: anticipation of him or hangover of the house? Could be grim there.

The talk in the car was all what time they had left here, arrived there. After every question and answer, Sam would turn to glow over the seat at Gino giving him quick encouraging glances as if he might get carsick.

At his place Sam followed him to the kitchen to help stash the beer and deli stuff, while Gino sagged in the big red armchair Annie had always sat in. She leaned on the kitchen table braiding and unbraiding her glossy hair as she talked, not from nervousness but spare energy. "Been dying to get you together. We listened to you last night. He won't say so, but he was impressed—had to be."

"How were things in Gary?"

She made a sad puckered face. Looking down at her sneakers, her soft lashes brushed her cheek. "The doctors want him to have another operation. He's refusing. I can't tell if it's because of the money or because he hates the hospital. I tried to talk to the surgeon, but you know how they are. You should go out there and find out what's what." Yente came rubbing against her legs, and she picked him up baby fashion.

Leaning against the stove he felt his body turn gross, waterlogged. "Maybe."

She hugged Yente hard to emphasize. "You've got to! Make him go if he needs it."

"Sam, how can I? What have we ever been able to make him do? I'll find out if it's only the money."

"He says he can't leave Mom again. But she could go with Harry."

He made a fending off gesture. "Look, he was a man who felt himself there. He pushed on things. He made things happen. Now all he can say is she needs him home."

"If he doesn't have this operation, how much longer . . . ?" Her voice had dropped to their old muted tones, conspiring. In the next room Gino was pacing noisily.

"I can try to get an estimate from the surgeon. If he knows."

"Harry came over last night."

"Mother called him?"

"I did. Thought Gino might as well see the worst of the family with the best." But she was grinning as she nuzzled the cat. She had a soft spot for Harry.

"How's tricks with Harry? Have they taken him into the Syndicate yet?"

"Actually he's been giving Mom money. But he called Gino a commie dupe and said the Army would teach him to be a man."

"Harry's always been patriotic. Probably his greatest regret is he was a kid during World War II and couldn't corner the black market."

"Hey," Gino yelled, "are you still in there?"

"Half a minute!" She put the cat down. "What happened with Anna?"

"Maybe we got tired making it. Year's a long time."

She slid off the table to punch him in the arm. "Liar."

He laughed and reached for her but she ran out. In the living room Gino sat crosslegged leafing through his books. He held up one stuck full of notes. "What's all this Bobbie Burns stuff?"

"I'm doing a special on him. Songs mostly. That is, the ones I can get Cal to let me do."

Sam knelt behind Gino rubbing her chin in his haystack hair. He was surprised at his embarrassment. She had never doted. Gino gave him a look of disbelief. "To a wee mousie? To a mountain daily? Have fun."

"He wrote fine raunchy songs. No poet has knocked out better." The kid was ignorant. "So, what are you studying?"

Gino knotted his fingers in his meager goatee. "Are you going through the standard parental bit? We already did that twice."

"Got some preferred way of sending information? Use it."

"Why give you labels? Make up your own. Her other brother had plenty last night."

"Gino, don't go defensive on him." Sam hugged his head but he ducked free. The look she threw Rowley said, isn't he fine?

"You want us to sit and stare until we achieve a holy vision of each other? Or do I just wait for donations, like are you even a student?"

"I told you he was. But Gino doesn't believe in letting ourselves be compartmentalized by administrative convenience," she said proudly, kneeling behind the kid with her strong hands on his rickety shoulders. "College is a man-power-channeling factory, along with the draft, to service the needs of the system. Gino talks about the guerrilla student who operates inside the university making it serve radical ends and his real needs, a grasp on your own society, your body, your brain, your history." All the while she talked Gino made faces of anguish but offered no comment. "Rowley believes the same way you do about education. You have lots in common." A sneer hung in the air between them, before her highcheeked intent face.

"Is he from around here?" Rowley asked.

"From Midland, Michigan."

He squinted, thinking. "Company town?"

"Stifling," Gino said. "Dow Chemical. Model community when you're not downwind. Little white houses in a testtube. Grass for a town of cows."

"Your father work for them?"

"He's a chemical engineer."

"Oh." Middle-class kid with grass on his face and a lot of crap about selfdevelopment. Par for the course.

"We have to go see them next." Sam pulled her glossy hair together under her chin. "Maybe at Thanksgiving."

"If you like each other, why care if your families think you smell sweet?"

"Because you know, families get excited," Sam said patiently. "They might think we're young to get married."

"You are. I'm still too young."

"You don't understand. Even though there's enough in our

family to do it, I'm not scared of marriage like you are. Really.''

''Fine. A man who's not afraid of fire isn't required to jump in. Take your time, Sam. You've little call to be afraid of being single, either.''

''You're turning into a bachelor!'' Her dark eyes narrowed, her elbows came in. ''I'm surprised at you. It isn't always the woman who wants to get married. Some men *want* to marry a particular woman—''

''Get off my back. I guess you'll marry someday, but there's no damn hurry. Those couples tied around each other's necks before they're out of school. Wife knocked up, barrack existence—''

''Stop being superstitious. Getting married only changes my name and his draft card.''

''Then why bother?''

''Because if you feel around long enough we'll get into a fight and break up. Like you and Anna. That's not my idea of what I want to happen.''

''If something busts you up, then you better not get stuck so tight you need a lawyer to untie you.''

''Oh Rowley, everybody fights. If we weren't related how many times we'd have written each other off! You're being trivial!''

''Sam, the way people act in school has zero correlation with what they're going to sound like later. Everybody's an intellectual, everybody's a rebel. Everybody's set to lead a life honest to their values—whatever those turn out to be, when things start costing.''

''Everybody doesn't sell out, Rowley! You don't believe that either. Don't you have faith enough in me to think I won't, and that I wouldn't pick somebody who will?''

A look of intense irritation had been growing on Gino. Now he hauled himself up off the floor and stood head forward like a stork with rundown heels. ''She means this whole scene to be pablum, but it's not working. It's only making it worse on you, thinking you can change things. Don't choke on it, but we are married.''

The kid dared to pity him. ''Shit!'' Rowley found himself

crossing as if the floor tilted, walking into his desk. He stood observing that he had not paid his telephone bill.

"I'd never act this way if you did something you really meant!"

"Like shoot the mayor? Well, now."

"Look at me."

He swung around. She flushed. "When? How? You notice I don't ask any more, why."

"The weekend after I called you." She went to stand beside Gino, who rested an elbow on her shoulder, and looked at him directly now. His eyes were a slatey dark blue. She asked, "Want us to leave?"

To smash Gino's flimsy long head against the basement wall. He drew a deep abrasive breath. "I don't want to quarrel with you."

"No annulment threats?" Gino drawled.

"She did what she wanted. You don't have to worry about our folks. They're scared of courts. The old man served a term for a sitdown strike, in the sweet past."

"My family can't do anything they haven't already, for other reasons. It's what you might call a very loose connection."

"Gino organized a demonstration at Dow. About eighty of us went down there and leafleted and did guerrilla theater in front of the gates. When he got busted, his father wouldn't bail him out."

"He was scared." Gino shrugged. "I wasn't. I can't bail him out of where he is, either. And he's in for life."

Cheap imitation of me. She was too young to have developed a taste in men. "Notice I don't ask how she'll be supported either. I know."

"Rowley! Help me only if you mean it. Don't beat him over the head. You're acting just like they want you to, putting him down on sight, ready to think you must know better. Big brother, you're acting like a trained seal, and it brings me down."

"Look," Gino said in his flat drawl. "I'm used to making it on twenty bucks a week, and she'll learn. And no apologies from me. She's got a brain and muscles, and she won't starve unless she wants to. She's tougher and smarter than you think—and less than she thinks.'' He gave her a little more of the elbow.

He could not realize it. Harry he'd never been close to. But she had been his person since she was a baby. He had first been pleased with her when she was six months born, with moist black curls and enormous eyes. He considered he had had a lot to do with bringing her up and setting her straight. His parents named her Sandra, but he had called her Sam, and his name had stuck. Now this skinny cretin from a company town, this gangling, sourmouthed lichen-chinned heir of a chemical engineer had the right to call her anything from Sandy to Tootsy, haul her around, give her orders, read her mail, pump her full of limp fuzzy babies, and decide when and if he saw her. He could not believe it. He picked up a glass ashtray and smashed it on the desk. Broken shards exploded. He had to pick splinters off his shirt, out of his moustache, out of his palms. Her face was drawn tight with strain. Another girl would be crying, but he had raised her tough.

He marched up to Gino. ''Look you aren't exactly pre-possessing . . .'' which made the boy laugh before he brought back the high horse expression, all nose and goatee. ''Sam isn't stupid, so you must be good for something. I guess you're both pleased with each other . . .''

''There, see! I told you.'' She threw her arms around Rowley in a quick strong hug. He could not respond.

Gino shrugged. ''You aren't so pretty either. She thinks a lot of you.''

He found he could plod along if he thought of her marriage as a temporary state, like the spring she decided she too would sing. Not that she had ever been as lusterless as poor Caroline. He must see that she stayed in school.

He took them for chicken and ribs at the place on 47th. Gino liked it because it was soulfood. Oh well. The kids did act pretty, obviously in love and giddy with joy at being somewhere together. Gino seemed frozen in his affection: he called her Sam or Smartass, and when he touched her, it was with a roughness that apologized, that claimed it was not sentimental. Yet Sam beamed.

"Promise me you'll tell them. I just can't," she said. "I just can't go through that scene with Dad."

He showed them around the studio and took them to a coffeehouse with good rock. Then he drove them through the greenlit tunnel roads under the Loop and parked near the river. Lights from the *Sun-Times* presses. The wind sawed into the back of his neck as they walked through a light dusting of snow on the bank. The cold entered him like steel as he followed them joined and embracing, and bits of their laughter struck his set face.

That night he slept on the couch and they shared his bed. He lay awake, pitching. He tried not to listen, he put his head under the pillow until he felt smothered, but their whispers and rustlings and jinglings and mumbles worked like hot sand into the inner part of his ears.

Tuesday—Wednesday, November 11—12

They were sitting around the diningroom table with the remains of mincepie and icecream and the second round of coffee. "Not bad pie," Harlan conceded, who thought Shirley cooked too bland. What they used to call the General Foods syndrome when they were always on the lookout for a free meal. After Shirley dragged the kids off to bed, Harlan held out a cigar, gesturing for Rowley to sniff it appreciatively while he lit up one for himself.

"Hey!" Long time. His nose tickled.

"No, tobacco, man. Hot red tobacco—no cooler smoke."

"Who brought these in?"

"We'll never know." Harlan puffed, wrinkling his forehead. "Had a call from Sheldon Lederman, renewal's iron man. Invited me in for a chat before the public hearings. First I heard of them. Turns out the University has their consents already—"

"He was bluffing. There aren't that many defeatists here."

"First, the University owns more real estate than we ever suspected. They been buying under dummy corporations. The old hospital signed—there are connections."

"All right, that's maybe forty percent. They need sixty."

"Remember our surprise they included some of their own lily blocks? Our neighbors over there signed in droves their approval for having neighbors no more. Lafleur down the block who's taking his family to L.A. That amazing ofay bitch on the corner who recalls sunflowers nine feet tall and figures this was a lovely village before all the riffraff from Chicago took it over."

"A city board has to pass on it. That's our real battle."

"And we are going to make it a loud one. I want every person in these blocks at the hearings. But we have to submit names ahead of time, and time's running short."

"I'll testify. I'm willing."

Harlan tapped ash gently. "You look bohemian."

Rowley drawled, "You calling me a Polack?"

"Second, you're only a tenant." Harlan held up his palm. "God will record your willingness. In the meantime, raise money, cause we're going to need it. And get us publicity! I can't see why we can't get anything in the papers. I keep calling up and getting the royal runaround."

"You wait till I do a program on it. I'm seeing Cal tomorrow. I've got the script blocked out already and I figure we'll use some of the tapes we've made at meetings."

"I'm seeing UNA tomorrow night—meeting with their steering committee. I figure they've got to support us. I'm taking Blanche and J.J. and maybe Short—I think he's come around. Those UNA types are all liberals and interracial. I figure if they send some of their University types to the hearings to testify against the administration experts, it'll look pretty good. They claimed these blocks weren't organizable, but I'm taking our membership lists, and they'll have to eat crow . . . This is some cigar.''

"So Lederman gave you a couple of cigars imported I imagine through Canada, and told you to reflect upon the moral of luxury?"

"He said as how he was sad to see me wasting my considerable energies obstructing the public good, and he was sorry I was going to lose this house. It had been brought to his attention that I had tried to buy a house nearer the University. A very attractive one is just coming on the market, right near a good school for my children, and if I thought financing would be a problem—"

"They tried to bribe you?"

"Don't be crude." Harlan sucked, sucked on the cigar. "We're discussing a great institution—one founded on oil needs a little grease to keep it running."

Rowley leaned back in the chair till it creaked, bracing his nape on joined hands. "I can't help but have the feeling something is missing. All this fuss for a couple of dormitories.''

"He said something about a research park too. I don't quite get it. Some sort of institute that does defense contracting? Besides, they're putting up townhouses too, at thirty-eight thou.''

"Some of the financial goodies are plain enough to me now. In urban renewal, the city uses eminent domain to clear land and sells it off to the developer dirt cheap—often less than half of what the city has spent in tax money to buy and clear it. Then the FHA insures a bargain-type mortgage for almost the whole damn cost of the development. Add tax concessions, and the redeveloper doesn't even need to lay out much hard cash to clean up. All this is to build places that will rent or sell for the upper third economically. So you end up subsidizing the redeveloper and the upper middle class.''

"Racism for fun isn't good enough any more, now they got to make a profit." Harlan snorted. "Lederman told me to stop acting as a race man and act more as a member of the middle class. This only two years after one of their agencies kept me out of a co-op that voted us in. All day long I fight a nasty colonial war against the down and out. Society rates my job with trash collector. Human garbage disposal. I punish my clients for being black and poor and female.''

Tommy appeared in the doorway in striped pajamas. ''Daddy! Read me about Pollywinkle. Daddy?''

''Tomorrow, Tommy. Daddy's talking.''

''You never do. You never do any more! Daddy?''

''Shirley!'' Harlan bellowed and Shirley led her son away, consoling him in a high voice meant to be overheard. Harlan shook his head. ''Don't know what I expected. A crude man who was going to try to put me down. But Lederman was urbane, genial. He really did think he was talking to me for my own good. Like he was admiring the fuss we've created, and warning me it's time to cash in or back off.''

''He has a mind like a hungry pike and the ruthlessness of the just. The joy of the real operator. When you walk into his office, you know you're in the presence of a man who is happy in his work.''

Harlan gave him a puzzled stare. ''When did you meet him?''

''Remember when I roomed with Joe and that kid Leon? That was his son.''

''The circles you moved in. Now look at you.''

''Leon's a jagoff. He got into trouble at the University. The dean contacted Sheldon—big alumnus, committeeman. How would he like them to handle it? Treat him like the hooligan he is, says Lederman: kick him out.''

Harlan raised his brows. ''Sounds like facesaving. What had the kid done?''

''Boosted some books from the University store.''

Harlan made a face of disgust. ''That's sick. His father could have bought him every book there.''

''Lederman believed in making the kids struggle. Don't give them anything they really want. Know what you get? One kid who can't put a dime in a parkingmeter, and the other who can't admit to wanting anything.''

''His son.'' Harlan winced with incredulity. ''Of course I

see what Lederman's up to. It's the Jews' interest to keep us in the ghetto because they own the business there—''

''Man, if you think Lederman cares for some palsied refugee with a candystore in the Black Belt!''

''How's your kosher girl? Haven't seen her lately, worst luck.''

''You ought to work for the CIA. Haven't seen her myself since last summer.'' Corpses of the cigars lay in the ashtray. ''I looked into that housing authority study on relocation, and there's meat for us. Proof people displaced have to pay lots more rent. I've located a batch of similar studies, some with racial breakdown. When you figure the statistics are collected by agencies who benefit from more of same, the odds loom even higher.''

Harlan was not listening. Dipping his finger in ash he wrote on the oiled walnut veneer. FUCK he wrote and wiped it out with the side of his hand. ''Did you know that joining the middle-class is like ordering one of those pink light-up phones from the telephone company?''

''Well now, how is that, Mr. Bones?''

''Because you never stop paying, you pay every month of your life, and it would be cheap at one tenth the price.''

Lederman had sent for him after he'd stumbled on Leon's suicide attempt. Sent him, questioned him, tried to charm him, ended haranguing him. What a need that man had to be right, to be acknowledged right. Forsake my son and cleave only unto me. In a strange way he had made Rowley think of his own old man, and that set his spine stiff. Both had been true believers in the American dream, both had looked on the bottom of the Depression and called it hell. Sheldon did not want to be beholden to him, but Rowley had told him that he didn't want a job or a letter of recommendation or introduction or a scholarship. ''There's nothing you've got to give out that I want.'' Sheldon had laughed in his face and finally sent him on his way, calling him a fool and meaning it, but slapping his back.

Finally he stopped at Vera's—an impulse he had been ignoring. Climbing the narrow stairs, he knew he would find her with a man. He felt raggedly a fool plodding up through the dim smells of wet worn wool, soft coal, male cat and piss, cooking oil and porkfat. Her voice questioned down at him, "Paul?"

Jealousy struck him before he remembered, walking into the light from her open door, that Paul was her brother. She sucked in her breath with surprise and danced backward. "It's Rowley. Come for my head, remember?"

Across the hall a door opened a crack, an eye watched.

"Oh?" She stood aside, her eyes razory. Wearing a loose olive sweater over slacks, she was lean and wiry, a girl on a smaller scale than he usually liked. Her thighs in the slacks looked resilient, hard. In one nice arc of movement she nodded him in, let the door shut and turn. Still moving she reached up, one knee on the bed, took the mask, spun around and handed it over. "Here you are."

"Come on, want to rob me of my pretext?"

"For what? It's the only thing could interest you here."

"For seeing you. Why not?"

"Do you usually chase after black girls?" The faintest of smiles: delicacy not of china but of the forelegs of a deer.

"Don't usually chase after any kind."

"Don't start on my account."

He noticed with a pang that her feet were bare: small, narrow, with a sharp bone jutting in the heel. "Do you think you have a special reason to mistrust me?"

She stood with her hands locked behind. "Whatever you think you want, you won't find it here. If you don't listen now, you'll lose your temper by and by as well as waste your time."

"Because you're involved with someone?"

Her mouth thinned. "I don't belong to that whole messy game."

Her words resonated strangely. "You mean people?"

"That isn't all there is to being human. If it were, yes, I'd be something else. Why not? Half those I pass on the street don't think I'm a person anyway."

She stood like an exclamation point, ticking conviction. "You sound like a stubborn twelve-year-old." He saw a child, skinny with wiry pigtails and broad ashy part, straight fragile colt's legs, black and arrowy body. Bastard image, half the young Sam, half the girls of his gradeschool, the despised haughty colored girls who fought it out with him for the top of the class in the fifth, the sixth, the seventh grades. Thelma Hawkens, Rosetta Townsend standing with him in tense agonistic spelling bees. He let the wicker rocking chair tilt far back. Vera suffered his stare with cold presence. Girls who could read and sum and spell to the top of the class but never were chosen to play the princess or act the Spirit of Christmas to Come.

"You're from a small town, right?"

Plainly puzzled she sat down in the armchair. "Green River, Michigan. Going to tell me I'm a product of small town morality?"

"No." He smiled. "Caroline comes from your town too."

"If you think I judge her, you're mistaken. I only think she mixes with people who make use of her and leave her unhappy."

"Small town. With many blacks?"

She let out a silent laugh. "All in the way you look at it. In one of these suburbs they'd get excited. Ten families."

"Were you all very close?"

"We knew each other. We lent a hand. But . . . my father's an educated man."

"With money enough to send you to an expensive school."

"I went to teacher's college in Kalamazoo and Paul is on a scholarship." At that she got up and began clearing the small table by the window.

"Were you just going to eat?"

"No!" Rapidly she packed the plates away in her corner kitchenette. "Our father's a farmer." She sat back down. Coming aware of her bare feet she took her sharp heel in her hand, squeezing. "You can see I'm a country girl."

"I'd believe you came off the moon. Caroline has more of that Michigan flatness in her voice."

"You mean I don't sound colored? You aren't the first to comment." Her face screwed up monkeylike. "Our father was a stickler for proper diction."

"In Green River you must have been isolated when kids

started dating. Even around here gradeschool kids play together block by block, but highschool kids sort out. People begin to watch them together.''

"If you see me dramatically alone, you're dead wrong. For one thing, there were four of us. Sylvia married too young, but the rest of us were close. Particularly Paul and I.'' She glanced at the clock.

"You're expecting him?"

"Yes." Her face contracted in anger, smoothed.

He thought if he politely asked if he should leave, she would surely agree. "An educated farmer. What was he doing there?"

"Our family has farmed in Green River for five generations," she said with glacial precision. "Our greatgrandfather, a freedman, came North and settled there . . ."

Hearing the lock turn he looked. With her back to the door she went on in the same tone. "The farm we have is the original minus a few acres lost in depressions, plus what our father has added since the last war. The farm has always passed to the oldest son, the others being trained for teaching or the ministry and moving out, except during hard times when the farm supports the extended family—"

"God! The holy Jamesons, chosen to rake manure by the Lord himself. Pure, pennykissing, squeaky with religion, highminded in the presence of their cows, anointed with grade AA butter, even their pigs decent and clean!"

"The brother," Rowley said with satisfaction and got up, extending his hand.

Tucked up even tighter in the armchair Vera introduced. "Mr. Rowley. He's a friend of Caroline's."

After a perfunctory shake Paul collapsed on the bed. At Caroline's name he threw Rowley an amused curious look: like, are you getting a piece of that?

"Would you mind wiping your filthy boots on the mat rather than my bedspread?"

"My boots—if you'd look instead of sticking your righteous Jameson nose in the air—are clean. I did not get them wet, because I had a ride here."

"By way of Alaska? You are a mere two hours late."

"I wasn't aware I was being timed."

"What did you expect me to do with supper?"

"Eat it." He giggled in simple enjoyment. The boy was tall but loosely built, a couple of years younger and shades lighter than Vera. Family resemblance, yes, and they probably all were handsome. But Paul's face was softer, easier. It lacked that cameo precision that caught his nerves: he was pleased it was so.

Paul caught his examination and swung around to stare back. Then he laughed. "I know you now. Yes indeed." He rose on an elbow to scan the wall. Scanned it again. "Vera, since when are you so polite? Where's his head?"

"I am not! I gave it to him."

Obediently Rowley held up the mask.

She folded her arms, drumming her fingers. "Well, where were you?"

"I ran into some people."

"Hard enough to knock you out? You could have called." She hugged her thin arms. "That's the last time I cook supper for you."

"You bore me when you make threats you have no intention of keeping." Leaning back he played with the braids of a lewd/innocent face of chintz and straw. "It was someone I owe a favor—"

"That *toad?*"

Paul made a warning face. "You don't know him."

"I'm surprised you want to. Your taste is rotting."

Paul rolled to his feet and glared equally at her and at Rowley. "You never annoy me so much as when you don't know what you're talking about but think you do. The family arrogance."

"Lately you've been down on the family." Tipping her cropped head toward Rowley. "What do you think, is he too old to put himself out for adoption?"

"I come in to find you reciting the litany of holy groans."

She laughed: a clean rapping in her throat. They appreciated each other. They had a common notion of style. Perhaps that was what he would find himself knocking his head against. She was leaning back in the chair, her smooth long throat tilted and the pants sleek to her thighs. He got his gaze off just as Paul caught him. Letter yesterday, Mrs. Eugene Warwick. Eugene into Gino, progeny of chemistry. While Rowley meets the farmer's daughter, jig-a-jig-jig *très bon*. By Christmas, at this rate.

"Besides you have no cause to complain. You had company." Paul's gaze flicked him.

"Uninvited. About to depart." Standing he shrugged on his jacket. Politely Vera rose and followed him toward the door. He saw her notice the mask on the floor beside his chair and her lips part on the impulse to speak, then shut. Smiling into her eyes, he went out the door.

Still smiling down the steps he considered it his right to interpret that silence not only as wanting to keep the thing she had made, but as his license to come back. He was on his way to hear some new field tapes, and if he had time there was a party for a visiting rock group he should make. Damn that kid brother for having a key. Descending he had the sense of entering his whole life as if all of Chicago were open to him now except her room, which existed in another dimension.

"Why did you want us mixed up in a neighborhood ruckus, Rowley dear?" Cal sat at his cluttered desk with his hands together in Gothic prayer. "Why, I beg you tell me?"

"Because action never hits one community: people dumped from my blocks will crowd other neighborhoods, giving the real estate boys a field day. Because housing for anyone who makes less than ten thou is scarcer than dragons these days. Because this scene bugs me more and more the harder I look. Once again the comfortable are looking after their greater comfort and the powerful are making money, and it's all being done to slogans about urban renewal—and who wants to say they're for slums?—and the usual liberal rhetoric."

"I know the left wing of the Church is up for justice and the right wing because they don't want Negroes in the West Side parishes. The old line CIO actionists are mad. The Communists are dancing. And you want us to join the picket-line? This is a music and art station, not the thirties revival rally of the air.''

''If you're scared, come on before and after with disclaimers. Give the opposition time. But let me put a program together. We've done controversial things before. We did Berkeley and Selma.''

''Rowley, the University is the only thing that keeps Chicago from turning into a vast shallow pool of warm beer. It's so flat here. Civic planning always involves shoving the poor around, from Burnham on. That's how you create parks and boulevards and expressways and civic centers. They're always in the way.''

Rowley crossed his arms over Cal's view: the slate gray lake, a freighter on the horizon, the black blattlements of the Loop. ''During the Depression when there was first talk of turning part of the Black Belt back to white high income housing, someone asked the real estate spokesman what would become of the poor shits living there. Perhaps, he replied, they could all go back to the South.''

''We're a liberal station. The advertisers we attract aim at that clientele. But that clientele works for Inland, graduated from there. The middle class has to protect itself, or there won't be a thing but Negro and hillbilly slums from Evanston to Calumet City.''

''It's that increasingly hereditary middle class I want to reach.''

''Buy an ad in the *Tribune*.'' Cal's fingers strummed. ''Wake up, sweetheart. Who keeps us slinging culture? Remember the Moss Foundation grant? Our subsidy from the American Steel Foundation? Who pays your salary? Moss and Barker are both Inland trustees—''

''That's why we can't get a story in the papers, because Moss owns—''

''Because there isn't any story. Curtis Brothers own this building, fifty percent, and John Curtis sits on the board of Trustees, and John Curtis builds all the new university construction.''

''It's a conspiracy.''

''It's business as usual. Don't turn into a revolting paranoid. Curtis Brothers really are masters of steel frame construction—they're almost aesthetic at times. Really. For instance, the big New York firms are so much grosser.'' Cal rose and clapped him on the shoulder. "You're getting bored, Rowley, getting flat. Looking for trouble. Such a bother. But not on the station I've built from nothing. Someday you'll take my analyst's name. You do look a bit haggard."

"Yeah, so I went into that UNA meeting, you know, to try to talk to them. They're so respected and interracial and reformist. I started out to get them to support us, but before an hour passed I was down on my knees putting it to them, if you go before that city board and defend this proposal, you're shooting us down, that's all. I was wheedling and dancing like a real Tom."

They were slumped at the diningroom table. Harlan's mouth was slack, eyes bloodshot, voice hoarse and drained. Rowley kept rubbing at his eyes. The corners felt swollen. The last pot of coffee sloshed in his belly. "It was the first time Cal's ever slapped me down. He always gave me a free rein, so I never knew till now I was on one."

"When it comes down to brass tacks, these black blocks scare them. They can't see past that. They've all got a piece of something they want, and they're hanging on. The black bourgeoisie shoulder to shoulder with the white bourgeoisie. And this guy Asher who's on their planning committee gives this rap about how they've finally got good channels into the mayor's office, and they have to give and take now. What they're set to give is us, baby."

"Asher. He used to always be screaming about machine politics and municipal corruption."

"Oh, he was putting down Lederman as a crook. They all put Lederman down. I got so mad finally I said to them that he was more honest than them because at least he bargained, he recognized he was screwing us and was willing to offer a little piece of the action in return."

"This case we're putting together." Rowley waved at the papers and papers all over the table. "It's iron."

"Got to be. But oh my, this thing sure separates the sheep from the goats. Feels like we're taking on everybody. They got all the good words and they believe them somehow. I feel like ten miles of rough road. Already I'm getting sick and tired of talking. Talking a foreign language that they made up.''

Saturday, November 15—
Sunday, November 30

Black Jack's sister Lucille filled the overstuffed chair like a ton of medium brown lard. If he had expected anything, it had been that she would resemble his image of the man who sang: lean, bone dry, with leather muscles. Lucille Thompson's round face was propped on layers of chins, her arms overwhelmed the wide plush arms of the chair. Yet the slenderness of her wrists and ankles, a shapeliness in her bulk was feminine and she preserved the manners of a pretty woman. She served his coffee and cake about the time she began to talk instead of poking sentences at him on a pointed stick.

''Now what you expect from a man like that, no good from the word go? True they lay him off, no excuse, just goodbye one afternoon.'' She forked her cake daintily, separating the layers from the icing to eat that last. Her slightly clouded maple eyes watched him shrewdly. ''Another man go look for work in the Yards or for the city. Not him. Jack too mad. Since he was a bitty thing he got a temper like a shotgun. He want too much and he don't get nothing.'' She shook her head. ''What you aiming to do if you find him? What you want him for?''

He had explained and he explained again, feeling foolish. The room depressed him: essence of childhood visiting rooms. He felt the wrong size and half asleep. The air was hot and thick, the house creaked to itself. In an upstairs apartment a baby cried persistently as a squeezed bulbhorn: waaa, pause, waaa, pause, waaa. In the bay window plants reared from china spaniels, burro with pannikins, curtseying ballerinas, wishing wells. Plants with glossy leaves, with purple tongues, with fuzzy throats and spiny antlers, with waxen white flowers. An upright piano gloomed against one wall, a fringed shawl hung over the top. The past could open its hippopotamus throat and swallow him whole. If the people want a real architecture, Sullivan had said, let them become real themselves. But Lucille was all there, rooted in her stifling house.

From rickrack tables a garden of faces pushed up toward the light. Among them he could follow the slowly swelling Lucille through her annual rings. Once she had been only a buxom girl, sweet and melony, but always she had faced the camera jaw first looking it square in the lens. Nobody had got her to say Cheese.

"Do you have a photo of your brother?"

Politely she eased herself from the chair and rummaged in the next room, brought back a shoebox. She set it in her bulging lap and as she talked put the photographs down one by one on the coffee table, stopping in midsentence to smile at one or tap it. "Now the police, they had it in for Jack but they couldn't touch him for the numbers. He even cut him a couple race records." She shrugged. "On account of the numbers he made money hand over fist. He live with this girl Teena Lewis, nothing but a cheap hustler. A user. I told him one hundred times leave that hooker alone. We wasn't brought up that way. But hardheaded, good Lord, Jack was a great big old rock! That girl twelve years younger but she lay it on like she think he made of sugar."

She pointed to the tables of photographs. "We were raising three boys grow out of their clothes every time you turn around. Then the police got him for possession. Sure as shooting it was her stuff. Mr. Thompson been saying, you keep that brother of yours away from the boys. This time he put his foot down. Jack out I know . . . but . . ." with a slight flourish she held out a picture.

Two men and two women stood in front of a late forties

Dodge. One he could tell following the receding Lucille was her merely plump stage squeezed into a long broomstick skirt. Lucille put her thumb next to the man on the left. "This here my brother." She chuckled, down under her third chin.

For all his staring he could tell nothing from the broad brimmed hat, swishy trousers flapping in the wind, jacket wide as a playing field. The dark face squeezed among the clothes evaded him.

"You going to find him all right," Lucille said wading to the door to let him out. "My boys all big now. you tell him Lucille ready to see him. With me so big and fat, you think he can tell his own sister?"

Vera had left town for vacation. Thanksgiving he worked, but in the evening he drove out to Gary. Sam was in Midland: Mrs. Eugene Warwick meeting the Warwicks who would probably piss all over her.

> *Sam, Sam, Railroad Sam,*
> *washed her face in a frying pan*

he used to sing her, curly on his lap. The wind slashed through chinks of the frame house. The television uttered scraps of the day's football. The set was working badly, the picture blurred and gray as his father's skin. The old man had been ruddy, maybe as much from booze as naturally, but it caught at Rowley to see him looking like something soaked in water too long. The flesh had come loose from his big bones. He sat drinking beer and cursing the teams that had let him down, for he had dozens of small bets going.

The TV showed carefully chosen clips of a demonstration and that started the old man. "Some movement you got there. We worked hard to clean the reds out so we could run our own union. You nincompoops invite them in."

"You wasted yourselves redbaiting. Used them organizing and tossed them out, and your brains with them. Wanted to be more American than the Legion."

"Think you'll get somewhere with a bunch of students? Always the first scabs. Queers with whiskers waving signs."

The old man yelled at him, but he was almost as alien from the kids. Gino and Sam out there somewheres. His father was seven feet high to a kid. His father had been to jail for the union. His father had taken on two thugs and beat them with their own tire iron. When had he first seen that his father was also a bigot and a loudmouth and a smalltime tyrant? Always ready to knock them around, including their mother. At times the old man had enjoyed his kids in a direct hearty way their mother never could, but more often they'd been burdens piled on his hardworking back. Always trying to pick his pocket, leeching away money he needed for things that made a show with the boys, a new Chevy, a good rifle, a fancy spinning reel. An old prairie radical with a mistrust of anything he couldn't heft. A man who made trouble as often as he healed it, twitchy under discipline—not unlike himself. Yet the old man delivered what he promised and took shit from no one, there were things he had enjoyed and he had done them, and now a cancer was eating his body out in slow progression from organ to organ.

The old man snapped suddenly, "Let the dog in."

Rowley got up and opened the door for the bleary-eyed retriever. "Hi Rumpus, old boy." The dog rose to paw at him perfunctorily, then plumped down with a loud sigh. "How'd you know he was out there?"

"If you got as good ears at my age, you'll have something to swell about. Those kids, the kids going to school right here, don't have a notion in their thick heads what it was like in the mills before we got the union. They don't know what sweat is. They don't know what they got to thank us for. Makes my blood boil. This was a tough town. Named for a hanging judge—Gary of U.S. Steel who hung the Haymarket stiffs and proud of it." The old man glared at the dog, who thumped his tail and drooled on Rowley's shoe. "Students marching," he snorted. "They got a new sport. They're too chicken to play football any more. They get their degrees and four years later they'll be voting Republican and saying what the state needs is a good right to sweat law."

His mother came into the livingroom to call them the way she always did, a little diffidently. If you wanted to talk to her, you had to go to the kitchen. The kids used to hang around leaning on the icebox to tell her their troubles.

At the foot of the table she propped her chin wearily on her hand. "I don't understand Sandra not coming home for a family holiday. Putting some boy's family ahead of her own." Her iron hair was pulled into a tight bun on her nape, emphasizing her cheekbones. Harry across the turkey had the same dark eyes, but their father's bones. Harry's wife and two girls, all more or less blond and made of chewed bubblegum.

"She has reasons. Pass the stuffing," Rowley said.

"Just foolishness," she muttered. "Don't you like the turnips? You always stick by her, no matter what she does."

"She's crazy about that punk," Harry whined. "You should have told her she couldn't go, Dad."

Rowley tried to keep the edge from his voice. "You couldn't. She's married to him."

He was sorry at once when the old man's face went sick and grayer than ever. Then anger brought the color in. "What kind of daughter did you raise?" he shouted down the table in his old form. "Runs off with a weirdo without telling her family. What kind of sneaky lying slut did you bring up?"

That was Thanksgiving. He shoveled the walks front and back and fixed the mangle. He stood on a ladder to look at the kitchen fluorescent light and told his mother that she must buy a new starter. He promised to install it the next time out.

"I bet that won't be till Christmas," his mother said, brushing at his jacket arm. "You ought to come more often. He's going back in the hospital next week. You're not going to have your father long."

As if he and the old man did not affront each other. As if the old man wanted to be seen shriveling. As he was leaving his mother whispered he should find out what Sam wanted for a present. It was a sour tribute that they all assumed he had connived at the marriage. "Keep your chin up," he said to his mother and plunged into the cold with relief. Oh Lord, going down slow.

* * *

The babysitter was late coming and by the time Harlan, Shirley and he got loaded into the car and on their way, Harlan was tense with worrying they would be late.

"Sure there's a black vote now, but how long will it last?" Rowley was arguing as much to keep Harlan's mind off the clock as to continue supper's conversation. "There was a Socialist vote once—I mean on the local level like city councils and mayors. The millennium ain't come yet—we have all the problems we had in 1890 and the permanent poor, the elite incorporating itself, inequality in the courts, jails and schools, and a foreign policy of blood-and-guts rightwing meddling. What happened to that vote?"

"Just protest voting. Issues got swiped. There wasn't enough force from the outside. We got no cause to complain about that, ourselves."

"Every group rising in radical protest has been coopted by the power structure after bloody skirmishes. A few leaders go to jail, the organization men get incorporated into the middle-class and the others are squeezed out to stagnate at the bottom with the other losers. You win a few special demands but lose the will to justice. Get to be a proper pressure group with your own lobby and piety and belief there's no more room for change."

"If you get some of what you need, what do the members care if the founders' goals get lost? People join movements for ninety different reasons—like to meet girls, to help their business, to up somebody else. Don't bug me, Rowley. You don't know how to change a damn thing either. It's hard enough to keep my head clear. I don't even know where I stand on compromising with them. Like I feel they've got so much money and they own so many buildings, they don't have the right to touch one house that my people need. But I got to face the fact that probably at that hearing we will have to compromise. And that makes me feel sick."

"That's too abstract. Every house they don't tear down is a victory."

"No, baby, that is too abstract. A victory to hold on to what you got, which is so little? A house you paid too much for to begin with, with cops on the streets who are just waiting to lay their clubs on you, with mediocre schools for your kids instead of plain rotten ones? We are still just a defense committee. Park anyplace.'' Harlan made a face of anguish. ''Jesus, I hate to speak. I get pains in the belly every time.''

''You'll do a good job,'' Shirley said from the backseat. ''You always do.''

''Yeah? In a way it takes a lot of brass to come to a black group and try to stir them up about us. Because we made it out of the ghetto. Asking them to help us save what they can't even get. Come on.''

But when they were in the hall on folding chairs and Harlan was introduced, his face was different. He had begun to have a public manner. Rowley still experienced the shock of how well Harlan spoke, that magic of voice and manner that changed the air in a room. He spoke fast, his voice sometimes faltered, but he was learning. He had special appeal in the ghetto, but he worked for some white audiences too. The great pressure Harlan was feeling to save his home, his community, what he called his ordinary life, that was a commodity that could be sold. Rowley had written some songs for the Defense Committee, none of them good but all of them good enough. The money they raised hired a lawyer to help them prepare for the hearings which would start Monday, December eighth. Ten days, That was all.

Vera's absence caught in his head like a burr. He figured she had to return Sunday night, and sure enough he found himself on his way, walking over. A winter obsession. If he could have her and be done. He passed a bar, the grind of the bowling machine and warm beery lap of voices. Ought to stop in, have a shot, and go home and work on his Burns program. His steps did not slow. He turned into her dark street. The ice felt more steeply rutted. Half bare she struggled on the cot, under the masks. Her head was pressed back on the pillow and her body felt like short piled velvet. With outthrust hand he broke ice-capped twigs from a hedge. He had never forced anyone. Clots of racial phlegm.

To clear out the poison he sang:

> *"Green grow the rashes O;*
> *Green grow the rashes O;*
> *The sweetest hours that e'er I spend*
> *Are spent among the lasses, O!"*

He passed the blind facade of an abandoned synagogue. On either side of the wide steps—a smooth slope of snow—iron candelabras lifted jagged, broken globes.

> *"For you sae douce, ye sneer at this,*
> *Ye're naught but senseless asses O,*
> *The wisest man the warl' e'er saw*
> *He dearly lov'd the lasses, O!"*

To make Burns come through: a drinking man, a leching man, of the left and proud of his work, with wit and temper. Annie wouldn't care for that program either. Or didn't she listen now that she didn't have to?

Though that reaction was not typical. He crossed the Moorish lobby. For some reason he could not get rid of the image of her laughing. She laughed with her whole body—laughter as sensual and total as her sex. Leon liked to talk about fucking, he was full of mystique. Yakking about the Zen lover, after tripping holed up with that skinny kid he'd used in his first flick. Like people who got high talking about grass with maybe one roach between them.

He realized he had forgotten to buzz. He rapped on the door. Nothing. Again. Then the creak of the springs. "Who's there?"

"Rowley."

A longish pause. Then the chain slid off and she opened. One side of her face looked puffy from lying on the bed, but even more the expression in her eyes and a purplish cast of fatigue about them made him ask, "What is it?"

"It's me, I suppose." Her thin hand came up to guard her mouth.

He took off his jacket, drew the armchair toward the rocker and sat. "What's wrong?"

She tossed her head. "What do you want? I'm tired!"

"Something happened at home?"

"Paul has gone out of his mind." She curled into the rocker, retracting her knees under her chin. She wore a wool dress in a soft dusky pink, a loose dress like a child's smock with wild embroidery across the top. Hugging it about her slender legs she hid in the dress, snuggling into it like a blanket. "Clean out of his mind, oh, completely."

"What did he do to get you so angry?"

She hugged her legs tighter. "What do you care!"

"We've been through that. Come on, you'll explode if you don't talk. Dump."

She rocked, rocked with her chin dug into her knees. "He's very bright. You probably couldn't tell the short time you saw him. You bet they were put out when they gave him an IQ test back home. They made him take it over."

"Sure, I could tell he was quick." Hero worship.

"My father was thirty-six when Paul was born and nothing but girls. You might say he took it as a personal favor from God to get a boy." Under her lashes she watched, poised to take offense.

"Are you as religious as your father?"

"No. We are not."

"You're saying that Paul's spoiled."

She frowned her nose at him. "*No.* You don't understand. He is special."

He slumped way down, hands clasped on his belly. "He must have done something special this weekend."

"It's that disgusting ofay toad he's hanging around. Poisoning his mind—I mean it. Like a sewer. I never met him but twice and the first time I didn't say boo. But he told Paul I'm trying to run his life. That I domineer over him."

"A kid in school?"

"Your age. Paul is stuck on him. It's disgusting." She stretched her legs out and flung her head back, an arch of protest. "Listening to every vile thing."

"Such as?"

Her hand came to her mouth. "All sorts of warmed over Freud in a special ugly sauce of his own . . . you know . . . penis envy, sibling rivalry, the whole bit."

"So he was spouting at you, trying to convert you."

"Worse." Shooting out of the chair she crossed to the bed, jerked the spread flat, straightened a couple of masks. The images of violence that had swept him on the street seemed absurd here. From across the room he explored the curve of her tall neck, the arm turned like a vase on a wheel. Fragility/resilience.

"When I say he's out of his mind. We've been close all our lives, you can't understand. But he loves preposterous ideas." Her hands drew across her temples, ironing. "Our folks went to church. We don't. We made that an issue last year . . ." She trailed off, silent for so long he almost gave up. Then she looked up and said with rising inflection, "He said I wanted to sleep with him."

He laughed, not wanting to.

"You laugh because it's silly. Isn't it?"

"He marched in and accused you?"

"We'd been fighting all weekend about this domination business. Then he said, what I told you. He was watching me with his face all sly, feeling clever. Oh, I could have killed him!"

Rowley grinned still, he could not help it. "Did he expect you to confess? Or take him in?"

"How do I know? He's such a goose." Once again she coiled in the rockingchair with her knees tucked under her chin. "He was acting in a play. Being so adulty, so damned sophisticated. Oh, I wished I'd smacked him."

"What *did* you do?" The laughter he had quelled still leavened his muscles. He had been jealous of the brother; but the brother could not make her either.

> *What you got in mind ain't going to happen today.*
> *Get off of my bed, how did you get that way?*

Literal children captured by an amateur analyst: who would have said what, had Paul come strolling in after vacation announcing he and his sister had established perfect sexual rapport?

"I don't know what to say. He went on lecturing, Basically our relationship is incestuous! I said, Basically your head is a pumpkin. Finally he sashayed out telling me I would never serve my reality principle intelligently until I faced the darker forces of my Id, end quote. I threw my best early mask at him and broke it."

"If he's as bright as you say, he'll wear it out."

"It hurts me to see him acting . . . stupid? vulgar? He hasn't been doing as well in school as he should. He was flunking science. The toad helped him in some way he won't tell me, but all of a sudden he's not worried."

"Does he have a girl?"

"Usually." She smiled. "Girls chase him. Even white ones." She gave him that filtered look again.

"Do you really think being black is the most important thing about you?"

"Of course not. That I'm black is the most important thing about you. You can't ignore or forget it."

"Why should I try?"

"Want a medal? I have some gold foil on the workbench."

He got up and stood in front of her. "I want you, in that bed with your arms around me."

She laughed with surprise. Her voice came a little muffled. "Well, at least you don't insist that's what I want. Don't stand over me."

He took a step backward, but as he did he caught her hands and slowly pulled her to her feet. "Look at me."

She did then, her eyes in her face of slightly flattened delicacy playing on him in open observation. She was amused. In the arms he gripped he could feel no sexual response, not fear, not desire. "I'm not any more successful with you than your brother," he said softly and closed the gap. At the last minute she turned her face so that he brought his lips against her smooth warm cheek. As if he were operating a tiny rickety crank, slowly he tightened his hold and drew her against him, first the soft fleecy wool of the dress, then the warmth of her, then the first resilient touch of her breasts and belly through the cloth. Slowly, slowly he brought her against him. He thought he felt in her a stir, a slight catching of the breath. Then she burst out laughing and broke from him backward, rubbing her cheek. "Your moustache! It's like being kissed by a dog. You tickle me."

Forcing himself together he started after her.

"No." She dodged behind the rocker. "I don't want to be kissed and mauled and handled."

Stiff and sore with wanting he sat heavily in the armchair. "How do you know?"

"Anyhow, your moustache tickles. It's funny."

"It's soulful."

"Off with it. Shave it, and then maybe, maybe I'll kiss you." She leaned forward on crossed arms on the rocker's high back. "I don't hate you any more, the way I did when you came clumping in here with Caroline like you were going to die with your boots on."

"Thanks, sport. You mean I listened like a good doggy."

"Can't you believe I don't want any part of that?"

He looked at her in momentary defeat and thought he had never yet fully seen her. The puffy fatigue had passed from her face, leaving the skin like ripe plum. The emotions that lit and went out in her face held nothing gross, murky or demanding: nothing of Caroline's turgid narcissism or Anna's bitter aftertaste. It was not a case of taking her from someone, but persuading her she wanted to share her possession of self with him.

> *"I'll tell you, mama, and I'll tell you true,*
> *If you don't want me, baby, it's a cinch I don't want you.*
> *I got those bullfrog blues, and I can't be satisfied . . ."*

He was singing with the guitar and Yente both somehow on his lap when Harlan came down. "I saw your lights were out. Is my playing keeping you up?"

Harlan shook his head. "Soon as I lay down I start thinking of things I should have said. Or things I have to do. I start repetitively going through the next day's scenes, making speeches and correcting and changing. If I do fall asleep, I come awake with a scared hard knock like I'd dozed off driving."

"You'll be in a hospital bed soon if you don't ease up."

"Talk sense. The hearings start the eighth. How can I ease up? Though I sure could use some tranquilizing." Harlan paced the record shelves pulling albums out randomly. "You keep any grass around nowadays?"

"You asking that as my landlord?"

"As a dying man begging for water."

"Why if I give it to your kids, I don't see why I shouldn't share it with you." Harlan hardly ever turned on with him any more. A thing they used always to do. "What do you want to hear?"

Harlan picked out some jazz tapes and he set them up. They passed the joint and soon Harlan started talking. Ritual soothes. "The bind is tightening on me. They have their ways of letting you know you've been rocking the boat in Welfare. Every routine form I send upstairs comes bouncing back. I can't get a paperclip without petitioning, and they keep making us reinvestigate. At home the kids feel neglected. Maybe I spoiled them. And Shirley . . ." Slowly he rubbed his nose.

"I thought she'd been taking it pretty well. She's put a lot of work in."

"Sure," Harlan mumbled. After a while, "But she can't get away from thinking making a stink is plain wrong. She's scared I'm going to get in trouble. Deep down she blames me for not making it all disappear. The world is my business like the house is hers."

"You satisfied with the materials I've dug up for our case?"

"I'm not satisfied with anything these days. All my thoughts got spikes on them. But I bet you haven't done that kind of research since we were in Dugan's class."

"Happens you're wrong. I research my programs."

"How'd you ever get started playing blues?" Harlan stretched way down in the chair, slowly letting out the smoke. "You been doing it since I met you, but you sure didn't grow up with the blues."

"If it's black music, what's a white man doing thinking he can own it—the old problem of blue-eyed soul."

"Now I put you down a lot, but you have feeling for it. I

like Miles better any day than all the old funky country blues you dig or those screaming rock singers. But why?"

"Every white musician has a conversion experience. The real thing. That's what I mean, or it means, or He means. Besides nobody really white comes from Gary. Real white people wouldn't live there and work there—right? Like Detroit and Cleveland and Newark. That's why the working class is so racist. It's the physical bloodstream music of where things are at now and that's why a kid in Stockholm or Berlin can hear it and have to make it—and if he can make it well it's his—right?"

"So the Jews had the book and we have the beat, and both conquer. Though in both cases the victories belong to converts from the outside who didn't quite dig the message." Harlan grinned. "And we're still outside and damned."

"The fate of all peoples who invent things beside weapons."

"You know what? Blanche got me. That's what it amounts to. Oh, my."

"Does Shirley know?"

"Is the roof still on this house? You know, I've been so wrapped up in this I didn't see it coming. She's a real worker, but she's a real hustler too."

"Isn't that going to cause a few difficulties?"

"No more late night sessions, for nothing. I like Blanche—she's quite a woman when you get down to it—but she's not getting me down to it again. Too much wildcat there."

"It's all that charisma you've been building up."

"Sure, Georgie. She really is after me, though. I hope she keeps her mouth shut. I got enough trouble upstairs. We got enough trouble all over. I went to a meeting of that big central renewal wingbat, the mayor's planning and housing council, and I looked around very careful waiting to make my little appeal. And I saw that one guy sitting on the board is the president of the alumni association of Inland, and another is on the board of trustees, and another is a politician they gave an honorable degree to last June, and another is vice-president of Curtis Brothers. When I finally got to make my little presentation, I couldn't get much oomph in it."

Why didn't he tell Harlan about Vera? Since Harlan married they hardly talked about women. Still he had the feeling he was keeping something back. Come on now, nothing had happened. Tell him about what? The jazz threw mandala patterns shifting and slowly turning on the air between them. Sitting a few feet apart and sharing the third roach, they were close and easy in their fatigue, and it seemed pointless to bring up a thing that could scratch the skin of a good, rare moment.

Asher

Asher woke taut, clenched. His gums felt sore, as if he had been grinding his teeth. He was not sure who he had been confronting across the desk, Sheldon Lederman or Boss Tweed. Someday he would slip and call Stan that to his face. Funny that he couldn't be sure which man it was making him squirm in the dream, they were so different. Stan had the professorial manner, softspoken, pipe smoking, big boyish, how-are-you-smile.

Whereas Lederman. Should never agree to go see him at his office. That enormous desk like a decapitated racing car, broad dully gleaming expanse of lustrous designer plastic. Then the view of the city: almost all of that wall. Sketches of garden cities and double helix skyscrapers on two walls. They waded in through his carpet, gingerly fitted themselves into the arty molded plastic chairs. He had them already. Out of their depth. Even Muriel had kept tugging at her skirt, uncertain about the angle.

He had headed the UNA delegation to argue the matter of school expansion with Lederman. But Lederman had thrown them all off balance by starting out so sympathetically, delighted to see them (beaming at Muriel of course), subtly flattering them about their expertise in neighborhood matters and then landing the punch about UNA not being the real grassroots. Chiding them gently for calling their group of professionals a grassroots organization, oh come now.

Catching them smack in the middle of their class shame, of course, liberals who are afraid they aren't as real as blacks or workers. Should have challenged Lederman directly, instead of letting him operate by innuendo and nudge. Pointed out they were the people the neighborhood was being renewed to keep and to attract, and thus they damn well were the neighborhood's grassroots. How had he let Lederman catch him offguard, when Lederman's position was statistically unsound? He could prepare a case that would blast Lederman's sly aspersions to kingdom come.

Button off his pajamas. New too. Planned obsolescence. They didn't care about bachelors, sewing buttons on by two threads. He pinched his belly folds meditatively. Got up and went to brush the sweaters off his teeth. Could never decide if the electric toothbrush represented technology in the service of hygiene or his weakness in the face of gadgets. Pleasant sensation. Maybe worth it on the animal level. Buzz in the mouth. Insect noise.

He put the water on to boil and toasted Friday's bread. Tomorrow he would find out if they had landed the transistor quality control contract. Could he charge some of Schmidt's time to it? Expensive man to ride on overhead. Boss Tweed was watching his overhead. What was he supposed to do when the research money dried up? Freeze half his department? Thaw them when the money thawed? Give Mavis two more weeks and if she didn't start producing, he'd have to ax her. If the contract didn't materialize, how would he get through Monday afternoon with Boss Tweed? A bullshit line, but what? He spooned sugar into his instant coffee. The difference between the bachelor and the married man is that the bachelor gets instant coffee and an imaginary quarrel for breakfast, while the married man gets both in their true form.

Not bad. He had a dry sense of humor. "Not dry, dried!" she had screamed at him. Lederman dropping that hint about the place for a good statistician in demography studies at the University. Um, to do research again. He had been, he was twice as good as Schmidt, and here he was reduced to worrying about how to support a department like a family without birth control. Demography indeed. Get out of the ratrace and do some work again. But publish or perish, and could he still?

Letting Lederman outmaneuver him. Vulgar old swinger. Vain, posing around, giving Muriel the leonine profile. Old fraud, old gouger, speculator and board room policitian. He, Asher, had his competencies and his fields of interest or knowledge, but he never thought of himself as exceeding the sum of his parts. Which is why an ambitious manipulator like Lederman could run circles around him. But Muriel wasn't impressed with that old tomcat.

Yesterday's mail still lay on the kitchen table, including a notice that the maintenance in his co-op was going up. Again. Where did the money go? He spent as much as he had when he was spending for two. Maybe if he could get an offer from the University, he could use it to raise his ante at the office. Best to go slow, feel his way. It was a good building anyhow, architecturally interesting and comfortable, even if the central poured concrete hall did act as an echo chamber. Money, money, where it went. Down and out. Dissolved. Taxes punished the bachelor. Sometimes he thought he should start his own consulting company, but the trouble. The capital.

Asher drove to Muriel's as much to give his car a little run as to avoid walking through the snowpiled streets. If he left the car too long the engine might not start Monday. A car in the city was madness: if only there were clean efficient public transport, silent Unirails as at the Seattle Fair or bus-sized helicopters. A car was a joy briefly while new: like a wife. He studied the *Consumer Reports* roadtests for he hated being cheated, hated the idea of buying with his eyes and being manipulated by his weaknesses. Whether he was buying a car or a watch or a camera, he wanted the object to be dependable, clearly the best and biggest of its class, a New York *Times* among merchandise.

On Sunday he went to Muriel's because that day her ex-husband had the children and she was lonely. With the children away they could make love conveniently. Finally, Muriel cooked a nice Sunday dinner.

The French provincial livingroom smelled of the roast. He felt his hunger, enjoyably. They sat on the blue couch while

Muriel spread the redevelopers' prospectus over the marble top of the coffeetable. He turned over the glossy pages. "They made a goodlooking job of it this time."

"I've been on tenterhooks to see the proposals." Her delicate perfume tickled his nostrils. Her soft pale brown hair lay sleekly against her faintly concave cheek. Muriel was a tiny graceful woman with something always tinkling at wrist or earlobe, dressed well but severely except for that flutter. They were both on the planning committee of UNA—not the usual reactionary neighborhood falange but liberal, full of professionals and dedicated to a balanced interracial community, and effective—at times. He sighed. Though a little too addicted to studies and at times a little too redolent of group therapy. Last Thursday's meeting had run till eleven thirty, with all sorts of people not even active in UNA up in arms about the renewal effort in their blocks.

"Let me tell you, I have my suspicions who was behind that attempt to pack the meeting." At her throat an antique cameo rode with profile clear as her own. "The same reds who tried to take over the school committee are behind this."

"Muriel . . ." he protested mildly. Rhetoric of her ex-husband, a Nixon man. Tedious but she was growing out of it. In time.

"I could have died for poor Dr. Palmer. Imagine that man getting up to say the doctor couldn't speak for local Negroes. As if he isn't one of our finest community people."

About two thirds of the way through any project those people turned up objecting, indignant, ready to shout. Who are you? their eyes challenged, but if in return you asked one, Where were you at the preliminary meetings? where were you when we were sweating over plans and knocking heads with officials? he would look at you as if you were crazy. If you asked him why he hadn't joined UNA if he was so interested in his neighborhood, he would say, *Them?* What would I want with them? I work, I got no time. A blank wall.

"If you knew what that big house looked like when Dr. Palmer bought it, the money he's put in. He told me the sweetest thing. He's so pleased with the grounds and the big elms that he's taken up feeding birds—with seeds? He's fed them until he has a flock of sparrows like little butterballs, almost too fat to fly.''

"If we could have persuaded the families who fled how well men like Dr. Palmer would fit in."

Muriel's small princess face looked wistful. "The panic! Real estate sharks going door to door, telling people, 'They're moving in nextdoor, the neighborhood's turning. Sell while you can get your money!' "

The white inhabitants who had stayed all liked to recall the harassment, almost in ritual terms. It was a remembrance of battle and a mutual reinforcement of purpose. Staying was an act, after all, but he grew tired sometimes of congratulation.

Muriel nodded at the bay window on the street where two old frame houses dripped ugly carpentry. "If those roominghouses don't go! I was talking to the head planner yesterday. A little park would be perfect, like the one you got for your old block. He said Netty Fox was pushing the site for some of that scattered public housing she's always steaming about. Well, I said, put the public housing on *her* corner, then, right in her front window!" She turned her tiny firm chin to him, leaning closer with a subdued rustling.

"The banks won't permit it, never mind Mrs. Fox." He patted her hand. After dinner, must. "The planners write it in, but they know it will be cut." He had mixed feelings. When he drove past a cleared slum, chaos formed into clean towers, he was impressed by how reason and moderate expense in the public sector could improve the city. But he knew all the arguments against the building of cleaner ghettos. And everybody said, not on my corner, and every alderman said, not in my ward.

Muriel gave him a trusting smile as if he had fixed the banks for her. She had cute ways: every flick of her wrist or tilt of her head were bouquets for him. He liked that. Together they bent over the prospectus. Towheaded girls with doll buggies and freckled boys with catcher's mitts played on spanking white sidewalks under big shade trees. Crystal towers set in a park of dewy lawns. A fenced playground where slides and swings and a jungle-gym invited. Some woman

had got up to ask the planner whether neighborhood kids
would be allowed to use the playground. "Oh yes," he had
assured them, "until the first incident." A suburb in the city.
He did not know.

He did not like the idea of putting people out of their
homes, and those at the meeting had been emotional. The
University was not exactly a liberal force in the neighborhood. Its administrators had opposed UNA many times, pre-
ferring white covenants and real estate deals. Now with the
University working with them instead of against them, doors
opened, businessmen listened and contributed, city officials
were helpful. In the past, what a roundabout course he had
had to pursue when trying to get something as simple for his
neighbors as a stop sign for a corner where two children had
been struck. To keep that working relationship, one had to
make compromises sometimes.

"I have to decide not only how to vote at the next meeting,
but whether to sign a consent. My co-op is in the area."

"But your block isn't *blighted*."

"We're not scheduled for any demolition. We're just part
of the planning area."

Muriel beamed at the wide lawns. "I'm sure you won't
have much trouble deciding."

"I wish they'd go at things in a more democratic way."

Muriel's potroast reminded him of his mother's and he told
her so. She kept passing dishes. "The children will be sorry
they missed you. They adore you. Mikey said the other day,
Why does Uncle Asher have to go home? You can give him
my room and I can sleep in Judy's. Isn't he a riot?" Her
delicate face pinked to match the cameo at her throat.

He was embarrassed for her and forced a chuckle. "Mikey's a little devil. But a good boy." He had thought of marrying her. Taking more potroast, he thought of it again. She
had a nice house and Mikey was right: there was room for
him. She was truly interested in the same things that he was.
She was a good woman, settled, not about to jump out the
window or rave about Relationships or start staying out late
at night. "Oh yes," he said elegiacally. "If my marriage had
not . . . I'd have a son of my own. But dreams break as well

as bones, Muriel, and no doctor knows how to set them."
A fanning of humidity disturbed his sinuses. He took more
potroast and asked for bread.

Pie and icecream for dessert. The pie was warm. "So you
made this yourself! Wonderful." Even as he spoke he was
surprised at himself. Actually he was sure it was from the
Co-op, where just yesterday he'd almost bought the Dutch
apple.

"Well." She hesitated. "So glad you like it."

He finished the piece with dismay. Besides, two of another
man's children. After one such mistake.

As they sat on the couch she turned to him with soft
warmth, but he had overeaten. Fortunately she never hinted
around. They discussed the next meeting. He was mounting
a slow campaign for the chairmanship. They counted his
votes, and this time he lacked only one. they went through
the committee looking for their next conquest and worrying
how they could hold their weakest votes against the blan-
dishments of Netty Fox. Muriel was a real helpmate, and she
knew how to argue a point without antagonizing. Even that
scoundrel Lederman always asked after her and perked up
when she was on a delegation.

He drove home indirectly, through the streets of the prospectus. Dusk was settling. Puddles stood in the gutters:
better storm sewers needed. These streets seemed more
crowded, harder used than Muriel's or his. A gang of colored
boys were blocking the street, though when he blew his horn
they drifted aside. Then a tough threw a snowball hard against
the back window of the car. Narrow grimy crowded street.
Black smoke billowed from a chimney—burning something
illegal. Dirty obsolete wooden houses, cheap shingle-sided
multiple dwellings, apartments cramped together without a
bit of green space. Really, he was a snob to sneer at the
pictures in the prospectus, when a child could invent a
healthier environment than this. No plan was perfect. Political action always ended in less than you'd hoped for. He had
lived in the city eight years and he could not imagine leaving,
but its politics were as grimy and archaic as this street. The
machine of the city and the machine of downstate grinding

hopes of reform between them. Politicians who ran as Polish or Irish in the third generation, as if that were a program. People shrugging their shoulders and blaming everything on the Syndicate, like peasants talking about the will of God. Irrationality and interconnection and the payoff. Even businessmen were unwilling to cross city hall, because the mayor stood on the back of his machine and acted as the friend to business, jiggling ordinances, zoning laws and taxes to attract or keep industries.

Three white beatniks came noisily out of a basement, a girl with long black hair with her arms around both men, one with a moustache and one with a beard. The big hulking one struck him as familiar, but Asher had already looked away. Stare and you encourage them. He drove more quickly, afraid another hoodlum would throw a snowball and break his windshield.

He felt relief as he turned on his own street with its wide lawns, the gray Gothic dignity of the fieldhouse. In front of a fraternity some students were rollicking in the snow, having a mock battle, while the snow was flying. Teaching, what would it be like now? He could always do consulting on the side. He'd run into Tom Lovis at that fund raising affair for Senator Botts, and Lovis had given him the word about the possibility of a research park. If that came off, the other possibilities might open. Lovis had done pretty well for himself. He was moving up fast. Written some of John Roger's speeches when he'd run for the House. That was a role Asher had sometimes imagined for himself: one of the hard working politically knowledgeable cadre behind a good clean liberal candidate, one of those who helped him define his position, consulted in crisis.

He let himself into his apartment. Danish with clear true blues and greens: he approved of his livingroom. He liked it better than Muriel's. Undoing the button on his trousers, loosing his belt, he sat in his adjustable tilt chair and reached for his briefcase, settling it against his leg like a faithful dog. In a while. First he resumed his survey of the *Times* with the magazine section which he read completely except for the recipe and school ads, but not excluding those many advertisements featuring lissome, elegant, bare but never vulgar ladies, erotic and soothing at once and somehow in the public interest.

Anna

Monday—Sunday,
November 10—16

In midmorning a boy strode in with an envelope, asking for her. She nodded him gone and slid it into her desk, unopened.

"What's that?" asked lean virtuous Mrs. Cavenaugh. "We can't let things pile up without attending to them."

"No," Anna said meekly. "I'll take care of it."

She kept hopping downstairs but her chance did not come until noon. She told the girl who ran the machines, Oh, go to lunch, I have a little job but I'll xerox it myself, and showed her a letter she had been holding up. As the girl left, Anna tore open the envelope and without pausing to look at the pages, ran them through, crammed all back in the envelope and went at once.

The snow had melted, leaving the lawns a faded watery green. In a block she unbuttoned her coat. The big yellow envelope felt conspicuous. Never had she cheated when she was in school and she had never given her students exams they could cheat at. Nevertheless when Leon had assumed she would help she had not hesitated. Ducking into the Oriental Institute she hurried across the lobby past the guard. Leon, Leon where are you, damn your eyes? Slowly she walked the aisle between cases of Egyptian artifacts. That unreliable bastard. Why couldn't he get up when he had to?

Letting the envelope trail the floor between two fingers she headed toward the great Assyrian winged bull, toward the sideways-walking, wallhigh winged bull with the face and beard of a man. Strong, full of dignity, he surmounted photographs of his excavation. Muscular pillars for legs, sexual cannon, broad and deep man's forehead. The beard extended square and curly like a cultivated field. Beast labeled a cherub: how did your name decline to pink-assed tutti? As she stepped back to admire the brawny legs, stout chest and heavy fullfeathered wings, she knew it reminded her of Rowley.

Hand fell heavily on her shoulder. "Hi gang. Got it?"

Turning she handed the envelope over. "I made two copies."

"Good girl." Leon peeked in. "I'll keep the other, you never know when. Tonight let's take in the old Bette Davis flick at the Clark."

"Aren't we going to have lunch?"

Shook his head. "Promised to have it back by twelve. Let me tell you, if my Uncle Burt wasn't such a big slob donor to his old frat, we'd never have got a touch of this." With a salute he turned. She watched him shuffle off, one long arm swinging loosely in the rhythm of his walk, the other stiffened against his side to hold the envelope in place. A patch of sunlight came to life on his orange hair, then he passed under the arch and out.

She drifted after slowly. Fake spring. The campus squirrels waddled across the lawns. If she looked at them they caught her eyes and stared back, expecting food. On a day like this she would have found herself energized, ready to shout at her classes in angry joy. She would have cursed, my god, half the semester over and what have I taught them? Finished the day with a good fatigue, despair at results, but pleasure in the process. Well, she could climb a bench and lecture squirrels: mountebank to nutlovers.

Wednesday, November 12: The streets were dark as she walked toward Leon's through no man's land of leveled buildings, a slough of mud pocked with stacked bricks and loose rubble. In mid air the elevated Illinois Central station lights blinked in the wind. She walked fast, for the empty fields had no protective passersby. The arc lamps dipped like branches, the cold-colored lights bobbed. Near the tracks new townhouses (suburban living in the city) were building. On a completed wall someone had chalked FAT CITY. Oh yes. Then the long arcaded viaduct past columns columns columns, echoes of mayhem and cars whooshing through puddles.

She rapped. In an island of light Leon slumped in the director's chair, brows meeting. Facing him Paul was centered on the swaybacked couch. Turning, Paul looked surprised but not pleased. Tête-à-tête interrupted. She understood. So clear out, it's my turn. Paul slid toward Leon and she took the other end of the couch, collapsing with a loud sigh.

Paul said shyly, "I wanted to thank you both for the exam." He picked at loose stuffing through an old burn.

"Did it help?" she asked.

"Mainly just having it. I studied as if I didn't, but it kept me cool. Finally about midnight I sat down and took it, and it was a snap. Then I went, had a hamburger and came home to bed. All collected, I walked in, finished early, even the essay part that was out of the blue. . . . Almost didn't look at it. I had qualms, then I figured it was harder for me to look than not to."

Something in his voice puzzled her. "What's wrong?"

"Never cheated before."

"That wasn't cheating," Leon drawled. "You had the questions, not the answers. Every fraternity jackass in that course had that advantage—why not you?"

"The University shouldn't be like a payphone you can monkey with. And I've been trained to do things the hard way. You know, public display of virtue. The Jamesons all think they're God's dummies, you know, walking ads for black justice."

"What do you think you were scared of?" Leon asked.

"Failing. What else? Losing my scholarship."

Leon spread his big hands. "Then why aren't you flunking everything?"

"That would take work. Maybe I'm just not interested."

Leon grinned like a trap. "But you were supposed to be an archaeologist. A kind of scientist."

"I saw myself playing Schliemann. Uncovering brilliant civilizations in some jungle. Kid's dreams."

"You saw yourself—or that sister of yours saw you?"

"Of course, it's been a mutual thing—"

"I wonder." Leon watched with hard narrow eyes. "You're smart, kid, so why are you stuck under your sister's thumb?"

"Don't be ridiculous. You think she dominates because she's older. The truth is that half the time I make decisions for both of us."

"Why?

Paul cupped his neck, staring. "What do you mean, why?"

"Why don't you make your decisions and she make hers? She pressures you to decide what you're going to do. What business is it of hers? You don't owe her a life."

Anna sat forward. "Come on, you think my relationship with Estelle is healthier? Lock me in a room with her and I'd lose my mind."

"Yes." Bam went Leon's fist. "I do call his bond with his sister sick if it keeps him from doing his own thinking. If he acts under blind compulsions coming off it. If he flunks a course because that's the only way he can say with his life, *no*! If he can't move out freely toward others. What is it protecting him from, that he should be learning? He's married to her—and he's too young to be married." The passionate baying of Leon's voice rounded through the high dusty room. Paul looked moved in spite of himself. Moved, yes, and intrigued. A strange halfsmile touched his face. In that moment he looked very like his sister.

Leon stirred. His hand fell on his belly, kneading. "Anna, how come you haven't made us supper?"

Paul frowned at his wristwatch. "I have to be going."

"Stay," Leon said. "Plenty of food. I like company when I eat."

As she worked in the kitchen she was overhearing seduction. Paul mistrusted Leon. His dark highdomed face would tense suddenly, harden to expressionlessness. Yet he was too much the young intelligent unsure male held on the leash of his vanity before someone older who wanted, holy shit! to discuss him, to resist Leon long. Perhaps the narrow domestic encounter began to bore Leon. How had she grown dependent? She must get out and see other people instead of plodding over here every night to curl up involuted dialogue.

He had the urge to make disciples. He had been born lonely and must continually manufacture a family to replace the first and second he had lost, that had failed him. As he had collected her he was trying to collect Paul. It meant much to Leon to have others do as he advised, to believe he was helping. Like any man he had to feel himself in the world.

"If love isn't just a bullshit word for neurotic grasping needs, if it don't mean I own you, I eat you, I use you for a crutch—then it's seeing, then it's attention. It's that heightened insight into the other person, as much what she could be as what she thinks now that she is. It's unfolding attention, attention that creates. That's what you understand in film. What you see, is. 'A fool sees not the same tree that a wise man sees.' Blake. The eye creates."

They ate in the livingroom. Paul looked at his flatware and seemed relieved that it was clean. "If you'd return those popbottles," she said plaintively, "we could eat in the kitchen. All this balancing."

Paul strolled in to see what she was talking about and gave a low whistle. He moved with a ranginess at once graceful and awkward. "Tell you what. This weekend we'll load the bottles in Leon's car and return them."

"Ought to be ten bucks, maybe more," Leon muttered.

"Oh, you're such a baby about money," she said.

"You must drink soda like a car burns gas." Paul laughed flatly, like a box stepped on.

"I used to take other things. Anything. More a holocaust than a habit, you might say."

Paul made a face of respect. "Not any more?"

Opaque eyes fixed on the wall. "The places I got to that

way, they got worse and worse. Hardly worth taking a trip if you don't get out of your bag but only farther in.''

"Did you ever take speed?"

Leon shrugged, slapping mustard generously on his span-ish rice. "Three interviews today. Pat my back. Bitches talk-ing about how demanding, how ungrateful old people are, and you can see in their ugly faces and bleached hair skinned up on top in pink curlers what kind of turds they'll dry into. The *in*-ter-*view:* what a crock.'' He chugalugged a Coke. "Tell you what I'd love to do. Get fired in a day. You start off to gain the subject's confidence. See what they want to talk about. Seem to write everything down. People hate it when they talk for five minutes and all you do is check a box. They want to register on you.

"After you snagged them good, you begin. You want to give the subject an illumination. You want for one minute *to turn him on to himself.*'' Leon heaped more food on his plate. "You persuaded the person they really shocked you, revolted you. You appear terrified. You faint. You retch on the car-pet.''

His eyes commanded, visionary, cold. "Suppose you're interviewing on sex attitudes. You move in slowly on the subject till, bingo, talking, talking, still asking questions, you make out on the couch. What do they think? What will they do? They find out. The truth is what they do. Or inter-view becomes fight. Or by subtle questions you lead him farther and farther on a limb, then cut! educational process. Leave every subject more alive—''

"Or the interviewer dead." Paul glanced at his watch.

"People think they think all sorts of nonsense. The main thing is, will they live it? You home that on them." Leon leaped up. "SATORI! ARGH!" He stabbed himself with his fist.

"Suppose your subject went raving mad. Or attacked you. Or began crying her eyes out," Paul said.

"The interviewer would have to be hip to the psychotic episode signs and cool it if he hit them. He'd have to know judo and karate. As for tears, that might represent a success-ful climax for an interview." He glanced at Anna.

"I think you're giving those interviews already." Paul showed him a thin but not unfriendly grin. "I have to move on, I'm late, but this subject just couldn't pry loose."

"But I make myself a subject too. Admit that. What's your appointment—girl?"

Paul tipped back and forth before answering. "Yeah."

"Pretty?"

He nodded.

"Good luck. Remember if you can't score, bring her back for Papa to try."

Paul looked between them in surprise. "That's not a safe comment in front of longhaired friends."

Leon said when the door had shut, "Bet she's white, or why so tightlipped."

Anna smiled. "He's on his way to see Vera."

"Maybe so." He lolled back, grimacing at the half-smoked cigarette in his hand. "Should stop smoking too. Then eating." He smote his belly folds. "Fat slob! I used to be in shape. In school I went swimming all the time. I was a good catcher." Thrusting his head forward, he held out the glove and signaled the pitcher. "Then I was in condition." He flung out an accusing finger. "You want to get into condition too—diets, exercise, cut out the crap. You're too soft."

"I'm supposed to be soft!"

He giggled. "Tried to get the kid talking about Caroline. He claims to know nothing."

"What are you worried about?"

"Why don't we run into them? The other night I happened to stop by the Rising Sun for a cup of coffee—"

Quick flush of heat as if at betrayal. "Now come on, we agreed you'd get nothing out of hounding her."

"Hounding, my ass. I was walking by. I'm no different from any other slob goes in for a fifty-cent coffee and a cruddy pastry from a tray."

"So what did she say?"

"She wasn't around. The waitress said, Who? I made her go ask another waitress, and then she told me Caroline quit almost two weeks ago. How do you like that?"

"Well, it wasn't much of a job."

Leon scowled. "Sounds fishy. She liked all those people looking at her fondling a guitar and making coweyes into space. Why would she quit, unless Rowley found her something better?"

Anna shrugged. "Your turn to do the dishes."

"If you keep me company." He wrapped a towel around his waist. "Films could be like the interviews I was describing. People come into a room, they sit themselves down and stare where they're supposed to, and they're saying Do me something. They have expectations. You start by breaking those. Immediately. Their brains are done up in plasticwrap and you have to get through it. The people who come to see underground flicks like that shock of surprise, but it's the others I really want to reach. And won't. And can't."

Friday, November 14: In the middle of the bombedout area a shopping center had opened, a double arcade of shops about a green space of four benches and a limp fountain. A few local merchants had survived the gap in time and financing, but mostly chain stores had taken over. As Anna carried out groceries, Caroline emerged from a zippy neon drycleaners just ahead. Anna halted on one foot tempted to dodge, but just then Caroline saw and froze also. For a moment they regarded each other with bleak dismay. Then Caroline broke into a performer's smile and hastened toward her with hand outstretched, which dug into the sleeve of her worn black coat as if streaking for earth.

"You're looking great!" Anna said with more surprise than she had intended to let show. Caroline's hair had been simply but elegantly cut short to her cheeks and lightened. On it sat a swoopy hat: a hat. She was dressed in dark mannish gray that made her even blonder. Lustrous vast leather purse. The coat with broad mink collar was new. Great, no. Caroline looked expensive, soignée, processed. Anna could hardly keep from gaping and asking questions.

"And you too, of course, you always do." Caroline's large slightly vague brown eyes kept asking some question of their own.

"How are things? I heard—didn't see you in the Rising Sun the other night."

"Oh, Bruce had me quit. I don't have that kind of time lately, and after all . . ." She nodded helplessly toward the street.

Following her gaze Anna saw a man in a sportscar brooding sullenly on them. Jagged suntanned face blatant on the snow. Longfingered hand in leather glove tapped the wheel impatiently. Edgy, longnosed, handsome face. Very Anglo-Saxon. His eyes grated on her and she turned, fluffed up the limp collar of her coat against him. "Bruce . . . ?"

"My fiancé." Caroline's hand with the ring bulging the glove rose between them in explanation.

Did Caroline drop Rowley for him? Or, no ring forthcoming, went back where the goods were handy? But the difference in her. Caroline's eyes studied her asking their questions. Yes, I am shabby, yes, I am older than you, yes, I have lost weight over him, and no, I do not care any more at all. I will survive you.

"I'm delighted to have him here. Really!" Caroline swallowed, turned and leaped in another direction. "Bruce is going home for Thanksgiving with my family, and—"

Bruce leaned on the horn, brah, brah braaah. "Oh dear, I've kept him waiting, lovely to run into you, my best to everyone . . ." She ran waving, her heels pittering over the ice. Elaborately he swung open the door, said something briefly that made her burst into explanations as they roared off in a plume of exhaust.

Sunday, November 16: "What kind of sportscar did that stud drive?"

"Oh Leon, how do I know?"

"A Porsche? A Triumph? An Alfa?"

"I tell you, I didn't notice!"

"Just like a woman," he said to Paul, who looked on bemused. "He was goodlooking uh?"

"I wouldn't say so. Not a type that would appeal to me."

"But to Caroline?"

Paul suppressed a laugh. She said, "That girl was dressed.

Not that she ever has worn cheap clothes, but now she's out of *Vogue*. Is he paying for it?''

Leon made an enraged chimpanzee face. "Why should he? Her father's a banker.''

"Caroline's father? You're kidding.''

"They always did hold a good chunk of the money and land in town, but since the plant was built, her father cleaned up on real estate. Even her loudmouth brother's a promoter these days,'' Paul said.

"When I was seeing her, she kept wanting to give me things—lighters with my initials and ties. Try to explain that to Joye.''

"But, why do they let her knock around? Don't they care who she marries?'' Anna asked.

"You can bet your last tootsieroll. She brought him back from Italy to Green River and her family gave the okay.'' Leon scowled.

"They don't want her fooling around at home, where it counts,'' Paul said. "Her mother's a lush and her father can't stand her. Thinks the sun rises and sets in her brother.''

"I know all that! Better than you do! I know that girl inch by inch. What do you think keeps me going in this shitstorm, my rotten life, except that I'm going to save her.''

"Save her? She's something to spend, baby.'' Paul drew his hand over his domed forehead. "What do you want to save her for?''

"To marry,'' Leon said coldly. "Then her family couldn't interfere. They'd have to make terms. Maybe send me back to school. I'd start re-educating her. Start showing her very slowly what she really needs out of all she thinks she needs, and what she needs that she doesn't know about yet . . .''

"Leon, listen,'' Paul said urgently, "She's going to marry that cracker, I'm telling you. He's just the dish her family ordered, and she wants to—she needs to get in good with her family.''

"She didn't even ask about you,'' Anna said timidly. "She must know by this time you're still interested—''

Leon kicked at the teak table. "The two of you are so naive I can't tolerate it! Must I teach you everything about the world?'' He stormed across the room, came back with a *Film Culture* and started flipping through it. ''For your information, kindergarten, people love without being able to say so. People hide their love, for fear of being hurt. I let her down once, for your information.''

He began ostentatiously reading, his face drawn into a jowly frown.

Paul and Anna looked at each other sheepishly. The room was quiet except for a scuttling in the wall and the turning of Leon's pages. With a sigh she went to do supper dishes. She turned the transistor radio on to a rock station, stuck it on the sink and began running the water. After a while Paul came to lean on the doorframe and finally took a towel and dried. When they finished, Paul carried the radio back to the livingroom. Deadpan Paul began to dance about Leon's chair, a slow snaky athletic movement with his arms casting long shadows over Leon and the magazine. He motioned for Anna to join him.

She laughed. ''I can't! Nobody my age can move that way.''

''Easy. Look, let your arms carry the weight forward. Your hips follow.''

Feeling her clumsiness she imitated him. ''No,'' he said. ''Loosen up. Don't push.''

''I can't. I'm too tight.''

''That's better. Vera's tighter than you are. If she can do it, so can you. Let yourself rise with your arms.''

She could feel her muscles stretch. She would know it tomorrow. She laughed again, partly with pleasure and partly because she imagined the sight.

''For shit's sake!'' Leon exploded. ''If you don't look obscene. It's a goddamn playground.'' He yanked himself out of his chair and stamped off into the bedroom, slamming the door.

She stopped and so did Paul. She kicked off her shoes and went quietly over to pick up the director's chair. She leaned it against the door and padded over to one of the half-packed or unpacked boxes of papers. She stacked that on the chair. Smiling serenely Paul heaved her chair up, tiptoed across and piled it upsidedown on the director's chair. She added the two kitchen chairs stacked, while he pulled the cushions off the couch and wedged them in. As they were carrying the coffeetable between them, the door banged open against the barrier.

"What?" Leon tried again, bumping the door. "Hey?"

"It's a caged lion," Paul lilted. "A lion behind bars."

"What'd you guys do?" Leon rattled the door and succeeded in thrusting it far enough to get his head around. "For Christsake. What a bunch of infants." He slammed the door and they heard the springs wince in the bed.

Paul snapped off the radio and stood looking uncertain. "He's really mad."

"For the evening. You should go home and study."

"You know, this Caroline thing?" He paused at the door. "She's pretty, sure. Like she's made out of icecream. But he had her, didn't he? As much as he'll ever get."

She unpiled the furniture. When she had cleared she knocked, smiling. Leon made a noncommittal noise and she came in.

"Oh, *you*." He pulled his head back under the blankets. "You put all that stuff back where it belongs."

"Done. Big deal." Sitting on the bed she poked at the woolly mound. "Anybody home?"

"Ow. Quit that."

She poked harder into what she supposed to be his ribs.

"Hey!" He wriggled his head out to glare. His hand pinned her wrist. "Want me to hurt you? I said quit that. Paul out there?"

"I sent him home to do his schoolwork."

"The kid thinks you're the hottest thing since little red peppers."

"I'm flattered. He'll be an attractive man, himself."

"He's not that young."

"A bit young for me, though."

"Why? In France . . . Or isn't that the only reason?"

"Are you pimping for him?"

He gave her wrist a halfturn. "Just asking. Just curious. You must get frustrated under the status quo."

"Not enough to start experimenting with kids, thank you."

"He thinks I'm out of my mind for not . . . making it with you."

"Oh?" said Anna with ice and high wind, and yanked her wrist free.

"But we would eat each other like cat and dog." He sat up among the pillows, his pale blue eyes narrowed and lewd. "We'd destroy each other."

"I'm sure," Anna said politely, piqued and finally amused. He put such metaphysics into his sex. At times she looked at him and a brute physical curiosity played over her skin. She seldom thought of him as ugly now. His face had become part of his utterance. She edged away down the bed. "Leon, you can't go on with ISS," she said severely. "Your project is almost finished. You can't go on wasting yourself on stupid short jobs."

"I can't? Nothing easier." He groaned.

"It's too hard on you. Maybe you should go back to school."

He sat up glaring. "*How*? All that alimony to pay. How?" He was silent for a long while.

"Going to tell you a story, but don't you ever repeat it to Paul. Okay? When I was a punk in school one time I was drinking with guys from Skokie, where I grew up. Guys at school. One had a car and we were out cruising on Forty-third and we picked up a whore, a young spade chick. Anyhow we shook her down. We scared her and took off her the money she had—forty-five, fifty bucks."

She stared at him. "That's one of the nastiest stories I've heard."

"Why? The whores used to roll us all the time. They hated our guts."

"Why not? You hated them too, for using them."

"We felt very tough, very high."

"The suburbs proving they're tougher than the city folk. No, it makes me angry all the way through. Don't you see—"

He laughed dryly. "You know what I did the next day? I went to the University bookstore and I stole books. I kept stealing books till finally even those jackasses got wise and the store dick picked me up. I had seventy-five dollars in books on me and I could hardly walk.'' After a while he said, ''You're wasting your time with me.''

''It's my choice. And my time.''

He lay in bed on his belly sunk in depression. She called a cab for once. For some reason she was haunted by the first winter she was married to Asher. She had thought him fine, serious, complete. Asher had still been in school, and they had lived in two vilely pink narrow rooms off a parkinglot, rooms the sun never poked into: rooms lit by dim bulbs and joy. Before they had begun to buy the perfect, exorbitant townhouse.

Coming in she opened her mailbox. Official looking envelope. She recognized the name of the city board. Yes, she was informed. Slowly she went upstairs carrying one more dismissal.

Monday, November 24— Monday, December 8

Monday, November 24: The anthill of the project. Out in the field interviewers met their men and women targets, sat in their homes and offices which they afterward described with what wit they could muster, listened and were seduced, angered, shocked and filled with suspicion. They dreamed the power struggles of the city in their pajamas. They ulcerated and connived and cursed.

The digesters sat in windowless rooms and coded, ran statistical analyses, composed graphs and indices. They worked an eight-hour day, yawned and went home. The wit, the passion, the anger went out in their wastepaper baskets.

The queens surveyed the work and saw it was of high

professional standards and fulfilled the contract. They spoke
of methodology, dealt with the agents of monies and shouldered the burden of negotiation. In their names—Rand
Grooper, Norma Clay—all work went forward: they would
swell in the journals and hew out their share of honorariums
and consultantships on the repute of the vast labor. They
were the source of money and legitimation. All the coolies
ate their bread and slept in their shade.

Miss Clay had been in her twenties a supporter of Henry
Wallace. She gave money with leaden regularity to groups
launching sit-ins, kneel-ins and teach-ins. Of her recent projects two had been paid for by the Army, one by AT&T, one
by General Motors. A recent study under her supervision of
lack of panic during a blackout in major cities would be used
to prove the citizenry would accept nuclear bombardment
with frontier humor. She lived with her mother in an older
high rise with beamed ceilings owned by the University. Anna
delivered machine runoff there. Miss Clay collected prints
by coming artists and attended the ballet when there was any.
Born of a professor in Nebraska, she had attended Wellesley
and spent an occasional summer in Europe. Her prime interest was understood to be the dynamics of social change.
Anna wondered what that meant to Miss Clay.

Rand Grooper was quickspoken, and his lean body curled
protectively around an early ulcer. A meticulous dresser who
sought in his mirror images from *Playboy*, he found receding
sandy hair, the rednecked ironjawed face of an Ozark pig-
farmer. He owned a beautiful malcontent wife, four precocious children, a split level he could not afford in a suburb he
could not stand. He signed checks for the ACLU and read
the *Nation*, but he was mobile as a barracuda and in the world
were only those out to knife him and those he had cut. He
spoke often of professional ethics. His eyes were wistful.

Meek and lowly, chin tucked in, Anna sat in her tweeny's
desk washing their data and hanging it out to dry. They both
wrote as if they had been bitten by a government pamphlet
on payroll addressing procedures. In the questions, in the
choice of interviewers and interviewees, in the definition of

politics and leaders and meaningful acts, lay the results of their study beforehand.

The citizen participation required by law had certainly occurred. Neighbors met and met again. The meetings of blockgroups could generate powerful feelings of concern, could be the closest these people ever would come in their lives to feeling themselves involved in meaningful decision. The blockgroups met and considered with passion the planners' proposals and hashed out a consensus yes or no. Of course they really could not vote no to the whole plan, that would be irresponsible. Maybe they could suggest a different use for a lot or a different placing of one-way streets. The proposals were drawn and the issues joined elsewhere. Ideas sent up from the groups, unless they were minor and convenient, died. Never in the whole study would anyone ask, Who gains from all of this? Who owns Chicago? Who's getting richer? What does each man control or own? At Inland University and at ISS, sociologists did not ask such questions: that was never in the contract.

Thanksgiving: Over the city of blackened stone, the charcoal ramparts of the Loop and the steel men breathed, the lead gray battlements of the University, the frozen turmoil of shore, the cube houses laid out on treeless streets once prairie, a mile of K's (Komensky, Karlov, Kedvale), a mile of L's . . . Over all the tall snow stood in the air and filled the rutted streets and capped the sluggishly moving cars. Snow flittered past the plate glass. Night settled in damping everything but the muffled ghostly falling, the spook snow materializing around the greenish streetlamps. Leon's was cold but not nearly so cold as home where the city was skimping on coal. Food smells softened the air, roasting duck with apple and onion inside.

They ate, picking the bones and passing the brown rice, salad and spiced cranberries back and forth. Leon had dug out a yahrzeit candle and its light merged with the ghostshine from the street. After they had eaten to drowsiness for warmth they crept into bed dressed, huddling under blankets. He let the candle burn on his high chest of drawers, left on the light in the other room that threw long shadows and a path of light across the bed.

With his hand Leon made shadow pictures on the wall, rabbits and stagheads and striking cobras. He was cold, cold. Her nose pinched.

"Paul should've stayed with us and had a good feed instead of going home where his sister can pin him down again."

Anna giggled. She felt ten. "There isn't room in the bed."

"If he was here, you think I'd set such a lax example? I am a father, after all." Silence trickled between them. He flopped onto his back staring at the ceiling. Candle flicker rippled across his broad face. "A year," he mumbled. "Seven more months to go. Got to get money. Got to get a film financed. If I just had enough bread to do one I have in mind, it would knock people on their asses. But I owe the processing lab, I owe everybody. . . . It was the kid being born as much as old Joye finding out about Caroline that busted things up. All of a sudden Joye started singing about how she couldn't raise her child around drunks and perverts and colored dragqueens—that last for Elliott whose stuff I really dig and besides he's very gentle with kids. Jimmy needs a nice safe lawn, good schools where he won't get his head bashed in. All of a sudden she's become her mother, she has fangs and teeth . . . But the most significant thing about your breakup is who you picked. Asher was Jewish and you chose a nonJew to haul you out. Knowing you wouldn't marry him, right?"

"I could say the same about Caroline, but it's nonsense. Rowley's real. The most evident thing is him, not a label."

"Is your being Jewish a label?"

"It was only an issue once. My parents saved up and went to Yellowstone. Like mice, Leon, so furry and scared. I don't know where my father got the *chutzpah* to close the store for two weeks. They called me, they're going to stop: they're dying for a piece of meat. For eleven days nothing but lousy fried fish. I go to a Jewish butcher for a beef roast and carry it home to kosher. Rowley watches—he can't believe it. You're killing that meat! He is laughing and at the same time, shocked. He thinks it's the most primitive bloodfear he's ever witnessed. I get furious and start yelling, antiSemite!''

"Choosing him was a revolt against your whole Jewish past."

"My past is not Asher! Maybe Asher's what my parents think they want. Maybe not even—you couldn't pinch his *tuchus*. I don't know why he married me. He didn't trust me. And by his values, look what I went and did!'' Her hands twisted in the blankets. "I thought he wanted what I could give him, but people give themselves what they want. You do not marry your complement as Asher and I tried to do, because what you aren't you aren't because you don't want to be."

"I don't know. Maybe I love Caroline because she's goy-ish and blond and smalltown and not too keen upstairs. Because she's my red, white and blue *shiksa* made of ice. Because she wants so bad to be loved and doesn't know what it means. She could sit on a pile of corpses and look soft and cute."

"Maybe you like her better as a symbol than you would at the breakfast table."

He laughed, but his voice emerged in a groan. "Got to get to her before time runs out. When I'm here alone at night the top of my head pulls off. I talk to Paul, I talk to you but you don't believe me. You don't see!''

Monday, December 1: The air smelled like a furnace room. A gray lid of clouds rested on her head as Anna marched down her street, just returned from the Loop where she had picked up a document for Miss Clay and incidentally a new red brassiere. Fire? The sidewalk was crowded ahead. No firetrucks, only an ambulance pulled over. One of the wreck-ing crew? People were milling around the front of an empty building. Its stores were already boarded up and two doors nailed shut, but the third in the eye of the crowd stood open.

"Come on, get back." A cop pushed on the crowd. "You never saw a looney before? I'll bet. Come on, get back." From the fringe she found herself thrust forward as people surged and shoved back under pressure and counterpressure.

Two attendants hustled out an old woman half their height clutched between them in a straightjacket. Her thin hair was on end and in her pinched, frightened face her lips moved constantly. Her dress was a bad joke, dirty, drooping, down at the hem: but her eyes pleading with onlookers were lucid. "I told them I couldn't pay more," she kept saying in a dry whine. "I just want to stay where I am. That's all. Just want to stay put. Thirty years, that's a long time and never behind in my rent, you ask them." The doors of the ambulance shut.

"It's disgusting," the woman next to her muttered, shaking her sleek feathered head.

Wednesday, December 3: Paul leaned toward her as they walked. "People find us an interesting sight."

"Because we're gorgeous. They think I'm a cradlerobber."

"They think you have bizarre tastes."

"I must, to do this. Don't you feel silly?"

"No, in a way it's fun," he said stoutly. "Now that her fiancé's here, what does Leon think he can *do*? Picket her?"

"Search me," Anna said bitterly.

"You'd be much better for him." He caught up a gloveful of snow and walked packing it.

"Thanks loads. Everybody has the right to choose his poison."

"Takes two to choose, and whatever she's after, Leon can't buy it for her." He let the snowball fly out splat against a telephone pole. "Where's that architect's office?"

"Ought to be this block. There's the car," she hissed then, grabbing his elbow. "There."

He looked toward the parkinglot. "You sure?"

"Of course. That funny green."

"British racing green. That's a Jaguar XKE."

"What does that mean?"

"You wouldn't exactly trade one in on a Rambler. Leon will be sad."

They passed the windows of the office and both took a quick peek. Bruce was looking at the model of the Suburb in the City, his handsome still-tanned face puckered as if he were silently whistling in high spirits. He leaned forward and gave a building a flicked nudge forward. They hurried on out of sight. "And you claim you don't feel silly," Anna said.

He corrected the fit of his gloves, tugging. "Vera's jealous of Leon, you know?"

"I also have the feeling she does not care for me."

Paul smiled. "Vera's a small woman and she doesn't like big women. She thinks they're going to sit on her. And she doesn't understand you."

She slung back her head to laugh. A stray lock jiggled against her cheek. "Do you?"

Paul pulled his long sophisticated face. "Better than Leon does, you can be sure."

"I will not be understood by someone ten years younger."

"Seven."

"Eight."

"Besides, Vera's more sensitive than I am, more cautious. She doesn't mix with the ofay, except a couple of old girl-friends from home. Which is why I know it's pure spite that she's letting this stud who must be thirty hang around with his tongue out. She says Leon knows him."

"What's his name?"

"His last name's Rowley. I don't know his first."

"George. He's thirty-one. How that cat does get around."

"You know him, uh?"

"We've met."

Saturday, December 6: Rubble, snow and local merchants' seasonal cheer. The stamped tin ceiling of the old A&P hung down rumpled and awry among its smashed walls. Loaded with Hanukkah presents for Estelle's kids she peered over the top of her bundles as she plodded along, idly watching a man walk toward her. Not a graceful walk but swinging, a big man who walked well in a loosejointed, rambling . . . Rowley! No moustache. Embarrassed, staring at him staring back, she turned and blindly crossed. A soft plop of pain. "Annie! Hey there!"

She clumped to a stop. "Hello. Didn't recognize you."

"I had no problem," he said dryly. "Listen, you know what? Sam got married."

"Your sister? What on earth for! I mean—"

"Who knows what for? To some halfassed suburban rebel with fungus on his chin."

"Did Vera make you shave your moustache? That's how come I didn't know you right away."

"The hell you didn't." He grinned in anger and she leaned away from him. "Say hello to Leon."

"I usually do." She turned with a shallow wave and trotted off. Why did she say that about Vera? Stupid Anna with the big flapping mouth.

That night she went out with a computer technician from ISS, as much because Leon and Paul were clearly planning something without her as because he held any promise. The evening went accordingly.

Sunday, December 7: "What good is a paper with no comics?" Leon asked his weekly question and fingered his unshaven jaw. "Why isn't there coffee?"

"Anna's too busy studying the paper," Paul drawled from the floor. "Then she'll recite it."

"Wait your turn," Anna said righteously from the forest of the Sunday *New York Times*. "When I finish I'll make coffee."

"That's what I call real gradualism." Paul was lying partly wrapped in an old Army blanket. From its drab roll his head stuck out into a sunpath shining like bronze.

"Dit you have a good time last night?" Leon asked archly.

"Moderate," she said.

"We went down to the Birdcage. No drinks served but lots of ginch. Jazz wasn't half bad, uh Paul?"

"Not bad, Lion. They had a flautist with soul and a good baritone sax. But the bass player was a zombie."

The guy on drums was a winner too." They exchanged the bored glances of connoisseurs.

"So? All culture makes Jack dull. What are you giggling about?"

"We hung around awhile." Leon made a gesture indicating duration. "Then we cut out with a couple of chicks. Brought them back."

"How old?"

"Mine said eighteen and so did his." Paul shrugged. "Maybe."

"Were they pretty?"

"At that age, what girls aren't?" Leon rasped. "Both stacked. Mine had a great ass."

Wincing Paul leaned out of the game. "She was a cow. They were stupid. Not hip, just dizzy. Always a little confused, sticking together because they don't know anybody else. Sweating anxious to be liked and getting layed instead. But you should hear them in the confessional act with those clods." Paul rubbed his chin back and forth on the blanket. "Before the lion we're all vacuum cleaners with bags that need emptying."

"Here, have a paper." She rose gathering the paper high and let it cascade over Paul till she had buried him. "I'm going to make coffee."

"If the car will start I have a plan." Leon squeezed a boil on his neck, squeezed grimacing till it bled. "We're going out to Palos Hills tobogganing."

"Just so I get back to the dorm for dinner," Paul said.

"How come you live in the dorm? You ought to move in here. Plenty of room." Leon gestured widely. "Save money too."

Paul laughed in surprise. "My roommates tell me I'm a monster to live with. Anyhow, I'm paid up to the end of this quarter."

In the kitchen Anna brooded. If Paul moved in . . . Didn't he distinguish between them at all? In a pique she shouted, "Well, I'm not going to break my neck in the snow. You can drop me home."

Leon strolled out to the kitchen, tugged on her loose hair. "What are you sore about?"

"Nothing."

He pulled harder on her hair, drawing her back. "The kid won't move in. He thinks this is a pigpen. Besides, you won't do it. I don't like to live alone." He released her and went back. In answer to Paul she heard him say, "Course she's coming. Just wanted coaxing."

Monday, December 8: When Anna came in from work she bumped into a stubby red-eared man with hair the color of cigar ash wandering in the dim upstairs hall. "What's your name please?" He approached her.

A little alarmed she fumbled for her key. "I beg your pardon?"

"What is your name? Are you a tenant?"

"As you see." She put her key in the lock.

"Number two." He ran down a list. "Miss A. Lev . . . Levinowitz?"

"Right. And who are you?"

He was Mr. Bradley, her relocation officer. He gave a quick discomforted peek around the kitchen, his gaze rebounding from the Cretan mother goddess to the freestanding nubbly pot a friend had thrown, to the Che poster she had tacked up over the place where there had been a photograph of Rowley used to advertise a concert. Not that she had thrown out the photograph. It was too good. And she hated waste. No, she had put it away in the bottom drawer of her desk under a file of material on courses she used to teach.

"You have how many rooms here?" he asked looking.

"Two." Swinging her leg in a neat arc of annoyance she sat at the kitchen table across from him. She got her alarm clock and stuck it between them.

"Are these rooms rented furnished or unfurnished?"

"Everything but the stove and refrigerator is mine."

"But most of the apartments in this building are furnished?"

"But not this one."

Mr. Bradley made slow copious notes on a form he took from his attaché case. Anna swung her foot in small angry circles.

"How much rent are you prepared to pay in your new location?"

"I pay fifty-five here."

"But this building is substandard. We will pay your moving expenses—pay the moving company directly, you understand—but only if you relocate into standard housing." Every word spaced out patiently for her to look at, a typewriter talking who was willing to repeat, repeat, repeat. Because that's how you make those stupid cases understand the rules.

"Standard housing—a great term. My needs are not standard."

"Now what are you able to pay in the way of monthly rent?"

"Sixty-five top."

He made more notes. "Now I doubt we can find anything in this neighborhood, but farther out . . . ." He recited the names of flat parkinglots on the end of buslines.

"I'm sorry, I can't live there."

"Why not, Miss Levowitch?"

Who and how is this stodgyfaced clickclack-voiced ass sitting in my kitchen using up my free time, inquiring why I must live where I live as I live? "I expect to look for my own housing, Mr. Badnee."

"Bradley. But you won't be able to find anything we can approve in this area. Why won't you consider a neighborhood where we can locate you more easily? In order for your costs of moving to be paid for by the city—"

"My friends are here, the things that interest me are here. My activities center here. My job is here. This is my web."

He contemplated her with ashy rebuke. "You could relocate near public transportation for your job. Families relocate every day and they find friends where they go."

"I doubt it proves so easy for every family, and I'm no family." She stood. "Good evening. You are not shipping me out past sex." Out to West Wahoo where I can't leave the house at night for fear of long dark streets with no people and hedges all over. Streets of boxes with nobody easy but all packed in place, no loose corners for new meetings, no cracks for the shaggy.

She had just got rid of him when Leon arrived. "Never mind changing," he said, "just comb your hair and let's go. Leave on your office clothes. You want to look respectable."

"But why? Where are we going?"

They were going to his Uncle Burton's office. His secretary had gone home but the evening switchboard operator announced them. Buoyed up next to Leon on a long leather couch she had plenty of opportunities to study the reception room before his uncle, a man shorter than Leon and five inches wider, summoned them. She scanned him without finding resemblance other than the strong bones of his head. In the inner office paneled with driftwood and accessoried in slate another man lounged. Even as Leon visibly caught his breath, stiffening, she knew the man was Leon's father. About the same size, his shoulders had that chimpanzee slope, his hair was yellowed white with a tinge of carrot, his eyes were hard, opaque and arctic blue: but the features had set in a harder mold. Lantern jaw, baroque nose, firm thin mouth, broad forehead fronting the massive bones. Sheldon Lederman was still a goodlooking man, and his appearance suggested that Leon had started with the same set of features and out of slow infant spite distorted them. Sheldon, who sat like a vain man, who posed his head leonine the moment he became aware of a woman entering, must see in Leon a willful distortion of his own loved face.

"What are you doing here?" Leon whined.

"What are you doing here?" Sheldon mocked. "I'm here more often than you are. I'm here for money and it would not surprise me if you were too. My son, the beggar, the *schnorrer*, eh, Burt?"

"Like father, like son," Uncle Burt wheezed. He looked much older than Sheldon, with a sad also-ran cast to his face, well irrigated by canals that drained downward. "Why should I give a thousand dollars to the University for its neighborhood dealings? They're rich, I'm not. Every day they expand their holdings. I'm having trouble getting tenants in my medical building, since the property across the street changed. They should give me a thousand dollars."

"The University has, Burt. The tens of thousands they've poured into planning to protect their investments and consequently, yours. The time top level people have donated to this. But they can't go it alone. How would it look for a noted alumnus like yourself to hold back?''

Uncle Burt tilted in his chair swinging slowly from side to side. "Too little too late. Money down a rathole, listen to me.''

Sheldon Lederman polished his firm gleamy jaw. "Burt, you used to be a shrewd operator. You're not keeping up with the times.''

"When colored people start getting into an area they destruct properties. They deteriorate properties and the neighbors move.''

"Burt, you know you are making more out of your apartment buildings than you were. Those kitchenette apartments are bonanzas.''

"In fact some colored people are clean. Take the Japanese. It's people of the deteriorating class, don't let's discriminate. Hillbillies are worse than the colored people. Now you take this plan. The do-gooders keep talking about public housing. Now you spend all that money to get lower-class people out, and then you turn around and move them back in. Is that smart? Take a destructive element like that and you're back where you started, your money down the drain and more burden on the taxpayer.'' His cheeks sagged.

"You know, I get on the phone and talk to anyone else of your rank in the business community and they're tickled to do what they can. There's prestige in being associated with top men in the administration. Would the trustees be wasting their time on a losing proposition? I'm being kind to you, Burt. Wouldn't you like to find yourself at a luncheon with John Curtis on your right hand and Gideon Moss on your left? We didn't wait till we were dealing with a slum, because Moss and Curtis and Barker and the chancellor went to Washington and talked to the President and got the enabling order to go ahead. Top flight cooperation, Burt. There'll be token public housing on the side toward the Black Belt and whatever else goes up will be financially sound, to bolster the tax base. If I didn't know we could persuade the commercial money world that investment in the area is sound—

that renewal will prove profitable—if I couldn't count on capital, you think I'd be wasting my time?''

"Should I come back later?" Leon drawled. He sounded fourteen. "It's dandy how you guys got eminent domain to pack the unwashed into dumps where you can pile them seven deep. A lot of them burn up every winter anyhow. Maybe you can schedule a selective second Chicago fire to finish off the rest.''

Sheldon was annoyed at being interrupted. His *macher's* charm disappeared and he grew testy. "I hear you've been pestering your uncle with schemes for getting back in school. Still can't make it in the world, eh? Think it would be easier to get yourself supported for killing more time. And you've been begging money for your girlie movies.''

"Did you complain to him?" Leon turned to his uncle.

"I didn't complain, Leon. I'm glad to see you. But he kept *hoching* me to tell him why you were coming.''

"Burt, money poured over that one washes nothing off. That is real money down a rathole. Thousands spent on him and he's like something the police pick off the dirty streets.'' Sheldon blew his nose in linen.

"Thousands and every penny counted. Every day you asked yourself if we deserved all you were doing for us, and every day you slapped yourself on the back and said No.''

"Remember, Burt, when we were starting off, I'd finished law school so green birds would perch on me and you'd bought out old Busby to find the books had been queered? That set you back on your ears. And the only place I found was with that incompetent shyster nincompoop who couldn't stand brilliance and competence. What kept us afloat when the going got rough and the nice boys went down for the third time? The idea that our sons would rise on our shoulders, that here in America we were building something they would take over and take farther—right, Burt?'' His hand played over his brother's sleeve. They were both well tailored, but Burt's clothes rumpled on him as he sat. Sheldon's voice deepened, mocking again. "Now see this manly object slinking in to beg for something he's ashamed to ask his father for.''

"I wouldn't ask you for a rope to hang myself with."

"You'd flub that too. Don't pretend you don't go wheedling around your mother for whatever you can get."

"I see her because I like her—you wouldn't understand."

"Burt, promise me you won't throw good money after bad. The University won't take him back. Nothing but a matchcover tradeschool would let him in, someone his age who can't earn a living, his wife left him, the court took away his son—if it is his—"

Anna stood. She could hardly believe the acid wash of anger that scalded her chest. "Come on, Leon. We have to leave." She took hold of him and half dragged him out, out of that field of magnetic hate and soured love that fixed them head to head.

"Leon, you call me again. You come out to the house and have a good meal with your aunt and your cousins and me."

Sheldon craned after them off balance. "What does he want to study this time, or pretend to? Why is he running out?"

"None of your business. I had something to discuss with you, Uncle Burt, and advice to ask. But I see I can't trust you, so just forget it." Leon marched out. Going down in the elevator, she could feel the waves of lavathick humiliation coming off him. "They pretend they want you to submit," he muttered, "but you can never crawl low enough. Because they don't want to help. They want to pretend to offer help and make you refuse."

The depth of her response alarmed her. She felt bound. She felt condemned to try to mediate between him and the world. His face was gutted with anger, dark and swollen. When the car reached the lobby she had to lead him out. On the sidewalk heading into the rasp of the wind, she took his arm and he let her guide, bumping blindly against her as they walked.

Friday—Sunday,
December 12—14

The first tape waiting to be transcribed was an interview with
a local politician who was for urban renewal but against its
abuses, for the planners but against their mistakes, in favor
of public housing but not in his ward. He favored responsible
government on all levels.

The second interviewee was Tom Lovis. She did not recognize him until he had talked for a while. Yes, acquaintance
of Asher who'd been publicity director for UNA, the neighborhood organization (University-Nesting Affluents, Rowley
called them, Ur-liberal Node-seeking Ass-kissers, and Us-
Nice-Animals, and Universal Nose-Clean Aunties, and so
forth). Had a tall blond wife and a pretty kid named Rhoda.
Whole photogenic family. The tape announced that Tom
Lovis was now a member of Penman, Bates and Lovis, As-
sociates, Communications Counselors, retained till recently
by the planning unit.

Mellowly Tom Lovis told the interviewer that he did not
think himself as a PR man, for the work of his organization
was largely education. They kept the public informed, a vital
function in a democracy and never more important than in
our increasingly complex exurban civilization with its heavy
reliance upon mass media.

With respectful voice the graduate student nudged him
subjectward. Were they satisfied with their consulting for the
planning unit? "We came in there," said Lovis sadly, "prepared to engineer a favorable response and we've handled a
number of consulting activities in the field of community
projects. We've lent our skills to some of the biggest corporations in the Midwest, as well as serving municipalities and

governmental agencies. But from time to time we run into a real lack of understanding of the importance of carefully manufactured consensus in a community. Stone age minds."

Tom Lovis described successful community organization. "You go in and identify the potential sources of conflict. Then you set up a committee and invite spokesmen from those groups that could cause dissent to sit in on it, being careful to keep it balanced and maintain its prestige. Now if the University had taken the trouble to negotiate consent, say, from key Negro leaders—businessmen, professionals who live in the area, plus the leftlibs in the unions—that would have nipped charges of racism in the bud, and you'd still have the same plan. You take some of the black business interests, real estate investors, insurancemen—they have sound business sense. They aren't looking for a quarrel with the banks or the mayor's office."

The graduate student, in phrasing a question, referred to Sheldon Lederman as a decision-maker, and Tom Lovis chuckled. "He's just a crude noisy lawyer. Mind you, he's devoted to the job and moderately inventive—but he has an oldfashioned style. He charges into battles wiser men wouldn't need to fight. He's useful now. But the only power he has is who he represents, and after the bulldozers are through, Lederman will be through too."

The graduate student asked Tom Lovis who then he would credit with the success of renewal in Chicago.

"It's a case of really topflight men getting involved in saving our central cities. The same thing is going to have to happen in every major city in the country. We've just been luckier here to have the local talent ready to move in and act before the situation reached crisis. While other cities are rotting at the core, look at the new construction going up here in the Loop and around it—new office buildings, new apartment houses. We've reversed the cancer some oldfashioned types were calling inevitable a few years ago. Here's a case where you have the banks, the utilities, the topflight insurance companies, the industrial giants, all giving of their best administrators or directors to take a hand in civic responsibility. Some of the most important men in the Midwest are sitting on mayor's commissions, serving on the boards which have prepared the urban renewal plans and mapped strategies. That's why urban renewal here hasn't been simply a matter of tearing down a few slums and putting up a few cheap housing projects. We have men here with the vision to see how the city could be revitalized starting with its economy, using urban renewal to bring back industries and keep the ones already here, attract the prosperous back from the suburbs and into the center of our city again. You have here a mayor with an efficient machine friendly to business interests, able to get the legislation we need through, and a business community shrewd and able enough to see its interest and plan for it. There isn't another urban renewal program in the country that's been as skillful and efficient and profitable as ours.''

They went step by step over the consulting, discussing what should have been done. The words flowed in her ears and out her fingers. When Tom Lovis said, ''Rowley,'' she jumped and the tape advanced several sentences before she could reverse it.

''. . . Harlan Williams and the socalled Defense Committee. There are a number of longterm reds or fellow travelers—I don't know what you'd call them—who've operated in the neighborhood for years. Tried to infiltrate UNA. They've captured Williams and they're using him in an attempt to obstruct the plan.''

The graduate student asked for names and Tom Lovis obliged. ''One is a folk singer named Rowley who comes from a leftish background. I personally know he's involved in narcotics.''

Anna sat hands poised typing nothing. Why did Tom have it in for Rowley? The student would never read her transcription. She produced a smooth version without names.

Lovis finished with a panegyric to the trustees and administration of the University, who had finally awakened to their responsibilities and joined the most forward looking parts of the greater business community in civic decision. Near the tape's end the graduate student, alone now, described Lovis' office in its glory and Lovis too, who had retained his slim athletic looks. He described even the paintings, impeccably violent and chic. The student added that he would attach high validity to Lovis' remarks as he was an informed observer with a background in the social sciences. Anna longed to add her own comments on Tom Lovis drunk and sober, at work and play, propositioning her in the kitchen while Asher held forth on reform from within the Democratic party in the next room. She giggled, but nervously.

Saturday night she went to a party at Marcia's, intentionally without Leon. But she could interest herself in no one. She caught herself wondering where Leon was, what he was up to. Simply to describe herself to a stranger seemed more work than any small pleasure could justify.

Then Rowley arrived. Vera wore sheer white wool. Her face burned above the dress very dark: reverse image of a candle. Her expression was a sulky curiosity but Rowley looked hot in the face, excited. She waved and turned her back.

She had to look again. Had to look for Vera's body in the dress. Skinny for him. Was Vera's being black like her being Jewish, something he ignored, something he desired, something he needed? Not a line on the girl, smooth as a ripe plum. He walked behind her warily. He thought her a prize someone might take from him. Anna laughed, she danced, she talked and heard herself emptying her lungs. She went home early.

"Tonight, dress. Like you did for that party you went off to on your own, prospecting. We're going up to the North Shore. Some film society—I'm going to suggest they rename themselves the Sons of Eisenstein and see them writhe—are paying—poorly—for a bunch of us to come and show our uncouth experiments. Afterward some broad will raise her hand and ask why is it depressing, and how come Caroline don't have no clothes on." He grimaced in pain.

"Vera insists you used to go out with that Rowley," Paul said, picking at the side of his boot. "I told her she was crazy."

"That she is, but she's right." Leon slumped in the director's chair, his broad ass filling it.

"She was at the party with him," she said.

"What's this?" Leon glared. "What about him?"

Paul fitted his chin into his cupped hand, spoke through his fingers. "She's acting funny. Still mad. I don't want her to seize on me again, but I wish she'd admit the truth—"

"You want to take her with you." Leon scowled.

"After all, it's bad for her not to be able to talk."

"What's this about Rowley?" Leon repeated.

"They've been seeing each other," she said.

Paul muttered, "You mean, he's been hanging around."

"Come on. Nothing obliges her to attend parties with him. Rowley is not an unattractive man."

"To Vera? You don't know her. She's not interested in men. Especially not white men."

Leon extended a palm. "You don't mind it. Why should she?"

"She's straight with herself. It's her way. Besides, she knows how it looks."

"How it looks. Now it's your sister, and out comes the race trash. Not my sister, not my daughter, keep it clean." Leon turned away in his chair.

"Look, most of the girls who . . . come after me they want the same thing, black or white, it's simple." The breath sang in Paul's throat as he held his temper. "She's not anybody. Not like that."

"It all comes down to you believing in good girls and fallen women," Anna said coldly. For an instant she hated them both.

"No!" Paul clawed at his close wiry hair, set it on end. "It's a matter of what people can do. I don't say this because she's my sister. I wouldn't say it about Sylvia or Loueen. She's proud, she's tight, if she believes in anything it's form—beauty, style."

"You have got to let go. She is twenty-two, Ace, she is none of your business. She's a woman and she's going to lead a woman's life or lose her mind. See that. Know it!" Leon leaned from the director's chair, his voice grating with passion.

She stirred, moving her thighs. "She's bright. So few men would attract her you shouldn't wonder some of those few will be white."

"What I don't like are Rowley's motives," Leon mumbled. "Trying to keep an eye on Caroline, you think?"

In a muted voice she said, "I did see them together. He looked wrapped up in her."

Leon drawled, "We have noted what a wonderful sense of observation you show toward men."

"Why shouldn't he be interested in her if he's not blind?" Paul snapped, looking up. "Think that's abnormal?"

"Are you soreheaded tonight. I've screwed all sides of the line myself—"

"Every lynching cracker can say the same."

"Listen to yourself. Listen! Then ask if you're so free of your obsession as you've been boasting. Maybe your sister's the one who really pulled out."

Paul looked from one to the other and then at the street, already darkening. "You think she's *involved* with him?"

She said, "Get Leon to ask Rowley."

"Are you kidding?" Leon strained back in his chair. "He isn't going to tell me anything."

"Why not? I bet he would."

"*Because.*" Leon's voice rose in scratchy exasperation. "I have you. I took you away . . . so to speak."

Paul smiled naturally for the first time in an hour. "I like that. Having a woman 'so to speak,' that's very spiritual. It's near ethereal, by god."

Leon cleared his throat. "Something important happened yesterday when we stopped by Macphersons for a bite. Who was there but Caroline and her fi-yan-say. We sat at their table."

"They were glad to see us as a couple of kingsize roaches, I'll tell you." Paul let out his breath in a hard, flat laugh.

"You mean that *klutz* Bruce was negative. Caroline was glad. Didn't you see the way she smiled at me?"

Paul tilted his head scarecrowlike on one thin shoulder.

"That's her way. I bet if we walked in on them humping away, old Caroline would give you the glad eye and the time of day and invite you to sit down and have some too."

Leon went doggedly on, "She doesn't love him, she can't hand me that bull. She doesn't turn on when she looks at him. She's fidgety and tense."

"That Bruce is a cold fish. All the wheels turning. Can I make anything out of this one? Anything here for me?"

"Did you see her take my hand? If she won't give me a chance she won't let go either."

Paul winced. "She flirts, she comes on. That's her style."

"Then when we were getting up, she reached out and touched my arm. Just reached out . . ." Leon produced a girlish imitation. "Not as if she meant to, not something thought out, but just as she was saying good bye as if she didn't care, out shoots that hand and says unconsciously, *stay*. You heard her invite me over."

Anna sighed and Paul held his head in his hands. "Like my granddad with his Bible: that's how you interpret that piece."

Leon's face turned sullen. "Maybe I just want her because it's something to do. My project. Ever think of that? It organizes me so I don't fly apart. Maybe. Did Dante really want Beatrice? Not that I couldn't give him a few pointers on hell." He grinned slyly.

Paul went home to eat and change, while Leon got on the phone to his brother and yelled. Then he spent ten minutes putting on and taking off various ties she had never seen before. Finally he collected his stuff and they drove to a new building up on Schiller to borrow Sidney's Porsche.

Sidney opened the door with a grumbled peevish greeting. He was shorter than Leon and even fatter than she had remembered. His hair was brown and fine and slicked down over his face of a dyspeptic rabbit. "That's an expensive car, Leon," he whimpered. "A delicate mechanism. I keep it in perfect order because I know how to drive it and I watch the tachometer. You'll get carried away making the engine roar and burn it out."

He had glanced her over with sour envy, peering around

Leon, but she decided he did not remember her at all. He could not distinguish faces in the swarm of women he imagined around his brother.

"Come on, I was driving cars while you were still pedaling a bike. You're getting hung up on things, Sid. A thingmiser."

"If you don't think it's so good, why are you always after me to borrow it?"

"Not for months."

"In September you asked for it."

"You wouldn't give it to me, so why remember? Tonight I need it. The Buick is falling apart, no lie."

"I told Dad you'd asked for it and he said it would be a mistake. He said not to trust you—"

"Going to listen to him? Old Divide-and-conquer. Okay, come on, Anna—"

"He always liked you better because you're older, anyhow."

"Get off it, Sid, he hates my guts."

"He says I don't have any." Sid giggled. He fished the keys out of his pocket, swung them from a fat thumb. "He wants to know what you're doing. He says you'll get me into trouble. He wants to know if you're getting money from Mother."

"What do you think?" Leon brought his face almost to Sid's.

"I think you're trying, anyhow." Sid let Leon slide the keys off his thumb. "It's redlined at 5500, and listen to me this time, Leon, don't drive like a lunatic. Don't race it. I'm going out but I'll be back by eleven. You get it back to me by twelve, at the latest."

"You don't drive to work, what do you care? Seeing a girl? Hey, Sid." He prodded his brother's belly gently. "You getting any?"

"Let me alone. Listen to me, Leon, or it's all off. Don't put garbage in the jumpseat, don't shift gears as if you're a racing driver, and get that car back by twelve."

"At twelve it turns into a VW bug, ha ha," Leon said as they rode down in the elevator to the basement garage. They left Leon's car on the street and transferred the film into Sid's white Porsche. Grinning like a demon Leon drove her home to change. She took her clothes across to the bathroom. He prowled restlessly. When she came back he paced round her, then nodded, "Okay, okay." But her coat made him frown. "Jesus, that won't do. Wonder if we can get something from Fern."

"No! I won't. Besides she is two sizes smaller. Wake up, Leon, what's wrong with you? Think those people give a damn how I'm dressed?"

"Exactly," He said. "That's all they do see. Her old mink—"

"Nothing is going to make me look that kind of respectable."

"At least we got the Porsche."

"You'd do better to leave Paul and me here, you know that."

"Eh." He shrugged. "Go up there alone? What a bore."

Paul sat in front with Leon and they chattered about the car while she was jammed in the jumpseat with his attaché-case. My relationship with Leon, she wrote across her mind, characteristics of: ascetic, verbal, emotionally charged, manipulative (largely him of me), analytical, nutritive, flirtatious, exclusive, and commanding of loyalty. Based on a role model of brother/sister. We are not however b/s. What are we doing? Games. Feint and withdraw.

Leon was to show *Moonblood*. Imposing, flawed, selfindulgent: she felt a deep physical unease to think she must sit through it. She had tried to talk him into showing something else, *Our Lady of the Nikes* for instance, but he said she had no taste.

"I'll never be any good while I'm dragged by money problems," Leon was saying. "I'd like to shoot everything that goes through my mind. But I can't afford to waste film. I have to use damn near everything I take. If I don't get what I saw, there's no way to do it over. Can't even get hold of the same people twice. Course there are strengths. The same hardness reality has. Is, is, and gone. No second chances. Forget your own preconceptions and react, really react, with what's there. Film's an aquarium where people become themselves with a difference—like Caroline.''

"You shouldn't try to get your family to finance you—even indirectly,'' she said, leaning her arms on top of his seat. "It costs you more than it's worth.''

"They can afford it,'' he said shortly. "They ought to help. Where else am I supposed to go? It's mine too.''

"Only if you're theirs too. You think you have a right to goodies. Maybe it's better to come from a family who couldn't help if they wanted, like I do, because there's no temptation to manipulate them.''

"I'm not interested in the bourgeois virtues.''

"But she's right,'' Paul teased, "you're interested in the bourgeois comforts and toys.''

"If you want to drive this later, shut up.''

The film society met in the auditorium of a very new school. A couple of guys she had seen at Leon's were on the first half of the program, and a woman was scheduled to follow Leon with a documentary in the second half.

The audience was inert for the most part, occasionally restive through *Wet Bag Dream Soup*. She sat between Paul and Leon and their obscene muttered comments. Images of commercials and bodies, politicians and penises, the world with red paint running over. She could sense Leon's consciousness of her body in the flickering dark. Heat gathered where their arms brushed.

During the second film—sharp blinding black and white scattering shapes, screeches of glassy color, bleeps of motion, Paul put his hand over his eyes and went to sleep. At intermission he got up, posed carefully and centrally, and they let him alone. Boredom relaxed the edginess from his body and he truly did not care what happened up here any more than these men seeking out Black Belt prostitutes believed they acted in the world. The women came to him and he played his putdown role with the same joy he played their own ramshackle games.

Leon was on the make following the smell of money. He argued with society officers that they should underwrite a film he would make with them, become involved, immersed in it themselves—then they'd learn what film was. People wanted to look at her. She felt pricked with foreign eyes. Their faces caused her unease. They seemed impermeable, bland and hairless. She could imagine them attacking her like pigeons pecking up seed. She would be glad to sit down in the dark.

A night moth hovered over a flower, slowly put out its proboscis, sucked. Paul had not sat down with them. He sat with a tall rangy redhead all in beige but for a large glossy platinum wristwatch whose dial glowed in the dark nervously tapping, marking time. The huge blindseeming moth hurled against a window screen in brutal persistence. Again again again. A fine dust came from its battering wings. Again again. Caroline lay wrapped in a twisted sheet, distorted, mummified.

Caroline tied to a rock: tied with bits of rubber hose and a jumprope and nylons and two gauze curtains and a string of Christmas tree lights. A black bird pecked at her small vulnerable breasts, at her smooth belly: a bird of the shadow of a hand. Slowly her legs parted. The bird diminished into her and disappeared.

Caroline stood in what looked like a large ashtray, washing herself. She bent and straightened rhythmically, splashing water up over herself, washing at herself. Slowly the camera moved around her watching the water slide over her radiant flesh, watching a web of shadows, filmy then hardedge then filmy shadows move across her, despoiling her as she bent and rose washing at her body. Her face was shrill with fear and twisted.

The lights went on though the projector buzzed still. Anna swung around blinking. Everyone was turning. Leon muttered a curse. Two uniformed cops and a round man in a business suit were standing at the back. The projectionist was arguing. Leon got to his feet and pushed into the aisle.

Everyone was standing now and she could hardly work a path through the crowd. By the time she reached the back and got up close enough to hear, the portly man had confiscated all the films including the still unshown documentary on learning in schoolchildren. It seemed for a moment that the projector would be confiscated too, perhaps for contamination, but it turned out to be rented from the school.

"We had a complaint after the first half of your program that some of the material being shown here was questionable and lewd . . ."

Anna puzzled. The light and dark patterns? The first film, a soft silly homosexual fantasy? Go on!

". . . what we saw ourselves is certainly not the sort of thing allowed in our community. I'm surprised at your bringing this sort of thing in, people like yourselves."

"We didn't know what it was going to be like," the club secretary said. "But it's not right to interrupt—"

"You're on taxpayers' property. How would you like the schoolchildren to find out what goes on here? As long as I'm captain I'll make it my business to keep smut out of our city."

The members made their way out with all possible speed, and Leon was left to argue with the society president for his promised fee.

"We're in enough trouble because of your film. You didn't tell us you were bringing something obscene."

"You're the obscenity, you and your fucking town. I want my print of *Moonblood* back and I want my money. You think I got extra goods to donate to the policeman's ball?"

Threatening to sue Leon stomped out. Paul appeared at his elbow near the door. "Want company back? Or don't you care?"

Leon paused, his face gone blank. Then he cracked Paul on the biceps. "Follow your own scene. My mind's blown tonight. I just want out of here."

She barely got her door shut before he started—not in the direction of the city but north to the tollroad.

"Bastards, bastards," he sang in his throat. "Turn your skull inside out and all they got to say is, dirty-dirty! What do they think's inside their own? Shit, that thing's beautiful. Blind hedgehogs. Touch them on their bellies and they curl up."

The moon was halved but ice-bright in the cold blue night sky. After they got out of the traffic of the northern suburbs the road was empty except for an occasional truck. Even with the top up and heater on the car was cold. Nestling into her bucket seat she almost wished for Fern's old fur. He pushed his foot on the gas and the line crept toward her, 70, 80, 85, 90, she watched it come 95, 100. He sat as if in a trance with the lips drawn back leaving the teeth a little exposed, but his eyes flicked from the speedometer to the road and back again. High whine of the engine. The night was a narrowing funnel. She felt numb. They would be smashed to bits against a bridge and she did not care. She was too exhausted. The line inched toward her, 105, 110, 115. For an instant it rose higher, 117, 118, and then sank back to 115. Slowly Leon eased his foot on the gas and gradually the car slowed. At seventy they seemed scarcely to move past the blurred embankments. He laughed. "We won't mention that to Sid."

"All we needed was to get the state cops on our necks."

"You were right, I should have brought *Our Lady*. That would show them who's obscene. God, that they dare use that word. That guy Mel who runs the society, he evaluates weapons systems all day—efficiency in megadeaths. Obscene?"

"You've never wanted to use me in a film."

"Nah." A couple of moments later he blew out snorts of laughter.

"That's so funny?" She made her voice grate.

"I was picturing you in that washing scene. You wouldn't look guilty or fearhaunted or pathetic. No, you'd look like a *balabosta* giving herself a good scrub in a poorly lit bathroom."

She would look worse than that: she was too fleshy to photograph well. Embarrassing vision.

"Could've picked up something myself better than what Paul got. Couple of those girls—nice ginch."

"So sorry. Wasn't my idea to go along, remember?"

"You could've picked somebody up. Think I'd stop you?"

No, just make life miserable the next day. "Idiot, I'm not looking for *ginch*. If I want anything, it's a relationship."

"Aha." He turned off at the exit for Wedge's Corners and

headed into the Fox Lake region near the Wisconsin border. "Looking for one with me?"

"I don't have to look every moment." She could feel herself being manipulated, but could not tell if he was pushing toward or only playing one of his late night games of hide-and-seek.

"I don't think you know what you want from me."

He turned off the highway onto sideroads. After the tollroad the pavement seemed to twist and barely dodge among the trees. Though he drove more slowly the speed felt greater because of the trunks flying past, the crests and dips. She felt the road in her feet and buttocks. The night was crisp, clear: the air stood frozen up to the frozen stars, up to the frosted smear of galaxies. Lake was hard to tell from meadow except for the cottages outlining the shores. On one bigger lake the ice had been partly cleared and shanties for ice fishermen huddled out on the bare expanse. She felt occupied, crowded with lostness, speed, images, dark, cold, him. "I suppose I want . . . what happens."

"What will happen?"

"Do you know?"

He drove actively, shifting for curves, pushing the car at the road. "Can you imagine what it's like being married to me? The night the shit hit the fan. Because I'm not different. I'm like I am now—the same. You see? Do you see?"

"I don't think I'm marriageable myself."

"Because of that dimwit."

"Asher was kind, gentle. Only I felt I'd been put in a box. I tried hard to be a wife and turned into a sleepwalker."

"Go on, you need to be married." He accelerated, sending the Porsche pouncing over the brink of a short steep hill. "You're just saying, me too."

"Sometimes I think you're a great coward, Leon."

"Sometimes I think you're a great tease."

"Not as big a one as you."

He grinned.

"Besides, you wouldn't be the same with somebody else

as with Joye. People differ, so they prompt different faces out of you.''

''I'm the same, can't you see that?''

''You're not the same with Paul as you are with me.''

''Who're you kidding?'' His voice rose savagely. ''I don't act with either of you. I make myself available. You want to do something? I'm ready. You want to sit around? fine. You want to deal with your problems? good. I'm a catalyst. I make things crystallize in you. I talk about what you want to talk about, I'm a thing you bounce off of and learn . . .''

A fine tension of exasperation lit her nerves. ''I almost think you believe that.''

''Even with Joye I was only a catalyst. I gave her something to react to. But she couldn't learn from her reactions. She couldn't become a free agent, and she's still reacting. But I stay the same, I sit in my room, I wait. Nothing acts on me.''

Under halfclosed lids she looked at him, annoyed. She drew off her glove and put her warm hand on the back of his neck. Slowly she drew her hand along his neck, dipped into the collar of his jacket, deliberately she kneaded her fingers into him. Then she took her hand back. She smiled.

Coming out onto a highway he turned back in the direction of the tollroad. ''When are they tearing your building down?''

''Don't know. I got my eviction notice.'' Finally she told him.

''Yeah? Why don't you move in.''

''Leon, I told you about my marriage. I can't crawl into somebody else's bag.'' She hugged herself. ''We'd turn into people quarreling about who left the water running. You eat each other till you're both digested to nothingness. You find out how even two people with no particular talent for torture can fix each other. It's more than that: it's what people won't allow of each other, and there you are day after day grinding bone on bone.''

''You're trying to fit me in the kind of deal you had with Rowley. See each other three, four times a week, all needs serviced. No thanks. That's not an I-Thou relationship, that's an insurance policy.''

"It isn't the same now—obviously! But start off with two opinionated people used to living alone and having their own way—"

"Shut up! Don't bargain with me! Forget it!" He ground his teeth in rage.

They drove forever on the tollroad. She could not fall asleep or pull herself together. What did she want? She could not tell if she wanted him. In the burnt ends of her nerves she wanted another body against her. She wanted to hold somebody and sleep. Finally they were in Chicago on the inner drive. Huge red lips hung puckered advertising a rugcleaner. On the left a sign: SUPPORT YOUR MUSCULAR DYSTROPHY CAMPAIGN: HELP KEEP CHICAGO CLEAN.

They were home. They sat on the bed. He was grinning, looking at her sideways. She burst out, "Oh, you have me on a hook!"

"What's the name of the hook?"

"Maybe it will never have a name."

"Remember your fairy tales. Name the dwarf and he goes away."

"Proving you can kill anything with words." She began unpinning her hair. One by one she took out the pins.

"Once upon a time there was a lion who lived in a bedroom . . ." His voice was patient, weary.

"What did he look like?"

"Oh, sad colored with snotty eyes. Don't interrupt. Now this lion could only tell lies. He couldn't even tell he was lying, because everything he thought was a lie. He didn't know how he'd got into the bedroom and how to get out. He only knew that it was getting colder and colder."

Handing him the last pin she shook her heavy hair free. "That it is."

"One day a little girl came in who liked to tame lions. And she fed the lion and patted his mane and asked him if he liked that." With one finger he touched her loose hair.

"What did he say?"

"Oh, he lied, because he could only tell lies. Don't interrupt. So the little girl and the lion lived happily ever after in the bedroom. But after they'd lived ever after for a while, the liontaming little girl kept asking the lion to let her put her head in his mouth. The little girl kept telling the lion how she used to do that in a circus and everyone would applaud. The lion kept saying No. She would pull on his tail and climb on his mane and ask and ask to put her head in the lion's mouth. Finally one day the lion said, Okay baby. He opened his mouth as wide as he could, and the little girl stuck her head in. And the lion bit it off. Then he ate her down to the little toe.''

"He was much lion." Anna tilted her head letting her hair fall forward over her cheeks.

"The moral of the story is, there is only one way to get the lion's inside story."

"The little girl had perverse tastes—as did the lion. However, I've heard variants—one ending with a furcoat. As well as quite another. But don't let me interrupt."

And they looked at each other with bleak but unflinching interest.

Leon

Our Lady of the Nikes

He had had to film in black and white. He was content except for the statue itself which had been recently regilded. He wanted that gold.

Columbia stood in Jackson Park near a missile installation, an enormous figure bearing aloft a large bushy cross and an eagle perched with its claws dug into the world. She wore voluminous robes and had a small head. In the sun she flashed and blinded, visible for blocks and though labeled the Republic, obviously a goddess of Empire.

The camera dwelt on her size, her glitter and flash. The camera crept up and circled humbly far at the three-stepped base from which rose another stone base mounting up to her robe-hidden feet. Overhead jets streamed in military formations for Armed Forces Day.

Before her came a pimply-faced hood. He was miserably dressed, baggy where he should have been tight, and pinched where he should have swaggered. He was covered with scars and the memories of scars. He was ugly and misshapen and his skin looked as if it were covered with a layer of eraser crumbs. At her base he knelt, looking up at her gold. He extended his arms, he beat his breast, he pantomimed his misery. The goddess stood remote with her head in the slanting sun near the bombers and interceptor-fighters. Finally he rose and skulked away into the park.

As the sun was setting, the hood returned bringing with

him an unwilling old man. Once again he addressed the Lady,
invoking her. Then for the Lady's edification he began to
beat the old man slowly and ritually, with continual shy
glances up at her remote small perfect head. The old man
tried from time to time to spoil the boy's style. He groveled,
he dragged at the boy, he made himself limp and wept and
embraced the boy's legs. The old man even staggered to his
feet and for a minute or two clumsily fought back.

The boy knocked out the old man's remaining teeth, broke
his arms, legs and jaw, plucked out his eyes and hair and
smashed his skull on the pedestal. Finally he burned the old
man, crumpled but still living, at the base. At this juncture
as the boy dropped exhausted, bloodspattered, at the end of
his poor abilities and strength, while overhead the jets still
proudly tore the skies, the statue fleetingly nodded. The boy
half rose, took a position on his knees. An aura of soft light
suffused the scene. The boy hid his face in his hands through
which slowly tears flowed.

Rowley

Saturday—Friday,
December 6—12

Saturday: The tombs cast blue shadows on the bright crust of snow. On the blacktop road sparrows hopped among puddles and pigeons. Names of fortunes winked from classic portals—names of streets and theaters and hotels and University buildings and department stores.

"Hundred years back when they were making Lincoln Park from a cemetery on the outskirts of town, they dug up the stiffs and moved them here. The fashionable boneyard for decades." He paused before a pyramid four times their height, complete with poker-faced Germanic sphinx. Vera gave him a look of complicity and disbelief. He said, " 'The grave's a fine and private place/But none I think do there embrace.' Just like your livingroom." But this noon she had let him kiss her. From indifference? She had told him he reminded her of Nancy and laughed at him almost with affection. Who was Nancy? One of her pupils. "A tough one, a bad girl. She arches her back and digs in and nothing can move her. She'll be the death of me yet."

She stared at the guardian sphinx with delight: but when he took her hand she hopped away. "Don't be pulling on me."

"At least you'll admit nobody's staring here." Sometimes he thought she could become a recluse, hole up in her room with its windows full of sky and never venture farther than her classroom of children. She always had excuses for not

179

going somewhere. ''People think it's shameful that Arab
women wear veils,'' she told him. ''I wouldn't mind that one
bit. Then every animal on the street couldn't wipe his dirty
eyes on me.''

Her coat was a deep vivid blue, her face less closed than
usual. Long neck, precise-cropped head against the background of snow, delicate dark face. She walked easily as a
deer.

Pullman's tall Corinthian pillar. ''A much hated man. Built
himself an ideal company town—couldn't get a glass of beer
in the place; he resold—at a profit—city gas and water, and
even their humble turds he used for fertilizer on his farms.
Everything was uptight until he lowered wages and kept the
rents high, claiming no connection. Anyhow, when he died
they brought out the body secretly in the night. Coffin covered with tar to seal it. Enormous pit dug, concrete poured,
coffin lowered, steel girders crisscrossed over, and the whole
shebang filled in with concrete. Safe till the first H-bomb.''

''Suppose there was a last judgment and he couldn't get
out?'' Her thin fleeting smile.

Pond, winter frozen. Little castles of death on this inner
circle. Ionic temple of the Potter Palmers. Ryerson money-
box with polished stone sides in which they saw themselves
passing. That was Sullivan too. ''Still, you have to thank the
ostentation for something. Of the pitiful few buildings Sullivan was allowed to build, every year more are torn down.
Like the Walker Warehouse. Used to dig going by it, anon-
ymous, just, solid. Like a second-grade teacher—she doesn't
have to be pretty, but what a nice surprise that she is.''

She looked with amazed eyes at an angel of death recording under a colonnade. Streak of her breath on the crisp
air. Her velvet lips slightly parted. ''You think it's funny that
I teach. Me too. Sometimes I think I'm hired to stand there
and paint them all gray. Layers and layers of institutional
paint, battleship gray, over their mind.''

''There! Sullivan built that for a woman—you see?''

She stood at the intersection of service roads looking at
the Getty Tomb, pale limestone lighter and less dense than
the snow that lay on its cornice, tomb that flowered and

danced. Her face went blank and sulky until he thought he had failed with her again. Then she gave that clear china laugh and went rapidly around it kicking up plumes of snow with her boots, kicking up the snow and grinning. Her legs were slim, the boots slim. She played in the snow like a kid. Around she went in the triangle of trees, poking at the smooth blocks of the base, the snowflake designs, the intricate diminishing arches of windows and door. The bronze doors stopped her, foliage colored with verdigris. "All right, you win!"

"What do I win?"

"You don't find that out till the game is over."

He quoted, talking it to the rhythm:

" *'Bring me flowers while I'm living, please don't bring them when I'm dead,*
And bring them to my bedside, ooh, well, to cool my achin' head.
Don't bring me flowers after I'm dead, a dead man sure can't smell,
And if I don't go to heaven, I sure won't need no flowers in hell . . .' "

"Rowley? Look inside." She pressed against the twin gates crowned with foliage. "The door. Oh!" Drawing off her gloves she wriggled her slender wrist through the space between the gates straining to touch the design that flowed over the door, a graceful wreathed calligraphic image of seeding life. "I could live here."

"He was big on natural cycles, never forgetting decay. He wanted buildings that expressed and didn't repress."

"Don't tell me what to see." Once again she circled, kicking up snow, patting the sides, and fingering the interstices of cut stone. "Your Mr. Sullivan, was he young when he made this?"

"He had his success young. Then the taste went to Roman banks and civic centers. The Columbian Exposition did it. A commission a year for country banks in Ohio or Iowa. Buildings grew ripe in his head and rotted there." He led her off the road across unmarked snow. Reddish stone. "Friends put that up later. He couldn't afford a stone. Died in a flophouse where Lake Meadows stands today—those flashy blank-looking buildings.''

He sat on the small cushion-shaped stone for Louis, and she, submissive for once, sat down on his mother. ''He haunts me. This was his city. He came here young, learned whatever he could be taught; made it big, and lost—to a Roman dream of empire he couldn't fight, a dream of empire that stinks in the air and the newspaper still. He went on losing for thirty years. Once he spoke about dying, leaving so little, what he called a few seeds under snow, when he was so filled with fertility. When I read that I wanted to knock my head on the wall. Buildings to him were honest or dishonest, like the society that pays for them. The Chicago they wouldn't let him build haunts me.''

''You believe in history.'' She smiled faintly. ''You talk about Chicago. Maybe it's different cities that have occupied the same space. City filled with people who don't see it, don't know it, lacks a history.''

''Then its people live in that history like a cage.''

''We're each living in our own heavy history.''

''Speak for yourself. I'm inviting you out.''

''Ever see a turtle out of its shell? Only in the kitchen, when it's about to be cooked.''

''More folks die of boredom than pleasure, I think.''

''How come you shaved off your moustache? I was teasing.'' Her widest eyes probed cautiously, with distrust but also with curiosity. ''It amused you. Made you feel superior to yourself.'' She rubbed the fur cuff of her glove against her chin. ''You have such simple desires. Can't you want something more interesting in this world than my poor black ass?''

''That you're not too respectable to say that cheers me up.''

''You forget I'm a farm girl.''

''Yes. I do forget that.''

''Think, then. Every morning I used to milk my two cows while Sylvia was on the other two. I'd go out with a pail and a pail of water to wash their bags. The cow would be eating, I'd be milking and day-dreaming. I used to like it except in the winter, because I could take a long time and daydream, against the warm hide. It was my secret time of the day—''

''What do you think you're doing?'' The voice cut the air with a plainsman's nasal sneer. ''Get over here. Come on.''

The police car had stopped on the service road between two mausoleums. She tensed and rose stiffly. She gave him one look of fury before her face stretched blank.

''We were visiting Sullivan's grave,'' he said as they approached the cop car. ''That's it.''

''Ya relatives?'' The second cop snuffled at the joke.

''This is private property. Got a good mind to take you in.'' His eyes were bored and lewd, his mouth worked around some small obstacle (gum?), sucking and mauling and ruminating. ''This ain't lovers' lane. Some kind'll do anything. Let's see your ID.''

Vera never turned her face, set in a mask. She took out her teacher's ID and handed it over. When the cops had both pored over it, the first said, ''You're lucky she's not underage.''

''Considering I didn't touch her, I don't see why.'' A slow rage built in his chest. But his balls shrinking hard in his crotch remembered the going over they'd given him at the last antiwar march.

''Too bad.'' The second cop snickered again. ''Where's your ID?''

A few years ago he would have known what to do from the beginning, but these days it was hard to tell. If the cops took them in, it would be ugly. If he risked a bill, that might clinch it. Or it might be what they were looking for, besides their idea of fun. He folded the ten under his license and handed it across.

They both looked at his license, but mostly they were staring at Vera. How she must feel it, the simple threat of rape. Anytime you ran into the cops, it was encounter with power pure and simple. If you had clout, if you were somebody or knew somebody or somebody owned you, then you won. But otherwise it was their game to play you. They might want money, they might want a little fun, they might just want an arrest, they might want to kill you.

"Keep your lip buttoned and haul you ass out of here," the first cop said finally. "Some people got no respect. Now move."

It was humiliating to feel so relieved. Relieved that they had taken his ten bucks instead of a couple of his teeth or ribs, instead of Vera's job or skin. Vera did not walk quickly but she remained frozen inside herself, even when he had brought her back to the car.

Tuesday: He finally tracked down Black Jack's old girlfriend Teena to a rambling house on the near West Side. It was big like a farmhouse, extended in all directions till the end of its small plot or some neighboring structure brought it up short, wedged between a drycleaning plant and a cannery. He had looked over several possible doors with an equal appearance of disuse, when he saw a sign pointing back to a side entrance in a cul-de-sac between the house and the drycleaning plant, under the heavy whoosh of escaping steam. Reverend Roger Bates, Spiritual Psychologist, Healer of Souls, Divine Doctor: Help on Love, Business, Vice Habits, Health, Marriage, Lawsuits. Classes & Private Sessions. Strictly Confidential.

Should ask him how to find Jack Custis, how to make it with Vera, how to halt the renewal bulldozer, how to preserve his community from dispersal. The waiting room had the drab misery soaked discomfort of a welfare office or clinic. A tall august black woman in nurse's uniform except for the veiled headdress viewed him from the corridor with suspicion and disdain. He explained his errand. She stood impassive until he had gone through the story again, then disappeared. Middle-aged women clutching their handbags came and went. A young man reading, rereading a letter was called and dismissed.

The Reverend Bates greeted him from a long immaculate topped desk, a light smallboned man with pale brown eyes, hands with long still fingers poised together. The top of the desk was highly polished. On its walnut finish the face of Bates floated upsidedown. The room was in contrast with the anterooms: thick beige carpet, rich brown draperies, Danish office furniture with orange accents. On a wall hung a degree—an MA in psychology dated fifteen years before, labeled indeed Roger Bates.

The Reverend Bates listened in silence, his graceful hands touching his temples. His smile when Rowley finished was milk chocolate but mocking. "Mr. Custis came by to see us himself, not too long after Sister Teena joined our organization. You want to find him? Drag the river bottom. Dredge the sewers." A sweet smile with a touch of almond. He slanted his long hands together. A ring of turquoise and silver glinted. "Sister Teena used to play the piano herself. Infrequently she favors us with a gospel tune."

Rowley found his eyes returning to the diploma. The Reverend Bates remarked gently, "Yes, as I'm sure you're aware, the day of the white collar Afro-American is upon us, somewhat. I was ahead of my time. Growing weary of running an elevator, I have found a way to make myself useful, if not inside the research or welfare system, then outside. There are sufficient unhappy clients for all of us . . . I see no reason why you might not have a chat with Sister Teena, briefly. We are all busy with the Lord's work here—understaffed and overburdened. I'm sure you wish to leave a contribution for our good work?"

Rowley did not ask what that was but produced a five, and was led off by the same woman who had brought him in, angular and deliberate in her walking as a heron. He followed her stately journey through the high drafty halls, the doors open and shut with an air of dormitory or camp. Sister Teena was located down on her knees scrubbing the floor of the huge kitchen.

Her hair grew in tight natural curls conforming to her Nefertiti head. Her back was long and muscular, moving under the loose maid's dress. Her headdress hung neatly on the back of a chair standing high on a workbench out of the way of her scrubbing. Her legs were slender, her feet shapely in spite of old sneakers. Crooning softly she scrubbed at the linoleum punishing it rhythmically, and her buttocks firm, wellturned as bakery bread, jiggled.

"Sister Teena," the heron-woman said in a low grating

voice. "You got a visitor. You stop a while. The Reverend
says talk to him if you want to."

She turned to look over her shoulder. His throat closed.
Her face was old. Worn, twisted. Her cheek was seamed with
a purplish-pink scar. Her eyes hung in loose pouches clinker
cold on him. He began to speak. She let him talk on for a
long time, holding the brush while slow drops gathered on
the end and trickled down her arm. She and the heron-woman
exchanged a long look, and then the other tapped briskly
away.

Oh yeah, she remembered Jack Custis, yes indeed. With
a slow, pinched smile. She didn't think she'd forget him. But
she didn't follow that old life any more. She was saved and
meant to stay saved. Jack had come here for her and the
Reverend had let him in, that was his way. The Reverend
knew she was born again, he wasn't scared of Jack. She had
never seen Jack again, after that time he came and made the
ruckus. She didn't go out.

"Not ever? You don't go outside this house?"

"Out there?" She shuddered. Drops fled the brush down
her arm. "No!"

A chill touched him. Vera. She had been a user, she said
flatly and described her habit. He had the feeling she had
said this all many times, the phrases were worn to her tongue.
The scar she'd got in prison, when another woman attacked
her and nobody would help. And why? Because they were
all lost, all blind. The blind can't lead the blind . . . She
paused, drying her arm on her loose dress. Out there she
couldn't get a job. Who did he think would hire her? She
laughed sourly. She couldn't live. They'd lock her back up
and throw away the key.

She seized the scrubbrush and began working again.
"Black Jack, he was on welfare a long time. Try them. They
keep track of everybody. They don't have no respect for you,
but they sure like to write things down. That time he come,
he try to drag me out of here. Even after he see my face is
all messed up. I told him, I told him, Jack, I'm through, I'm
worn out, and he hit me upside of my head. He never bring
nothing but trouble." Lowering her head she worked fu-

riously, purifying the floor, and he left. Around the next bend of the hall the heron-woman waited aloof under her veil to guide him out.

He had come on the bus, for the snowplow had buried his car. For five, ten minutes he waited on the corner. Getting dark. The air creaked with ice. Suddenly he turned and began walking on Grand Street, he did not know why. Aimless lately. He might have pressed Teena to remember old addresses, details, but a sickening indifference had come over him. He kept disconnecting. He forgot for a moment how to talk. He was used to enjoying his job, used to working because he enjoyed it. Now he had no ideas. All was labor.

As he walked east on Grand past the Salvation Army, the emblem on the watertower caught the last light. Wooden bridge over railroad. With the passing of trucks the old planks jigged under his soles. An iron bridge followed, crossing the North Branch. He leaned over the railing toward the Loop. Intricate web of railroad and car bridges, high buildings which did not at this point compose so much a skyline as a sharply lit compacted maze. Blunt hulk of the Merchandise Mart. Along the mushy shores stripped sumacs and cottonwood saplings stood ankledeep in frozen gray scum. Fish reeked from a processing plant on the bank he had left, and overlying all floated a strong aroma of chocolate from a factory a couple of blocks south. Streetlights cast his reflection on the garbage laden water. Sluggish, peristaltic. Would anyone drown himself in that?

He struck his gloved hands on each other, rubbed his numb nose. Could not move. Will had dwindled. What was eating him? From boredom he read the plaque on the bridge. Carter H. Harrison, Mayor. Historians' favorite. Handsome and less the gouger than most. To contemplate mayors of American cities is to get a bellyache. He too owned real estate in the vice districts. Simple empire of the First Ward based on an army of whores and control of booze and gambling: the first innocent syndicate of Hinky Dink and Bathhouse John. Convenient, centralized vice district with its own newspapers— pimps' house organs—its annual ball, its social leaders.

He leaned over his reflection that crept and shuddered on

the oily surface. The past. Which did not exist. Catching him in a stupid error yesterday, Cal had said with his ordinary sarcasm, you must be in love. Watching the river ooze past, the lights from the Loop austere on the condensing dark, he leaned against a bridge support and something in the pressure against his side jogged him.

Smell of grass phantom on the fish and chocolate. Fireflies. A day when idyllic summer floated over the prairie miles, the cottonwood streets, when the cliffs of glass fronted a crisp serene sea. He had spent the day staring into the blue with Harlan and family. Their transistor radio pumped out the summer blood beat. They drank beer from cans in a bag and Shirley had brought chicken and potato salad.

He had got it out of Marcia that Anna was going with her to a concert at Ravinia to escape from Asher, her indecision, him. He had let them get settled. Then casually in the dusk he had come over to their blanket. He could makes Ives' Second Symphony sound in his head and feel the nubby worn blanket where he lay, his hip grazing hers through the soft cloudy dress. Tunnel of green and hilly sideroad. Walking in the tall grass. The green was new and fresh, the city was new and breathing, the ground was under their feet. Twelve gates to the city, hallaloo. The city, the woman open to him, new, alive, to take and shape. His life before him warm and mapped like a hand. Prairie with sunflowers eight feet tall the settlers found. She was a sunflower turning to him, seedy and warm and coarse and strong. Love was a map. She had come to him and his life was in his hands like a woman. Vision of the city of long prairie streets and sunflowers, of his friendship with Harlan, of her summer body, him knowing and about to act of his fullness. Himself in his life in his city.

Icy water slid by, filmy, slow. Vera had cast him loose. He had felt brutal impatience for people who couldn't find a thing in the world to give themselves to. Now he was flat except for his desire. Nothing he did had meaning to her. She was in tangent, in one quick bounce of judgment off again. Before her he stood a bloated clown, wearing the lewd gross self-loving mask of Mr. Charley.

GOING DOWN FAST   189

Well, sun going down, moon begin to rise in blood,
Well, sun going down, moon begin to rise in blood,
Well, now, life ain't worth livin' if you ain't with the woman you love.

The formlessness. That he could not grasp himself as actor.
Could not grasp his own actions or possible actions. That his
society appeared as a series of masks and obfuscations and
hidden forces. He cursed and leaned over the filth to spit.
Jammed his hands in the pockets of his hunting jacket and
walked off.

   Monday, the hearings started.
   They had a good turnout from the neighborhood. The
hearings room downtown was rapidly filled. Harlan argued
with the officials to move it to a bigger room, but he was told
that would be impossible, and some of their people who had
not signed up in time to testify but who wanted to be present
were not allowed to stand inside and had to leave. Shirley,
with Tommy squirming on her lap, sat between Harlan and
him, with Blanche on Harlan's left side. Blanche was being
very circumspect. She was wearing a black wool dress with
white collar and cuffs and gloves and only two bracelets. She
sat there clutching her purse and looked straight ahead. J.J.
had parked his burly self on a folding chair just behind them,
and he was leaning forward to talk in Harlan's ear. Beside
him was the little man whose name Rowley had never
learned, but who had brought his soft mild insistence on
justice to every meeting and every strategy session. Mrs.
Samson, the widow with six kids who'd been relocated twice
already, was present with the three oldest wearing somebody
else's suits. They all leaked nervousness, they all had little
bits of paper with what they wanted to say written down,
they all kept looking anxiously around to try to judge the
enemy.
   First came the Corporation testimony. The chairman of
the division of social sciences of the University was called
first. This was not the announced order, but Lederman
hopped up to explain that Chairman Wangler had flown in
especially to testify and he was needed back in Washington

where he was working very hard on the President's committee on crime in the streets. He shook hands with the commissioners, beamed around and launched into a smooth exposition. He was followed by a demography expert from ISS.

The experts proved by census data and their own surveys that population density in the area under consideration was greater than in white middle-class areas to the east. Ages of structures were higher (smartly printed up comparative tables were distributed), and their potential obsolescence militated against soundly financed renovation. The area showed the perfect type of a sector in transition. Most inhabitants had arrived recently: such high transience destroyed stability.

"How'd they enjoy it if we talked about them that way? Those professors always picking up and going where they make more!" Blanche was prickling with anger. Harlan reached over to quiet her, then pulled his hand off her arm as if he'd been stung. Tommy was whining and Shirley was trying ineffectually to quiet him.

Blight was widespread, the experts reported. Inspectors working under Corporation auspices had found violations in building after building. In its racial composition the area resembled other districts of blight. Conversions by use were common. Let alone, the area could only hasten downhill, infecting property values in adjacent areas and further depressing the urban tax base.

The Corporation testimony was clear, vigorous and backed up by table after table of statistics (Table I through VIII). When the hearings broke for lunch, nobody in their group was feeling lively. Their mood was not improved by watching Lederman and Wangler go off with the commissioners to lunch. The Defense Committee people ate in a $1.39 steak place down the block, pulling three of the formica tables together. Tommy collected the foil from everybody's baked potatoes and made a big ball of it.

"Maybe we made a mistake not finding out more who these commissioners are. Rowley, think you could check them out tonight?" Harlan had eaten quickly and shoved his plate away, sat tracing figures in spilled salt.

"The business library's closed tonight, and besides, I have to be at the studio by six."

"Okay, get what you can this afternoon."

"Come on, man, I want to be at those hearings as much as you do."

"I don't want to be there at all. We need some discipline. Blanche, you go with him. He'll show you what to do."

"What's come over you, Harlan? You know I got to testify."

"We aren't getting a chance to testify today. Can't you see that?"

Testy and insistent Harlan sent them off. "You give in to a man one way, and pretty soon he's bossing you all around the map," Blanche said. She was as pissed off as he was at being exiled. They played round robin all afternoon through the library shelves: *Polk's Directory, Poor's Register, Who's Who in Illinois.* One of the commissioners was a member of the real estate board. He had his offices in the Midwestern Title and Trust's building, but they could not figure out his connection with the bank. The other white commissioner was a middle-level executive of a world agribusiness corporation, active in his church. His wife had furniture store money (People's Friend Discount, active in the ghettoes). The black commissioner owned a small paper box plant.

They could make some connections between men who sat on the board of directors of Title and Trust and the agribusiness corporation and some of the central corporate kings they knew were behind renewal, but no more than they would turn up out of almost any business in the city that dealt with banks and interconnected with other corporations. The men serving as commissioners were not big shots—they weren't the mayor's favorite giants for committees with real power—just middle echelon men anxious to please and do their civic duty with distinction in the eyes of their superiors. It meant everything and nothing.

Tuesday the University administrators took the stand to state the needs of a great institution. A color film was shown depicting the contribution of the several institutions of the area to its economic viability. A vice-president reminded the commissioners how Inland served the community, the city and the nation. He cited potent federal officials and senators on the need for student housing and the expansion of educational and research facilities, the importance of advanced technology to our national defense.

"We have to shift our emphasis from the elimination of already existing slum jungles to something far more important, the use of urban renewal to develop our urban economy itself, to support our critical institutions and attract vital new industries and to create attractive neighborhoods in our city in which solid and civic-minded men and women can live safely and raise their children, neighborhoods in which normal cleanliving families want to settle and go to school and work. Inland University is ready to face its responsibility to its city and its neighborhood."

On Wednesday the Corporation finished its exposition. Attendance from the neighborhood had fallen. "What can I say?" Harlan counted his flock. "A lot of them are just clerks and domestics. They took off the time they could, but they're afraid they'll get fired if they stay out longer." Harlan had had enough trouble getting a leave of absence, while Rowley continued to work the late shift. He slept odd hours and never felt rested. Sometimes he fed Yente several cans of catfood and sometimes he didn't get back to feed him for a whole day. Shirley was back home with the kids, and he hoped she would remember the cat with an occasional handout.

The last witness called by the Corporation was a spokesman for UNA. Rowley winced and shifted in his seat. Old Asher.

"On behalf of UNA I would like to state our reservations about the plan," Asher said and did at length, dwelling especially on the lack of provisions for good relocation for those who would be displaced. Studies using the city's own statistics showed that the relocated ended up in overcrowded, deteriorating neighborhoods and usually paid far more than they had. "However, we feel in the absence of any genuine alternative plan for preventing further decay, we can not do otherwise than to offer our support to the Corporation proposal. I don't know how representative this Defense Committee claims to be—how many of them are here? fifteen?—but I would like to enter in the record that UNA has made repeated attempts to organize this area without finding interest on the part of the residents. Repeated attempts," Asher said again as Harlan rose protesting.

Asher had documents too, results of surveys and studies and projections carried out by UNA. He had a trim helper bustling about him producing each document as he cited it, fluttering, perky, with a silken efficiency: "Scalpel!" "Scalpel!" There was Asher slitting their throats, droning on in his colorless but crushingly authoritative way while his wee houri danced around him. It made Rowley squirm to recall how Anna had ministered to Asher: Asher had a knack for getting women to wait on him. "Where's my pipe, Anna?" "What did I do with that report?" "Did you get those films developed?" "I wonder if you could stop at the library and check a reference for me." Nice legs. They were always something special, Asher's women. Asher appeared not to see him.

Mrs. Samson's three kids had had to give back the suits to whoever they'd borrowed them from. They were bored and angry and started horsing around till one of the guards reprimanded them and said they would have to leave if they didn't know how to behave at an official city hearing.

On Thursday Vera came. She sat at the back sketching while her brother lolled beside her. She sketched with a spidery line, steel wire, and would not sit with him or let him sit beside her. Paul looked all legs in the narrow seat. He listened with his forehead frowning and his hands playing with his pen, his hair, his buttons. Their side-by-side heads balanced. He did not see them speak. When Vera looked at Paul her face tightened. She sat watching him, remapping, judging; while Paul stared at the hearings, hurt, obsessed, confused, during noon recess full of questions. There was plenty to react to.

One by one homeowners from the area got up to speak. "He can't call my house decrepit," piped a gnarled little man who worked for sanitation. "Why, I painted that house top and bottom, inside and out. Every inch two coats of good paint.''

Mrs. Samson with her six kids: "What have we done? What's wrong with us? We bought homes here and fixed them up. I spent my life's saving and my poor man's insurance money on this house. We love this neighborhood with the grass and trees and flowers. It's not overcrowded. Before we found this house we lived in two rooms. We had to look for months. Why can't the University just buy a couple of apartment buildings? Why do we have to keep moving? Mr. Judges, why don't you come home with me and visit my livingroom, and see if we live like animals the way they say. See for yourself.''

Finally Harlan took the stand with questions of his own: When would the University integrate the buildings it owned? When would their real estate combine allow black people to move into the area around the campus? If the Corporation really wanted to promote stability, why hadn't the residents been allowed to participate in planning for their own area? The way he saw it, the whole urban renewal thing was a way to use public money, the taxes that sat so heavy on people like the ones in this room, to make life easier for those who had it easy already. It was a sort of socialism for the rich, to insure their investments and get them land cheap to make profits on. "When will the University and the redevelopers take the same chances I have to, of buying what they want openly?"

The Corporation lawyer had only a few questions. "Mr. Williams, you've stated your objections to our term 'conversion by use.' You've stated that housing in the demolition area is sound and is being increased in value by its present occupants. Mr. Williams, do you own property in the area under discussion?''

Harlan gave his address and described his house briefly.

"A single-family cottage. Now, Mr. Williams, how many families reside in your house?''

"Just mine. And a friend who rents the downstairs.''

"Mr. Williams, isn't it true that you have rented the cellar as an apartment? Isn't it also true that you rented the unfinished attic as another, to another family with children?''

"That's my wife's brother. It's not unfinished.''

"Have you put in a bathroom?''

"There is a bathroom.''

"For your tenants? Or is the bath shared?''

"It's my brother and sister-in-law and their baby. We have relatives staying with us because it's a lot better for them upstairs then where they were. It wasn't safe there. It's not a permanent arrangement, and in fact I plan for my own kids to take over that floor when they're older.''

"Three families occupying a structure intended to house one none-too-large family is exactly what we mean by conversion by use. Thank you, Mr. Williams.'' The lawyer smiled.

When he brought the car around, Paul half shoved Vera into the back, leaping into the front.

He turned his head at the address Paul gave him. "Leon's? So he's the toad.''

"Vera likes people for strange reasons and dislikes them for plain bad ones . . . Is it true you used to go with Anna?''

Something in the kid's tone made him bristle. "Yeah.''

"Yeah?'' Paul turned limpid eyes on him. "Guess it's a stage girls go through.''

"While Leon is a very young man's disease.''

Vera laughed sharply from the backseat.

"Leon is about the most generous person I ever met,'' Paul said with hauteur and a slight whine. "It's not just big liberal talk with him. Knowing him is an education in how people can exist with each other in a nonrotten way . . .''

Was Anna eating this up too? Leon always had a swinging line, that he swung till he tripped. Like saying he got married to save Joye from her home environment, to educate her. He married Joye because he'd been in the sack with her on and off for months and her family was fussing. A nice piece, maybe a little thin upstairs, but nothing to make up an ideology about. Bitter now.

"You disgust me,'' Vera lilted. "Foul abstract words filling your mouth. Once you knew what it meant to talk. Don't you spill over me the leavings of some fat fake's lectures.''

"Talk? You mean we made up our own language. Any two kids can play games, Vera. What were we risking?''

"What are you risking with that toad except your own decency?''

"You just love shiny Jameson words like decency lately.''

"No wise man has been making me ashamed of where I come from, and who.''

They were pulled up out front of Leon's storefront. "You're so closeminded, you make me weep!'' Paul flung himself out.

Rowley held that door open till Vera got the idea and moved up front. "Scared someone will think you're my chauffeur?''

"In a VW?''

She sat straight with arms folded. Now and again a spasm of anger bit her features.

Perhaps it was like taming a unicorn. She had stopped jumping at his touch. She would let herself be kissed. She would even curl up on his lap if he kept talking or listened to her. Once he asked her as she waited under his kiss, "Didn't anyone ever kiss you?''

Her amused face. "Do you think I come from Mars?''

So little trace. As little as he was leaving. Sometimes he grew sick with himself and thought he would take up molesting little girls. But she was a child only in stubborn pretense.

Friday he came to meet her where she taught in an ugly redbrick warren in the Black Belt, stinking, overcrowded, its dank halls and packed classrooms jangling like sore nerves. As he loitered smoking and waiting against the wire fence with the pitiful bleak schoolyard before him, he felt young, mean, truant. The wall was splattered with fucks and hearts, Candy Loves Willy, the names of gangs and would-be gangs. Someone had lettered carefully in purple PUSSY IS GOOD FOR YOU. A used scumbag fluttered off a spike in the fence.

The smell of fear choked him, continual buzz of the scatological sex of childhood, the warfare, the petty oppression, the unremitting oily boredom. The status world of the young hustler. Always someone to face down. Fear, fear. The bratty shrillness of the bells across the gravel yard made him think of the airraid drills of World War II. All of them sitting by classes crosslegged in the halls singing "The caissons are rolling along!" They had to sit crosslegged, their feet turned just so, because otherwise they might be comfortable. Still everybody enjoyed them so much the board of education had to issue a warning against too many airraid drills in certain schools.

Midmorning watery milk. Teacher prying, How many children brushed their teeth this morning? took a bath? The screws put on them to cough up dimes and quarters for defense stamps, for Christmas and Easter seals, for teacher's favorite charity. The smell of the gym floor and hard gray mats. Whether baseball or basketball the team leaders were Al and Babalu, and they would choose up the other colored kids first. He was always one of the first whites chosen because he was tall and a good hitter, but it incensed him that they'd choose PeeWee, who was as little as the bat, before him. Even mild prejudice always got whites indignant.

Other kids went to all white schools. His crowd learned that early. Something must be wrong with them. They weren't as white as other kids. But the real white kids were stupider in lots of ways. They didn't know the other language. There were many things they didn't know. Though school was stacked against the colored kids—like for Auditorium they always had to be giving oral reports on Booker T. Washington, George Washington Carver and, by infection, Lincoln till the walls wept while the whites had Everybody—still something was exchanged. Soul, style. If he could explain about that, with his music.

One last bell and the volcano spewed kids. Landslides of kids. Hundreds, thousands poured out, they poured out. His first impulse was to run for his life. The building could not have held them. They must be jammed in six deep. As the hordes of children squeezed out the old massive double doors, he thought he heard the snapping of bones, he was sure little kids went down underfoot and were trampled to jelly. For ten minutes children thundered out, delirious to reach air. The pavement quivered. The air rang like metal with their cries. Finally the explosion dwindled to stragglers, and teachers began coming into the parking lot and through the door near him toward the busline.

A number passed before he saw her walking alone with small, tired steps lugging a black case as if it were full of bricks. He was amused how much a schoolteacher she looked, slight, spinsterish, weary. Then she saw him. Her head whipped up, her shoulders froze. He thought she would walk past without speaking and he swore if she did, he would forget her. With a twist of her lips she stopped in front of him. "What brings you around?"

"Thought I could give you a lift home."

"Nothing like a little scandal to enliven these biddies. Is this doing me a favor? I'm too tired to know. Yes, I'm glad not to pack on the bus and stand all the way. But don't do it again. I'm not a regular teacher yet."

When he came upstairs with her she kicked off her shoes and let him pull her down on his lap. She did not sit on him as if he were a chair the way she usually did, but collapsed, burying her face in his neck. "One of my boys is in trouble for having a knife. He's just a baby. I'm sure it's his brother's and he was showing off, but the principal's treating him like a criminal."

She taught, she attended evening classes at the Art Institute. She had a friend, an older Negro woman, Mrs. Hamilton, who went around with her like two nuns elbow to elbow in the museums, galleries and exhibitions. Mrs. Hamilton was earnest and admiring. With her Vera's face was closed as the trunk of a tree. Afterward she would tell him the flashes of charlatanism, of pomposity she had seen.

For that she needed him: to share her sense of absurdity. When she made her masks of derision, of wit and even of wonder she must have someone to see them. He measured her need and moved in. No wonder his days had gone hollow.

Returning late from her that night he was coming down

his street, walking from the parkingplace he'd found around the corner. One of the streetlights was out, had been broken all week. Trash scattered around the sidewalk. City was cutting down services already. He saw the kids coming toward him but did not think twice. Neighborhood kids. Perhaps he knew them. They split to pass him. When they were level, the one on his left lunged into him.

"Hey, Whitey! Get Whitey!" The kid on the right closed in, ricocheted off.

His thigh burned. Then cold air. He swung after them, his hand going down. Touched torn cloth, touched smear of wet. He let them go. They had not cut him deeply but the wound stung.

Yente rose stifflegged from under the steps yowling welcome.

"Hi, tuxedo-cat." He stooped to ruffle his shaggy fur.

The door opened above them. "Rowley? Where you been?"

"With a girl. What's wrong?"

"The commissioners voted this afternoon."

"Already? They didn't take long to decide."

"No, they didn't take long. They passed it two to one."

"Shit. Look, I'll be up in five minutes."

"Don't. I got no stomach for talk tonight. No stomach at all."

"Tomorrow?"

"Maybe."

In the john he examined his leg. A slash ran half the length of his thigh in a jagged seam. Maybe a froe? Some kind of broken knife. The blood rolled over the winter-sallow skin and dripped on the white toilet seat. With plaintive meows Yente rubbed against the leg he was standing on and nuzzled his boot querying, hey?

"What's the world coming to, cat? The power structure deals and I get cut. Aw, tonight I feel rotten."

Then he heard Harlan's words and let the cap of the tincture of Merthiolate fall into the basin. They were beaten. They had made a good case, they were right and within their rights. But they had lost. A huge baffled anger formed in him as he went over the steps of their case again and again. The last thick syrup of bleeding oozed over his thigh.

Saturday, December 13

The breaking wave of her breasts against the white wall. Firm small breasts like fists. The musculature of her sleek back was marked and beautiful.

"I'm strong for my size. All those generations of farmhands." The vaccination mark showed in the resilient flesh of her upper arm: bite of closeset pointed teeth. Shadowy hollows in her throat.

"Don't keep saying I'm pretty, it leaves me cold. Bodies are jokes."

"Then some jokes are prettier than others. What do you think you're defending now?"

"I must be the first female Jameson to commit immoral acts in four generations, since freedom. Think of it, the shock among the elder saints up there watching."

"If I think of that there won't be an act. You're fighting."

"What you call fighting, I call breathing."

"Breathe through your skin then."

"It was silly mysticism to suppose I'd be any different when you got my clothes off."

Yet the fruity silk of her thighs, warm against warm. Belly's dull gloss. At times her body would answer him, follow.

"I've wanted *objects*. Certain drawings downtown. An Egyptian cat. A Japanese monkey screen." In the slack flutter of her eyelids the sheen in the plumage of grackles. Color of very dark tulips. One hand rested on his back.

"I began making my clothes when I realized they didn't like me trying on clothes in Ransom's. I understood why my mother ordered from Sears. I learned to sew then. A woman from the church gave me lessons."

"Do you blame me for wanting you?"

"Of course."

The wall of masks watched, among them his own lewd face. With her he felt conscious of his bulk, his hair, the buried clubs of bones. Her small hand floated on him without pressure or urgency. She said, "I never know how much I should be watching out for you. You seem so clumsy with your guts dragging and your pockets full of yourself. But you want, you want."

"Well, you wanted that monkey screen."

"I have a cold faith in myself." Her eyes mirrored him in obsidian. He was dug in for a long siege, prepared and patient. "If I really want that screen, I can reproduce it. It may take a year to learn brushstroke technique and longer to master it, but then. Suppose I make a screen? Is that what I wanted? If not, what did I want?"

"We have different problems."

Her fresh laugh. "Friend, you noticed that?"

She never completely shut her eyes. Sometimes she filtered him through long lashes. Sometimes she fixed on middle distance, above the ceiling. Sometimes she challenged his eyes. He laid his hand on her flat midriff. In her free floating a bubble world: two dark skinny minnows in clear cold water, in a hard early morning light with the colors sharp as scallions but few. In his arms, her: in her, that water world. She spoke of her brother.

"We kept each other's secrets. We were always acting stories. We like the Bible best but we'd do King Arthur and Robin Hood and Tarzan and lots of martyrs. He'd be Moses and I'd be the children of Israel—all of them. That's how the masks started."

She sat up against him suddenly, groping. "What's that? On your leg there?"

He winced. Rough scab. "Accident."

"You cut yourself shaving? What kind of accident?"

"It's getting tough in the neighborhood. Ran into some kids the other night."

She lay back still touching it. Line of lamp on her cheek.
Her nails teased his back indolently. She moved her head
slowly to and fro on the pillow. Hollows came and fled in
her arched vulnerable throat. The breaking curve of her
breasts interminably against the wall. In a slow teasing voice
she told a story. "Once upon a time in a cold country lived
a king who had two hundred daughters. Finally a son got
born named Peter Moses Joseph George Washington Fred-
erick Douglass—"

"A heavy name for a kid."

"You don't know the half of it. Of all his two hundred
sisters, now, he liked Joan best, just older. The kids found
out that much was expected of them at home—only perfec-
tion—and that out in the world people had expectations too
but the opposite. Once they got off the farm the world seemed
pretty mean and badly run. Even the folks who depended on
their father thought the family stiff and proud. Their sisters
became giddy and boycrazy or household drudges under the
strain. The boy Peter was spoiled, yet beaten by his daddy
so he'd improve. And he tried and she tried all through their
childhoods to be *good*. Their daddy was superintendent of
the little Sunday school, where every week in trepidation and
glory and cold, cold sweat they performed like tortured par-
rots.

"Now in everything Peter led and Joan came running after,
cause she was trained always to give her brother the bigger
piece—which meant in practice she let him do the cutting.
Their relations with the town whites were sometimes tense,
sometimes muddy. But they were never afraid of their white
teachers the way some colored kids were, because their daddy
was much scarier. And they could trust each other. Old Joan
had had it so dunned into her that her duty was to her brother
that she would even lie to her daddy to protect him and then
wait for God to cause her wicked mouth to be sewn shut.

"Things went along like that till Peter was in highschool
and Joan was in teachers college. A mean pablum-minded
school where she paid tuition and the cost of a dreadful room
five nights a week by doing domestic work—but that's an-

other fairy tale. Now through wide reading, Peter lost his faith. He started pointing out flaws in their religion."

"Did Joan lose her faith then?"

"At first she argued, but then she couldn't stand to be outside, so she joined him. In fact each time she came home for the weekend she would bring new contradictions she had worked out. She'd always been thorough in her lessons. Peter was sick and tired of the whole project long before Joan had finished busting up their tight little world. It was busted good, too.

"Summer came, and Joan came home. But Peter, who'd always had his charm, was discovering what to do with it. Life was nature, he said, to replace the broken world, and sex was natural. He picked out the daughter of a man who did odd jobs. Not one of her father's churchgoing families but those bad niggers on the outskirts of town they'd been raised to scorn. One hot Saturday Peter went off to town nervous like before an exam and selfimportant—oh! Joan lay on her bed and read and reread a short story of Hemingway's called *Up in Michigan* which seemed horridly appropriate and her zoology book's vague chapter on reproduction. Of course she's seen animals together though told nice girls didn't watch, but thinking of chickens and cows and dogs made it worse until she cried. This grubbiness was clearly not the sort of thing that could replace that tight world in which they'd tried to be saints, together."

Experimentally she touched him, her hands for a moment less weightless. He was fighting now. To quiet that voice of cold water running he kissed her and kept her mouth. He let her slip from him only momentarily, then fastened on her again. Slowly her breasts heaved, her breath quickened. Fringe of lashes screening her sliver of gaze, wary still. Plumage tones in the flesh that slightly gave to him and answered. She was with him now, obedient, following though the eyes scanned him and would not go under. He did not dare let go of her mouth for fear that voice would start up like an airconditioner, so with his hand only he worked on her parting her thighs. She was small, firm as her breasts, yet he could not be sure she was a virgin. He had expected a tangible hymen. Perhaps some poor bastard before, laboring on her black marble belly veined with his sweat, died leaving no trace.

Finally, slowly he slid in using a condom. She had said, "You do something. You do it." She was tight on him as slowly he worked in. He could no longer keep her mouth but it pressed into his shoulder. He tried bearing against her, but a wince crossed her face and her eyes opened wide. She felt good, she felt good, but he had to hold on. Her face was borne on the pillow, the lips slightly swollen, the eyes watchful and bright. He brought his mouth over against her lids and got them shut. Let go, come on, let go. If only he could get her to cast loose.

Her tightness brought him to the edge. He stared at the floor, counting boards beyond the little rug, counting them back again. He could feel a pulse in her beating against him, a slick pressure growing. Could feel her coming up to him. He clenched his teeth and worked. That pulse answered. He was so sure. But after a while she turned her face free of him. "I'm beginning to get sore," she said in clear gentle tones.

He shifted, slowed. "Better?"

She shrugged, still looking away. The resilient pulse had died. Her flesh shrunk away. He came, working up grimly, and got out. Sitting on the bed's edge he felt heavylimbed, as if he had just climbed out of a lake after a long swim. She hopped to her feet, plucked her underwear from the floor and went to wash.

She called from the bathroom, "Anyhow, if you still want me to go to that party with you, I will."

Second sudden surrender. He dangled the loose sloppy pendulum of condom. They should get out of here or they'd get depressed. He told himself as he got up to flush the condom away that many virgins could not make it for a while. Next time.

She shut the bathroom door with a slam. "Wait till I come out!" He had to kill time on the bed, the clamminess of the condom making him sit with his thighs far spread. He kneaded his belly folds. Well, he had lost weight recently.

Was skinnier than he'd been in four, five years. He felt no satisfaction. Thirty-one. Anna's face as she leaned into the mirror sometimes: he had called it masochism. This was such a dryshod moment when he thought, what am I doing here? Why did I want that? What am I trying to do?

Out of the bathroom she strolled coolfaced, coppery high-lights in the forest of her skin. Her walk was lightlimbed and relaxed. Her eyes were wide, the soft pushbacked curve of her nose was raised, inquiring. No fingerprints. But a brief cat'spaw of smile touched her face as she met his gaze.

When he came out he caught her at the mirror, examining. At once she swished away, brushing imaginary lint. He laughed, getting her coat. "No, you don't look different."

She stuck out her tongue. But let him take her arm. His depression had blown off. To have got her to bed was only a step. In the car her head on its long neck inclined toward him. Slowly she bent. He drove through the icy streets enjoying the extra effort. He felt good in his body.

"Afterward, come to my place tonight."

She shook her head no.

"Why not?"

"You mean, why not *now*. Because I went to bed with you."

"Don't nit-pick. Why not anyhow?"

"Because of your friend."

"Harlan?"

"Yes. It's his house."

"But you'll have to meet him sometime. He's going to learn about you anyhow."

"I have to live in my world."

"One you keep shrinking."

"I'm going to your party, aren't I? Like a proper trophy."

He parked down the block from Marcia's, the narrow house lit and uttering pulsations of shout and bang and crash and twang and ha ha. Her head lay lightly on his shoulder. "Should I tell you a thing that pleased me?" she asked.

"My modesty would survive it."

"That you didn't say you loved me."

"Why?" Because if she'd asked for words, he would have.

"Because people do that, presenting a bill. *I love you.* As if you'd asked them to. Sticking their need at you."

"Have you been billed that often?"

"The other thing I liked was that you didn't ask indecent questions. You didn't behave as if you had a right to know."

Setting her ground rules. Far from minding he felt the surer of her the more she was careful to set up new barriers. On the stairs she shrugged off her coat and he took it. Who knew what would happen and for how long? For the first time he noticed the dress she had put on in the bathroom, worn with boots. He looked at her clothes because he was aware she made them. Soft folds of white wool. Bridal nightgown. Whatever happened she was going out of his hands into the world, not back into that damn little room. He would make her see and smell and taste and hear a hundred new things. He would drag her around the city until its streets buzzed in her head.

She moved into Marcia's livingroom ahead of him with a hint of swagger in her walk—partly the boots, partly her good mood, partly her nausea at appearing in public with him that usually caused her to go sullen and stiffspined.

The room boiled at them. "Rowley, marvelous! Yes, I'm really leaving." Marcia embraced him gustily. From kelly green shadows her soft eyes inspected Vera. After introductions as they were turning away, Marcia pinched his arm. "Not bad. By the way, Anna's—let me see, where did she go?"

Across the room. Dark yellow Mexican sheath he had given her. In sensual repose against a doorway, the bow of her hip was taut for a tall guy who filled her ears, leaning close. Deeply she laughed. She never wore a girdle. He felt like touching her. Not gently. Like coming up behind and giving that shelving ass a pinch. As if his eyes hurt she twitched then and looked over her shoulder directly at him, without apparent surprise. Waved and turned back with that heavy flowing ease in her movements. He looked for Leon but could not find him. Maybe that was over. He felt no satisfaction. The guy in a tweedy sportsjacket, big build, peered at her bust. Suppose he was what she'd call handsome in a sort of openfaced rube way.

Some kids and some not danced by the phonograph. A girl with an ecstatic freckled revival-meeting face and long straight hair flying out, sharp pointy hips in orange pants, spun her ass like a propeller. Opposite a lean bored boy flopped. Two pretty brownhaired girls did a sedate roadrunner alongside. The talkers, his age or older, were nose to nose in every room. Permanent graduate students, lower to middle faculty, research types from the institutes, actors, personnel from FM stations and museums, proprietors of book shops or galleries, a smattering of editors and union staff, a psychiatrist, a poet, some social workers. No one on top. All partly defeated and partly on the make and partly arriviste. All interested in who were sleeping together, but more interested in who got the grant and who the ax. On sofas wives talked babies and appliances and the neighborhood association. Twenty percent black, thirty-five percent Jewish, more men than women, a good slice of the gay life.

"Well, Well!" Sally stood at his elbow: Marcia's roommate and once his. Curly darkbrown hair, blue eyes in a face of olive. She stood there squareshouldered with feet planted as if in oxfords, and shot off her eyes. Short, deepening lines dragged the corners of her mouth. "Your newest discovery is up to the mark. But young. Eighteen? So young, so dark, so fair—just what the hip folksinger brings to a party."

"With a little luck, sure. What are you doing these days?"

"Editing a reader on urban problems." Sally worked for a textbook house. She had been a poet. He had set one of her antibomb pieces and sang it, until? Until the bomb itself stopped being the focus.

"You writing anything?" he asked her.

The mouth dipped. "Some of us give up our youthful pretensions."

Sally herself had rather gained focus, in selfpity not to be explained by any event in particular: bitterness she had leaped into pulling the cover down. He felt sad seeing a woman he'd had rusting. She said to the world with her bitter mouth and squared off stance, You don't love me! Said the world, No

kidding. Patiently he waited for her to release him. Vera let
herself be talked at by a glib fairskinned Negro kid, well
tailored—what she would marry? Displaying before her an
inflated smirking male pride as no doubt he himself. Her
provoking air of resignation and mockery.

"I *asked* you if you'd talked to Anna lately?" Sally's voice
croaked with annoyance. "Anna Levinowitz. Remember
her? Or is that too ancient history?"

"I haven't seen her for a week or so. She's over there,"
he pointed, then saw that she wasn't.

"Oh, she just walked out with whoever that was." Her
large blue eyes blinked at him from that face of olive. "We
were all surprised that dragged on so long. Anna is such a
self-defeating person. Leaving graduate school to get married. Leaving her marriage for a quick affair."

"She's tougher than you think. And she would have walked
out of that marriage if she'd never met me."

"Is that what you tell yourself?" In blue-eyed wonder.
"Heard she'd been fired from her teaching job. Wonder what
she did?"

"Are you sure?"

"Some man hired her at the University. I thought you said
you'd spoken to her last week?"

Jesus, a couple of months sharing a bed five, six years
ago? and she thought she had a license for kicking him in the
shins every time they met up. Had it in for Annie, no known
reason. What would have got her fired from that sweatshop?

He joined Vera and they began making their slow way
toward some station people when Vera said, "Oh, there's
Caroline." Still wearing a coat she stood near the door talking to Marcia while her eyes combed the room. "She told
me she was coming tonight. She asked me special if we'd be
here."

"Yeah? Where's her boyfriend?"

"She said he couldn't come. She only has time to drop by
for a while."

He felt a vague uneasy boredom as Caroline steered toward them. She stopped to squeeze an arm or exchange a
hug, but she kept glancing in their direction to check that

they were waiting. By the time she came up to them she looked hot and fussed but kept on her coat.

"Hi, Vera doll, is that a mad dress. I love it! I'd give anything to have you make my clothes. Listen, come to the john with me for a moment, okay? We'll be right back. I have a personal favor to ask."

Now what? She had always been making sly suggestions that he push her as a folksinger. Yeah, out the window. He frowned after them, sucking on his cheeks. Caroline led the way with her hand on Vera's arm like a bracelet of flesh. Vera stepped along neatly just behind. Once she glanced back at him as they were going into the hall, a quick pout of what now? with a trace of smile and a tiny wave of her free hand.

He continued the interrupted journey to the group from the station. There were friends he never saw because they worked a different shift. Everybody was arguing about a new series they'd bought from the BBC. He kept his mouth shut and hoped nobody would find out he hadn't bothered to listen. A few minutes later he saw the girls already making their way back toward him. Vera was leading now, and when he saw her face, he excused himself brusquely and went to meet her.

She was walking stifflegged, her back tense and her face smoothed into that childish mask of no-one-home. Her eyes as he approached narrowed and spat at him a look of pure acid. I hate you, said the eyes, I hurt, I hate you.

He took her arm. "What's wrong?"

"What could be?" She stared at his hand on her arm. She made that arm stiff as fish skin under his palm. "Caroline has a few words for you."

"All right. Say them." He frowned.

Vera jerked her arm from him. "No. Get our coats."

"What's up?" He stepped close, meeting that scorched gaze.

"Nothing that won't come down. I would like my coat."

When they got outside Vera plunked herself down on the porch steps. "You go talk in the car. When you're done, blink the lights and I'll join you. Then you can take me home."

That he would settle later. He marched ahead of Caroline to the car, trying to figure out what in hell she could have told Vera. Getting in, she huddled in her coat. A faint smell of sweat came off her along with her perfume. Her hands sought each other. Caroline sitting in his car that warm night, hugging her own bare arms tentatively, at a different pitch of nerves. Annie felt he should just have turned her off—merely locate the switch. Who was that guy she left with?

"I didn't have a period last month." She waited. He turned, encountered her wet glance and shook it off, looked into the windshield instead. "I went to a doctor." Again she waited. Leaning on the wheel, he stared at the frozen street. Vera hunched in her coat on the steps. "I'm pregnant. I'm going to have a baby."

"You're getting married. Move up the date."

"I can't marry Bruce and have your baby!"

He cringed. "Marry Bruce and have Bruce's baby. I'm betting it's not mine."

"It has to be." Her voice leaked reproach. "I don't sleep with Bruce "

"In a pig's eye."

"It's true. He loves me. He wants to marry me."

"He loves you and doesn't touch. What do you do?"

Caroline pushed up the fur collar. "Besides, we did in Europe, then he decided we shouldn't till we're married. He'll know it isn't his, I mean it's physically impossible."

"Who else did you fuck during October?"

"Don't talk to me that way!" She flipped the collar down, turning to him. Large tears began to well from her eyes.

"It bugs me to hear you go on as if you had an inner voice could sort out the sperm and label that thing, Maybe by Rowley."

"I've been engaged. I only went to bed with you because I loved you. That was stronger than my engagement. But I haven't slept with anyone else since *July*, except for Bruce. It has to be yours."

Loved him. Hot pig meat.

"How can you sit there and treat me that way? No one has

the right to speak to me in that tone of voice! I loved you, and now I'm going to have your baby."

"You did not *love* me and I didn't *love* you. Is that what you told Vera in the head that got her mad?"

"I know you're dating her, but Vera doesn't like men. Her family would never let her become serious about somebody from a different background. Maybe you wouldn't expect that, but they're stand-offish. I asked her if she would mind if we started going together again, and she said, Of course not—"

"You stuck your foot in it."

"You can't be serious about her, and I have a right." She snuffled slightly. She had stopped crying. "Don't look at me that way! Do you think I'm enjoying this?"

"No. I think that, in a sly way, you expected to."

Her hand flopped in her lap. "You want to hurt me. You don't care any longer."

"Not you, and certainly not me, ever did." He forced himself to put out his hand and touch her arm—lightly, lightly, for fear she would turn and fall against him. "I'm sorry you're caught. Have you told your boyfriend?"

"Bruce? Of course not! I can't marry him now. He'd kill me if I told him!"

"He sounds like a gem. However."

"Everyone says he's on the way to being a very successful architect. Dad is going to have him do the new highschool." She slumped with hands to her cheeks, suddenly and truly aghast. "What a mess, oh, they'll never . . ."

"What kind of architect is he?"

"Oh, he must be good. He travels all over for redevelopers and people making subdivisions." She sat up, rooting in her purse for a handkerchief, which dispersed perfume on the frosty air.

Vera stirred on the step. Compacted and catlike. Goddamn it.

Her voice came out with a throaty quaver, "How can you question me about Bruce? I can only forget him." She turned her face into the path of the streetlight with lifted chin. Even now he was struck by how pretty she was, with soft mouth and melting long-lashed eyes.

"Want a baby?"

"If you want me to." Cautiously she smoothed at her hair, still holding that chin-up pose. She was offering what she had been taught to offer, her all-American playmate's face.

"Hell no. Look here," he said, "I can help you pay for an abortion and then you can marry your boyfriend and go on the way you were going. I'm short on funds but what I can scrape together, I will."

"You don't care if I die. If I can't have babies the rest of my life. No!"

"The Syndicate protects a man downstate, clean setup. If you don't like that, gynecologists in the Loop are available for the price of tears, crawling, and five hundred bucks."

"No. Why should I suffer?" The chin was down now, her fists clenched. She spoke with passion: cry of an angry child. "Why should I crawl? Or go to jail? Or let some horrible, dirty old man, no!" She cradled her belly. "I won't!"

"What do you want, Caroline? Get to the point. Vera's frozen by now."

"You can always go in and get warm. What do I want? You knew well enough what you wanted that night I told you Bruce was coming back and we were getting married."

He held his head in his hands. He felt like picking her up by the scruff and depositing her in the snow. Yet in the blue-green morgue light of the streetlamp he pitied her flowery face, her soft chin and soft body, her ridiculous dead animal collar and large compliant hands and hips and mouth. She probably sucked off her friend. He had never been convinced she enjoyed fucking. Her frenzy was all beforehand. Little lump of cells inside her going at it, half Caroline and half him if he could believe her.

"I'm not about to marry anybody. If I'd thought we had a strong thing going, I'd have let you know."

"You think you can get away with anything. You think you can just tell me, go away, and I'll disappear. My father would kill you, if he knew. He could do it, too."

"If you want to ditch this thing, I'll help you. If you want to have it, I'll help you. You'll let me know." He snapped the lights once, switched on the motor and hit the horn.

Stiffly Vera rose brushing snow from her coat and came toward them. With slow deliberation she walked and every tap of her boots on the sidewalk expressed distaste. Her gaze passed from one to the other with equal contempt. She got into the backseat without speaking. When she saw where he was going she spoke up. "You can drop me first."

"I can drop you second too. Hold on."

Caroline turned and said over the seat, "He won't marry me. He says he won't."

Vera said shortly, "Perhaps he'll change his mind."

After Caroline had gone tripping past the doorman, he drove a block before pulling over. "Would you come up front?"

"No thank you. This talk won't be a long one, and you can hear me well enough."

"But can you listen to me?"

"If I'd known there was a hanky-panky between Caroline and you, I'd never let you . . . see me. When she was staying with me, she was calling Santa Barbara every other night, so how was I to guess?"

"Hanky-panky is all there was. On that basis I am marching nowhere."

"That's your business. You'll do as little as you can get away with."

"Vera, listen. I did not pursue Caroline. I didn't even ask her, like. For you I'd feel responsible, because I've put a lot into this and asked a lot from you."

"I'm not surprised that a girl not pregnant should attract you more right now than another girl pregnant who attracted you last month. You know I'm not about to talk marriage, ever. Then let's keep quiet."

"Why are you riled up? I thought you'd guessed about Caroline."

"If she can't trust you, why should I?"

"Because I damn well never asked her to trust me."

"Well, I don't ask you to trust me. Or want me. Or pester

me. Or keep me sitting in this freezing car. I want to go home. I want to wash you off and forget you like a bad cold.''

"Stop slamming doors in my face!" He twisted around with the wheel jabbed into his ribs, shouting over the seat at her. A bitter fury took him when he saw from the depth of her anger how close to her he had got. He had got under her skin for real. His victory had not been sexual: he could not fool himself that he had moved her beyond simple bored acquiescence. But she had come almost into trusting him. "Tell me what you're blaming me for? Screwing around with Caroline before I met you?"

She pushed open the door and hopped out. "Your life disgusts me!"

He slid across and went after her, taking her by the shoulder. "Vera, get back in. We're not finished."

"Let go of me, or I'll start screaming."

Annoyed, he let go. "I'll take you home."

She got back, this time in front. "Then don't talk! What more could happen to me tonight?" Her voice was shrill, fraying. "Your talk makes me sick down to my shoes."

Hearing the pain in her voice he felt sick. He could have wrung Caroline by that soft throat. Coming and going she cast tacks under his wheels. He couldn't believe she had come to him tonight confident he would marry her. Of the girls he would not marry she was high on the list. If that made him a bastard, too bad.

Leaving the car doubleparked, grimly he followed her in. He felt ragged with helplessness. She half ran up the stairs. At her door she turned at bay. "Go home! Stay home! Keep your big feet out of my life!"

The door across the hall opened a crack. "Goodnight, Mrs. Martin," Vera said, biting her lip hard.

It was not in him to plead or wheedle, no more than he had with Anna. "Goodnight yourself, Vera, and sleep tight." He went down. The door slammed. He heard the lock turn over and the chain slide to. He went down, leaving her to the narrow bed, to the art nouveau rockingchair, to the worktable and sewingmachine and lesson plan for the second grade, to the sky of treetops and chimneys, to her neat tight body and her brother and her hard narrow life. Past old scents of soft coal, of child and animal piss, of chitterlings and disinfectant and cooked greens, he went down a staircase he would not climb again.

He drove home through the icy streets and found a parking spot three houses away, fatigue like lead in his boots. The Corporation had begun to tear down an apartment on the corner—and although it belonged to the University and they could have torn it down at any time, the sight had demoralized even the Defense Committee. The crane dwarfed the houses. He shouldn't have gone to the party. But Caroline would not have given up. He had a premonition she would be sitting on the front steps waiting, his special present from the world tonight.

He wanted to stop and talk to Harlan and pool their depressions. Harlan had been feeling really down. His job was easier on him than Harlan's—less pressure, less nonsense and a lot more joy. If he had lost interest, how did Harlan get through his welfare days? But the only light on the first floor was in their bedroom. He'd see Harlan tomorrow. They had to make a decision about trying to take their case to court.

So late and cold he was surprised not to find Yente at the door yowling, hammering his furry head against his pantleg. Maybe he'd begged his way in upstairs? The night was bitter cold. He called a couple of times, looked around a moment longer, then went in.

He was already asleep. He did not know what first made him wake, then know he had to get up. He had been asleep and he did not think he had heard anything, not anything real. But he got up, snapped on the light and pulled on his trousers and shoes.

When he opened the outside door he saw nothing and was about to shut it. His sleepy reflexes slowed the gesture long enough for him to catch sight of something moving under the steps. It moved again. An animal came dragging out. It pulled itself by its forepaws on the ice. It made a noise in its throat. As it dragged along in the ice it left bits of itself, charred flesh and burned hanks of hair. It came on toward him, dragging and made a noise in what had been its throat.

He knelt down. He did not know how to touch Yente, because he was burned too badly. Gasoline reek. Lynched cat. He tried to touch Yente's back, but half-mad with pain, the cat snapped at him and cowered. Then Yente stretched out his livid red and black neck, his scorched skin to which stuck patches of crisp hair, he craned out his neck and out of his one eye and out of his cooked opaque eye he looked and asked and made the noise in his throat.

Rowley knelt over him with his fists clenched. His eyes scalded. He felt guilty. He felt there must be something, something he could do that would turn Yente back into himself, return him as shaggy clumsy cat and make this tortured thing vanish. Napalmed cat. We do that to people every day. He shut the door and knelt over Yente. Yente was dying but slowly, slowly. He rolled to and fro in his frantic pain and made that noise. Gobbets of cooked meat came loose. The stench of burned hair and baked flesh. His fat smeared the floor. He rolled and snapped at himself. He turned to and fro, he crawled dragging toward Rowley's foot, making the noise.

Rowley straightened and went into the kitchen. He took from the knife rack the best knife. He could hear the noise behind him. He sharpened the knife on the grindstone. The knife swam and wavered and came back to itself.

He went back into the livingroom and knelt. Forcing himself to touch the charred living head, the blackened bone exposed over the cooked eye, he held the head and drew the knife across Yente's throat. The cat gave a weak spring as the throat opened and the blood came spilling over his hand. The noise stopped. The body shuddered, again, and went still.

He found a box for Yente and put him in. He wiped the floor as well as he could. He put the knife in the box too. Then he put on his coat, took the box and went out. He could not think where to put Yente, because the ground was frozen. There was never anybody to blame, for each man only does his job and hopes for a promotion to a job where he will do more of the same. There were only the needs of great organizations.

What could he do with his dead cat? He carried it to the house of the chancellor of the University and put the box down before the door. That was the best he could do, though he did not hope that anyone would understand his justice. He did not care. He had no place to bury Yente. He went home and went back to bed. It was very cold in his apartment. He thought it was the coldest it had ever been.

Friday, December 19—
Saturday, December 27

"I don't want Whitey in my house. That's all."

"Don't throw slogans at me. I've never been Whitey before, and it's not me who's changed."

Harlan reached up. His fingers brushed a pipe. "Can't help it. I'm not saying I'm sorry. What's the use? There's only so much water in the bucket and it's all gone dry."

"They push you back toward the ghetto, so you turn and leap in."

"I can't balance my mind like a tray of dirty china any more. Let it fall, let it drop, let it bust. I'm making allowances for nobody. I'm done giving credits or green stamps."

Harlan looked tired through and through. He'd lost weight and he was down to sore nerves. Rowley looked aimlessly around his livingroom trying to think how to reach him. "It wasn't the way you lived, when you could help it. Now you hang a big sign on me Whitey, Guilty. I'm not taking that sign."

"That's your problem. I can't afford to care about your feelings. Besides, I can't have you in the house and join the FBM. They wouldn't take me. Not that I'll be having a house long."

"The Free Black Militia. Of all the pseudo-fascist splinters."

"You can't win from the city and all you win in court is words. I can't work for them any more. I played into their hands too long. Riding herd on poor black girls with their miserable illfed kids, driving them out of their heads trying to find out if they're getting any. I've had it. Please, White Father, let me pay twice as much for this lousy little house and you can forget about cleaning the streets and picking up the garbage, we'll just eat it. At least in the FBM they're men."

"It's not the black supremacy stuff per se that bugs me. It organizes people who have to be organized, and what group doesn't think they're God's own peepers? But this talking violent is an old scene. When violence hits, who gets their heads broken?"

"You lose every time till you win. But that's how you get pride."

"Look, the less actual channels exist for action—given the being hurt, the anger and outrage—the tendency exists for the words to get hot. Like the Wobblies who talked sabotage a lot more than they practiced it—but the union got broken and the leaders jailed for enraging the public. If you talk violent enough you get the government down on you. Are you going to fight the real estate interests and the corporate interests with codewords and karate practice?"

"This society is trying to box me, is trying to tear my balls off and stuff them down my throat. I got to fight. But not fair any more. I can't afford it."

"You're saying I got hurt, so I don't care how effective this action I'm going to take is. It's an outlet for my feelings. The race be damned."

"When they drive the nails in you, let's hear what you yell. You're yelling now, cause you been comfortable and now you're getting pushed around a little. I'm saying they're killing me, and I'm going to choose my death. And it sure won't be ulcers or hypertension. And I'm telling you, clear out of my house."

He looked at Harlan. His shoulders felt heavy with sadness

and the acid residue of useless anger. "I'll move out tomorrow."

Harlan shrugged, looking away. "You're paid up to the end of the month. Just start looking."

"I'll move tomorrow. But we'll both be poorer for this, and I don't mean at the end of the month."

"Don't you see why I feel like a fool?"

"No. I'm the fooled one. I thought I belonged here."

"Look, I had you into my house and we pretended like this is a world where that makes sense, where people are naturally together. All the time my black brothers *need* places to live, need them desperately. You can find yourself an apartment anyplace. We have been pretending, and that's why I say we are both fools."

"When you got this house you wanted your mother upstairs of you and me downstairs, because we were friends. If none of that finally worked, it's not hard to see why, but it sure doesn't mean it's wrongheaded to try . . . I'll have my stuff out by supper time."

He parked his boxes in the basement of a friend's house. If it were spring he had the feeling he would keep on going down to the hiring hall and sign on a lake freighter.

> *Done laid around, done stayed around*
> *This old town too long*

Herb let him sleep on his couch, a thin pillgulping announcer born of the alliance of American Legion and WCTU in the dry prosperous northern suburb of Evanston, born wrong and running. Since Herb had just been divorced again and was sleeping at his new girl's, there was little pressure on Rowley to look for a place.

Herb had a suite in an apartment hotel a couple of blocks from the lake on Wilson Avenue halfway up the North Side— a location chosen by the vectors pulling him: Evanston, Loop job, girl on the near North Side, exwives and children in suburbs. A gamy and exhausting neighborhood with cheap kitchenettes jowl by jowl with uniformed doormen, girlie

bars, secondhand stores and the rococo Waikiki nightclub.
Rowley was growing his moustache again and out-of-work
men in bars with veins of steel string, hill twang in their
voices wanted to pick fights. Like the men in the mills. Men
he would belong with except for the University, except for
his music with its black roots. Under the El on Broadway the
stores were festooned with plastic poinsettias. In the lobby
an aluminum tree turned bathed in a blue spot.

Christmas Eve at cocktail time he was leaving the studio,
passing the Blackhawk, when the Lovises emerged with a
small party. Tom was thick with a portly tanned old man,
but Nina svelte in leopardskin saw him. Saw him, looked,
looked through him. Turned away her perfect chin and
slipped her arm through Tom's, laughing.

Christmas he worked the six A.M. shift. Then he drank
sour mash while a blizzard howled in the streets, and played
Herb's records. After a while he took out his Gibson instead
and began to feel a little action in his blood. Herb was off
splitting Christmas among his previous begotten households
and his girl, with a visit to god's country also on schedule.
He would arrive late and drunk. A mirror was hung to reflect
the couch, giving him the feeling of the WCTU watching.
Feet up he played and sang to himself:

> *Did you ever wake up lonesome—all by yourself,*
> *Yeah, did you ever wake up lonesome, all by yourself,*
> *And the one you love was loving someone else?*
> *My friends don't see me, they just pass me by,*
> *Yeah, my friends don't see me, they just pass me by,*
> *Wouldn't mind it so much, but they hold they heads so high.*

Ragged moustache, leathery face, bloodshot eyes. He looked,
he felt, mean. So, so let her go, he thought about Vera with
a raw angry ache. He lacked the gall to try her iron virginity
again. He missed the way she tilted her head, her fresh laugh
and the taut line of her thighs. But he could not want to see
her. Nothing to say.

> *That makes me evil, oh Lord, so evil,*
> *Yea, I get evil, baby, when my love comed down.*

Caroline carrying that lump she called his. She had phoned before he left Harlan's and gotten truly angry, truly indignant. She could get in touch with him through the studio. He knew his mother and Sam were disappointed he did not come to Gary, but he could not face them, play older brother and sturdy son, play man with the answers. He didn't feel like going to work or fucking or talking.

If you want to have plenty women why not work at the Chicago mill?
You don't have to give them nothing, oooh well, just tell them that you
will.

After Harlan bought the house they'd gone to see his mother. Harlan wanted her to live upstairs and he told Rowley that they'd just go and move her. A hot dusty July day. She had been living with one of Harlan's half sisters on South Buffalo but they were all gone. Rowley sat in the car while Harlan asked around and finally they found them a couple of blocks away on Green Bay, living in a shotgun house—the rooms getting smaller as it backed off the street.

His mother would not move though it was obvious they were in bad times. "At first I didn't like Shirley for nothing," his mother said, shaking her head with a blank, benign smile. "Now I know she good for you. But she wouldn't be good for me. Now every week I wonder how are we gonna do, how are we gonna make out. But if I come and live with you, I know how: war!"

They went out with two of the boys to a shingled rickety corner store for icecream and beer and a few groceries. A little money infused in the house made everybody happy. Mrs. Williams cooked a crazy hot chicken stew that Harlan and Rowley ate till they were stuffed. Near the turning basin in Calumet Harbor. Cottonwood, sumac, patches of tall weeds. A rubble dump and towers of high tension wires. Railroads crossed at grade level. Dogs trotted through the dusty streets and kids hung around on the corners. Remote, hot, isolate. Ships came and went slowly, potently, past the scrawny handmade looking houses. Near the grain elevators a big gray ship was hosed down. Highway 41 stood up on end to let a frighter pass. In the sky trucks trundled along the expressway. A concrete rainbow of no particular promise arched over the deadend houses. Harlan stayed hours past the time he had promised to be home, and he did not go out to a payphone and call Shirley, he ate supper and drank with his brother-in-law and nephew and mother, ate till he hurt, laughed himself silly: and that day they were close and understood each other without needing to talk about it. Gone.

Maybe in a place like that he'd turn up Black Jack. He had let that slip, let that go. Maybe it was the one real thing left for him to do. The one person he could talk to, that he had anything to say to. And one other. On the seventh day of his drinking, Saturday, he rose and drove in glittery sunshine past the frozen baroque of the lake to the South Side to see Leon, for friends are friends and what the hell.

He remembered how he had come in that morning, stopping off on his way to class to shower and change, and found Leon. When he went to see Leon in the hospital and after, he had felt closer to Leon than Leon felt to him. Then Leon got married and moved out.

Leon had admired him, imitated him, dogged him. He was a shy pimply suburban kid. When he got excited his voice would go way up. He was so awkward around girls that he sounded rude. Sometimes he courted insult. Always he came obliquely at what he wanted. Grimacing, Rowley called up time after time when he had known what Leon was getting at (wanting to meet a girl, wanting to be taken along, wanting Rowley to say out loud that he was welcome, wanting Rowley to come out to his folks' house with him) and pretended not to, pretended to him and Leon that as long as Leon hadn't spoken out loud, there had been no communication. Why? His mean streak, only. Leon had been a vulnerable kid, and they'd all had a crack at hardening him. Yes, meanness.

The plateglass window was steamed up. When he banged on the door he could hear Leon moving but when the door opened, Annie stood there. She stared. He thought she was about to slam the door before she produced a broad smile, perhaps at her own shock, and motioned him in.

Her dark tangled mane was caught back on her nape. She wore no makeup. Her face was flushed with exertion and looking around he saw a vacuum cleaner plugged in. The room looked bigger, lighter than he remembered. She seldom wore levis—thought herself too broad in the beam—but she was wearing them now with a striped jersey. She looked younger, leaner, yet domestic: the vacuum, the splash of cleanser on her pantleg.

"Leon's out, probably for the day. Let me think where you could look . . ."

"Forget it. I'll catch him some other time. Are you living here?"

"Me? Sure."

His impulse was to march out but he was too curious, too annoyed. He sat down heavily. "You've left your mark. Can Leon bear it?"

"He likes it clean, but it's hard for him to throw junk out. He hoards every last butt and popbottle of his life. I understand that, I'm enough that way myself. Maybe I'll learn to dispose of my own collections." She laughed easily, throwing herself into the chair opposite. Quickly her eyes covered the room, measured her progress and allotted herself a break. Her embarrassment had evaporated, and obviously she was relaxed with him as any casual visitor.

That was her style. A little bitterly he recognized the ease with which she had played hostess to married couples and bachelor friends. Once Herb had fluttered round her in the kitchen while she was making sesame lamb: she had turned on him and said sweetly if he did not exit at once she would roast him. Herb had scurried into the livingroom, convinced that she would. She presided where she sat now ankles crossed and head pensive on hand, eyes cleaning the rest of the room.

"Been living with Leon long?" He wanted to ask her what had become of that independence she used to rub his nose in.

"My building's coming down. Half the tenants are out and the city's using indirect persuasion. Heat's off. Last week two people got mugged in the upstairs hall. So Leon insisted

I clear out, and I'm staying here—my stuff's still in my apartment—and looking for a place." Her large eyes flashed over him.

"I'm looking for one myself."

"Is Harlan down already? My god."

Then he wanted to tell her. He wanted to talk about it and he did, even drawing out the story. Trying to convince himself? Or trying to make her react to him?

"You shouldn't have left like that, getting your back up. How do you know he wouldn't have changed his mind? He was sore. You have to leave doors open for people."

"I've never been able to force myself on somebody or stand around biding my time while they cool down." He was doublesaying but damned if she got it.

"But you've known him so long. It has to heal."

"Nothing *has* to work out." He shrugged. She was insufferably friendly, helpful, remote. He felt like punching her. "I didn't mean to startle you. Just looking for Leon. Had no idea you were here."

"It's just that you've been the missing man all week." Pushing the hair from her face she smiled into a corner of the room, smile of recollection and something harder. "Caroline's been around."

"Did she come to you with that story too?"

"Too?" Her gaze twitted him. "She's been crying on Leon's shoulder, and you'll admit, won't you, she has something to cry about? Couldn't you have been more careful?"

"Caroline can reach me through the station any time she wants."

"It's all coming down on Leon. Clearly he invites people to use him. Me, for instance, now. But still—"

"Are you saying you're staying here platonically?"

She looked at him levelly. The amusement that had been working in her face along with a submerged tension, surfaced. "I am neither saying that nor its opposite. I am not saying anything like that, since it's clearly none of your business."

"Insofar as I know both of you—"

"Oh, in a way." But she was not truly interested in scoring off him. "I'm scared Leon will let her use him."

He was not grateful she had let him off. "I think you'll find Leon taking care of himself. He never gets more involved with a woman than he means to."

She made a wry face. "You're both bigger improvisors than the other thinks."

She was wrapped in Leon like a flag. "I was always defending Leon and you were wondering why. If we've changed sides, it's not because Leon's changed any. He's the same confused guy."

"As Leon says, last year I didn't see who he was. He claims Caroline has to be made to see who he is, in a similar way. I'm scared that she will and take him for the patsy he is. I mean, in regard to her."

"You have the field in hand."

She threw that away with her right hand. "But her need, her obvious urgent need is much greater."

He felt dizzy. The conversation proceeded by rules known to her, not to him. He had a sore urge to make her talk about him instead of Leon. "Are you straight that I should marry her?"

"I know you're not up to that. Besides, I wouldn't, but I'm prejudiced, as Leon says. I told Leon in September you wouldn't marry her."

"Thanks. I could have told him that in March. You know Vera broke up with me over this?"

She nodded. "Paul's relieved, of course. By the way, how is that fight coming? Are things happening there?"

"What are you talking about?"

"Where Vera teaches. The parents were trying to get the Board of Ed to bus the kids out to white schools with room. Finally they got fed up and then they were organizing to try to take over the school. You know anything recent?"

He did not know anything unrecent. How little Vera communicated to him. "I knocked on that door a long time. That's all I know."

"Paul's a strange one too. Unlike Leon, I liked to see them together. They played with style. That moved me."

There she coiled in the chair, the bow of her hips, breasts rubbing against the striped jersey. That he couldn't have her if he wanted seemed unreasonable. She had passed beyond him, miles past Sally bitter still at the party. Anna was not bitter. He had the bizarre feeling he could tell her his troubles and she would listen and cluck, thinking of Leon all the while.

"Leon says you're being nasty to Caroline because you feel guilty. And I do think you could make your position clear without being brutal. It isn't her fault you knocked her up."

"If you use the expression 'Leon says' once more, I'll pick you up and shake it out of you."

She laughed. "Ah well, new disciples are the most earnest."

"What are you a disciple to?"

"You've never taken him seriously."

"Once or twice," he said dryly.

"Well then." She shrugged her round shoulders. He caught her glancing at the clock.

"If you'd got stuck I wouldn't have felt this way."

"Gee thanks, dad. Why don't you go talk to her?"

"Instead of hanging around here? I can't argue her into an abortion. Jesus, she'll be some mother."

"Leon thinks motherhood will redeem her—in spite of what it did to Joye. He has his illusions. Thinks it will fulfill her."

"What would fulfill that girl? Disneyland?"

"Are you finding her a nuisance?" she asked with syrup and looked openly at the clock.

So he left. Climbing over a snowbank to the VW he shook his head. Then he grinned.

He used the newspaper first and then walked the streets. Got two narrow rooms at the top of a gray stone building back up in Herb's neighborhood, but on a poor scroungy street. A real place anyhow. To begin trying to figure out who the hell he was now. He wrote a check, got the key and sat back to the wall on the floor of the room with the bay. Not even shades. A period in his life had closed down. In almost all ways a good one but defunct, already the stuff of nostalgia and revision. In the interstices of a rich society he had lived. A society that paid him to entertain it and to preserve pieces of its urban folklore for future entertainment,

and paid him better than his father had ever been paid for
making its steel. Now he was cutting down his standard of
living. He was preparing for something else.

Cracks, crevices. One time he had stayed in the Mecca
with a friend, jazz composer who was making a living playing cocktail piano. He was working the freighters then, he
was in between and somebody was getting married. So he
slept at Fred's.

The Mecca had been built in the nineties as a fancy U-
shaped block. Inside you walked down block-long arcades
dim and echoey with the only light leaking through skylights
four floors up and sixty years of city grime. Wrought iron
balconies. Two thousand people lived there. It hummed. No
sound came at you sharp. The building mumbled, kids playing in the interior streets, people yelling off the balconies,
music. An elderly white woman lived there and a girl married
to a bass player, but aside from them the only whites he saw
those ten days were a bill collector and a social worker. Torn
down. Two thousand gone noplace as cheap. Another institution ate it. He had lived in the cracks where people could
now and then get together, disaffiliated but easy among themselves, and when a crack closed he found a new one. Thus
he had lived in his society without confronting it, and now
he did not know where to begin.

Saturday night. Not the local bars yet. He drove back down
to Woody's. He drank at the bar, keeping to himself. He
wanted to prolong his new mood until he understood it. He
felt the bones of his life setting into a new form. He had been
passive for too long. Vera had finally crawled into his arms
because he seemed less menacing than the rest of the world.
He had not been honest with her. He had waited around until
she had shown him how she should be seduced. He had failed
to make her want the risks he offered. Leon had been more
successful with Anna: Leon had taken thorough possession.
How much did he dislike that?

The beer made him feel bloated, so he switched to bour-
bon. He drank more from the habit of the week than desire
for that thickening of mind tonight. Several thoughts seemed
on the point of articulating themselves, but never came

through. At the bar no enlightenment was going to descend. But he stood there and drank because he considered the night wasted already and because he did not want to go to Herb's couch but hardly relished sleeping on the bare floor. He exchanged a few words with friends but stayed at the bar because he felt too clotted with ideas and longings to talk.

The guy had been standing beside him a couple of minutes before he felt the stare on his face and turned. A guy his height, fairhaired, whose face was reddened with a tightly reined anger. A guy who stood in Woody's as if it stank in his nostrils, who wore a handsome tweed overcoat, leather gloves, and a hat. The hat should not be forgotten.

"You're George Rowley?" The thin lips opened just enough to emit the words. Piss on the tongue. "I'm Liggott. Bruce Liggott."

He waited, puzzled. Guy wanting to pick a fight?

"Bruce Liggot, Caroline's fiancé."

"Oh." He looked into the blue eyes squinched with anger. He wanted to laugh, but invisibly.

"Are you coming outside, or do I hit you here?"

"Sure. Outside we go." He finished the shot he didn't want and waved at Gus. Paid him. Followed the back of that handsome tweed overcoat out. Man to man. The jerk kept marching around the corner, toward the alley. On the way they passed a Jag at the curb. Caroline lowered the window as they went by and opened her mouth. Under the greenish streetlight her face looked pale, her open mouth very dark. She did not speak. Her breath stirred the fur of her collar. Rowley followed the jerk into the alley.

Anna

Friday, December 19—
Saturday, December 27

"It was a goddamn madass stupid thing to do. Get yourself
kicked out of school. Find yourself drafted next, cannon fodder. Jesus, you were thinking with your elbows!"

"It's not clear I'll be kicked out. And those people are
losing their homes."

"So you want to be a hero," Leon muttered. "Fight cops,
look for a little action. Fed up with your own life and problems. Time to run around the streets and feel like a man."

"If a student isn't a man, what am I? Come on, these are
my problems. I'm as black as anybody in those streets."

"How much you got in common with a numbers runner?
Think you could talk to him for five minutes? He's going to
find you white. It's like I decided to identify with the Jews
in the Mea Shearim who throw rocks at tourists."

"Maybe I have to talk to him. Maybe he has to talk to me.
Maybe that's the problem." Paul slipped down on the couch
with his legs stuck way out, his hands in fists.

Leon rubbed his hands against the cold. "Look, maybe
I'm no one to talk. I got myself tossed out for boosting books.
But—"

"It's not the same thing!"

"Damn straight it's not. I needed the bread."

"Look. You're telling me I was raised lucky." Paul felt
for the words. "The cost of being black has eaten me less

229

maybe than the cost of being a Jameson. Of course people have kicked me in the face and so on—"

"Has anybody ever kicked you in the face, I mean for real?"

"Of course not," Paul said. "You know what I mean."

"You know what I mean too," Leon drawled.

Oh god. She stared from one to the other. What was eating Leon?

"I was trying to say that being black had worked to my advantage too. Not for Vera, even. I could choose my school. I got a good scholarship. Frats approached me. The first thing I liked about you was that you didn't come any further for me than for anybody else—you came that far for everybody."

"But now you don't listen. You don't ask advice. You go around with plans in your head you're not open about—"

"A thing I had to do. Since I went to those hearings."

"With your sister and Rowley. He's all for dashing around. If he's a sort of sloppy pink it's because it runs in his family, like being Baptist or Lutheran. Sing him 'Solidarity Forever' and he takes off his cap. Mushy politics, mushy thinking, mushy feeling."

Paul was drawn up now, staring. "Who cares about my inner hangups? Haven't you said time and again you can tell a person's real ideas by what they do? What they put on the line?"

"What did you put on the line playing tag with a bulldozer? Throwing rocks at a wrecking ball, is that what you think?"

Paul shook his head helplessly. "The bad part was, there were some black guys on the wrecking crew. They felt like we were trying to take their jobs away. They were ready to fight us."

" 'I can hire one half of the working class to kill the other half.' Jay Gould. A favorite quote of Rowley's. Throwing yourself at a bulldozer can't do anything only because the wrong man is driving it."

They looked at her blankly. Intruding in their private quarrel. Leon felt betrayed because Paul had acted without him.

Paul felt betrayed because Leon could not understand his act. They nursed their betrayals. It ended with Paul walking out, slamming the big door so the glass rattled.

Leon sat in a thick brutish silence, picking his nose. On the sagging couch she skimmed the newspaper fat with Christmas ads. "Why are you taking it this way?"

He gave her a grimace deploring stupidity. He looked sunk into his chair. His depression yellowed the air.

"Want to go to a movie?"

"We've seen everything twice."

"We could go to Woody's."

"Alcohol is a notorious poison."

"Are you hungry? How about a pizza?"

"We're always feeding our faces. You never think of anything else."

"So get out the projector."

"Why don't you just ask me to slit my throat?"

"It's a pity you don't have music," she said helplessly.

"Joye took the hi fi. That bitch."

She did the supper dishes and read and worried. The rooms were cold and she fiddled with the stove. Then it was late and Leon stirred himself and they went to bed: like husband and wife, unspeaking, indifferent, in the double bed.

After five minutes of dark he poked her with his elbow. "Hey, you want to?"

She laughed and put her arm around him. She had no sense of doing a new thing. His warm, blocklike, somewhat inert hairy body was familiar. Worry had left acid in her muscles, and she could not gather herself into great excitement. The room was cold and its iron air pressed on them. They huddled under the full load of covers awkward, fumbling, patient. Like children, children figuring it out. They were quiet. She felt a little shy. He was gentle, his hands and mouth light, cool, careful—leaves on her.

They wriggled out of their clothes. Side by side they lay under the blankets and quilt and shifted here and gave there and poked around until he had come into her and still they were side by side facing. Slowly he moved in her and she seconded him cautiously. The bed hardly creaked. Every once in a while he would slip out. Each time he fitted himself back she grew more excited. Coming into her freshly he felt hot. Side by side they lay at ease except for the slow cautious fuck with its more and more but still localized excitement.

It was a game: that each scarcely moved. That she held her breath tightly controlled and never let it break from her. That his hands on her and hers on him were casual open palms that did not close. The roots of the game ran into childhood furtive curiosities and explorations, into the attics and basements and garages and tents of that first green and snotty sex. They did not challenge or threaten. Side by side they met in subtle exercise and the excitement was local and intense as an itch and full of teasing.

He worried about everyone, she thought, but no one took care of him. She would love him gently, almost remotely. What came off him more and more strongly as she knew him was a sense of waste, of good human material and strength and caring and willingness, wasting. She must stop tending her independence, stop worrying so much about herself, and see what happened.

She woke before him. She was already bathed and dressed and making coffee when the phone rang. She stood over it biting her lip, then answered.

Paul asked her, "Is he still mad?"

"Wait a second." Going quietly to the door she looked in. He slept on his stomach with his hands tucked under. "He's still sleeping. Why don't you call back in a couple of hours?"

"I'll be gone. I'm on disciplinary probation—a drag but could have been worse. But I'd better go home and explain it to the old man. I've been talking to Vera and she thinks we can put it across to him in a way he can take . . . What's wrong with Leon anyhow?"

"You didn't discuss it with him first. He can't see any way to act himself, so he can't help jumping when somebody else gets moving."

"I'll have it out with him when I get back. Hey, how come you answered? Suppose I'd been his exwife or his mother?"

What the hell, Paul was on her side. "Think I'll move in. Might as well."

"Does that mean what I think?"

"You have a dirty mind. Anyhow, we can try it. So don't worry about him."

"Because you'll take care."

"I will try, baby."

"He's come to his senses. Don't get married till I get back, okay?"

Later she was glad she had talked to Paul, because that confirmed her memory. Nothing else did. Leon got up groggy and dawdled over breakfast. Then scowling into the mirror at length and squeezing imaginary pimples on his nose, he listened to her tell him part of the phonecall from Paul.

"Back into that bag again. Jesus Christ. Hopeless kid. He'll be back, but if he thinks I'm going to sit here and listen to him rap about his independence with a straight face . . ."

Probably she would not have brought up moving in except that when he took her home, Matt Fenn opened his door as if he had been waiting and put out his still bandaged head.

"Well! I'm not the only victim, and now they're not waiting till the middle of the night! That poor old pensioner Mrs. What's-her-name who's always coughing. Well! When she came in yesterday evening, no later than seven-thirty, she was knocked down right in the hall. She was pushed to the floor and her purse snatched from her hand. How do you like that?"

Leon turned a face of disgust. "You got to get out of here. What are you waiting for, to get raped?"

She left most of her things, for she was by no means sure she could live with him. With only a suitcase, a few cookbooks and a box of toiletries, she shifted roofs.

Monday she edited interviews: A noted Negro urologist, happy owner of an early Frank Lloyd Wright, pointed out that the planners were professionals and just as when a person grew ill he must call on top professional advice, thus when a neighborhood ailed and grew blighted . . .

A lady high in UNA spoke of the pains and pleasures of

working with various officials, the planners, and Sheldon Lederman, that wise and slippery facilitator. If he respected one, she implied, he revealed charm and even honesty. His most dubious maneuvers were carried out with a twinkle, so to speak—and without his ability and contacts and political acumen, where would they be? The neighborhood had lost more of its important families than it could afford, but since Sheldon and his superiors had entered the scene, new confidence had been infused among the stable elements.

Certainly the planners had revealed themselves responsive to the public. When she and her neighbors had noticed certain homes belonging to desirable elements were scheduled for demolition, they had gone to the planners. Not just to carry on, mind. It was wise to have alternate proposals when dealing with busy people, and the offstreet parking problem had to be dealt with. They suggested tearing down the Tyler Hotel—a place with a poor reputation and a late hours bar, and the planner had obliged.

It was her feeling that local groups could accomplish much if they didn't imagine that officials were against them but saw them as busy hardworking people. Instead of shouting one should sit down and work through the problems on an unofficial basis in a mutually considerate way. Her father, Judge Alwyn, had often said, Never push someone by taking a public stand if you can avoid it, and she thought it good advice.

The last interview was with an organizer working for a grubby tenant organization in a nearby area. He fenced with the interviewer, who tried to get him to admit he was involved behind the scenes with the Defense Committee. He delighted in going off in long explanations of what his group was doing in their own neighborhood. He was, the interviewer noted, young, shaggy, dressed in a work shirt. He left abruptly to keep an appointment with a building inspector, saying he was sorry he couldn't throw the bull longer as he always enjoyed meeting people from the University when they came into his area for any other reason than to tear it down.

"Something wrong?" asked Miss Cavenaugh.

"Maybe not. See you later." She put on her coat, picked up an envelope at random from her out-basket and headed for a payphone. She asked for the name from the interview. He was not in.

"Look," she said to the young suspicious voice in the receiver. "From the interview I just wanted to pick up on what you're doing." Only she did not even know what questions to ask. She got the address, another name, left the phonebooth feeling silly and vaguely expectant.

The next day she called in sick to ISS and went over. The office was a storefront—a couple of desks and tables, posters of Che and Malcolm, a phone, a mimeograph machine and a hot plate. Except for a Puerto Rican woman from the neighborhood, everybody was younger. She talked mainly to Rick, a short pudgy growly-voiced kid with rimless glasses and an intense brown stare. They were living off the neighborhood, occasional contributions and what they made on a paper they put out.

"You couldn't live on less than what I used to get downtown, believe me."

But they did. She shuddered and persisted. They were organizing a tenant's union, there was a day-care community school project, they had picketed a few landlords and held a rent strike. They were keeping an eye on the University's real estate dealings. They were starting some draft work. There was a staff meeting late in the afternoon and she stayed for it. It was agreed she would start coming in on weekends. In the meantime she would give notice. By the first week in January if she still wanted and worked out, she could come on staff, a mix of students, neighborhood people and two organizers. "But everybody's an organizer," they said. "You'll see."

The street outside was crowded. The squat weight of the El kept off the mean sky and kept in the precious heat of cars and bodies. At four it was dark. Neon sputtered under the girders, spicy barbecue smoke, roasted chicken. A player's street where boys and girls learned young what they could sell and what they could buy.

As she turned north into a sidestreet the air felt colder,

harder. The day was stiff and windless with a light dry snow flaking down on patches of slick ice or black heaps of rocky old snow. Going home to Leon she felt good and stopped to buy a chucksteak, ripe bananas and sourcream and a frenchbread.

The kids working for the project were most of them living close by the office, and in the back of her head she could hear Harlan's sarcastic voice, "Yes, them poor sentimental old maids at Hull House didn't comprehend how social work had to be done. They done it social-like. Moved right into the neighborhood, soaked themselves in it. No wonder they got to agitating for new laws. They didn't comprehend the first thing about how you treat a client, and how people turn into cases and how many cases make a load. If the client wasn't sick, would he be a client? The problem is obviously with him."

Fall, a year ago. The Gypsys were arriving in Maxwell Street for the winter, setting up in storefronts. Pushcarts heaped with old toasters and chipped pots and transistor radios and doublebreasted suits and patched galoshes. Parodies of her father tugged at her, wizened, insistent. The old ghetto. From a Mexican lunch wagon they'd brought long green banana peppers that had been so burning hot she had cried out with pain and had to drink soda while Harlan and Rowley laughed at her and ate more of the damned fiery things, showing off.

Nearby on Blue Island they used to go to a Greek place that had good cheap lamb and retsina. Sailors in from Greek ships would get up to dance to the funky wailing clarinets, when the bellydancer or the sturdy fatlegged singer wasn't on. She had been by lately: gone. Another institution had expanded. The people living there had shown a sense of possession and roots hard for the power structure to credit. But their misfortune was that their roots were set into land too near the Loop, part of that coming golden girdle of high rise, high income apartments, new glass office buildings, institutional complexes and expressways to seal off the financial heart from the festering human stockyards. Hull House was a redbrick sore thumb amputated in the failure of what it stood for.

Should she really quit her job and the University matrix? Cross to the other side. Exactly what did she still fear? They weren't bribing her with much. The difference of a couple of new dresses and a coat. Better to get a new mind and a new body. It was her only life spending in their cycle of the meaningless into the pernicious. The job was aging her into a toady, a technical serf, a cog squeaking and grinding as the machine turned out its nets of social control.

Lights on. With packages in her arms she did not fish for her key but banged until Leon came. He looked at her blankly. His face was blotchy with excitement. His orange hair stood on end. Caroline sat sharply erect on the couch gaping. A twinge went through Anna at her breast. Nodding she went directly into the kitchen to put the groceries away. "Stay to supper. We'd love to have you."

"Oh dear no, I can't," Caroline said. "It must be late. How the afternoon went. I had a million things to do, too."

Anna turned to see her come close to Leon and pat his cheek. "You've been tremendous, really. After all!"

"Let me know what you decide, hey?" He stood awkwardly. His face was heavy with feeling, his voice thick. "Don't forget!"

"I have to talk to him again. He has to reconsider, I mean—"

He gave a harsh laugh like a bag popping. "Listen, forget him. Don't let it get you down." Lightly he hit her shoulder. "Don't panic. Above all, don't panic."

"You've been a darling, Leon."

"So call. Let me know what's happening. If you feel down—"

"Thanks, love. I don't know what I'll do, I just don't know." She held out her cashmere trenchcoat, and after a moment he grabbed it and helped her in. When she had left he rubbed steam from the plateglass and squinted out. His face was a mask of interesting pain. He looked years younger and shriveled.

He wandered around holding himself by the arms, went

to the window to rub steam and look out at nothing, gave the mobile of bicycle parts a tinkling shove to send it grinding through space above his head floating soot and dustclots down.

"Hey!" he shouted. "I don't know, let's get a Christmas tree."

"What for, Jew? With a blond angel on top?"

"And a baby underneath." He snickered. "Caroline's knocked up. You hear me?"

"So. She's getting married."

"It ain't his. It's Rowley's."

"How does she know?" She felt like pulling a knife from the rack and driving it into the wall. Into Caroline. "She has a third eye?"

"From dates. Has to be his."

She snorted. "I bet that paternity changes three times in the next three weeks. She'll have you convinced it's yours, by telepathy."

"Anyhow, he won't marry her. Just said a flat No."

"I'd hope not." Bang with a pot on a burner. "I sure wouldn't."

"She still hopes he will, but she'll realize."

"I'm surprised he didn't offer to help her with money?"

"For an abortion. Sure. Cut it out and forget it."

"If she wants the baby, it's to put him in the wrong."

"She wants the baby like any normal woman. She's opting for reality."

"I wouldn't call it that. What about her boyfriend?"

"She says he'll take off when she tells him." He rubbed his fingers across his mouth. "So she came to me. Finally. I told you it would pay off in the end. Patience. The waiting game."

His pale blue eyes grew still on her, perceived she had interests. "Aw, who knows?"

She gave notice at ISS. Leon was not pleased but he could not spare the energy to argue with her. He called Caroline at least twice a day and late every night. His voice thickened and softened and died into soft mumbles. She was afraid

Caroline would use him, then toodle-oo. She offered to look for an apartment but he frowned and said, Ah what's the hurry? His caginess amused her. Indeed, he hated to live alone. Would he like both of them? She wondered at her lack of indignation.

Friday he came home with a thin feral grin. He held up his paycheck by a corner. "Take a good look. One more arrives and that's it, kiddie."

"The project's over? I thought it had a month or more."

"It, not me. Haven't been completing enough interviews lately, they tell me. Destroying social science single-handed."

"What are you going to do?"

He shrugged heavily. "There's always the post office."

Saturday morning Caroline called while he was still in bed, and within forty-five minutes he was dressed and out, leaving her astounded and wryly amused. She had just started cleaning when someone knocked. Oh, she hoped it was Caroline, that they'd missed connections, because she wouldn't mind at all having a few private words. She opened the door and there stood Rowley. Perhaps she was too startled to feel anything. He jumped to see her, though. He asked for Leon. She pretended not to know where he was, although for a moment she was tempted. Sort of committee meeting.

"Forget it. I'll catch him some other time. Are you living here?"

"Yes," she said firmly, enjoying it. He plunked into a chair and looked glum. She had the advantage of better intelligence service and of seeing him in an awkward fix. Not that she could relax. His eyes made her restless. She kept turning to the vacuum cleaner in the corner to look away from him. He was growing his moustache again. Paul said Vera was through with him. He looked thin and tired and his eyes were bloodshot.

He wanted to talk. Once he started it poured out. She wanted to put her hands over her ears. Harlan, the Defense Committee, their defeat, Yente's death, as if she were still his he poured his troubles into her, he grappled for her attention and sympathy, he demanded. But she could not help being curious and gradually involved. Briefly she was angry, as if he should have been able to keep Yente alive, then she pitied him.

She was almost enjoying herself—she felt in a way superior and that was new. Perhaps she did feel a sort of friendliness as she'd imagined before that night in Woody's. He left and she stood leaning against the bedroom door feeling short of breath. Somehow the encounter had blundered through like a package falling downstairs. She looked at her levis. What a way to catch her . . . Why should she care? Every encounter between them was worn or lost, for her.

She did sit down with the ads for apartments and call a few. Leon came from lunch with Caroline, high, whistling, swinging his arms. She looked him over from boots to Van Gogh hair. He would be hard to save. They went off to do the week's shopping at the Co-op.

They loitered through the spacious aisles of the supermarket, clean, airy, a monument to the educated consumers who created and owned it. People shopped there because it was vaguely liberal to do so, because it was well stocked and because the help were friendly. It was pleasant and sumptuous and made her uneasy. Much time and effort and idealism went into making shopping nicer. Suppose they had gone toward solving some lethal problem?

He strolled beside the cart she pushed, with his hands in the pockets of his worn peajacket. "No shit," he mumbled, "she's coming around. She's beginning to *see* me."

She puttered along the meat taking chucksteak for goulash, chicken and a pork loin.

"She can't trust that stud whose diamond she's toting. Rowley doesn't give a shit if she dies under the knife—"

"That's a little strong."

"But I care, and she's beginning to sense that." He popped a box of imported biscuits into the cart. "I'm not making her promises, dig. I won't bribe her. I'm just saying trust daddy, loosen up. If she'll do that—come home and ask for help and put herself in my hands . . . She's got to choose it. Otherwise it's useless."

She shopped the peanut butters for price. "You like chunky, right? Planning to marry her and have the kid?"

"I've had worse ideas." He dropped Port du Salud into the cart. She took out the English biscuits and left them on a shelf among catfoods. He muttered, "I'll never get my hands on my own kid. Joye'll see to that. Should've been Caroline got pregnant two years ago, instead of Joye. Simpler all the way around."

She was reading the labels on rice: 59 cents for 22 5/12 oz. as opposed to 69 cents for 1 lb., 7 13/16 oz. She could not see Caroline sharing the rickety concession stand, the shack from the Great White City of the Columbian Exposition with its fainthearted stove and Joye's mobile shuddering under the ceiling, his old catcher's mitt moldering in the closet, disciples and cronies and wounded old friends shuffling and moaning in the stall of kitchen with its unsurpassed collection of popbottles. Yet Caroline had fallen for him once and come to him in trouble now. Joye had married him. Nice cleanlimbed girls from Winnetka and Park Forest had taken off their clothes for his movies, and he mostly had not bothered to seduce them. Their pores were recorded and they were back in Winnetka and Park Forest with their clothes on. Here she was pushing his shopping cart. This misshapen red man.

"I bet her family would send me back to school. They'd have to, huh? Have to give a hand. With a degree I'd land a decent job. Or get foundation money." He tossed a can of albacore tuna into the basket along with a jar of caviar.

She replaced the tuna with a cheaper brand. "Could be."

"We can have dozens of big fat pink babies." His harsh laugh. "I come home at night and yell about how she doesn't keep the house clean—and she won't—and why didn't she water the lawn. I'll get fat, I'll look like a vulture too."

"Hey chief, what do you want her for? And what kind of bread you want—French or a nice dark rye?"

"Rye. Because we're each other's best hope. She's a narcissistic woman. But she made it with me once. And I bet she never really made it with anybody else. I can keep her from coming apart into little plastic pieces. I can make her grow up the way she should have, with me instead of her pig father. And I like her soft hair. The way her face is. The bones in her throat . . . Remember in *Moonblood* when she puts her hands over her eyes, and they're like slugs moving on her face, and her mouth is so sad? I like it. She moves me.''

He grinned at her over a head of cauliflower she was fingering. "I warned you. Remember?"

She smiled back, adding the cauliflower to the cart, removing the caviar. "Would you like grapefruit for breakfast tomorrow instead of juice?"

Caroline

Saturday, December 27

101. = PROGRAM XX2

Caroline woke Saturday morning feeling oppressed. Her avocado waltz-length gown clung faintly damp to her. Only ten fifteen. Awful dream. She snapped on the clockradio. Really, she wished she were still in therapy to have someone to tell it to.

MAKE OWN STORAGE FUNCTION

She had been walking out of Woody's bar with a man. He had his arm around her, they walked together from the crowded bar. At once she saw that many more buildings had been torn down. The sky was black, the streetlamps lay roots up. The sidewalk petered away in a rubble field. They were walking pressed together, his arm supporting her across a desert of gritty sand and broken bricks. Thinking that she did not know where they were going, she turned to him. Then she saw he was changing. He was falling apart. His big head cracked like the turret of a sandcastle, cracked and before she could cry out, ran crumbling down his shoulders. She tried to scream but the wind blew the stinging sand into her mouth. She was blinded and choked by her scream.

EXIT TO CONTROL ROUTINE

She tuned the radio to music, programatic, familiar. Pushing the pillows against the headboard with its sliding doors she peered into the distant vanity mirror, reached for her brush. She was a touch nearsighted. Just enough to make games difficult. Just enough that entering a room she could not look to the right or the left for fear she might look at someone and not recognize him. Her brother Orland always acted as if she missed the ball on purpose.

Fingering her throat she sighed. A world of bright feathered dead birds, oiled guns and smelly dogs: her father's world had once seemed never far from the neat order of the house, but thanks to his own success in land development, the fields and swamps were gone now. In the back of her head she could hear her father's flat deep voice. "You're lazy and inept, like your mother, and her biggest exercise is lifting a glass." Images of mother were fuzzy, even from before, when mother wouldn't touch a glass of sherry. Her father had been an officer during the war, and trekking from base to base, mother had begun. Mother belonged to rooms with blinds drawn, bottles of pills, chenille bedspreads and pale quilted robes.

UNCONDITIONAL JUMP

She squinted into the distant mirror. Dingy at the roots. This time she must get Dominic to restyle her. She had seen a cut in *Vogue*. She had felt a need of change, had felt herself sagging. She reached for the princess phone to wheedle her way into an afternoon appointment. Dominic claimed he could scarcely fit her in Monday. Thanks ever so.

She ran her hands lightly up her body. On the belly her hand paused. A chill spread. Sandcastles from summers on Lake Michigan. Orland had always devastated her castles. Sibling rivalry. As the therapist had indicated, she must not live in such a way that she proved the contempt of father and Orland justified.

CONTROL STATEMENT REJECTED

As she cradled into the pillows, music billowed over her and she drifted in vague murky wistfulness. "Darling, why . . . ?" Her hand touched her belly again gingerly. What did Rowley mean by having his phone disconnected? Perhaps he was drinking trying to forget. She saw his dark face set in that smoldering sullenness that melted her, bent over a table in some sordid bar. The night of the party he had been harsh from shock. He was afraid of the attraction and afraid he would weaken toward her. His behavior was not difficult to interpret. That was the woman's role, to understand, not to withdraw as her mother had. Strange how hard he found speaking about his feelings when he was so glib on the air. But after all he made long tedious notes to himself. She had always thought his programs spontaneous.

ERROR   TOO MUCH TIME BETWEEN CHARACTERS

If he didn't come through for her . . . Perhaps she shouldn't have fallen on him by surprise, but how could you prepare a man if he lacked sense to realize the consequences of his own actions? Lacked conscious sense, *bien entendu*. That night when he had understood that Bruce was truly coming and that she would be lost to him he had fallen on her in the hall. His arms came around her in naked assertion, they fell together, their mouths fusing. Her nipple hardened under his curious fingers. Then in the shock he had acted before he could stop himself, creating their baby. Unconsciously he must be made to recognize his own motivations. He had wanted her, had.

TAKE REAL RESULT

The phone rang. She held her breath, afraid to answer. "Caroline here." *Ici Caroline, j'écoute.* Settings are everything, she had told Bruce once at Amalfi, where they had stayed in the villa of his friend who had not liked her, and Bruce had agreed.

"Yeah, how are you?" Leon.

"Bearing up, ducky, bearing up." Of course she had been

a bit disappointed, for what they called a villa was no bigger than the cottage where her father went fishing. She had been wise to conceal her reaction. Bruce could not bear feeling that he had not got the best. He and his friend spent the whole time skin-diving while she went sightseeing and the Italian men drove her mad.

"How are you really? Don't chatter at me. Are you meeting me for lunch?"

"Lunch?" Anyone else would have put off till she had her hair done. Once she decided something was below par, it was dreary to go around where people could look at her. But Leon was not a materialist. He belonged to that period when she had been seeking her identity. "If you want, pussycat. Love to. Where?"

BEGIN STATE

Looking sideways into the mirror she drew mist nylons up her legs slowly. Would be great to be an American in French films like Jean Seberg. After all, she spoke French perfectly and everyone told her how good she was in *Moonblood* and *Grokking Wholeness* and *Viaduct Rock*. *"Je suis triste ce matin,"* she murmured with her new pout. She drew her hand up her leg watching. *"Comme tu vois, je suis seule, absolument seule."*

Slipping into her little boy suit she turned from side to side. Was she beginning to show? Already? Anyhow she could not, absolutely could not wear it without a girdle, and she could not crawl into a girdle feeling so done in and the day just begun. "They're murdering me!" she said, turning back and forth in hopes she could persuade herself her belly didn't show. But it did. She knew how she wanted to look: slim, understated, somewhat innocent. The sailory knit would have to do.

She sat down to add lashes and brush on makeup. Durrell's for lunch was no treat but she would not run into Bruce or his friends. She had a vivid foretaste of Leon across the table and yanked off her lashes. He could embarrass her about the most ordinary things.

INCONSISTENT ENTRY

As she completed her face her eyes traveled from photo to photo around the mirror. Herself at seven in a white dress with darling smocking: Might need one like that soon enough, oh dear. "Everything is grim lately!" She had always been a beautiful child. Herself in the professional pix right after she had won the Teen Queen contest and Mother and she had been sent on that ghastly trip to Hawaii. She had tried to break into modeling, but finally she had the grim news: her hips were too prominent. She would never call modeling a loss because she had learned ever so much and it was priceless training. She drew her fingers along her cheek, her eyes growing wide into themselves. They thought it was all glamour, but the incredible discipline . . .

SYSTEM AWAITS NEXT INPUT STATEMENT

Leon was already at a table. In spite of the nagging of her hair she felt good and to be looked at. The *très élégante* wife in a French movie going to meet her lover—or else her husband after she has been with her lover? That was better, for Leon was giving her a truth-or-else look that made her suddenly unhungry. Why had she told him?

She ordered a grapefruit salad and tea. Leon immediately increased his order to two roastbeef sandwiches, thundering, "You're in no condition to starve yourself." She was sure that the dimestore blond waitress had heard him.

"I don't know why I bothered you. Really, it's nothing to concern you, and—"

"Don't you know why you told me?" He glared from under bushy brows till she felt confusedly that at any rate, he knew.

"In a way. I've been desperate."

"You know I'll help, right? You know you can ask me to help you in ways you can't ask others."

"I tried to talk to Rowley again, but he's had his phone disconnected! I mean, how could he?"

"He's desperate too—to get away. Expecting anything from him is a waste of time."

The waitress brought the orders. Leon plunked a sandwich in front of her. "Eat. We have to take care of you."

"I must talk to Bruce. But I'm terrified."

"Promise me you won't talk to him yet. What's the hurry? Let's give ourselves time to work out a solution. Who needs him?" Leon swept him off the table. "Rowley and Bruce are only thinking about themselves. Forget them. Think about yourself and what you want. You're going to *do what you want to*. Screw them, Caroline. Yourself, your life, your baby."

"Suppose I do have the baby. In one of those dreadful charity hospitals? And give it away?"

"Long as you have him, you might as well hold on to him. We can take care of that too, if that's what you want."

"Will Anna take care of me too?"

"What's she got to do with it?"

"I was surprised to see her walk in with an armload of groceries. Is she living with you?"

"She just got kicked out of her apartment. She's looking for a place and sleeping on the couch. Nothing to get steamed up about."

When she had called and Anna answered, she had almost hung up. What stopped her was a fear Anna knew it was her on the line. Anna was divorced and older and dowdy and fat besides, absolutely nobody out of a hole in the wall, but Caroline had always been a little afraid of her. Anna was quiet but hard, arrogant, dreadfully serious. The wrong sort of woman for Rowley. They must have spent night after night in glum sulfurous silence. She had pointed Anna out to Bruce once and he'd called her a peasant. Rowley wouldn't talk about her.

END IMPLICIT SUBROUTINE

INDEX RESULT

"It does seem a bit funny that she'd stay with you."

"Why? Lots of room. Rowley treated her rotten too, which

should have given you fair warning. Anyhow, forget Anna, she isn't your problem." He pushed the sandwich at her.

She chewed it doggedly to please him. Lowgrade stringy beef. "I don't see any way open to me. I feel trapped." Tears wet her eyes and subsided. "Why can't Rowley act like a human being?"

"He's being very human. Cowardice is. He don't want no consequences." He tapped her arm. "I said I'd help you, and I will. But you have to trust me. Decide that you want my help. That's a decision only you can make."

UNDEFINED INTERNAL CONNECTOR

He wanted to reopen the affair. She was a little surprised. After all she had changed. She had been dreadfully young and he had impressed her with his psychologizing. He had actually talked her into therapy, but of course once in she saw the affair as destructive, with him married. Then too she'd been impressed because he did make films, even if they were poor things that hardly anybody saw: the sewer cinema Bruce called them. Though he'd never seen any. Of course Leon was divorced now. "I do trust you, you know I do. But how can you help me?"

REQUEST KEY

He grinned, a painful grimace. "Think about it." He drew his hand nervously across his mouth. "You know I've got a position at ISS now, fieldwork, and with that kind of experience I can move up to something better. I've got a thing going for me at the Council of Arts, a grant that looks like a sure thing. A longer flick, no more one-reelers. This idea is going to blow your mind. You come over tomorrow afternoon and I'll tell you about it, okay? Elliott's got a New York distributor now and if I can bring off this new one, he'll screen it for the guy. A new way to shoot you I worked out, wait till you see. We'll finally get that quality of your skin, right? That dull bony glow. My mother Fern, she's not a bad sort, she had a soft heart, you just got to get her by herself. You'll like her. . . ."

RESET CLEAR

Afterward she went downtown and bought baby suede gloves, a new afterbath called Silky (leaves you silkened from head to), and a cashmere scarf for Bruce. Then she bought a Countess Mara tie for Leon. After all, he was trying to be a true friend. And she detested his ties.

She could not tell if Bruce liked the scarf. "I thought we had Christmas two days ago," he drawled. On the other hand he did not seem annoyed. The evening would have gone well if only she had had her hair done instead of having to wait till Monday. Perhaps Dominic had not liked his Christmas present? Bruce was hypersensitive to slight defects or carelessness in her.

Bruce was wearing a shirt Mother had given him (though of course Caroline had bought it), which brought back the Christmas scene she had succeeded in forgetting all day. Her father liked Bruce fine, her brother thought he'd do, Mother was vaguely pleased. She had thought she would tell Mother what was wrong—or had she really thought she could? Each time Bruce went home with her he was perhaps a little less . . . nice afterward. If only Rowley . . . They would be poor but her family would have to help. And Rowley could do better, she was sure.

MEMORY OVERFLOW, FIELD LENGTH TOO SHORT

The color TV was playing but Bruce had the sound down and the stereo on, some demonstration record with earsplitting brass. "How does it sound?" He frowned from his Corbusier chair.

He did not trust her judgment anyhow. She assured him it sounded great, looking around to see what he had changed this time. Actually the battering of the noise suffocated her.

"I don't know. It's fuller yes, but it lacks something that Gil's set has. Why should that be? Poor room acoustics?"

He looked bored. He shut it off in the middle of the record but left the TV on. He usually did. He had a small set in the bathroom where he often sat for an hour on the toilet reading the stockmarket. He said that helped. He had promised they would have two bathrooms in the condominium rising on the far North Side they were signed up for.

They had prime ribs in a place with early American motif. Afterward they stopped to look at the skeleton. Bruce wanted to go poking around the site on the lakeshore. Although she tried to beg off he made her come along. A watchman was sitting in a shack with smoke puffing from a makeshift chimney, but Bruce led her down the next lawn and through a hedge. Counting floors he pointed out where their suite would be. The thing she liked best so far was the word ''condominium,'' which was a game to say to people, to see if they knew what it was.

The night was bitter cold. The ground was rutted, and piles of lumber and metal joists blocked them at every turn. She twisted her ankle and ran her stocking and finally she felt like sitting down on a joist and never moving again. Of course it would be great to live here, of course. There would be a doorman, of course, but also closed-circuit TV as a security precaution. All-electric wall kitchen. Central air-conditioning. A balcony. A view.

INVALID JUSTIFICATION IN COLUMN XX

Usually on Saturday they went to his key club, but last week the comedian playing there had annoyed Bruce. Bruce said he drank in a key club to avoid types like that. When they got back to his place she was frazzled. Not the bedroom yet. She had a scotch and ginger ale and then got sick, just making the bathroom. After she'd washed she winced at herself in the cabinet mirror. It was just too much. How could she trust Leon? For all his talk and his big ideas and his famous insight, what could they do? Sit around that barn and make home movies?

COLLAPSE

She began to cry. Bruce sat across the room in the Corbusier chair hearing her out with a funny expression, almost a smile, as if he'd been expecting something. She told him how when they'd been separated for weeks and weeks she had been racked by doubt and wanted to be sure. She left all that vague. But she did tell him the important night. She told him how when she had informed Rowley that he was coming back, after they'd left Vera's and come downstairs, he had seized her in the hall and carried her into the courtyard . . . Tears poured down her cheeks. He had not loved her, he had hauled her around like a rag doll. She saw his face. They were jammed against the fountain in the dirty courtyard and he was fumbling at her pants. He pushed her clothes aside and came in hammering at her. She saw his face, his brutal face huge, inflamed and almost laughing, laughing at that moment. Then all the joy and excitement and sureness that she had him after all, went: went like that. She was rammed against the stone fountain afraid, and she begged him to be done. Again she saw his animal face and she was scared and did not want him any more at all. She wanted that face smashed.

BLOCKING FACTOR

Bruce was very angry. She was twisting her hands in her lap. She felt nauseous.

"If you throw up again I'll rub your face in it."

He told her to powder her face and come on. She thought he was going to take her home and demand his ring, but he told her they were going to find Rowley.

They drove first to his house. Bruce made her go in. The basement was dark but she banged on the door anyhow. She came back and told Bruce that Rowley was not there. She remembered his phone being disconnected but did not dare say she had called. Then she rang the upstairs bell. Mr. Williams answered, a big dark Negro who had always been polite, but this time he told her he did not give a damn where Rowley had gone and she could clear her white ass off his porch. She did not repeat that to Bruce.

Bruce started in slowly, not looking at her. His handsome straightnosed profile stood out against the streetlamp. "Where would he be, then, on a Saturday night? You must know his habits. One would presume you had learned his habits?"

SEARCH MODE   CHECK MEMORY

They parked around the corner from Woody's. She mainly hoped they would not find him. Bruce grasped her elbow until her arm felt numb. As they walked in she saw Rowley down the bar, huge, relaxed, nodding: just the same. She stiffened with anger. The same, the same.

"Which one?" Bruce had that earlier smile. When she pointed, he took her by the arm, steered her outside and sent her toward the Jaguar. "You can wait there. And I mean wait."

A few minutes later they came around the corner. Bruce marched first, not bothering to look back. His camel coat and blond hair passed under the streetlamp and moved palely through the shadows toward the alley. Rowley came more slowly, ambling. He had been drinking. Slowly he turned his head to and fro. He looked puzzled, not unfriendly. For a moment she felt sorry. She almost called out to Rowley not to go into the alley. But he shambled past and was gone.

INNER DO LOOP NOT CLOSED

She waited and waited in the car. She couldn't just sit there. Finally she slipped out, leaving the door ajar on the curb side so she could pop back, and crept to the alley corner.

They were both tall, turning about each other. Rowley was heavier but moved more slowly, with drunken awkwardness. With anger to help him Bruce was landing many more blows. Rowley mainly tried to keep off. Bruce circled, jabbing. His hat lay on the snowy lid of an ashcan. They looked heavy and slow and lethargic in the dim light. Rowley's face was smeared with blood, his lip was split. Bruce bled from his nose which looked lopsided—his fine straight nose. She breathed down the urge to giggle. They were snorting and panting, and occasionally one slipped on a patch of ice as he lunged.

Bruce kept going at Rowley, jabbing at every opening. Rowley tried to keep him off and struck out rarely. He seemed bored. When he did hit Bruce she heard the impact. Then Bruce would move in cautiously for a while. They looked comical, padded in coats, shuffling in the dingy icy alley and snorting whitely. Maybe she should trust Leon. At least he seemed to care about *her*. When she told him she was pregnant he did not drag her out on a freezing night to watch him dance in some alley. After all, what good were they doing her? They were not even hurting each other. Her father could lay them both out, as he had done to Orland that time he'd got fresh.

UPDATE BUFFER

Bruce hit Rowley hard on the jaw and Rowley rocked back. Then he straightened and walking into a flurry of blows, picked up Bruce and slung him though the air into the back wall of Woody's. In her excitement she stepped free.

Rowley turned and saw her. "What is this?" he mumbled. "Want me to kill this guy? Who needs it?" He stood squinting at her. His left eye was shut. His face looked dark, bruised. "You are a real busy broad, you know that?"

By the wall Bruce was getting to his feet. He rose with something in his hand—a broken board. He came at Rowley swinging it. Rowley caught the movement and turned but too slowly. The board crashed into the side of his head and he went down on his face.

She was too startled to duck back, but Bruce did not seem surprised to see her. "Let's go."

"Did you kill him?"

"Don't be silly."

She should kneel beside Rowley to make sure he was not dead but the alley was trodden into black slime and Bruce was already walking toward the car. She hurried after.

"Never leave the door open. Never," Bruce said evenly. "I forgot my hat. It's on the ashbarrel."

She realized he was waiting for her to go get it. "I can't!"

"You will."

EXECUTE RETRIEVAL FORMAT

She hurried. The hat was on the ashcan. Rowley was still lying face down. As she trotted back she brushed the loose snow from the hat. Bruce had got in on her side, and he tossed her the keys. "I hurt my hand, I'm afraid. You may drive."

Nervously she got in the driver's side. He had never before let her. Rubbing her gloved hands she stuck the key into the ignition. "Is first up or down?"

He showed her the plan of the gears. "I meant to fight him like a gentleman until he pulled that wrestling hold. I certainly wasn't about to wrestle him. How do you happen to know toughs?" But he was smiling, dabbing at his nose with cautious fingers. "Are you surprised that I know how to fight?"

STORE IN MEMORY

She took a taxi home. She felt exhausted and even the doorman asked if something were wrong. She crawled into her avocado gown and unmade bed, turning on Music till Dawn. She kept on the small lamp. Should she call Leon? She wanted comforting. But if Anna were there. She did not like that. Was he really not sleeping with her? Anna was lumpish but she wore her sweaters too tight. Anna had heavy thighs and a big behind. Leon couldn't want her. She drew her hands along her own thighs. The emptiness of the apartment coagulated, the wind tried the locks. She had to force herself to turn and look behind her. She touched the phone and turned the radio louder. But if someone broke in she would not hear. She lowered the volume.

ILLEGAL FUNCTION NAME

She squinted at the light through her ring, twisting it back
and forth, then burrowed into bed. How the wind moaned
off the lake. Her hand came slowly up her thigh, gingerly.
She shut her eyes tight, clenched the lids. Her muscles waited.
She saw herself strapped to a table, a narrow white table,
conscious, naked, powerless. She was strapped to the table,
her arms bound above her head. Two men in white surgical
masks drew her legs wide, wide apart. They strapped them
down. She could not move. She strained her muscles rigid.
Things would be done to her. Others watched. The eyes over
the masks looked at her. Naked she lay in the hard light,
spread open. They would make her suffer pleasure and they
would watch. Deliberate as an insect, long nails catching,
the hand walked up the inside of her thigh.

INPUT COMPLETED TO TERMINAL

Leon

December

He had been invited to show at the Cellar Cinematheque with three others, but Elliott had made it painfully clear he had to turn up with something new. They grew bored with him, they put him down with a shrug. Mindless bastards who could play with color film and Nagra tape recorders. Him with his Bolex. He could splice something together that would blow their minds all over the ceiling. Act fast. Get Elliott to let him use the Moviola at that place that did training films. Work all night. Clean up before they got in in the morning. Twist his arm.

Shots from the reptile house: Live mice were put in with the small boa constrictors. They took hours to swallow a mouse. Boa's mouth: mousehead in. Mouse kicking. Mouse swallowed to mid-belly. Then all in but the snakelike tail.

A girl danced in front of a big concave mirror he'd borrowed and set up in the livingroom. Dusty floorboards, attic gray light. Sound of mindless crooning. This girl was a college dropout whose parents had since shipped her off to a sun-and-ski school to get her away from him. Bones poking through her skinny back. Shuffling back and forth in front of the mirror with a birdcage in her hand: image of despair, image of narcissistic trapped adolescence.

The projector ran dry. White screen. Wastepaper images from *Black Orpheus* and *The Trial*. Mounds of wastepaper, coils of paper stirring. He would prefer bones, tincans, beer-bottles and condoms and autobodies rusting in the sun. He would prefer:

CAROLINE VISITS THE SANITARY CANAL

Out through the railroad yards that on the map looked like bundles of muscle fiber, past quarries and claypits and gas storage tanks and the Hawthorne Race Track. The Sanitary Canal: the name evokes old kotexes floating down the Mississippi to the sea. Drowned Caroline borne along with churning sewage pumped out of the city daily, nightly.

Her face with eyes closed perfectly suggested soft death. Her eyes full open with the chin lowered became the mask of a tortured child. He had not used her well enough. He had not unwound a coil of past from within spieling images that would explode.

Another reel. Badly exposed, useless. He had sat in the last car of a ''B'' train coming all the way south from Howard Street and shot into the lighted windows: short glimpses of women stirring suppers, men looking out hopelessly from grimy sills, couples embracing, babies kicking in their cribs, old men playing cards around brief tables. The sequence was never quite in focus, grainy, underexposed, yet it hit him with a poignant restlessness that made him remember being sixteen: a sense of possibilities and random concatenations merging beyond his empty hands. There, there people were really living, out there where he could not reach.

He looked at one image again and again. A woman with dark hair and dusty skin—Negro or Italian or Mexican or anything from most places—a small, tired looking woman stood in a flash of plain dingy room with cot, washstand, wave of ashgray curtain. As the camera went by plucking her like an apple tasted only never eaten she bent to the cot, picked up the pillow and clasping it in her arms rocked it against her breasts, a limp flat pillow.

Sheldon Lederman's Dream of the City of Light

White towers. With brick and stone it had been a matter of piling little pieces. Something fussy in that that could never please a man who liked to think in terms of large functions. But now building was rational. Not like those older skyscrapers with frou-frou on top. Might have the Taj Mahal perched like a hat on a medical building. Victorian protocol: couldn't cut through the red tape. Like Fern who could never come out and say anything. Hinting, sulking, rustling in corners, moving little objects. Even when he knew what she was getting at, her prissy ways infuriated him so much he wouldn't admit he understood.

But a poured concrete building on a steel frame with walls of glass: that moved him. Light, cleanliness, order, totality. The truth was he was shrewder even in aesthetics than his wife with her Ethical Culture airs and his hippy son. His own desk was free form. No reason to think in cubes once you grasped that the materials created their own dynamic. Had to keep an open mind, up to date, receptive. Take the helix. Technology could render you obsolete as an old pen you would dip in the inkwell to write, rusty point, yes, penholder and point and clotty black ink. For a moment he almost liked remembering. Dip, scratch, scratch.

White tower after white tower with lots of green space: he had learned that from the professors' attacks on the first part of the Plan to go into construction, those middle-income high rises, Prairie Gardens. You spent green space lavishly, you surrounded your towers with parks. He had learned, hadn't he? The easy symbol. Grass was affluence and nicety. Learn their symbols. He had been doing that since college. Symbol of tie, symbol of cufflink, symbol of right restaurant for lunch. Mistakes like starting to paint the house himself when he'd first moved his family to Skokie, he made only once. Learn or die. Unless you were a lucky parasite like Fern or his ludicrous sons.

About shops he had his own ideas. You had a floor in the high rise, yes, but only small shops. Like the old corner grocery, expensive. Pay for the privilege of convenience. You also had a shopping plaza for each complex because women did want to get out and run into each other. Each shopping plaza was different: it would have a catchy name and a different motif. One would have big outdoor animal figures and cartoon characters. Another would have fountains. Another, a covered mall with hanging plants and benches. People would stroll in the plazas: no sharp dividing line between plaza and park. No line between leisure and consumption. Outdoor cafes, glassed in seasonally. People would circulate into the plazas, strolling, pushing babies, windowshopping and spending. Each plaza was different and they would spend in each. A woman's shopping was her business but also her play, her recreation. The more idiots men like his brother-in-law Sol with his dismal *schlock* shoestores. Put in a coffeebar and business goes up twenty percent.

Sol understood zero. Sol still acted as if people came in once every six months for their pair of shoes, and you had to cram it on them and get them out. People all had shoes. They wanted to buy entertainment and pleasure. Women wanted to buy youth and attractiveness and distraction and sex appeal.

In the White City lights would play over trees in the parks at night. Everything lit up. No dark corners. Light was better, cheaper than police. His other basic idea was a modular approach. Each complex would handle its own waste disposal, own maintenance, own road repair. Cut down on crippling strikes. Cut down on municipal graft by taking it out of the public sector. The University community had its own police force already, and used a private pickup service and its own snow disposal to supplement the city. Increasingly the contractor provides a life package for his client. Client would know what he was getting in the way of schools, shopping, neighborhood, life style. In some developments the housing package would include lawn, trees, barbecue pit, swimming pool, carpeting, furniture, appliances and even car. By the time most people were twenty to twenty-five, you could figure out their lifetime earning expectancy.

Suppose someone had thought they could figure him out? But if he were starting out now, if he were twenty-five and where he was now. It took so long to reach a point where you could see the long view. There was his boy Sid the kid, an old man at twenty-five. If they were to trade ages, the brat would never notice. What a loser, what a whiner. Every time he saw him he felt like asking him what rock he had crawled out from under. Been that way since four, five. Fern always acting the big protective buffer, getting between him and the boys. Sometimes he thought she'd done it intentionally, brought up those two idiots to mock him. Then Leon turning up with that big sullen slut, always some woman, always, always. He had no respect for his family, no respect for anyone. Her suddenly up and dragging him out of there in the middle of the conversation. Before he'd had a chance to say half of what he meant. Leon was always like that, explosive and slippery and gone. Leaving him raw with anger, hot with words.

No, don't think, don't think. The quickness of his own mind, the orderliness and mastery of details, the skill with people, all that he owed to his years of law: but never until he had moved into renewal had he felt his own scope. It was the breadth of the job that pleased him.

The trustees of the great and little institutions he had to work with by and large had the minds of caretakers. They saw nothing bigger than the far side of the ledger. They pinched pennies, they were afraid of planning as creeping socialism. They planned for their corporations and used computers for everything from taking inventories to mixing

steel, yet they were scared witless, they held on to their balls
at the idea of city planning. The timidity of institutional trustees about sinking money into anything they might be held
liable for made him feel like wringing their necks. Longterm
development needs made them quake in their boots. They
had to be wheedled along and diddled with a step at a time.
Big men, men with vision didn't think that way. Take a man
like David Rockefeller. He thought and operated big. Now
he was pushing down part of Morningside Heights, now he
was clearing a whole neighborhood for Lincoln Center, now
he was expanding Rockefeller Center or shooting up a huge
hotel, now he was moving into piers on the riverfront. Well,
if he personally had that sized piece of just Standard Oil, just
Jersey, he would think big too.

It was a historical moment, when the ride of decay was
being rolled back in the cities, when great stewards of corporations and banks, men honed on the law and finance,
turned their talents and vision into the rebuilding of the cities
into proper setting for such men and such corporations. All
the buzzards of gouging slumlords, those petty small thinking real estate hoarders and speculators—their day was over.
The day of the smalltime ward politician with their payoffs
not to enforce the building codes, to let in this saloon and
close down that one: they were joining the other dinosaurs.
Not that there wasn't a lot of porkbarreling left, but the mayor
kept it under control. It was rational, it served.

Those hearings almost drove him crazy. A whole burnt
offering of time on the part of some really valuable administration men and experts, for what? You couldn't have the man
on the street putting through a logical and rational plan. He
couldn't see farther than his shoelace. How could they re-
build a city without disrupting some individuals' private
plans? If they gave in to every group in the city that decided
their toes were being stepped on, the city would come down
around their ears before they got a move on. It was all win-
dowdressing for what had been decided two years before, but
it slowed them down, it wasted valuable men's time. All
those pathetic nobodies getting up to say their piece in public: "I'm Mrs. Homemaker and I don't want to move, so you

can't build your expressway." "I'm John Doe and I have eight kids I can't support anyway, so I refuse to let you tear down the filthy shack I live in, because I am so attached to it, my home sweet home." What an incredible ritual, all those nobodies getting up one at a time to say their piece and expecting the wheels of the world to stop turning. Like Leon, always expecting to be the exception, to get away with it, brazen as ever still, still. Persisting into the dirt, not one sign he had learned anything, that he felt what had happened to him, kicked out of the University, branded a common thief, judged in court unfit as father.

To remain clearsighted. Beyond the business district, the groves of high rise. Beyond, the garden cities, and beyond that ring, the industrial and research belt, then fancier wooded suburbs for semi-country living. The black plain of Chicago was obsolete. Most people on it were unnecessary or soon would be, because cheap labor was no longer economical. Managers, men of ideas and vision, technicians who put things through, these were components of the future. Communications men, media men, men specializing in design research, engineering consumption, market analysis, systems analysis. But the great unwashed, those clods out there, the restless noisy lumpen, they were obsolete. Society no longer needed stupidity and brawn, brawlers and breeders. The proles belonged with the dinosaurs. Consumption was increasingly the job of the upper middle class. They had a more and more dominant share of the pie. Slum dwellers were economically extinct. No city would rot from the center to accommodate them. No city would need to.

The city of the clean, the fit, the socialized, the acceptable, the good. An end to vulgarity and chaos and spoilers and those who spat on the right way. The White City would fill America to the brim like a city set on a mountain, the New Jerusalem, the next Chicago. The city of his mind.

Rowley

Tuesday—Friday,
December 30—January 2

Rowley sat in his nearly empty livingroom against the wall, eyes halfclosed playing against the 78 he had taped. Last Friday he had done his show on blues singers who had been based in Chicago on and off: Bukka White, Leroy Carr, Ida Cox, Lonnie Johnson, Big Joe Williams, Memphis Minnie and Little Son Joe, James Wiggins, Brownie McGhee, Peatie Wheatstraw, Big Bill Broonzy, Blind Blues Darby . . . In the taping he had hit another Black Jack, property of a collector from Madison. That by now familiar voice older, harsher, sang:

> *If all my sweet women were hangin' on that tree,*
> *Yeah all my women hangin' on that tree,*
> *Everyone would cry out loud, Jack baby, what you done to me.*
>
> *I was comin' down the street and I saw my daddy there,*
> *Yeah I saw my old daddy there,*
> *Shadow turnin' on the ground and his feet in the middle of the air.*
>
> *If I don't hang for what I done, get hung for who I am,*
> *Yeah, I'm Jack, I'm black that's who I am,*
> *I'm Black Jack, I'm keeping track, my life ain't worth a damn.*

He could hardly make out the guitar. A harmonica chirped now and then like a cricket. The voice was an insect from a dry year. He had been working on the song till he had a guitar

part that fit, it snuggled in there under the voice and lifted.
It was right. Then he started feeling bad. Here he was eating
up the record and the man who made it was down in the
bottom of Chicago getting nothing. He felt comfortable and
very white. For months he'd been talking about the man, how
he had to find him. He had leaned hard on the contacts in
Welfare and got what little they had, including arrests for
drunkenness and the curves that had not taken. Tomorrow
he would work through the black flophouses, start on South
State and see if anyone would listen. Carry his guitar. His
face still looked messy. People would edge away from him
in elevators. It was healing.

He put bulbs in the fixtures and hung shades. At the Salvation Army he bought a double bed and a table and straight
chairs. Otherwise his two rooms were empty except for boxes
and suitcases. Basic necessities. One was lacking.

Blues in my mealbarrel and there's blues on my shelf,
And there's blues in my bed, 'cause I'm sleeping by myself.

Nursing a hangover and bruises and thumps and great cha-
grin, he had come on his desire.

The phone rang. It was Shirley Williams who'd got his
new number from the studio. She got to the point pretty
quick:

"Do you know where Harlan is? I have to reach him. I
thought, perhaps, you might've seen him, not for me but for
the children . . ."

She was staying with her folks with the younger kids. The
oldest boy was with an aunt. Harlan was gone.

He knew then that he was fooling himself with his guilt,
going to do good to old down-and-out Jack. He needed him.
The last touch, the last contact to his own adopted past. The
roots of his own black identification. Go back and touch
base. Find out what's still real. Are you there? Will you know
me? Blue-black old man who made the music that's made
me. Got to find you, talk to you. Last connection for my old
sweet habit.

Late Wednesday afternoon, last day of the dying year, he

found Jack Custis in the Paragon, 350 Fireproof Rooms for Men Only. The staircase reminded him of Anna's, going from landing to landing steep and straight up, but for four floors. The lobby was on the second floor with a small wan TV, some straight chairs and a big old spittoon. Every chair was occupied by old men. When he looked more closely they were not at all old, they just sat that way. Slow dull murmur of conversation. The white man in the teller's cage gave him directions.

After climbing two more flights he turned into an endless, windowless corridor with doors every few feet. Wee bulbs bleared the dark midway down from the black ceiling. Piss hung like fog between the defaced walls. The corridor felt like a passageway in the bowels of a ship. Numbered door after numbered door. Someone was vomiting. Finally 319. He knocked. His hand felt heavy. Jack Custis was about to turn flesh. He must be old. He knocked again. "Mr. Custis?" Somebody garbled a word or two inside, and he opened the door.

A man lay on the cot as if he had fallen from a height, tall, black, wizened. His face was an oilcured olive that had shriveled into minute creases and puffy folds. The cot was narrow and tilted toward the wall stained with old puke. A grimy sheet and a dirty scrap of blanket covered him, lying in his shabby clothes. There was nothing else in the cubicle. In the ditch between the cot and wall Rowley squatted. No instrument visible. Must have pawned it long ago. He had brought his guitar, carried it partly as a peace sign, as a calling card, partly because he hoped to persuade Jack Custis to play. He stood it in the corner.

"I've been looking for you a long time," he began, "ever since I ran into one of your records in a secondhandstore." He talked about his program and his search. This broken old man sprawled on the cot could be anyone, could be another Jack Custis down and out.

But the bloodshot eyes opened and a lopsided grin pulled on the deep wrinkles around the mouth. "No shi! All 'is dime." He was nearly toothless. His words came out in a rasping lisp from the broken sump of mouth. Maybe a stained chip or two far back. Rowley felt sick. But false teeth could be bought for a toothless singer. He had trouble understanding and moved closer to the head of the cot.

"Sick," Jack said urgently, and a spidery gray hand came skittering out of the covers and felt for his chest, his throat. "Sick for days. Since Tuesday." His voice tore up in clots. "You like my old records, uh? How come, a white kid like you?"

He knelt beside the grisly cot in a position of infant prayer and told Jack why he'd tried to find him. The sound of a hack cough from the bottom of tubercular rotten lungs came through the chicken wire from the next cubicle or the next after that.

Jack made a face. "Yeah, raise hell all day, all nigh'. Can' get no rest. Bedbugs, roaches. You lay in your cage and they eat you live. Skinny old men in this place and fat cooties."

He bent close to hear. Some he couldn't guess out of the toothless mumble. Reek of acid vomit. Jack seemed eager to talk. "Moochers, jackrollers always hangin' aroun'. I pay by the week when I can, else they roll you and you out on the street. Got to keep walkin and scroungin around the Salvation Army or Union Station. Summer I don' mind, but winner is so bad. I can' take it like I used to. Just walk and walk. I go to places for work. Manpower places. They charge so much and half the time let you off right away. You stand around the state office all day."

Somewhere two thin voices yelled at each other.

"I get so mad, fed up. I just can' sit without a drink. I start thinkin and I get jumpy . . ." The corrugated metal wall behind him popped against his shoulders as Jack rose on his elbow to vomit.

He leaped up and moved out of range. Just brownish curd. He looked again. "You been sick three days? You know . . . it looks like you're bringing up blood."

Jack shook his head wearily and lay back on the stained pillow.

"When was the last time you ate?"

Jack shrugged, his eyes closing. He talked less and his words became harder to catch. Rowley began to get scared, feeling the man was fading out. "Maybe some food would help. And we should get a doctor to look at you."

Jack opened his eyes slightly. "You going?"

"I'll be back. I want to call a doctor."

Toothlessly Jack laughed. "Kid, you funny."

The man in the cage did not get excited. "The bleeding ulcers or one of them things old alkies get. They're drunk every day and trying to scrounge money for a bottle. He's not on General Public or they'd send a doctor. You won't find one to come down here."

"I think he's really sick. No joke."

"Listen, all winter the girl finds them in the morning, and the cops come and haul them away. There's always more where they come from. And I'll tell you, a third of the men down here, they don't drink at all, and they get just as sick."

He went along to the first lunchroom he saw and used the payphone. He couldn't find doctors in the neighborhood, so he started with the Loop. Most doctors had closed up shop for the holiday. He tried doctors south, but those he got hold of backed out when he mentioned the address. He tried calling the city. Most offices were closed. When he did get connected with someone, they speedily assured him Jack was none of their department's business. Jack was nobody's client. He had a pretty good idea what would happen if he called the police.

Afraid Jack would think he had disappeared he got some greasy soup in a paper cup, coffee and a limp sandwich and carried them back. Jack lay eyes closed while his hand moved uneasily on his chest. "Feel like jelly," he mumbled. "Old runny jelly. Wouldn't be bad but I feel so cold."

He touched Jack's clenched hand. Cold as the pavement. He took off his coat and tucked it around. Jack felt cold all up his arms and legs. Insisting, he propped Jack up to taste the soup. A few minutes later Jack vomited that up with the brownish curds and blood that looked fresh. "The bastards won't come. But I'll get somebody. I'm going to call again."

"Put your guitar down under the bed, boy, fore you go down." The spidery hand moved on the wide sunken chest. He had been a big man, as Rowley had imagined. "Sure as

shit they come in and lift it. I can't get up to lock the door.
Put it under me, or you come back and find your box gone.''

Rowley obeyed. Something scuttled from his hand. "I'll
get you out of this hole. I'll get a doctor if I have to drag
him. You'll get teeth and you'll record—record what you
want to.''

Deep in his chest Jack laughed. He winced then and as
Rowley left, rolled to the edge of the bed to vomit new bright
blood. Cursing, Rowley ran down the mountainside of rickety steps. On the sidewalk people moved out of his way. In
the bleared mirror over the hashhouse counter, he saw his
face red with anger, bruises inflamed, eyes glaring, hair on
end. He got back on the phone. What he finally settled for
was an ambulance from the county hospital.

When he told him, Jack twitched with fear. "Don' want
to go there. Uhuh. Uhuh." He moaned, his hand seeking on
himself.

To pass the time Rowley pulled out the guitar and squatted
against the partition. "Hey, you remember this?

I'm gonna lay down when I'm tired, when I'm feelin' good I'll stand,
Gonna ride when I get restless, and I ain't gonna be your man,
No, I ain't gonna be your mealticket, I ain't gonna be your man . . .''

"That's mine but you don't do it right." Jack rolled his
head to and fro. Rowley did not know if he should go on and
waited till Jack motioned for the guitar.

Now you want to cry, now you want to crawl
But baby, you been foolin' me, and I don't need you at all.
You been foolin', oooh, you been foolin' me!

Jack fumbled at the strings. "Pearldiving ruins the hands.
Get a cut and it never heals. Get it off of me, boy, too heavy.
I can't catch my breath."

Rowley took the guitar and Jack lay back with his eyes
shut. Time oozed by. He wanted to go down and call again.
He played blues and Jack nodded weakly and the bugs skit-
tered up the corrugated walls and through the chicken wire

came the sound of men retching and coughing and snoring and quarreling. A couple of men stopped their slow shuffle to the head to push open the door, listen a bit, and stare. Then they shut the door again and went on their way.

"Tell me the words to that song, 'Noplace left to go.' "

Jack shook his head. "Jelly. Everything inside feel like it going squish." For a long time he did not open his eyes.

Then he began to laugh and he laughed until blood choked him. "Sure as shit, here I am going down and some honky squat here ready to take my last words. Roll round a recorder and hand me guitar to blow. My, my. Things about coming my way. Success come to Jack, my, my, reprieve on death row with the old chair all lit up." He was choking and laughing and halfway sitting up with his eyes shining out of his head, the cords in his neck standing straight out.

"The songs touched me. Isn't that real? I started looking for you, and you weren't easy to find. Okay, I was doing ninety other things, too, and maybe—"

"They don't touch me. It isn't useful. The police been beating on me too long, they whipped me down to the ground. Don't nothing matter worth a damn but I'm cold. One thing be good for me. To see this supposed to be great city a hole in the ground. Then I get out of bed and dance all over it. White folks always been trying to use me and I seen they never make it. You come up to use me now and you too late. I so full of poison maybe what I do is drag my big old carcass down to Lake Michigan and pollute up the city water supply, so all them nice folks have a little sip of Black Jack and keel right over. Maybe I do that."

He choked again, brown blood on his mouth, and slid back. His eyes closed and he did not open them again.

By the time the ambulance came, he knew it was useless. He went along to help sign Jack in. That took forever. Then he ate in the hospital cafeteria and sat around the waiting room riffling raggedy *Life*'s. He called Lucille and she came down an hour later with two of her big boys and her tight-lipped, stiffbacked husband. A young doctor told them brusquely at eleven that Jack Custis' esophagus was hemorrhaging: common among alcoholics.

Rowley said to the elsewhere face that Custis was not a common alcoholic. Mr. Thompson looked grim while Lucille sighed and rubbed her fat hands on her fat knees. They had coffee from a machine and stared at their feet. At one thirty-five Jack died.

The Thompsons gave Rowley a ride home. He should not have bothered Lucille, for she would be stuck with the funeral and hospital bills. He apologized and she assured him he had done right: Jack was family. But he knew they needed no dying body from Skid Row. He apologized again and a furry silence settled in the car. He held his guitar upright on his lap and sweated.

He woke a couple of hours before dawn to find he had bedbugs. He couldn't remember at first what the sharp itchy bites were. When he understood he rose, bathed, soaked his clothes in the sink. When he lay down they swarmed from their hiding places. He would have to spray the damn mattress and boil his clothes.

Trying to sleep he found himself awake on the livingroom floor, awake and echoing like a big cold hall. He was going to scrap the show he had taped for tonight. He found himself planning a program to be a memorial as mean and angry as he could make it. Jack, he died of anger, he died of that bitter toothless laugh that scraped his throat raw. His blood turned to lye and ate him. Alcohol was the gentlest poison that he swallowed. Waste. The meatpackers used to boast that they used all of the pig but his squeal, and the workers swore that Gustavus Swift used to go snooping around where the packinghouse sewers dumped into a creek, on the prowl for traces of escaping fat. But a man could go out with the garbage whole, nothing of the good and talent in him spent, all his wanting and needing and loving turned to bile and acid. A man could be wasted as well as spent.

Who mattered? Who was needed? Cannon fodder every ten years? Would they have automated wars? The kids on the corners were not needed, the two million Indians, the tenant farmers, the unaffluent old and the students in humanities and the saints in canyon communities and out of work miners and poets and roustabouts were not needed. He did the show live.

He called from the studio and asked for Leon. Anna said he wasn't there, she didn't know when he would be back. He thanked her and hung up. Fifteen minutes later he parked out front. The metal of the knob felt cold through his driving gloves as he gripped it, waiting.

"Oh. It was you who called." But she let him in. Her hair was loose and slightly damp, spread tentlike on the shoulders of a wool robe with Leon's initials on the pocket. On the floor beside her chair a transistor FM was tuned to the next program on his station. Pad of paper covered with her scrawl.

"Did you like it?"

She looked for a moment as if she would pretend she did not understand. Then she shrugged, swinging the heavy dark hair. "Yes. You were good."

"Even though I sang?"

She would not smile. "Have you been in an accident?" She peered into his face. Hers shone with washing across the high cheeks.

"Caroline's boyfriend, out back of Woody's."

"She told him, then?"

"Behold!"

But she was wrinkling her forehead, plotting the curve of some private thought. "She promised Leon she wouldn't."

"She makes pacifier promises. What does Leon care?"

She smiled with her mouth sucked in. "Oh, he does."

"And what do you care about?"

"Him. Evidently."

"Anna, you are one big fake."

Her hair swung wide in indignation. "Why you son of a bitch! I don't come bouncing into your livingroom to make derogatory remarks on what you feel!"

"I've known Leon a lot longer than you have—"

"But I know Leon *better*." She was swishing around in anger. Was she wearing anything under the robe? Not much.

"Is that by way of rent?"

"I pay cash and Leon's out of work if you want to know."

"Jesus, Annie, what have you jumped into? You'll be supporting him before the winter's over."

"Not on my job," she said and smiled. "Because Leon has trouble making it in the world doesn't mean he's a worse person than those who thrive. Maybe he's better."

"How come you got mixed up with him? Why Leon?"

"Because he was nice to me, you nitwit! About time somebody was. He tries—believe it or not—to be *good*. He cares about people. He worries, he feels. He takes responsibility." She paced, one hand holding the robe shut and the other inscribing angry arcs.

"I want to see him being good to you and Caroline at once."

"Oh go stick your head up the chimney! He's my business, and what do you mean coming in here and trying to upset me?"

"You know, you have a worse temper than I do."

"Who says so?" In honest indignation, staring. "I have a sweet, yielding disposition. Ask Leon."

"Provoke me just a little more."

"You egotistical jackass! All you mean is *tsooris*. What did you come here for?"

"You."

Her breath stopped in her and she looked him full in the face with surprise. Before she could react he caught her by the arms: firm, warm, tensing under the wool. As he bent to kiss her, she stiffened and thrust forward to bite him on the chin. She pulled back, half expecting to be struck. He jumped with surprise and pain but held on. It was hard for her to hurt someone, and he took that moment of recoil to get a better grip. She tried to turn from under his kiss, writhing in the loose wool. Full and longbodied she struggled against him, her expressive earthy body and shuddering hair against him.

At the familiar returned feel of her he half wanted to laugh and kept trying to draw her closer. Then under his mouth hers grew warm and she stood still against him, leaning slightly. He had her, yes. Her loose hair spilled over his arm. He had her again, her mouth gone soft and warm and open

to him. Then abruptly with angry strength she wrenched free
and ran behind the couch, yanking the robe tighter.

"Bastard, bastard! Every time I find a man to live with,
you start wanting me. What kind of demented loving is that?"

"If you're living with him, you're putting up with a hell
of a lot. What made your neck so stiff with me? With poor
sticks like Asher and Leon, you make allowances and excuses till you fall over."

"Because he needs me. Ever think of that?"

"Nobody past fifteen and under eighty *needs* anybody."

"A warm body, that's all you want." She looked about to
cry. "A cunt who knows how to cook."

"I haven't had a decent meal in four months—"

"Choke! Starve!"

"And if I don't care who it is, what am I doing here,
getting bitten and yelled at?"

"I don't know." She shook out the folds of her robe.
"What are you doing here?"

Why didn't she make him angry? Because he had regarded
her as his and perhaps had never quite stopped. He came
around the couch. She drew herself up with her bust out,
glaring. "Don't you come mauling me again, I'll kick you
in the balls."

Of course she wouldn't. Instead she stood her ground
trying superior moral force. "No. I will not be touched."
Suddenly her face froze and she leaped backward saying
"Shhh." And smoothed at the robe, her hair, the robe again.

Leon unlocked the door. "Hey?" he called wearily. His
face was screwed into a grimace of despair or disgust. Then,
seeing him, Leon grew rigid. He stood near the door pulling
off his gloves, rubbing steam from his glasses, smacking the
gloves then into his other palm. "Long time. What brings
you by?" Leon looked hard at him and hard at Anna. Very
hard at Anna. Around the room once and back to him.

"I wanted to see Annie."

"You see her. Take a good look. Next time come around
when I'm here."

"That doesn't seem to happen often."

"Did you ask him over?" Leon glared at her.

"Don't be ridiculous!"

"I was by a week ago. Didn't Annie mention it?"

"I forgot! Everything's been so hectic."

"You forgot." Leon's face was drawn tight with mistrust and annoyance. Slowly he got out of his coat and dropped it on the couch in front of her. She went at once to hang it. Leon watched with coldeyed annoyance. Rowley did not like that look at all. Leon said flatly, "Look, man, you've done your time with her. If she doesn't want you hanging around, don't bug her."

"That's my business. Hold on to her if you can."

"I don't know what you're talking about." Leon walked into the bedroom and shut the door.

He took his jacket off the chair. "Goodnight, Annie."

She looked as if she would speak but did not. As he went out she stood behind the couch leaning forward on its pitted back with her elbow crooked and her hair cascading forward. Her eyes shown large and dark and wary above her heavy cheekbones. For a while afterward as he drove to his new empty apartment, he thought he could feel that dark unfriendly but not incurious regard.

Caroline

Monday, January 5

THE SCIENTIFIC TERMINAL SYSTEM IS NOW OPERATING

"What do you want to see her for?" Leon asked. He was
holding her hand, it was young and gentle with the snow
coming down. The afternoon had been beautiful. They had
watched *Moonblood* and *Grokking* twice. Maybe he did have
talent. Maybe she should grow her hair again but keep it very
blond. They had talked and talked, Leon had told her his
plans for going back to school and putting his life together.
He spoke to her in such a warm sure fashion that she thought
in his own way he *was* strong. Really he lived in a hole, but
as long as they stayed there she felt wrapped in a cocoon of
nurture and care, and she'd hated to leave. He wanted to take
her to a steakhouse to eat that was almost nice, but she was
afraid someone would see them.

UNDEFINED DATA REFERENCE

"Why do you have to go to Vera's tonight?" he repeated.
"She's an old friend, baby. I can't hide. She was very
understanding when I told her." And Vera might know where
Rowley was hiding. She might even be seeing him. Vera
could be stubborn.
"Don't tell everybody. You're making yourself trouble."
"Of course I won't. But Vera never gossips." Too true.

Vera wasn't interested enough to remember what was told her. Vera would say offhand that she had bumped into so-and-so—the very man Caroline was crazy about. She would ask Vera, what did he talk about? Did he say anything about me? Vera would wrinkle her nose and try and try, but she really could not remember. Maddening. Though Vera did notice clothes. She could be a designer, but she just shrugged off suggestions with a closed face. Meaning that Vera thought being colored she couldn't make it, but you had to fight handicaps: think of her hips, after all.

END STATE COMPILE

She gave a squeeze of Leon's hand to show she hadn't forgotten him, and his hand tightened around hers hard, too hard, till she wriggled her fingers to let him know.

"You're still wearing that ring. How come?"

"I haven't had a chance to straighten things out with Bruce." She would never expect Leon to give her one, after all, but she did wish he would be a little more specific. He created such a warm cocoon of understanding she just couldn't ask questions.

UNDEFINED STATEMENT IN DO LOOP

"Don't go into the present situation. Just tell him you don't want to marry him. That's what you ought to be taking care of tonight."

She sighed. "All right, I'll go over there later."

"Call me when you get home."

"If it's not too late." She patted his arm.

"You think I'll sleep? I said call me."

He wanted to come up with her but she managed to say goodnight in the lobby. Past the ghastly spot where it happened she hurried before he changed his mind. Could running upstairs cause a miscarriage? Too much to hope for. Things had been going smoothly till the accident, her family satisfied for once . . .

Vera opened the door and Caroline bussed her. "It's been days!"

"What a day this was. I think they're worse after vacation, always." Vera was wearing a loose tent dress in a soft green, one of those sheet wools she liked.

"Really, I'm going to have to start wearing dresses like that all the time. I can't bear to look in the mirror."

Vera scrutinized her. "Doesn't show yet. Why don't you just marry your fiancé a little early?"

"Is that fair? It isn't his, and all . . ." She had been avoiding Bruce, a wee bit frightened of him since that Saturday. "I think he's mad at me."

"Well, no wonder." Vera gave a small tired smile.

"What does Rowley say about me? Is he sorry?"

ILLEGAL CHARACTER RECEIVED

"How would I know?" Vera sat up quite straight in the rocker.

"I thought, if you'd run into him?"

"I told you I wouldn't deal with him any more."

"I haven't seen him in ages. He moved, and I don't even know if he hasn't skipped town."

"He wouldn't." Vera stopped abruptly.

She wanted to ask how Vera knew but did not dare. If she could find out where he was hiding. If she suddenly appeared there wearing her new winter white, what they were calling naked white, calm this time, yes, very calm, understanding . . .

VARIABLE GIVEN CONFLICTING TYPES

"By the way I have to leave by eight. I have a meeting."

"A meeting? I didn't think you went in for things like that." Caroline felt thrust out, uncared for.

Vera made a light hopeless gesture. "It's about my school. I promised a friend to go with her."

"Leon has been a real sweetie. A friend in need."

"He does seem a friendly type," Vera said with such acid she was startled.

"I mean, I think he'd marry me. Of course it wouldn't be like marrying Bruce. My family wouldn't be pleased—"

"Your father would drop a hydrogen bomb."

In a way. However she'd realized from Bruce's conversation that Leon's father was a respected man. Bruce seemed to value contact with him, though he made fun of Sheldon and called him an oldtime shark with no understanding of the importance of consensus. But Bruce said he was wellregarded even in Washington and that he had a kinetic approach to the problems of containing slums and building buffers. She made a genuine effort to listen to Bruce sometimes. She had understood that Leon's family though Jewish would prove acceptable.

VARIABLE DUPLICATED IN A COMMON REGION

"At least Leon cares for me. He wants me to have my baby. He isn't trying to pack me off to some grisly abortion mill. My family would have to help us get a decent place and something better for him than that silly interviewing job—"

"You seem to have thought it through," Vera said meekly. "But didn't Leon quit that job? I'm sure Paul said so."

"That's impossible! Vera, think. What makes you say that?"

"It was weeks ago. We've been in such a state what happened over Christmas feels like six months gone. Paul wants to quit school and organize in the black community but he's scared the draft will get him. Give him the privilege of dying in a colonial war on his fellow skins—I'm quoting. He's changed, Caroline. He's silly, of course, full of Our African Heritage and quoting Malcolm but . . . you should have heard him standing up to his father."

INPUT INTERRUPTED

She was afraid Vera would go on about Paul. "But what about Leon? What did he tell you?"

"Paul called there the day we left for home, and he called again the day we came back. I know that Paul said Leon had lost his job. I know because he was talking to that cow who lives there, and he said to me, watch, she'll end up supporting old Leon. What are you planning to do with her if you marry Leon? I hear she cleans the house, but . . ."

"She doesn't really live with him. She's staying there while she looks for an apartment. She's quite poor."

"I see." Vera smiled.

"You don't believe it?"

ENTRY JAM

"Neither would Paul, I'll tell you. Did Leon ask you to marry him?"

"Not exactly."

"How approximately?"

Her hands locked in her lap, she tried to remember. "He said he would help me. That I should trust him . . ." Her voice trailed off. She felt chilled.

"Caroline, I heard Paul talking to that woman the Saturday we left for Green River. I heard him kidding around and he told her not to get married to Leon before he came back. I know from what he said she's not staying there like girlscout camp. Perhaps that man really means to help you—I don't know him as Paul keeps telling me, and frankly I don't want to. But you better find out what he means by help. Ask him to find her a safer place to stay if he's serious. You've always been taken advantage of by men who aren't worth your bother." Vera gave her a rare look of pity.

She felt herself shrinking. Staring at her clasped hands she thought how the veins stood out. She ran her tongue along her teeth. Her mouth felt dusty. "Do you think I'm losing weight?"

"Your face does look thinner. Are you taking care?"

CANCEL JOB****

She cast herself on the cot, one hand on her belly. "What's the use? Who really cares?" She squeezed till her belly hurt and then in fear let go. "What am I going to do? If I can't trust him, what will happen to me?"

"All I know is what I heard Paul saying to that woman. When he hung up the phone he started laughing and recited a poem at me he said was D. H. Lawrence. Paul was big on Lawrence last year. 'The elephant, the huge old beast, is slow to mate . . . ' I wouldn't cut off from Bruce before I knew for sure what's going on over there."

"Everything is such a mess! What can I do now?" She would be caught. She would be caught out in the open without anyone. No one would have to take care of her, no one would have to care. "What's going to happen to me! I wish I was dead!" She went on until the tears began to flow, and finally Vera sat on the cot too and she cried on Vera's small firm shoulder. "I haven't slept with that many men, not compared to other girls." Vera's cool nurselike hands stroked her. "I'm still pretty, aren't I? Vera!" She cried and cried until she felt loose inside. Then she became aware Vera was glancing at the clock. It was five after eight. She wanted to beg Vera not to go to her meeting, but she had that terrible bare sense of being caught without shelter and Vera could offer her none that counted.

COMPARE EXIT

They left together. Across the hall a door opened a crack. "Hello, Mrs. Martin," Vera said, shutting her own door behind them.

In the lobby Caroline averted her head from the sordid courtyard with its broken cupid. Apologetically Vera left her on the sidewalk and scurried away into the wind calling back, "Be careful now what you do! Keep in touch."

Everyone had someplace to go, someone to go to. That song Rowley sang the second night:

I get full of good liquor and walk the streets all night,
I go home and throw my man out if he don't act right:
Wild women don't worry, wild women don't have no blues.

She sang it softly, seeing him with his big hands on the guitar looking strong and sensual, and tears burned briefly behind her eyes. At last a cab droned through the falling snow.

She curled up in the backseat burrowed into her collar. Even if Leon did marry her he was not of Bruce's caliber. Was he really the best that she could do? She gave the cabbie Bruce's address. Moving till she could glimpse herself in the rearview mirror, she gave herself a weak smile. Nimbus of hair. For an instant she saw her face gray and luminous on Leon's screen. Dreams, dreams twice he had sucked her into them. Cheating her. Deep inside a slow pain beat. She crept further into her coat.

PROBLEM EXCEEDS MEMORY

She could remember the wild electric kick when she realized at her coming back party that she could have Rowley. She'd watched him for a year. He was strong, he was masculine, he had a direct warm roughedged manner that always made her think about bed, but she had never been able to get his attention. That night after she'd finagled to get him invited, he had come in with Anna—still that woman—she had felt cast down. But he had not acted *with* Anna and then in chatting she had become aware that she could take him away. She had felt alive then, triumphant and utterly woman. Somehow she had felt that the ring she got from Bruce was a magic thing that would now bring her what she wanted. With Rowley she would have felt safe. Why couldn't he! But there was something animal about him, yes, and after all he lacked many of Bruce's . . . qualities.

DATA CHECK

Bruce would not be pleased to see her without warning but she must find out where they stood. Bruce came of a good family but his father was a failure. His company had been bought out and he was only a minor official. Bruce's mother wrote him weekly in a fine script with straight margins. She had met his parents briefly before he had gone to Green River with her and given her the ring.

Bruce was ambitious. He did well but he spent more than he made, though he did invest. That was one of his subjects with her father. Whatever he bought—the Jaguar, the stereo, designer chairs, sportjackets tailored from selected bolts of Scottish cloth—he took wonderful care of until he got something better. He fretted over his things but he had wonderful taste. Mostly. He read dreadful books.

After all, he didn't ask for his ring back. Perhaps he was still willing. Bruce had something that her father had, and Leon and Rowley both lacked: authority. He was handsome and really they had more in common and that's what marriage was built on, everyone said.

END BLOC COMBINE

Just after eleven as she unlocked her door the phone rang. She let it ring. Once she had gone to bed it started again. Finally she could no longer ignore it.

"What happened?" Leon barked so loud she held the phone out from her ear. "Did you tell him?"

"We had a wonderful talk! Absolute communication."

Silence. Then, "What does that mean? You break it off?"

"The splendid part was, it isn't necessary. He was completely understanding and supportive. He pointed out that, after all, we can't know it isn't ours, and—"

"You said you hadn't slept with him."

"Not just lately, but you never know for sure. And I do love him and except for all this turmoil, I'd never have doubted."

"Kid, what are you marching into? You *don't* love him. You're running scared into marriage with somebody you don't care for and never will."

"Leon, I wish you wouldn't talk that way. You don't know Bruce but if you did, you'd adore him. He's very mature. Now we've disagreed and had misunderstandings, but tonight we really worked things out."

"What does that mean?"

"We realized one of our sources of conflict was that when Bruce went out to Santa Barbara on business, I felt that proved he didn't love me, and I wanted to test his feelings."

"Who cooked that one up? This guy doesn't love you. Why does he want you so bad?"

NO ENTRANCE IN THIS MODULE

"Let's chat another time. I'm absolutely dead."

"Goddamn it, listen!"

"Don't yell at me, Leon. You've been a real friend, but I have to think of my future and my baby—"

"This afternoon, that was friendliness? Come off it. You know what we had together and what we can have again—"

"Darling, if you misunderstood I'm dreadfully sorry—"

"I misunderstood nothing. I can still feel your body—"

BLOCK

"Don't be difficult, Leon-love. You've been a friend to me all these past hard weeks, don't spoil it now."

"I'm on my way over."

"No! Please."

"We'll hash this out before you make a worse mistake."

"Leon, listen, everything's straightened out. Bruce will marry me, it's all right!"

"I'll be there in ten minutes."

"No! Leon, no!" But he hung up. Oh, he was unfair. She did not want to see him, she could not. No one took her condition into account with their incessant demands. Her impulse was to dress and run out. Suppose she ran into that mad Leon on the street? Cabs took forever to arrive in the snow. Leon would be yelling at her and pressuring her and twisting her words out of shape, just when she had everything set again. He would blur the lines of everything, he would soften her into a fake child, his harsh but persuasive voice would hypnotize her into his cocoon. She could not bear it.

ZERO SUPPRESS CODE

She called the doorman, telling him she was going to have a visitor she definitely did not wish, and would he be a darling and tell the young man who would ask for her that she had just gone out? Don't let him in. Thank you terribly. Fortunately she'd given the doorman a good bottle of scotch for Christmas.

She crept back into bed but fidgeted and could not sleep. The room rustled and shifted. Finally she got up and checked the windows, particularly onto the fire escape, and set a tilted chair against the knob of the doublelocked halldoor. Wheeling the TV in she got back in bed to watch a fifties Western. A great drag but it soothed her. As she watched she worked on her cuticles.

Then the phone started ringing. She leaped up and ran into the bathroom, turning on the water full force. She thought she could hear the phone going on and on, but when she shut off the water and listened the apartment was silent. She shivered with rage. How dare he persecute her. His face danced before her, ugly, grinning. He needn't think she would endure everything. She wasn't defenseless! If only she hadn't used up her tranquilizers.

EDIT DUMP

She had just gone to bed when the phone started again. "That idiot! That idiot!" At last she took all the extra blankets from her closet, tore open her recent laundry and buried the phone. As she watched the movie she could hear it ringing from time to time but tiny and lacking urgency, like the voice of an insect. Slowly she began to relax. After all what could Leon do? He could not touch her. Pretending to be her friend and then turning on her the moment she didn't agree with him.

She would phone her parents tomorrow and say they'd decided to marry soon. Mother would botch everything but thank god, Bruce was reliable. He would not let things be spoiled. It would be hectic and grisly, but then it would all be over.

JOB NO **** IS COMPLETE

Vera

Poor silly Caroline, in over her head. Better off married. Merely to picture Caroline embedded in a house made her look safer. A baby, a husband, and an electric carving knife: what more could she ask? Caroline had been a sweet, soft, generous child and with her own children she might quiet into that again, could be.

The little shrimp Petey, fuzzy and flatnosed, was waving his hand and making a pitiful screwed up face. Raisinface. "Teacher, I got to go. Teacher!" She gave him the pass. In the meantime Ronnie and Jason were up shoving each other, knocking heads like angry rams. "Miss Jameson, he call me a bad name!" She had to walk into the aisle to quiet them. Francine tugged on her skirt. "Teacher, my book tore." There was a general murmur by now and something fell behind her. Time for reading anyhow.

Pictures in the reader showed yellowheaded pinkskinned children chatting with friendly toystore men and grocers, visiting Grandfather on the farm with pigs (oink oink) and cows (moo moo) on the train (choo choo). They lived in a white house on acres of aching green grass with a dog Spot and Mother and Father. "Jack will help me," said Father. "Yes, I will help Father gladly," said Jack. "I want to help, too," said Joyce. They all played happily ever after under the koolaid leaves. "Paul will run the farm after me," said Father. "In a pig's eye," said Paul, "screw the family tra-

287

ditions." "It is your duty," said Father. But Paul was opting
for tougher duties. His new confusion.

Nancy cracked her bubblegum. Vera made her spit it in
the big wastebasket. Afterward, she had Nancy open her
mouth. Sure enough, half the wad was secreted between the
child's upper gum and cheek. Back to the wastebasket. Nancy's sullen slanted eyes glowed in her thin face. You stole
from me, they accused. My gum, my sweet gum. Who knew
where Nancy had found it? She never had anything, not a
pencil to write with or a penny for Christmas seals or a button
to close her sleazy rayon jacket against the winter wind. She
was tall for eight with good muscle tone and a quick stubborn
mind.

Petey was taking too long. She peeked out the halldoor
and noise spurted through the class. "Ow!" "Quit that!"
"Hey, look at me!" "Who got my ruler?" There he was
fooling around the drinking fountain, compressing the stream
with his thumb to make it arc out and pee on the floor. As
he saw her he came running. She hopped in for a moment.
Bob was slashing at Jimmy with a ruler. She should not have
let Petey go—the whole class was due in twenty minutes—
but if he got upset he peed in his pants. When she swung
around, Nancy was making a face. Mouth frozen instantly,
eyes dropped. Soon they would not drop. The gum.

The door banged open and in came Jason's older brother
with a message about a change in lunchroom forms. Jason
giggled and craned around to see if everyone knew it was his
brother and he stuck up his finger Fuck You at Ronnie. Some
kids called at him.

The room smelled always. She thought it smelled like anxiety, old murky odor of failure sweated from the baseboards.
Every desk was occupied and more shoved against the back
and between rows—and there were five absent. The kids had
helped take down Christmas decorations and cut white tissue
snowflakes for the windows. On the bulletin board were
drawings of firemen to be collected into booklets on Our
Neighborhood Helpers. The widening social horizon.

The afternoon stretched like an enormous waitingroom,
as long and dark and dingy as the halls of this vast rotting

school. Mary Ellen was sucking her finger again. His head down on his desk, Terry at ten was the oldest and biggest. Ronnie was drawing. Petey looked like he might be playing with himself. Maybe a third of the class stared dully out the empty windows. Whatever happened Paul must not end doing something halfway true, for it would destroy him. That speaker last night on welfare: regimented rot. Tall thin-faced man with probably some Indian in him. Rich voice with muscles in it. From some black nationalist group.

As she put the pass away she saw her unfinished lesson plan. The principal, Mr. Burns, had spoken to her again. Selfrighteous pink fink. The kids hated the school. They learned right away it did not belong to them: it had them, they were condemned to it for years to be bored and tortured and teased and lied to—here as outside, as that speaker had said. She'd gone to the meeting mainly to please Betty Hamilton who had a couple of girls in the upper grades. Betty went to galleries with her so she went to Betty's meeting. Betty kept asking her wasn't Harlan Williams wonderful and on and on till she figured out that Betty had a secret huge middle-aged crush on him. If she didn't leave off thinking about him, she could stop laughing at Betty.

Terry was frankly asleep. He was always tired, sagging on his big frame. She woke him. "Would you be my captain for boys today, Terry?" Jimmy gave her a reproachful pout. Teacher's pet. She regarded him with that mockery she saved for whatever she really liked. Uncanny in arithmetic. Intuition. Would it survive?

Terry shambled forward. Single file, boys in line, girls in line, march. They shoved and giggled and tumbled after. Half the teachers acted as if they hated the kids in the halls: like her mother walking down the street in Green River with them, hand gripping, wringing small hand. Show them you're a lady. Things had to end somewhere their long queasy spiral. Let the others complain.

She leaned on the doorframe, keeping an eye as they straggled past. Mary Ellen's dress was unpinned and she fixed it. Flo had a new purple bruise on her upper arm she was showing off to the girls in line. How starkly depressed Paul had been. Ultimately she thought his ego would save him but she tended to underrate his suffering: as she had the time he'd fallen off the shed roof leading an expedition up Everest. When he just lay there wailing she had lost her temper and made him get up. His leg doubled. The bloody bone poked through.

She clasped herself. So hard to be a kid. Carla was standing out of line buffeted by the girls as if she were a heap of rags, withdrawn, shoulders hunched, eyes half shut. "Come on, Carla, don't you have to go?" Let herself be pulled along. She had not spoken in three weeks. Her arms were covered with scabs. She had sent Carla to the school nurse and the school nurse sent her back with a note, *This child scratches herself.*

For Paul, pangs of action must be cured by new action: family tradition that used to lead to ministry or teaching. Paul was perhaps shocked that she had accepted his new radical ideas and projects. But she had long ago learned to live in a hostile armed camp. He seemed himself in company with those shaggy kids, whereas she had not recognized her brother sitting with that toad, plucking dirt from his naval and rubbing it into his hair. Last night listening to the pride and anger and power in that man's voice for all her repulsion to rhetoric she had been moved, and moved to imagine Paul in that role. The sketch yes, she had realized as she finished it that it was a pastiche of the dove hovering over the waters, the spirit on the waves, but the waves were people's faces upturned and the bird was no dove: more eagle, a phoenix-eagle black as a crow, a muscular broadwinged bird with talons.

The urine ran in quick streams to the drain over the cracked tiles. The toilets were too high for second-graders. Nancy slunk past in line. She put her hand on Nancy's round head. The child pulled away. She liked Nancy who arched her thin back and fought. Teachers in the higher grades could not afford to like the tough vigorous ones, but who couldn't put down a second-grader?

Mary Ellen pushed Francine so she stepped into the urine and wet her shoe. "Mommy'll slap me down!" Francine wailed. She dabbed at Francine's shoe with a papertowel. Above the bank of washbasins she floated in the weaksighted mirror, rosy in her dress. Rowley had come to her door and put his hand in, touching her face. She had pulled back like Nancy. Touch me not, this black violet. She had liked his energy, his way of moving, his voice with its patches of roughness. He did not use love or other obscene tricky words, but finally like every other man he thought he was worth that, he wanted to be loved. Love was not historically possible, not to be arrived at. He talked about history but did not think it applied to him: not even his own, witness Caroline. She frowned, tapping her foot.

She quieted sniffling Francine and flushed the toilet after Carla and washed her hands for her. She had not liked his hands, like loaves that had never been baked. Would Paul guess about Rowley? He never had about Will, poor Willy, wherever he was with his lifeguard's body, his smile and his, alas, commonplace mind furnished by Poor Richard out of *Ebony*. His handsome useless body.

Images of power: not No-Power, not holy selfrighteous puritan power like the Jameson fathers. Black phoenix, bird of battle, black horse galloping. His face was quick with intelligence. His voice blew the crowd like wind. They said his wife had tried to hold him back politically, been afraid and wanting him to give up. Most women were barnacles or cows. Clingers or selfcentered breeders. Much of what he said was all that black pride rigmarole Paul had been spouting, but he said it with pride. Almost everybody seemed to need their totems, be it old 78 race records or African kings.

She heard noise in the hall and told Denise to line the girls up. When she got to the Boys, Ronnie and Jason were at it again. Ronnie was banging Jason's head and shoulders against a locker. Some of the kids were yelling. Terry was numb faced, mouth open. Norman had wandered away to peek into other rooms. She collected them all and trotted them along while she brought up the girls. Back to homeroom. *Home*-room. They weren't fooled. If only she did not feel that Paul was luxuriating in his doubts and indecisions: might sit proliferating ideologies and swapping futilities with dormitory politicians until he grew bored and wanted distracting, and always there were girls who would oblige. Like her reaction to H.W.? The man said, We must make a new world, and the woman said, Honey, you so right, why don't you start with me?

The fast readers got a new chapter in the integrated reader. They got a colored chapter. Bobbie and Susan lived in the city in a big clean (Spotless) apartment with Father and Mother and Baby. Everybody in the white chapters was white, everybody in the colored chapters colored. Separate but equal chapters. Up yonder the hierarchy decreed that the new textbooks would motivate the children. Oh, colored balloonman with colored balloons. The children sagged and sprawled and yawned and picked their noses and drooled boredom. The fast readers read about the friendly policeman. They would not object though already they knew better, for they had learned already not to connect, not to believe. Their brains would turn to sawdust and their IQ's decline from testing period to testing period. Boredom lay over them like a worn hall carpet.

Wallie twisted a rubberband around his finger till the top swelled obscenely. Somebody's book hit the floor. Somebody else cried out in pain. A messenger from the office came in with a note that her class was using too much construction paper. A moment later came a loud muffled bang that shook the windows and everybody began talking, "Miss Jameson, what happen?" and getting up to look out the windows. "That was a bomb, man." "Nah, Mr. Burns sitting down."

Beatrice never would meet Benedict but then she did not expect to and laughed in the mirror as well as the world. The fast readers as a special treat tomorrow would reread the same story. Write Policeman four times. The slow readers sat in a circle, in the suburbs with the white children and their integrated dog Spot. "Show me the sentence which tells what color the house is. Who can show me?" Mary Ellen's eager hand waved, waved on an arm rigid with passion. Thin rickety girl with a love-me face. She would recite all the time if she were allowed—nine tenths of the time wrong. She could not read two words. Calling on her was adminstering a drug.

Norman's nose was running down his chin. She fetched another Kleenex from the box in her desk. He had a cold all year, one he had caught at birth. His first word doubtless a sneeze. Next to him plump demure creamy Denise sat in her impeccable smock, smiling faintly. Her PTA mother was deeply ashamed (her daughter an underachiever) and thus hostile. She wanted her kid bussed out and no wonder. Denise had started out eager but just given up.

The bell rang in the corridor. She flipped back her cuff to see her watch. Not time. Again. Again. Again. Surprise fire drill. Even though they would freeze in the slush for ten minutes and the kids would be wound tight afterward, it would wake them and use some of the slimy length of afternoon. She had them stand and form a column of fours. As they milled out, some pushing, some going bugeyed along serious and ready, others joking, she did a quick roll. "Where's Nancy?"

Blank eyes looked at her, away. The corridors were jammed already with four-abreast lines squeezing from every stuffed classroom to the jostling crowd outside. Exit Three for them. The end staircase.

"Where's Nancy?" she asked again. "Didn't she come out of the washroom?" She felt sick to her stomach. She always counted. But she had been rushed and thinking of Paul and last night and, "March along now, no shoving, Wallie. Flo, don't dawdle. Pick up your feet. Stay in your own line now." She got them moving. "Miss McBee!" she called to the bluehaired third-grade teacher. She hated to ask her but she was next in line. "Miss McBee, would you take my class down with yours? I have a child in the lavatory."

Miss McBee gave a knowing smirk. "I'll do my best, though when *he* hears about it, feathers will fly. If you didn't let them go running through the halls every five minutes . . ."

Miss McBee called the children animals. Well, she'd say in the teacher's lounge, back to the thundering herds. Welcome to the zoo, she'd say to new teachers. Vera walked from the stairhead, pushing against the current. She made her way past broken lockers, the leaky fountain, toward the Girls. Every time she passed a teacher she had to explain. Her cheeks burned. All for a piece of bubblegum Nancy must have taken off another kid on the playground.

She pushed open the Girls. "Nancy?" No answer. "Nancy Parks! We're having a fire drill. You come out at once."

Letting the door swing shut she squatted on a comparatively clean stretch of floor to peer under. No legs. Nothing to do but open every door. And if Nancy had snuck off or hidden or gone home? O lord! Outside, the stairtreads thundered, the stairwells echoed with a loud roar. She marched along opening every door. In the last cubicle before the grill-covered windows, Nancy curled on a toilet with her arms hooked around her legs. Big-eyed scared waiting look, with something of relief. Nancy must have thought no one was ever coming to find and punish her.

She grabbed Nancy by the arm and pulled her out. "You've been very bad. You hid from me and stayed outside class and didn't answer when you were called."

"Leggo my arm." Nancy yanked free and stood rubbing her arm ostentatiously.

"If you'd waited to chew your gum after class, I'd never have taken it from you."

"You could've let me put it in a piece of paper."

"But I don't do that with the other children. They'd get jealous."

"What you got to be yelling at me for? Everybody else always yell at me."

"Come on, give me your hand. We have to go down with the others."

Pouting but compliant, Nancy gave over her thin hand and let herself be yanked along. The bell sounded again. Were they done already? She'd be on the principal's carpet. She wasn't a regular teacher and never would be, the way things were going. Four bells. Then it went on. One, two, three. A fine time to pull that, or hadn't she noticed? Exit Three closed. Let's see, the alternate exit. "No, Nancy, we have to go back and use the middle stairs." Meant she would have

to use Exit Two and go all the way around the building to get
back to her kids. Everyone would see her. No! She'd run
down with Nancy the way the kids had gone and take her
chances on getting caught.

"Come on, we will take the end stairs. Your teacher's
crazy."

She held Nancy by the cold tight hand and went at as quick
a trot as she dared. No one was in sight but she couldn't be
sure. When they finally reached the end stairway and started
down, at the first turn they ran into thick black smoke. She
stood still a moment in shock. The school was burning. This
old firetrap. She could not see down the stairs and her eyes
began to water.

Nancy burst into tears and hugged her legs. She tried to
pull the child back upstairs, but Nancy clung to her legs and
her warm tears went running down the nylons. Stooping, she
gathered up Nancy, a bag of allwhichway bones, oh she
weighed half a ton, and started down the corridor to the
middle stairway. She heard something fall below.

Smoke was everywhere now thickening the air. Her eyes
burned. The floor looked funny and hurt her feet through her
soles. The bell began to ring again in one long ring that went
on and on and on. It came at her from all sides. Nancy clung
to her neck in a stranglehold while her big purse thumped
against her side. Finally she thought to drop it, right in the
hall. The bell went on and on boring into her head. Her side
ached, her shoulder and back hurt from carrying Nancy and
trying to hurry. The child's loosely dangling shoes kicked
her.

She started down the middle stairs. The bell sang inside
her head like a pain. Smoke whirled up the well. Then from
the second turn she saw flames. She stopped, holding Nancy
who clung to her neck, tough Nancy burrowing in and sob-
bing in deep shudders. The fire was orange and sometimes
bluegreen in the old masonry, in the old wood whose layers
and layers of varnish spat. The fire leaped and smoldered
and hung in wreaths. Her eyes were running hard and she
had to wipe them on Nancy's flimsy dress to see.

> *The buck clattered.*
> *The firecat went leaping,*
> *To the right, to the left,*
> *And*
> *Bristled in the way.*

She had disliked that poem in school because of *bucks*. When
would she no longer get shocks from neutral things, even
from neutral things? Get moving again. They had been raised
not to be frightened. Not to sit down. Not to cry.

> *Because of the firecat.*

There was no way through. She said the poem aloud to Nancy
as she carried her down the corridor, aching. All the doors
were closed. The last child was supposed to shut the classroom door. She could almost imagine classes in session. She
set Nancy down. "Do you think you could walk now, baby-
love? Come on, give me your hand."

But Nancy sank down crying. "Don't leave me, Miss
Jameson, don't leave me here! I didn't mean to make you
mad!"

She stooped and picked her up again, staggering. Smoke
was thicker and acrid. Down where the first stairway lay,
flames licked at the doorframes and seeped from the walls.
Nancy's tears dried on her neck in the heat. The child began
to cough, rubbing her face into her shoulder. She could not
seem to think what to do. Her head ached. Her head was
parched and the skin stretched drum-tight.

The bell stopped, abruptly. Sirens wailed and the fire spat,
the itchy licking and high rumble of the fire. The floor smoldered in the hall. Below things fell. Outside men were yelling. The floor scorched her feet through her soles. She could
hardly make herself keep walking. She felt as if she were
sinking. The air was hot and hurt her face. She could not
carry Nancy further. Her lungs burned and her throat ached
and her back throbbed. Heat stretched her face tighter and
tighter till it must split.

She pushed open a door into a classroom on the street side.

Fifth grade, Miss Barnaby. On the board the founding of
Chicago was pictured: Jean Baptiste Point du Sable, the first
settler, black like me. Here first and last ever since. Smoke
was pouring from the heating duct. She dragged her way
among the desks to the window. Found the window pole.
Nancy's grip loosened on her neck and she sat the child limply
at one of the desks.

Clambering on the ledge she pushed high the window. The
metal of the outside grill was hot to touch. Then she dragged
Nancy up. The wall was burning. The glassdoored book-
cases with pictures of jet planes and cars and rockets showed
flame. The glass was blackening and cracking. She held
Nancy propped against her and looked over the edge. Straight
down. She felt dizzy. Firemen were running hoses in through
the doors. A hose was struck in a smashed window almost
below. She yelled and could not hear herself. She yelled
again.

The children were mostly lined up across the street and
they were screaming with excitement. The older kids were
out of control, dancing and clapping and singing and urging
the building on. Even the shopkeepers were standing with
big grins. Everybody hated this old school, this monstrous
redbrick dungeon. They were cheering the flames and for a
long time nobody heard her. Then a kid saw her and soon
many of the kids were staring and pointing and finally some
firemen saw and came running. Her face felt blistered. Her
hands were flayed. The heat leaned on her, ate at her. Calling
a warning she could not hear, she rolled the limp Nancy out
the window and fell back. White firemen. She could not
jump. Could not. Into space. Skirt flying up. Her dress was
burning, the soft pink wool. Hideous odor of burned hair.
Tried to crush it out between her hands, beating at the sparks.

Poor Paul, what would he do? He never had hated. Fire-
wolf leapt. Flame in a sheet swooping. *Can't, no, please,
can't!* She was screaming and ashamed, though she could
not hear herself. She went twisting back and forth beating at
herself. Had Nancy landed all right? Poor Paul, what would
he . . . should have jumped. She could not stand it, could
not stand it, mumbling *I'm sorry, I'm sorry!* Pulling herself

up burning onto the burning ledge, she rolled over, and cold
air burned her as rolling over and over she fell, heard wind
and screaming, not hers, and fell.

Anna

Since she had gone to bed on the couch weary of waiting for
Leon, every sound had torn her thin sleep. Now the scrape
of his key in the lock woke her again. In the graying dark she
watched him make his exhausted way to the bathroom to piss
and cough up phlegm. Afterward he passed the couch and
paused. She shut her eyes. She did not know why. She lay
simulating sleep. Making an explosive noise with his lips he
lumbered into the bedroom. Two thumps as he kicked off his
wet boots. The rustle of the bed.

He must have been trying to see Caroline again: all night?
It was bad, bad. She snoozed till the dank light of morning
seeped through the room. At breakfast she looked through
the paper for an apartment without success. Meetings in the
afternoon and evening. In between she would hang around
the office taking calls: no heat, pipes burst, children sick,
eviction notices. The work was grim and slow, with a builtin
futility that sent the staff into apocalyptic daydreams for relief, but the work was human and would do. Already their
neighborhood was feeling the brunt of renewal. Rents going
up, apartments being further subdivided into tiny partitioned
holes, services cut back. The streets seemed visibly more
crowded.

While she was sipping a second cup of coffee, to her surprise Leon came shuffling into the kitchen. He collapsed into
a chair and blew his nose for several minutes.

"You've caught a cold."

"So?"

His eyes showed bloodshot even through the shades he had put on, his nose was swollen, his lips cracked. She said, "Why don't you stay in bed today? Maybe you can shake it."

"You'd like that, eh?" He squinted: elephant eyes red in his swollen face.

"I won't be here." What was she suspected of?

He gave a dry meaningless chuckle that deteriorated into coughing. "What did you do with those antihistamines Murray gave you last winter?"

"What?"

"Those blockbusters he gave you?"

Was he thinking of Joye? blending them into some general wife-figure? "Want me to get something from the drugstore?"

"No use without a prescription."

"Are you running a fever?" She reached out to his forehead.

He ducked away. "Let me along. Got things to do."

Her trailing fingers had made contact long enough to tell that he was burning. After she cleared breakfast she picked up the mail from the floor where it slid through the slot. For her.

"What are you opening?"

"My check. The last from ISS. I had it sent here."

"Yeah? You going to cash it?"

"This afternoon."

The air felt soft and filmy. The streets were filled with a gray froth like dirty eggwhites. Beside her Paul walked head bowed, but he chose their erratic route. The snow and the dim light of the air were yellowed like old streets. Their boots sucked.

He was five days back from Green River and the funeral. "Caroline was there, with that prick she's marrying next Saturday. They're saying they been secretly married since Europe, and now they want to do it again in church. She came over waving a hankie and saying that Vera was the best friend she had.''

He walked through the gargoyle gate into campus. To their left a pond straddled by a small stone bridge where he sat down. The gray ice was puddled. Digging into the slush and leaning back, Paul lit a cigarette and winced. His face looked closed and young and weary. He kept rubbing his fists into his eyes. The whites were sore-red, full of blood. Around his wide sensitive mouth the skin was broken out. Past him rose the Gothic lace of the corner tower. The guardian of what is, what owns.

''Leon never did see her. I lost contact myself. He thought she tried to run me. Not like that. She sunk a lot of imagination into me. She didn't want enough for herself.''

''What did you want for her?''

''Not enough. In gradeschool she was already good. They couldn't tell because they were big on having kids draw blue sky and green trees and white sailboats, and Vera was too easy with her paints to stop with that. But the woman who taught art encouraged her. Then one time her homeroom teacher was asking the kids what they wanted to be and when she got to Vera, Vera said she was going to be an artist. The homeroom teacher stopped and raised her brows and did an exaggerated doubletake. 'What's an artist, Vera, do you know?' Between classes Vera saw her out in the hall telling two other teachers about the funny colored girl who was going to be an *artist*. She walked like a little broomstick and she couldn't bear to be laughed at. The masks laughed at others, and if they didn't like them, well she made them to please herself.''

Sparrows hopping around some tidbit bared by the thaw. Paul stared at the gargoyle entrance, iron gates ajar.

''They're still saying it was arson, aren't they?''

''Fuzz are pinning it on the FBM. Harlan Williams said the school ought to be blown up, that parents should keep their kids home sooner than send them to that lousy indoctrinating firetrap to learn to be stupid and sick. The fuzz raided a garage and picked up some squirrel rifles and bowie knives and spread it all over the papers. Others say it was the

Marauders—a teenage KKK. I talked to the janitor. He says
if they're investigating they aren't trying very hard because
nobody will listen to him. Something exploded but he says
it was the rebuilt boiler. Construction graft, the Syndicate
connection, and who cares how the job's done.''

"You went over and talked to him?'' Before the funeral
he had gone into a fury if anyone discussed the fire.

"Yeah, at first I wanted to shut it out. But I changed my
mind.'' He rubbed his gloved hands slowly. "It's an issue to
organize around. I'm going to let them use me. That's what
I belong to, where I start. I'm going to let them use me and
her death.''

"Rowley called me. It hit him hard.''

"Yeah, he felt it.'' He got up and they walked among the
gray buildings and through a damp arch to the Midway. "He
wanted to go to the funeral. I said no but I was sorry after.
Would have introduced one note of truth.''

"Have you been seeing him?''

Paul made an ambiguous gesture. "He's useful. And he
cared about her. He sees what I'm trying to do.''

Traffic on the Midway was heavy already. Soon she would
have to leave for a staff meeting. "Come and see Leon. I
can't get through to him.''

"No.'' His voice clanked. "He doesn't see what I'm after
and he should. I can't forgive him for being blind. And I just
plain don't want to talk about her with him.''

"Paul, things are bad. He's sick and feverish. I woke up
in the middle of the night and heard him using the phone.
I'm sure he was calling Caroline—at three, four in the morning.''

"At the funeral she started to say he was bothering her,
but I cut her short. What does he think it will do him?''

"He blames me in his head for the way she dumped him.
That's why I have to move. I slept at my place just one night—
it's spooky with the building empty and the heat off. Next
day he made a scene. Claimed I was sneaking out to see
Rowley.''

They drifted toward the fountain of time in shape of a half
moon swarming with figures crawling out of and fading into

the muck at either end, cast in crumbling concrete. It was obvious, pompous and fine to look at. They sat on the rim of the basin facing the centerpiece of mounted legionnaire. Beyond the fountain and fringe of trees stretched an expanse of wintry lagoon.

"You can't pull out. Suppose he is acting crazy. You can't up and leave him when he needs help."

"But he doesn't want me there, Paul. At times he hates me."

"He's sick over Caroline."

"But I'm not doing him any good."

"How do you know?"

She knew, sitting on the basin, that her friendship with Paul had lost its home and she was saddened. There were no natural ways left for them to meet. "Can I do anything for you?"

He shook his head no. But a minute later, "Vera left some things at the Art Institute—drawings, papers. I want them but I don't want to look at them yet. You could get them."

She nodded. Just to the side of Paul the tall gaunt figure of Time peered from his hood like Lamont Cranston, the Shadow. "You think the way he eats us all he'd be fatter . . . It's late."

"Have to see a man. You know, take care of old Leon. He doesn't have anybody else who will."

At dusk the temperature dropped with a thud and the slush froze hard. Coming home her feet grew numb, her teeth ached with cold. As she crossed campus a meeting or lecture was just letting out. She picked her way along a glacier behind a couple. The woman was wearing heels and the man had to pry her over the crevices and catch her as she slid. Something puzzled her about them.

"Tomorrow night we'll present them with a fate accompli," the woman said cosily, crashing against him.

He corrected her pronunciation and equilibrium. "Do we actually have the votes this time? We're not forgetting someone?"

Asher. For a year and a half she had dreaded this accident. The woman played to him and he accepted it, the ritualistic recounting of votes. She would have been useless: would have tried to make him laugh or got amorous from the jostling or said right out, hey, you know you're going to win so let's have a drink or go to a movie or something.

When Asher drank he got silly and penitent and likable. He put his head in her lap and howled I'm no good, I'm no good at all, and then suddenly he would pull her off the chair smack on the ass, and giggle. They had had games. Games had been their best mode. He was fond of cheese fondue and when they both stabbed the same piece, they would duel briefly with their forks . . . Ay ay. A chill in the liver. To remember their quarrels was less painful. She hurried past them, slipping and skidding, and no one spoke. She smiled down at her feet, weakly. She continued and so did he.

If Leon found a job, he would steady. She believed in the therapy of work. Besides he couldn't go on taxing his mother. Fern kept nagging him about getting a job and claimed that Sheldon had found out she was giving him money. Leon's car had not started in weeks and now the plates had expired. At any rate she'd got him to write out a résumé the night before. Now while he slept she typed it. Details of last evening nagged. "Caroline said Rowley talked against you all the time." Did he believe that?

When the phone rang she hesitated before answering.

"Is this Leon Lederman's residence?" A woman's voice.

"Yes. Just a moment."

"Just a moment, you. Who is this?"

"His secretary. I'll call him."

"This is his exwife. Don't tell me you're his secretary!"

"Hi, Joye. It's Anna. I'm doing some typing for him."

"Anna? How are you? It's amazing how he always cons some girl. Anna, you're crazy!"

"If you'll wait, I'll get him. Hold on."

"No, wait. I'll bet he's in bed."

"He's sick with a bad cold."

"Not so sick he can't drive me crazy. You just tell him I'm informing my lawyer. If he tries to waylay me again with

Jimmy, I'll get a court order. And if my check doesn't come before next week, I'm raising the roof.''

"Has he been hanging around?"

"I won't put up with it. I didn't go through all that to have him in my hair. You tell him."

"But he really is sick. Don't run to your lawyer just yet—okay? I'll speak to him."

"I've given him chance after chance. I'm fed up. I'm calling my lawyer right now, and you be sure and tell him. His secretary! You must be crazy as he is. Not that I didn't throw away six of the worst years of my life on him."

Afterward she made faces, nauseated with worry. She hardly dared give Leon the message and dared even less to withhold it. She wished Paul were around to share problems, but she could not even call him until she had done what she'd promised. Signing Leon's name, she took the letters and résumé's to mail in the Loop.

The money was not in her purse. She felt an instant wild terror, imagining it stolen in the office, the street, the bus. No, she had still had it last night. She fumbled through her big purse, finally shook out everything and went through its contents a piece at a time. Ten dollars. The money was gone, all but ten dollars and change.

Leon's room was dark and smelled of menthol and damp clothes. He lay on his stomach with his face in the crumpled pillow. His breathing was hoarse and wheezy. Oh dear, oh dear. Trouble was the air they breathed. Slowly she drew out his top drawer and looked. A rumpled five, change. She must have left it someplace, but where? Her flesh felt heavy on her bones. Carefully she shut the door. Plodding to the IC she kept wondering should she move or stay, keep quiet or try to convince? And the money, where?

When she climbed up from the train at Jackson, the sun was bright and a clean wind spanked off the lake, pushing her as she headed toward the Art Institute. She came out with Vera's papers in a manilla envelope as the big Coca-Cola sign north on Michigan Avenue read ten forty-five. Sun bounded off the glassy facade of buildings. The city began abruptly at the park presenting a sophisticated, monied, bland

broad facade of gray worsted. Wind scoured the wide streets,
pale blue and dark gray, streets that ran along for miles and
miles across the prairies. The day felt clean and generous.
The skyscraper was invented here, a thrust skyward to
counter the thrust of the horizon. Leisurely she walked north
toward the slab of Prudential. The loss of her little cushion
of check scared her, but the kids in the office lived on five
bucks here and two bucks there. From affluent homes for the
most part, they lived below welfare level. They never made
budgets. The Movement would somehow feed its own. She
felt bourgeois beside them.

Prosperous people pacing along, furs, crisp overcoats,
cared-for faces. Leaving Peck and Peck a blond who . . .
Caroline? Couldn't be. But that cashmere trenchcoat. Carrying a small package and eyeing herself in shopwindows,
she walked north too. Seen her? No, absorbed in self crossing Air France, American Express. She quickened her own
steps, risking the loss of Caroline if she stepped into a shop,
but if Anna did not get ahead, she could not cross Michigan
in time. At Madison the light was against her and on a gam-
ble she kept going. When she looked back she thought she
had lost. Then she saw Caroline peering in at John M. Smyth
furniture. At Washington she waited for the light, catching
flashes of the trenchcoat through breaks in the crowd. Caroline turned the corner toward State just before the light
changed. Feeling silly she hurried after. As she came up to
Wabash Caroline was crossing Washington with the last green
of the light. She trotted under the heavy iron shadow of the
El, under the deep rumble of a train as Caroline did, opposite, and completed the square as she strolled into Marshall
Field.

Inside she caught up. ''Caroline!'' she said loudly, suddenly sure it was not.

Caroline turned, her face composing. ''Oh, Anna! What
a delight. How goes it?''

Slightly out of breath. ''Shopping?''

''In a frantic rush. We're getting married Saturday in Green
River and you can imagine!'' Caroline moved on a few steps.

She kept close, clutching the large envelope. "Yes, but I wondered—"

"Tonight I leave and Bruce arrives Friday. It's going to be intimate—just family and neighbors." Caroline danced along a few more steps in the moving crowd.

Great gray beard and glittering eye. "You've no doubt figured out that Leon is in a panic. Can't you talk to him, just for a little while? To reassure him. He's worried, you know Leon." She felt slimy-mouthed as she offered him up for mutual superior commiseration. Yes, we girls know poor Leon.

Caroline's face closed. She withdrew into her makeup. "Really, if you had any idea how he persecutes me! I don't know what gave him the impression—"

"You told him your troubles. How can you be surprised if he still feels involved?"

"I don't know what you mean." Caroline drew her gloves smooth, touching the ring. "After all! He's your boyfriend, isn't he? Why don't you keep him from making a nuisance of himself?"

"I thought you liked my boyfriends."

Clutching her purse close, Caroline half turned. "I had to have my phone unlisted, because of him! He waits outside Bruce's like a detective. When Bruce caught on, he was outraged. He knows Leon's father, and he said last night he'd speak to him."

"Are you going to let him?"

"What can I do? It's not my affair. After all, I can't imagine why you want to run around trying to force me to see Leon!"

She found herself staring at Caroline's belly through the coat. "You couldn't imagine. My, I'd love to give you a good kick."

Caroline colored and whirled, trotting away. She found herself sweating heavily and wandered off at right angles. Came to among aisles of sparkly mothers' necklaces. She had intended to buy underwear at the January sales, but with the money missing . . . From the gaudiness of State Street with its flashy many-armed fluorescent streetlamps she ducked down a subway entrance. A "B" train was pulling in and she ran for it. She would go directly to the office.

With a sense of prying she looked through the manilla envelope. Mainly figure drawings in a fine but cutting line. A number of quick studies of Paul, of an older woman with a pleasant homely face, of small children, then a series of talking, gesticulating people, black and white. Those faces reappeared in a careful sketch of a room full of people centering somehow on a brooding Paul at the back. Sketch for a painting Vera had contemplated? She returned again and again to a drawing of Rowley, more finished than anything except the room. A clear look at him, not caricature and yet not at all what Anna saw. It vexed her. Staring at it was like pressing on a burn.

The only warning she had was oblique. When she came in Friday evening, Leon was on the phone to his mother. He hung up saying thickly, "Got to hustle over there. Sheldon's rattling the windows with his righteous anger because those two finks, Joye and Bucko the Lord of the Ring, turned in complaints. I been causing trouble, oh shame and scandal in the family. They want a little blood on the walls tonight."

She had to bring up the money. "Uh, did you pay the rent?"

"Next month's? What for?"

"Leon . . . I was trying to call you this afternoon to ask you about something, but the line was always busy."

"Yeah? Some girl called. Wanted to know when you'd be back. It wasn't Caroline."

Sam appeared an hour later. "Thought I'd take a chance on catching you in. We're at Rowley's for the weekend." She tossed her pilelines corduroy coat on a chair. Her face was rosy with cold, her dark hair loosely braided. She wore levis and a faded workshirt. Anna decided she looked happy. "That's Gino, my friend there."

"Nicespeak for husband." He was prowling around on edge but curious, taking everything in with slow panning movements of his long head. After that first comment he ignored them for a good while, as she and Sam brought each other up to date with a fair amount of honesty. She had always judged Sam to be on her side, and she was confident Sam assumed the same for her.

"Rowley was awful." Sam laughed quietly. "You can guess. And Gino has to come on to everyone at first, particularly if they're older—"

"Not everyone," came the quiet voice.

"Rowley's warmed up since. He can't be pompous for too long, and Gino finally won him over by being himself."

Gino snorted disagreement, drifting out from the walls finally into the light. The type of some of her best students. Blossom head heavy with beard and hair. Thin as a saint, he had that sharp flayed boy's sexuality potent off him like the smell of paint. His eyes suddenly coming up to meet hers were a dark blue-gray that startled her, and she looked away without meaning to. She was making her lame explanation about what she was doing in Leon's rickety household when she had an idea. "Can you run a projector?"

He could and they had movies. They liked that. Gino even allowed himself excitement and spoke of what he would do with a camera. They had brought grass and got high in the screen-lit dark but kept talking, kept in contact. Last year she had fretted that Sam might never escape Rowley's domination. Obviously her relationship with her brother had trained her in the right mixture of independence and submission needed to live with Gino and his bruised cool idealism and the girls who would keep trying to immolate themselves on it.

Sam flipped her braid over a shoulder and drew her feet under her, blinking at the return of light. "Are you still mad at Rowley for being so stupid?"

"Of course not."

"He's awfully silly. But he's generous and gutsy and warmhearted—"

"Toward himself. Does he care about anyone else, finally?"

"Don't pretend you think that, Anna. Don't."

Lying on the floor, Gino opened his eyes. "Leave her

alone. You can't hand her over to your brother like a pacifier. Lay off."

Sam did. Anna told them casually what she was doing and they were careful to take it almost for granted. They kidded her on coming into the Movement an old lady. Gino probed about what exactly they were doing in the neighborhood and said he would go down to the office with her before they left town. They talked about organizing on campus, they told her dozens of names of people she must meet in Chicago. When they generalized with "we," they included her. She knew when they left they would discuss her, and Sam would say, see, see, I told you.

Saturday Leon got up as early as she did. While she ate he sat at the table making little notes and mumbling to himself.

"What happened last night with your folks?"

He fell into coughing and shook his head helplessly. "Eh. Today's the day Caroline gives herself away. Yeah. I'm going to celebrate it. Who was that girl who called?"

He insisted. He had the ability to sense the undertones of her silences. She told him.

"He sent her over, uh? Why did you talk to her?"

When she came back from the office, late because they had been putting out a mailing, the apartment was still empty. Leon did not come home until Sunday morning. Then he arrived too weak to make it to bed alone and she had to undress him.

"Now she's married to him," he muttered. He lay in bed wrapped in all the blankets. He complained of cold but his forehead was burning. "She's done it. Finished it off once and for all. All gone."

She made tea and he drank it. Then he complained of being hot and threw off the blankets. He got up and she could not make him lie down until he began to shiver. "Nobody gets anything," he muttered. "Nobody gets anything. Everybody gets nothing."

Monday afternoon his fever rose to 104.4 and she was afraid. She gave him aspirin and tried Rowley's cold remedy:

equal parts strong tea, rum and lemon juice, with enough
sugar to get it down. He cursed as he drank it and threw it
up.

Leon tossed in bed, his face shining under sweat. He was
simmering with fever. Restlessly he turned in the nest of
rumpled covers. His breath came harshly, his chest rattled.

"Leon, I think I better call a doctor."

He made a gesture of disgust. But when she started turning
the yellow pages, he said, "Call my cousin Murray. He's a
fat jerk but he knows what he's doing. Murray Lederman.
Burt's oldest kid. Call him, say I got a bad cold and arrange
with him so you go to a drugstore and he calls in the prescription." Then he grinned, facing half into the pillow.
"And pick up the newspapers, okay? I want to see the newspapers."

Cousin Murray was busy. After she explained, the nurse
said Dr. Lederman would phone her back. In the meantime
she called the office to explain she would not be in for the
staff meeting. Then she tried plain tea to sweat his fever
down. She fiddled with the stove and succeeded by constant
effort in keeping the bedroom moderately warm.

Leon turned his swollen head back and forth heavily. His
orange hair was plastered to his scalp. She was ashamed to
realize she did not like to touch him.

"So she's married," he muttered. "I'm going to get my
lawyer to fix it so I can see Jimmy. She's running around
with some dentist. Ought to be able to pin something on.
He's my kid, right?"

When she touched the pillows they were wet. She changed
the cases. It was dark before his cousin returned the call. At
first he was suspicious of what kind of prescription she was
trying to get. When she mentioned Leon's temperature, he
said he would come. He let her know how much out of the
way it was. When he called her Joye, she did not bother to
correct him.

She fed Leon hot bouillon and changed his pajamas.
Quickly she tidied, hiding her traces. When the doctor finally
arrived, she realized she need not have troubled: he was
wading into the unseemly and could not be relied upon to

discriminate between scrubbed and unscrubbed bare boards. He would not at first take off his coat: a short stout pigeony man whose scarce brown hair had only orange lights, although he retained the sad family nose and brow ridges. A weak chin: his head gave up. He knew by now she was not Joye and called her "Miss" though Leon introduced them gruffly. He bustled around Leon, clucking. Before he examined Leon he ordered her out of the bedroom, while Leon kidded him hoarsely and without energy.

"Ashamed to have anyone see how you treat me, you quack? How's your mother?"

When the door opened, Cousin Murray was obviously angry. Ignoring her he went to the phone and dialed, misdialing, quit and dialed again. "Hello, Fern? Yes, well he has pneumonia. No, of course not. How am I supposed to know? Gross neglect. No use upsetting yourself. What are you talking about? No, I didn't see it. I don't have time to read newspapers. Into the hospital, I'll arrange it. Always glad to. Yes, why don't you, I think that would be the best thing."

She went in. Leon was lying with the pillows pushed up and his eyes closed. "He says you have pneumonia."

"Fancy name for a bad cold. I'm not going to the hospital."

She kept silent, not wanting him to go either. She was afraid of hospitals. Leon would be taken and fitted into a white frame. Her fear made her guilty. She had to say, "If you're that sick maybe you better."

His eyes opened, the pupils large, the irises only rims of blue skim milk. "Eager to get rid of me?"

"No," She touched his hot hand. Gritty feeling.

"Better off here." He patted the bed. "You're not a bad nurse. You get a bang out of it."

"Not much. I like you better cool and healthy."

"Am I ever healthy?" His head lolled on one shoulder. "Born with a sick eye. See a gray world, color of ash. See you gray too."

"I'm not gray! I don't see you gray."

"Wash your eyes out." He said then in fitful eagerness,

"Tell Caroline I'm sick. She'll get over her mad. She'll figure I've been out of my head with fever. Who's that?"

She went out to see Sheldon enter, trailed by Fern and another woman. Sheldon was monolithic and glittering, florid from the cold with a vibrancy of joyful anger coming off him. Quickly he surveyed the room, her with the other furniture, before passing in a wake of cold air into the bedroom. He shut the door but his raised voice came through it. Clucking, Cousin Doctor Murray went after him.

The other woman sat gingerly on the couch. Fern stood in her fur, twisting her hands. "I must pack his things for the hospital, but how can I go in there with Sheldon so upset? Why does Leon do these things?" Fern paced around the apartment, running a finger along a table, giving the refrigerator a peek, peering without recognition at Joye's mobile of bicycle parts. "I told him Friday night to watch his step. Sheldon is furious!"

"He certainly has given you enough concern." The other woman was plump, corseted, with fat slack cheeks surrounded by blonded hair. She fidgeted with her shuddery hat and tweaked at her gloves. "He'll worry you into a stroke one of these days, what does he care? Trouble for the family. Everything the way he wants. His parents should give and give and he should take and take, a big boy his age." The woman's eyes scraped over her.

She leaned against the wall by the bedroom door, her arms crossed, incredulous. Amazing grace. The righteous shall forever stick the ungodly with pins and needles and laws and their abominable manner of being in the world. Holy fat wives and mothers, forgive me my body and loves, my hair and clothes, forgive.

Sheldon swept out. He slapped his gloves smartly into his hand and stood a moment frowning. "Didn't you pack for him yet?" he asked Fern. "Get a move on." His gaze fell then on her. "You can go home."

"I am home. And you may stay a short while longer."

The electric cold eyes of Leon's father looked and waited for her gaze to drop. A vain handsome irascible man who loathed her on sight. An efficient enemy who wanted to turn the world into himself. The eyes flicked on. He was too busy to challenge her at length. She perceived the source of Leon's gentleness. Also that puritan streak. He had eaten the father and could not cast him out and must always with part of his mind condemn his own pleasures.

Leon was forced to dress, bundled into his coat, a small bag was packed for him, and the entourage exited. They did not offer to tell her where they were taking him, and she was too proud to ask. After they had gone silence hummed in the rooms.

Leon

Invasion of the
Poverty Freaks

Saturday, January 17

He had little trouble getting his people together. There wasn't that much competing in Chicago and they liked him. Old goodwill. Elliott not only agreed to send his current stars but came himself in high drag and full of suggestions. Friday he rented the equipment and bought the film and started collecting the props and garbage they would need. Finally he had taped the words he had written. Saturday when they assembled he played the tape for his actors. He thought it went over pretty well, but he would make decisions on the basis of what happened and the kind of footage he caught. They assembled at his pad, skirted the park, marched under the viaduct and along the embankment; a route where few saw them until they arrived.

Saturday morning at eleven thirty in the new shopping plaza, zenith of local commerce and socialization. The prosperous burghers nudged each other gently in the wide malls. But before the drum Big Thelma (two hundred fifty pounds of ex-anthropologist-whore) beat they fell back. This was handheld camera with a vengeance, because he was jostled and shoved.

THE EXILES'S RETURN

WE ARE ALIVE TOO: WE ARE AS REAL AS <u>YOU</u>

WE ARE YOUR GARBAGE
YOU DISPOSED OF US

WE ARE BRINGING OUR GARBAGE
BACK TO YOU

He was glad that he had shot the footage of demolition over the past months, especially that summer stuff. The commentary spoke in his mind. *Our tenements crack like rotten eggs before the swinging ball of the wrecking crew. A sidewalk smeared with hopscotch leads to a pit. Gray with dust, a workman sorts bricks where the deaf shoemaker coughed at his oily bench. Feldman's candystore is a nondenominational parkinglot. There . . . are . . . no . . . smells . . . left.*

A hag in Army surplus overcoat shuffled raggedly, riffling every wastebasket they passed and strewing the contents. Doreen in town for the weekend from Ski U was made up as a tubercular beggar. His old girl Fran toted a sign NEGRO HUSTLER WITH AGED DEPENDENT DESIRES ROOM, with her brother and his friends as hoods marching together like a war party. They had magic markers and chalk and cans of spray paint.

FAT CITY

YOU SUCK MONEY

GARBAGE OF THE WORLD, REVOLT:
YOU HAVE NOTHING TO LOSE
BUT A TRIP TO THE INCINERATOR

BLACK SUN RISING
MOON GOING DOWN IN BLOOD

YOU STOLE MY BONE

The neighborhood is being facelifted for professional couples who wish nice companions. Gingerly the great crane nibbles the bar where many began and many more never could: the teeth close. (Zoom shot.)

Ghosts of dislocated alleycats slink at midnight under the fluourescent moons of shopping plaza. Halloween visitants haunt their bulldozed beds.

Pink and purple and green and gold and black. Tinsel and rags, sequins and burlap. The big cart filled with burned mattresses and twisted springs and broken mirrors and plas-

ter and bricks and doors and cracked toilet bowls was drawn
by Elliott's boys with Elliott himself in full thirties drag on
the driver's seat. Big Thelma beat a rock rhythm on the drum
and his parade came dancing after, clanking strings of tincans at their feet, wheeling dollies heaped up with suitcases
and boxes, moaning and lurching and weeping and shouting
out the slogans on their signs and banners. They came under
big emblems of roaches and rats borne above them, some of
the kids burning incense. But instead of flowers they tossed
garbage. The pillars of the mall dripped red and black. Elliott
would hand down a smashed chandelier or a bottomless chair
and another actor would place it carefully in front of one of
the onlookers or against the window of a store.

A boy peddled bright balloons labeled GRASS, ACID,
BENNY, PEYOTE, KIF, OPIUM, HASH, SPEED, HORSE. A girl
dragged a kid's red wagon with a plaster statue of St. Francis
wearing beads.

POVERTY = LEPROSY

YOU HAVE TAKEN OUR HOMES: TAKE US INTO YOURS

Into the shopping plaza jiggled the army of unwanted.

His heart rocked in his chest as if he was on a bad trip. He
was hot and cold in long woozy spurts. Even through his shades
the sun clawed out of the sky and fractured off the expanses
of new cement, and he had to take off his shades as soon as
he started squinting through the lens. He had not eaten since
yesterday, had had nothing but a cup of coffee and a candybar
and the glass of water with which he took two antihistamines,
yet he was high. On top of his fever, on top of his sickness,
he balanced on a bouncing wire. Colors struck on his eyes,
cries entered his ears and blood and burned there with a cool
rippling ecstasy. He had to fight to see black and white. Nor-
mally he hated color: it was anti-image. It was cheap pseu-
dorealism. It encouraged postcard reportage instead of seeing
it new. *What is seen, is.* The phonemes of cinema are images.
He found himself floating into abstraction. Hold on, hold on.
The camera felt heavy. His arm ached already.

WE BREATHE: DON'T BURY US
IN GARBAGE
IN GHETTOS
LOVE US, WE ARE YOUR SHADOWS
WE ARE YOUR GARBAGE

Images would intervene. A fence of doors: exits, invitations, openings, and places where locks are hung. Flash of a doorman barring an entrance. Around them shoppers surged, stopped cold. A hush of horror settled on some. Others yelled. Some tried to interfere and he filmed a couple of fistfights. Some giggled, some frowned, some stared, some turned and hurried away.

I AM BLACK BUT COMELY AND
I WILL NOT MARRY YOUR SON
(NOT EVEN FOR MONEY)

REVOLT OF THE GARBAGE
RETURN OF THE REFUSE

THE WASTE COMES BACKIn the center of the plaza where a small parklike area surrounded a fountain with an original piece of sculpture all brassy and nonevocative (unless it was programmed subliminally to whisper, buy, buy, buy) they began to deposit their gifts. They opened the tattered bags and dirty suitcases and stacked up the bags of garbage around the fountain.

Dream of freaks and razors. Barb your hedges, doublelock your doors, hire men to stand guard outside, put up wire fences, arm your cops with mace and flamethrowers and tanks.

NOTHING HUMAN
ALIENATES
LIKE COMFORT

The press arrived five minutes before the fuzz. So ended his parallel ceremony.

Rowley

Sam sat on the windowledge, one leg swinging and the other propped up. Her hair hung in a fat glossy braid and she clasped her hands behind her neck looking wise. "I could have told you six months ago you wanted her . . ."

She did not know what six months could hold. Vera haunted the corner of his eye by flashes: barefoot in pants and loose olive sweater. He felt removed from Sam and patient.

A goldbrown shirt brought out the blood in her cheeks. "Now you've let her move in with some guy and then you complain you can't reach her. All this static. I can't figure you both out. Are you looking for an excuse to give up?"

"Not hardly. But you don't patch up with someone by twisting her arm."

"I don't see why not." Sam looked with private meaning at Gino slumped against the wall. "If you do it nicely."

"You want her to come to you." Gino squinted up through the bottom of a popbottle. "Why should she? She has a scene going."

"But she always does have." In which she was just like him.

"Because she's open." Gino scratched his crotch. "If you want to get to her you'll have to risk being open yourself."

"All this good advice. Like the phony whipcream that squirts from a can." Ten minutes with Anna and the kid was

319

lecturing. Anna always turned gangly kids on. Sweet the kid would say if that word wasn't excised from his jargon: sweet, uh? also salty, spicy and bitter in layers the kid would never taste.

But what he minded the most was what he had come to think during the weekend, watching Sam and Gino and the friend who had come with them and slept too on his floor at ease, grubby from traveling and unsurprised and cheerful together. A few days before they had been busted at a demonstration at an induction center and they were full of comparative anecdotes about demonstrations and beatings and jails. That morning their friend had left on his way to the Coast. Sam and Gino would be catching a ride back in a few hours, hoping to arrive for their morning class.

He could no longer dismiss Gino as the son of a chemical engineer, though he found Gino still glib and fuzzy and product of Midland, still infuriatingly righteous and callow. He had watched them and saw that Sam was more theirs than his. They shared phrases and buttons and jokes, they sang scraps of rock and owned the same few books—which he had sometimes read but not in the same way. They shared more than a bed, more than a language and friends and style, though the style was important to them in ways he thought silly. They were at once open and closed, mistrustful of anyone who could not share their cool, easy style. They had political instincts different from his own, and perhaps more natural to them than his had ever been.

The kids were more and less isolated than he was. They had a total mistrust of the whole shebang that startled him. Where his generation had taken honors and bitched at the system, they dropped out. How will you make it? Oh, they said, by hustling. They turned seacold eyes on the establishments right, left, liberal, philanthropic, academic. There was scarcely a man with power or place they did not consider an enemy, yet they spent little time in the ritual cursing he remembered as the main social form of politics at their age. They struck him as naive because they thought meeting in their dingy storefronts and cranking out their mimeograph machines they could change the world: but already they had changed each other. They had a sense of identity and community he had had only in his music. They felt part of something, not in the disciplined but rigidly insistent way he had known with American Communists. Thrown down in random flat cities they found each other, in Fort Wayne and Davenport, in Tangiers and Guatemala City. They invested much hope in small countries whose geography was blank to him. They made him turn and examine his youth as a piece of history. They could say "the revolution" without giggling, without quotes, without a sense of absurdity. Harlan and he had called themselves radicals, but if they had referred to "the revolution" the quotes hung in the air and their tone was heavy heavy irony, self-deprecation and shame.

They struck him as good. Nothing would be given them but each other. They made him feel fat and sluggish. They made him feel that the pleasure he took in his work had drained something from his life that he must get back. He felt bought off. He had been allowed to do his thing and paid for it and sat on the shitheap studying blues archives, witnesses of past troubles. He would not be sorry to have them gone, for he was not used to envying. He was afraid for them, for Sam's rosy face and soft body. A few nights in jail were an experience: five years ground anyone down. No one had charm after that. He had met civil rights workers with the shattered reflexes of mental patients. This fat violent country wanted pretty longhaired radical kids no more than lice in its armpits and would squash them one by one.

A little after three in the morning they left, bookbag and laundrybag and bag of sandwiches and fruit, gone, and he lay on his mattress with his head echoing and did not particularly like being alone.

He stopped by concession row after work for several days before he was convinced nobody was there. First he sat parked in the VW hoping to catch Anna coming in or out. Then he took to banging on the door. Finally he leaned his forehead on the plateglass and peered in. Mail was piled below the mail slot, and lying nearer to the door was a key. Everything looked clean and neat and cryptic. Were they out of town together? Leon's old Buick stood at the curb looking as if it would never move, yet he could not get rid of the notion she might have gone off with Leon.

All they would tell him at ISS was that Anna had quit at the end of December. He hated to ask Paul, but they had other business. On Friday he picked up the kid after a meeting and they ate Chinese.

Paul was letting his hair grow—mostly up—and he looked tall and wild. Paul would carry a load of ornament. At first he had prized Paul for what remained of Vera in his looks and most his way of speaking. The resemblance had hurt but hooked him. He had felt protective of the kid and full of an unnerving urge to touch him. That had passed. Paul was Paul and not Vera (or only a little).

"What are you doing on your show tonight?" Paul asked him over iron steaks. "That Jack Custis thing, that was strong. That had pepper in it."

He winced. "Thought there'd be backlash. Cries of pain. But Cal, my boss, called me in to tell me how he loved it. It was too tough, too beautifully brutal, Cal said, the real nitty gritty, and why don't I do some more? . . . Jack's sister finally turned over the records she has and Psychedelic is bringing out an LP. I wrote the jacket copy." He took out a check for fifty dollars. "So the guy says, get in something about black power, that's very now." He endorsed the check and shoved it across. "I know you have FBM contacts. Pass it on."

"You meant to build a fire and only made fireworks." Paul put away the check, giving the waitress a cool eye. "I thought you were down on them."

"They're sitting ducks. And I want everybody in one movement, everybody wanting to change the system, shake it, break it. But I have nothing to offer except that I don't know where to start. Harlan's fighting, anyhow." He rubbed his chin. "What's old Leon doing these days?"

"You mean aside from busting up the shopping plaza?"

"That was *him*? But . . ." He shook his head. "Were you there?"

Paul looked embarrassed. "Don't see much of him. Anna called to say he was in the hospital."

So where was she? Saturday morning he went by her old place on the off chance she might have left a forwarding address. Her mailbox was stuffed with eviction notices. The hall hadn't been swept in weeks and a drunk had left an empty tenth and a stink of piss in the entrance. Dark as the mines. Feeling silly he knocked. No answer of course. Notice pinned to her door that if she did not remove her things by Monday A.M., the city would.

He knocked pock-pock on an empty room. He was turning away when he smelled something. Funny sharp smell like scorched food. He sniffed at the crack. Yes, from inside. He banged harder. "Anna?" Put his ear to it. Heard something, maybe. "Anna? Open this goddamn door, I know you're in there." Alternate visions of her roasting in bed and some bum burning the furniture to keep warm. Yet he was scared. He could see his breath as he yelled, "I'm going to bust it down, Annie." Old private eye flicks. Bust his shoulder first. Instead he took out his jackknife and slid it between the rotten wood of the jamb and wall until it nudged aside the bolt. He pushed the door open and walked in.

Woman. Anna. Wrapped in an old black winter coat, three sweaters and a scarf, she squatted behind a hibachi from which smoke curled. To her left was a pile of index cards she was checking one at a time against a typed list. Her hands were bare and she warmed them at the small flame. Over her the ceiling was smudged. She was bundled into shapelessness. She looked Eskimo, the skin of her face tight, the cheekbones slashes, the eyes squinted against the smoke black and tough with scrutiny. Stubbornly she went on matching the index cards against the list and making an occasional correction.

"Hello there." He got down on his hunkers. "Having fun?"

"Working. Remember me, I don't believe in fun."

"What are you burning there, old mice?"

She showed her teeth briefly. "My past."

"Glad you're finding it useful." He looked into the hibachi. Scorched notes. Letter fragments. Brown and shiny scraps with small gray lacunae of photographic images. "Here I am again, keeping you warm in war as in peace."

"You and half a dozen others. Heroes all."

"Including Leon?"

"Leon is in the hospital," she said in a flat monitory tone.

"So I hear."

"Did you hear which one?" Her eyes hoped.

He shook his head.

"*The* hospital." She snorted. "That's all I know."

"You're squatting here?"

"I slept at the project office last night. It got spooky at Leon's. The phone made me jump. I felt I didn't belong there."

"You don't."

Deep in the burden of wool she shrugged. She was round as a potato. Indifferent as the stone goddess on the door. She crouched behind the smoking hibachi with her nose smudged and her hands black with carbon and inkspots and the plume of her breath dissolving before her. Hobo over a campfire in a jungle.

He looked and looked, stymied. She took more cards and checked them. Only the faintest curl of her lips indicated she knew he was there. Her body was veiled and padded. She corrected a card and reached for another. He grabbed her by the arms and tipped her over against him. Her lips were cool and tasted of smoke. Her eyes widened in surprise and she tried to speak against his mouth. It was so much like embracing a large bag of laundry he lost her mouth and began to laugh.

"Let go of me, Rowley. I have a right to choose what I want."

"You moved out of Leon's. Here you are."

She glared. The scarf came off and her hair, warm from it, flowed over his bracing arm. "Maybe I'll marry him. He needs someone to look out for him—"

"And you need someone to look out for? I'll buy you a blind goldfish."

She shoved the heel of her hand into his chest. "Stop belittling him."

"Only want one thing he's got."

"Didn't want it when you had it."

"Older. Wiser. Hungrier. Poor Leon will get out of the hospital with his knees dragging and find this big strapping woman wanting to screw him back in again."

Her eyes snapped. She struck fullforce against his chest, trying to thrust free. She was too bundled up to exert pressure and he held on.

"Victorian Anna. How come you get mad like that?"

Her temper dwindled and she touched her tongue to her lip. "Suppose it's a matter of my repressive upbringing among what C. Wright Mills calls the lumpen-bourgeoisie— a name I find suggestive of the texture of my mother's kre-plach. I remember asking my mother what rape meant, and she told me that was what men did to women."

"And what do women do to men?"

"Your father told you that was marriage—no?" Her voice was urbane. "How is your father lately?"

"In the hospital again. I drove Sam home. Grim scene. They want him to have another operation."

She was covertly trying to wriggle out of his grasp, all the while asking nice questions. "Will another operation help? Do they hold out any real help?"

"Going to stick a warm poultice named Annie to him and watch the old king go. Come here."

"I am nobody's warm poultice," she said and spat in his face. Her eyes were narrow. She would not budge.

"With Leon hanging on your tit?"

"Ah, you're so sure you're better than he is!"

"For you? You bet I am."

"Ha. Well, turn it into a mysticism. Rave about it the way he does about Caroline."

"Caroline?"

"Don't you feel funny thinking she's married to that prick and going to have your baby? Don't you feel anything?"

"Hell, yes. It's a bad joke. The kid should come and shoot

me in twenty years, but he isn't reason enough to live with her.''

''And I don't have *any* reason to put up with you.'' Even her hands were closed against him into fists.

''Indifferent.''

''Hard as that may be for you to believe.''

''It's some good instinct makes you provoke me, because otherwise I might just give up and go home.'' He yanked on her and she came dragging against him with willful clumsiness, making herself bulky and inert and thumping like an old boot caught on a line. She hid in her layers of garments and turned her face into his jacket. He was left to bury his mouth in her hair.

He fumbled at her looking for flesh. Boots, thick texture hose, finally a stretch of thigh—under her coat and skirt and slip his hand found and closed on hot sleek skin. God she was warm. Almost burned his hand. ''Annie, I want you.''

''On rye or whole wheat? And who will you have for dessert?'' She spoke muffled into his chest, hiding her face.

''And I love you. Whatever that means. This time I admit it's not the same thing.''

''Go away then. Come back when Leon's out of the hospital. I have to think.''

''No. Can't afford that. I want you to clear out of here with me. If you loved him—''

''Whatever that means,'' she said bitterly, lifting her head.

''—you wouldn't be here. You'd have fought his family tooth and claw, nails and crockery. You'd know where you belong. You'd be sitting in that hospital corridor on guard.''

Gravely she met his gaze. He saw that she half believed him. A great lightness buoyed him up.

''In some sense it's because he never *left* his family,'' she was beginning. He kissed her hard, holding on to that sleek piece he had claimed, and her mouth under his turned warm and ripened. He gathered her closer with a nostalgic ache through his groin. Wanting, remembering wanting, remembered having, all the merged funny burrowing of bodies. His. He kissed her until he was sweating and heat shimmered off of her like a blacktop road in summer, till her mouth was

swollen and pulsing. Yet she lay in his arm withdrawn in her
clothing and taut with waiting. If he released her she would
spring away. He groped upward and into her bush and found
the truthful ooze of welcome. Her mouth came wider under
his, her breath caught and crumpled and the tautness faded
into her arms. He dug for her among the woolens, unbuttoned the coat and rolled her out, unbuttoned the ski sweater
and drew off the pullover, digging for the ample slow lines
of her until they were nested among the cast clothes. Her
breast heavy and filling his hand. Curve of hip into him.
Solid pressure of thighs under. Quick ripple across her belly
as he stroked it. Lips nuzzling, her urgent passivity gathered
against him and moving as he moved. Her large dark eyes
were open and watching and merry, almost amused. He
wondered then exactly when she had decided. He came into
her and slowly her muscles accepted him. Her cunt held him
in a smooth firm grip like her hands, and he was home.

Yawning she curled up in her coat, round and embryonic,
and smiled. He dressed and stood looking around. "Come
on. Time to pack up."

"Oh," she said languidly. "Didn't say I'd go back to you."

"Won't be the same. Nothing is. And I don't want it to
be."

Lying on her belly she looked at him out of the cocoon of
coat. "Something new? Or just the rhetoric of prick?"

"Come and live with me."

She shuddered in the coat. "We'll probably get pneumonia, it's freezing. I'm afraid you'll hurt me. I've always
been afraid."

"I guess I will. There's a lot of meanness in me. Did Leon
make you happy?"

"Happy was what Asher married me for. What an obscene
thing for any human to think they can do for another."

"I've asked you, Annie. I won't argue with you."

"You shouldn't quit so easy."

Standing over her he gave her a gentle nudge with his foot.
"I've used up my best argument."

"I'm coming already. What's the hurry?" But she did not
move until he began awkwardly pulling clothes out of draw-

ers. When she had dressed she came to stand beside him.
"Did you miss me, then?"

"Sometimes. Especially lately."

Marching off to pack her bags she called, "Well, if I liked
to fuck just a little bit less, you wouldn't get me back, not
yet you wouldn't."

"That cuts both ways."

"Five or six ways, Rowley. I was hoping you'd turn up."

"Why didn't you open the door?"

"Who shut it?"

That afternoon they spent moving her. He was inclined to
leave things and she to take them. She was quiet in the car,
downcast. Since he was fifteen, women had happened to
him. She had not happened this time. He had the advantage,
he thought as he drove north, of understanding better than
she could yet what that meant. She would find her footing.

As he parked her face questioned him. They loaded up
and she preceded him stopping at each dark and smelly landing until he nodded her onward. Worn coat. He had been
more giving with Sam, with Harlan, with any casual acquaintance. The coat was thin and threadbare. Was she cold
in it?

Hesitantly she walked in. "You didn't waste yourself fur-
nishing it."

"Figured you'd want to help." He ambled after her.
"Planning to take off your coat and stay awhile?"

"*Chutzpah* pays again. Well, if it wasn't me, it would be
another." She stood shy and flatfooted until she came to
unbutton her coat. She stepped out of her boots, then walked
slowly before him to the mattress past a witnessing row of
unpacked boxes. With a small smile she sat down neatly on
the edge of the mattress and gave a nod toward her left shoulder. "Pull down the shades."

He did. As he was kneeling to reach for her, she swooped
forward and caught him off balance, toppling him into her
arms.

At last they carried the final load up the three flights. Then
as she made supper he sat on the floor picking chords and
singing now and then.

Me and my baby was side by side,
Yes, me and my baby was side by side,
She said to me, Daddy I want to ride . . .

He was tired, he was hungry, he was pleased. He trusted that she was too.

Anna Rowley

Sunday, January 25—
Sunday, February 1

Putting away kitchen utensils she thought of Leon damply, with guilt. She felt partly as if she had run out on him, and partly as if she had escaped. Clearly there was nothing there for her, but equally clearly that had not mattered. In comradely love she had lived with Leon, on his terms. Now it was as if she had quit their game and said, Well that was fun, but now it's time for some real live adultsize sex and love and household. He would say she had sold out, and if what she had betrayed was vague, her sense of it was not. She had opted for bread and flesh and direct clang-clash argument, she had put away Leon's gods in a box like broken dolls, and they haunted her.

Rowley was at work. Though she felt shy about calling hospitals—encountering any bureaucracy—she forced herself to begin at A in the yellow pages. She called through D, went back to work in the kitchen, then did E-H. No luck.

Next she hung her dresses on the left side of the closet, one at a time with enjoyment. After she called through L she began supper, freed and tangled and vaguely satisfied. She put on a Bach cello partita. She had mostly wasted the day and that was a treat, pottering about in random gusts of thought and memory. She moved in her loose body listening, touching, fixing and in part waiting, because she was not sure of him yet—if ever she would be—but she was sure now of herself.

* * *

Though rationally he did not believe she could have left, because hadn't it taken them four hours to move her in, he was relieved to see lights up there. The hall smelled of chicken and cardamon and coriander. Strolling from the kitchen to greet him, she wore that grave sensual smile of the day before. Her loose hair shone. She looked at home and serene. He was struck by the knowledge sudden and painful as a muscle cramp that he no longer lived alone in his privacy. He followed her into the kitchen and told her his day.

After supper she said she had called through L and handed him the yellow pages. During Ns he reached the right hospital.

"Mr. Lederman was checked out this afternoon."

He repeated it to her. She gave a wince of dismay and took the phone. Waited, thumbnail at teeth. Waited. Finally she hung up. "But he's not there."

"So he's out. Or staying with his family."

"I can't call them. Anyhow, he must be all right if they let him out. Mustn't he?"

Monday when he came home she was more puzzled. "Leon's phone has been disconnected.

"Did you pay the bill?"

She threw her arms around him. "That must be it!"

She could not go on calling a dead phone. On her way back from work on rainy Wednesday she headed over, speeches bumping one another in her head: all crude, awkward, apologetic and stupid. Ho ho, guess what, old Leon, we've come full circle. Yes, I know I hated him last week, but the moon or the wind changed . . . She saw herself arriving. Leon would be sitting in his director's chair bundled up, tousled and still blowing his nose. "Why isn't there coffee?" he'd bark, and she'd trot out to the kitchen. He would launch into denunciations of his family, the doctors, the hospital, the wasted time. They would argue about his happening and why he had kept it secret from her and she would help him edit the film. He would have a new plot for reaching

Caroline or abducting Jimmy. "What's for supper?" She
would never, never have the nerve to tell him about Rowley.
She could not look him in the eyes and say, I'm leaving, it
was all a mistake. She would take his temperature and off
they would go to bed, clumsily, furtively, gently. All would
recommence. Ay. And then she would see Rowley, his eyes.
Had to, had to tell him.

She knocked and peered in the rain-streaked window. The
shade was up and the key on the floor as she had left it. She
hung around in the rain stamping her feet and watching her
breath, but it was dark and she felt Rowley waiting and suddenly wanted to be with him, with him at once.

The next morning the phone rang. They had finished
breakfast and he was going through a stack of new releases
while she measured the windows for draperies. When he put
down the phone she took one look at his face and got down
from the chair. "Leon?"

"The old man. He walked out of the hospital. That was
my mother." Turned on his heel. "Got to call the station."

She followed, waiting. "Do you think you'll be back for
supper? Or will you spend the night in Gary?"

He drew his hand through his dark bushy hair. His eyes
tightened, grew catlike and cruel. "Get changed. You're
coming."

She did not dare say anything but with suddenly fat hands
put on a teaching dress and pinned up her hair. In ten minutes
they were in the car heading south to the Calumet Skyway.

The thaw continued. Yesterday, the day before, an unclean
gray rain had fallen, not hard but constant like a bad cold in
the atmosphere. Everything felt clammy. The world had begun to dissolve. Sidewalks flowed between granite levees
stained tan with old dogpiss. Deep waterfilled ruts snaked
through the deeper ice of streets. Sand, cinder, turds, grit
and rocks were left exposed as by the retreat of a glacier. A
pause in the Ice Age. The winter would be continued after a
short intermission.

Covertly she fingered her hair and moved a bobbypin to
tighten the chignon, looked at him—his walrus moustache
and strong nose and coarse black tumbled hair. She touched

his thigh. From the Skyway the sky was low and battered, clearing in patches over the immense gray city. She could not lose the sense of going on a journey. "Hey you," she said softly.

"Yeah?"

"It's good. That's all." Tatters of the night lay warm and tenuous on her. Turmoil and compromise. She was humiliated to want him as she did, and nothing else was worth the sweat. Loving him justified nothing, changed nothing outside their coming together which would always be ragged and flawed and the strongest thing she had to assimilate into herself. He had come to her and this time he was putting himself on the line: but there would be other parties and pretty easy girls and invitations too sincere to be passed up. She would have to make her own peace with her pride. That was what she decided was Anna this windy wet February day as they passed a great storage tank where turning flights of smoke-colored pigeons like specks in a film flickered against the rusty sky.

He just drove. He disengaged his concern because traveling would take the time it took and then he would see what was up. What he must do. She curled on her side looking demure and sleepy. Occasionally her gaze turned on him and asked, Is it all right? are you worried?

The sky was dull red over the refineries. Squat orange flames blew off. Rolling down his window he stuck out his hand for a ticket at the tollbooth and handed it to her. Clark emblem on the low round tanks. He speeded some on the tollroad, running past the orange South Shore trains to one side, freight running contrary, E J & E on the other, high tension wire strung from towers he had called soldiers as a kid, soldiers marching tall in rows blam blam blam from the backseat of the old Terraplane, past dunes, marsh, scrub, approaching the vast steel mills. A nonlandscape, abstract. 90 East. It never failed to move him in contradictory spasms. The Calumet River steamed with chemicals alongside.

"Close the window. It's gassing me," she said.

Downhome smell. Clouds of stink rotting the lungs. U.S.

Steel as far as the eye could travel on the left. On the right gritty Gary led to the twin domes of downtown. An even line of slender stacks suddenly belched rusty smoke. They were putting oxygen into the open-hearth furnaces, making the flames leap and roar. A belt of coke cars pulled out empty. Parkinglots glittered cars.

Why hadn't he gone into the mills? He'd wanted to clear out of Gary. Fighting with his old man, girl on his back to marry her. The ships had drawn him. At least they moved. But through childhood he had been fascinated by the mills where his father went. Sunbright corn likker steel. The shapes of the buildings, the stacks, the towers, the furnaces excited him. Inhuman manmade scene. He remembered the long strike when the air had been clean over the drab houses. Steel shaped men and land: for miles the mills pissed into the lake and dirtied the sun. They were beautiful.

Gary West exit. He had a gut perception that slacked his foot on the gas, a slight queasiness that resolved in a shrug as he touched his tongue to his moustache. Overlap with the old man. Because he was bringing her home—not that it was. As he downshifted on the ramp she counted change and handed over the ticket. Then they were on Grant heading south. Because he was fulfilling the old man's pattern, choosing his own dark somewhat alien woman later then usual. A woman he damn well ought to treat more kindly and in better faith than his father had. Having learned something? Only Annie would judge.

The house was custard yellow with several cars already in back. The paint was peeling. Sparrows perched on the nylon clothesline. A birdbath stood in the circle of pastel stones near a bottomheavy snowman turning to slush. As they left the car a woman maybe forty opened the stormdoor on the second-floor porch and peered down. "How are you, George!" she called, giving it two syllables. "How's life treatin' you these days?"

He waved in answer and pushed her ahead through the kitchen door. She could have killed him. She didn't want to march in first with her nervous face hanging out. A sausage-shaped blonde powdered pink as a plastic baby sat at the table in a kelly green tasseled dress, her ringed hands spread flush on the tabletop and her mouth open. A tall hardbodied woman with irongray hair streaked with white chopped vegetables at the sink. She had to be his mother.

He introduced her by name without explanations. The blonde was his brother's wife, and his mother, who came from the sink wiping her hands on her apron, took Anna's hand in a wooden grip, abrasive and strong. "You made pretty good time," she barked. She did not kiss Rowley but insisted on taking his coat and brushed it carefully as she went to hang it up. "Hope you didn't speed, but I know you better, don't I?"

The sausage was looking her over an inch at a time, but she had expected that. His mother looked in quick sideways glances, shyly. An atmosphere of funeral hung in the house, food and coffee were pressed on them with that ritual insistence, but the man in the posie-covered easychair was alive. His skin was ashen, his eyes bulged in his pitted face, the cords stood out in his hands. Yet his face was alert with an annoyance she recognized. His sandiness had sunk into his children without a trace, but his strength had come through. He was the wreck of a big tough man. At his feet lay an old retriever blinking out of looselidded red eyes and thumping his tail.

"Got you to run down, did they?" He squinted at Rowley, gave her a close, suspicious look. "Dropped everything and came flying. Well, you can fly back for all of me. I'm not going to the hospital no more. They cut me open enough times to air out my insides. Let them practice on puppydogs. Every time they lay a finger on you, another two hundred, five hundred bucks. Some racket."

"Don't worry about the money. Hell with those excuses. Get done what you have to."

"Don't worry!" he mimicked. "It's my body, and I'm holding on to it. They can keep their drugs and bottles. No more." He pounded the arm of his chair. The dog gave a throaty bark and got up fatly to nose him.

She hung back at the archway beside Rowley's mother who

twisted her apron in her hands. Rowley planted himself in front of the easychair. "What are you planning? Going to sit there till you get enough worse you have to go in? Then they cut even more?"

"Think I'm going to hang around your mother's neck, don't you?"

"Listen to him," his mother said. "Listen to what that old loon thinks is an idea. He's lost his mind."

"What idea?" Rowley crossed his thick arms, waiting.

"Stop bearing down on me. Go on, get over there, sit down. What did you bring her for?"

Rowley ambled over to sit on the doggy couch, motioning for her to follow. "Figured she might as well see how mean I'm likely to get, if I live long enough."

"Tell them what you say you're going to do. Tell him, if you aren't ashamed in company," Rowley's mother said from the archway.

"Going down to Brown County, that shack Hanson's got on Bean Blossom Creek. You recall, I used to take you hunting. Old Hanson, he don't get down much any more. He's tickled to have somebody to fix it up."

"He's going off where nobody can take care of him and all I'll do night and day is worry. Oh, I always knew there was a lot of spite in you—"

"Would you be contented, woman, seeing me turn into a vegetable in the hospital? Into a yellow turnip?"

"Go down there and crawl into a hole like an old sick tomcat. Who'll know when you get the pains? Who'll know when you need help and what to do for you?"

"I'll get them to put in a telephone. There's doctors down there. I don't want nobody looking after me. I don't want nobody looking at me, period."

"Tell him he can't do that." His mother took a step past the archway, her eyes fixed on Rowley. "Make him see he can't."

Rowley sat forward against the slope of the couch, his knees spread and his hands resting on them. He bit down on his teeth. His eyes were narrow and bright. "No, I can't say that.'' Slowly he said through gritted teeth, ''He's got a right to the kind of death he wants.''

The old man broke into a grin. His face was sucked hollow but the grin was broad. He had his own dark yellow teeth. ''They don't use that dirty word in the hospital. But I know I'm a loser. I like that country. They're spoiling it, but they're just getting started. It'll last me out. I'm square with my policy, and the union'll bury me. Got my plot paid for out at Mount of Olives. The papers are in the bottom drawer of my chifforobe, in a tin box. You can check them over. I'm all squared away.''

''Feeling proud of yourself, aren't you, mister!'' His wife turned to walk out, then stopped to glare at Rowley. ''You're two of a kind, if you can't see how wrong this all is. The blind leading the blind!'' Two more steps and she turned again, jerking her head at Anna. ''Come on, you can help me set the table for dinner.''

As soon as they were in the kitchen, his mother took her arm in a hard grip. ''You talk to him. Make him see. Make him come back and tell his father he can't act that way!''

Mother stayed mad and he knew her well enough to guess that she would never entirely forgive him. Her feelings ran deep and sullenly, down in some tunnel where she could neither enjoy nor exhaust them. He pitied them both. Harry arrived at mealtime and started yapping at the old man. In the meantime Mother managed to catch him outside the bathroom. ''Are you going to marry her?''

''Maybe.''

''Figured you wouldn't have brought her otherwise.''

''You didn't blink an eye. Sam told you, uh?''

''I don't know what gets into that girl. Course I'd be nice to your girlfriend.''

''Were you nice to Gino?''

''He's not a bad boy. Your father can't stand him, but he shoveled the walk without my asking.'' She looked at the wall, the imprint of former wallpaper wearing through paint thinned by scrubbing. She was a fierce scrubber. ''She doesn't look very Jewish.''

He laughed then, leaning against the shut door in the bathroom, laughed till his ribs ached. Her sharp suspicious eyes
brooded on him, her mouth turned in. He saw himself bringing Vera, and would mother have said, She doesn't look very
colored? For a moment he felt winded and sad through and
through. "It suits me."

"Well, I suppose so." She was bristling.

He gave her a pat on the shoulder. "She suits me. You
know? That'll have to do."

After an enormous meal, plain in the main dishes but fancy
in the trimmings, they drove back. She felt worn out with
paying attention, staring at everything indirectly and being
stared at, not indirectly. She felt numb in her ears and eyes
and facial muscles. All the way back she sat in a mild stupor.
She hadn't even noticed where they were, except that they
were almost, almost home, when he said, "Look, they
started."

The crane stood beside her building with neck bowed and
suppliant, head resting on the ground. Her old rooms lay
open. The outer wall and circlet of windows were gone to
dust. The pale blue walls of her bedroom, the white wall of
her kitchen were nude to the passerby. She felt a dart of
shame. Only the poor were blatantly exposed, her walls with
their personal stains and bumps, the rub marks of her bed,
the smudge over the radiator, the Che poster and the lamp
he'd not thought worth taking.

The crane rose and leaned into the building. "Wait," she
said to him. "Park. I want to see." Rowley pulled over just
past the traffic light and she hopped out to watch as the crane's
teeth ate into her floor, her walls, and the pale blue cracked
and splintered, a rain of loose plaster dribbled from the teeth,
and where she had slept was space. Five, six minutes and
her rooms vanished and had never been. She got back into
the car and they looked at each other. "Didn't take long, did
it?"

"Come on," he said, "you can vaporize a man in two
seconds, what do you want?"

"Your mother asked me to talk to you."

"The old man's okay. Cancer won't pin on a blue ribbon for endurance. And if you go the hospital route there's a point where you stop being human, but no point where they stop making money off your carcass. I expect him to have an accident some time in the spring. He'll wait for the spring—it's pretty in Brown County."

"Why does he have to get away from her? That's what hurts her."

"That's the way they are together. I'm sorry for her. But I can't change the way they've been chipping at each other all these years. Can only try to do a little better myself."

"I'll remind you of that."

"Not too often."

As he pulled into their street, she said, "I have to send Marcia my new address." Yes, because Marcia would be pleased for her, Marcia would understand and be pleased.

When the phone rang after supper he hurried to answer it, thinking it was the girl who wanted him to back her up calling with the recording date: electric this time and so was she, a sloe-eyed part Oglala Sioux with a smoky voice. It was Paul, though, with news. He stumbled over words. When he stopped they both listened to the line static. Then he called Sheldon Lederman from whom he got nothing: not even anger. Then he called the station lawyer for background. At last, reluctantly, he came over to Anna. "That was Paul."

"Does he want to talk to me?" She started to get up.

"No. Listen, Anna—"

"Is he ever going to be friends again?" She grimaced, shoved the evening paper at him. "Know what? Sheldon Lederman is out. Reasons of private business and lots of eulogies. His replacement is Tom Lovis. I think you know him, which reminds me—"

"Listen to me. Leon's been committed by his family."

"What? Committed what?"

"Sheldon committed him to an asylum."

Her face folded on itself. "No!" she said loudly. "No!" It was a long time before she would admit that she believed him. She paced, she argued. "We have to get him out. Don't say it's impossible! Don't you care?"

For a long time she proposed tricks for getting Leon out. Finally she began to cry.

He could not touch her at first. He felt awkward, cut off. "It was that scene he put on in the shopping plaza. How the hell did he ever get the money for the equipment?"

"I gave it to him." She sat in a chair weeping, huddled. "I gave him the money."

Because she saw him. Burned by electroshock, yes, and swollen with the white thunder of insulin and bloated. Worse, she saw him surviving, she saw him settling in The lion would have his cage. The world would be a room, oh a big one with lawns and gardens and pingpong and tennis courts. He would get fat and diet, he would intrigue and push against the rules to see how far they gave. He would find his constituency and his opposition. Perhaps they would let him make films, or perhaps he would experiment with the aesthetic possibilities of psychodrama. He sat on a bench hunched with heavy shoulders, his orange head bowed and his eyes milky and only half open looking into himself, and then he let out that slash of grin and got ready to rasp a challenge, ready to push outward so that he might feel someone pushing back. He sat on a gray bench. His eyes met hers but did not see her. He and the bench were embedded in a shroud of cotton batting. They were systematized. They were digested. Something in his stance said that he believed a little less in connection, that he knew a little better what they could do to him. It was a good institution, simpler than the society and with the lines of control just as taut but more visible.

Her anger did not surprise him. Nor her clumsy vague schemes. But he was surprised by how long she cried.

"I loved him!" she said passionately into his chest. "I loved him but he couldn't love me."

"It's over now." He stroked her hair. Neither he nor Leon had taken each other's ideas as real but written them off as life style. They had had no dialogue. They had failed each other. Only she might have been a bridge, but he did not think that would happen now.

When the phone began to ring again he felt afraid and did not want to answer it.

"Rowley?" The voice was deep, peremptory. For a moment he did not recognize it.

"Yeah, speaking."

"It's me. After all."

"How are you?" What people say in shock. He cursed his clumsiness. "I mean I'm glad to hear from you. Where are you?"

"In a payphone. Where I'm staying the phone's tapped. Got the check and used it."

"Fine."

"Money is one thing we can really use."

"That was meant more like a letter than a check. I won't be having extra money. I'm quitting the station."

"How come?"

"Because I can't fool myself I'm doing anything to change the system in that job, and I can't fool myself any more that I haven't been fucked by the system too. Shaped, channeled, mutilated, dehumanized, squeezed by the balls. And I can't see myself happy as a concerned honky."

"The whole Black Belt's going to blow this summer, don't you know that? You got anything more real?"

"Not yet. But I better have. I start with the fact that I'm cut off from my own roots, powerless to save what was my community, cut off by a wall from a woman I loved and her wasted, burned, my music gone dead and useless, mocked where I've tried most to say something, turned into a commodity to be advertised and used up like any other. I start with that. I start with those busy kids who made me so pissed. I start with where I'm trying to live."

Harlan chuckled. "Well, Paul can always get a message to me, you know. If there's a good reason. Take care."

"You too. Don't let them bust you."

"I'm trying." Harlan hung up.

That was all there was and there might never be more. He

went back to Annie who lay spilled on the floor. "Come on. We might as well go to bed."

She got up. "I'm not crying because I'm with you. I really am with you. But they've got him, Rowley, and it's such a rotten waste!"

She lay in his arms damp with tears, tears that dripped slowly over his shoulder. He thought they lay at the bottom of a shaft of dim light and in the dark about them many circled. Not Paul who had cut her on the street but spoken to him, not Sam who lay with her love in their own pool of amber light. Through the dark drifted the ashlight bodies of burned Vera and Black Jack and Leon bound and Yente and his old man with a suitcase almost as old hiking into the past, and the thousands in the city burning with a stench more suffocating than the soft coal favored by its landlords, burning in poverty, in powerlessness, in blindness, in thousands of deadend graverooms where the smoke of their angry flesh and charred nerves rose in their nostrils and choked them. A sweet fetid odor of slow decay sweated from thousands of other rooms where in the aquarium of the TV objects pirouetted, objects glossier than any body in a shimmer of blurred lust and status and money-purr, while in the twilight contempt and desperation and cancer burgeoned like house plants. There were light high rooms where Nina's teak body banged toward some apotheosis of the nerves, some release from the spiral of golden sawdust, where Caroline sweated her odorless fears and reacted, reacted like a clean sleek white lab rat, where Asher sought the rational world that would reward his observance of the rules and found his new Olds and his living stomach betraying him.

All his life he had been dodging. He had opted for his comfort. Now he had planted his feet and from this point must begin. In the morning he would see Cal and resign. He'd keep only his own program. He could no longer live in interstices. He did not want to make a gesture or express his moral fiber: he wanted to act but could only push from where he stood and recognize that hardly anyone was going to feel the pressure for a long while.

Harlan had seen one thing: defeated you gave up and died

or fought from a new base. You began by recognizing your own oppression and once you tasted that, you could not go back to sleep.

He thought that he was lucky to have something he wanted in the dark, only lucky, for all things come down in the dark and the light, come down like ash upon the sleeping and those who stretch and rock with pain, and on him too who held in his arms the woman he wanted, though crying tediously, with patience through the long polluted night.

About the Author

Marge Piercy has written eight previous novels, including FLY AWAY HOME, BRAIDED LIVES, VIDA, WOMAN ON THE EDGE OF TIME and GONE TO SOLDIERS. She has published ten collections of poetry, including CIRCLES ON THE WATER (her selected poems) stone, paper, knife, and most recently MY MOTHER'S BODY. Her work has been translated into fourteen languages. She lives on Cape Cod with her husband, Ira Wood, the novelist and screenwriter.